CW01621938

Crossing the Line

Crossing the Line

J. Button & L. Hughes

ISBN: 978-1-9168985-0-9

First published June 2021

Front cover by JoZo Collection

Typesetting by David Siddall Multimedia, Dartmouth, UK
www.davidsiddall.com

Digitally printed by Amazon

Also available as a Kindle eBook

Published by
White Orchid House

To all fans of the beautiful game

Contents

Fulham Team
9
Zac Miller
(USA)
14
Leo Blake
(ENG)
11
Lucas Karlsson
(SWE)
10
Antonio Perez Alvarez
(ESP)
7
Javier Herrera
(ARG)
6
Eric Jovic
(CRO)
3
Aidan Rafferty
(IRL)
5
Phil Philopoussis
(AUS)
4
Jamie Crawford
(ENG)
2
Sunday Oyetoro
(NGA)
1
Davy Walker
(ENG)
Manager: Marko Maric
First team coach: Charlie Paxton
Fitness coach: Dario Kovatic
Team doctor: Andrew Brown
Substitutes:
no. 12 Mitch Masters (USA)

PART 1

There's a lot more to a football club than the people you see on a match day. Behind the scenes, there's an army of us grafting away so that the players and, of course, the manager can grasp all the glory. The fans think they've got the inside track, but they don't know the half of it.

Monday 9th December — Motspur Park

Zac Miller was the best striker in the Championship. The American looked calm and composed in front of goal, he was strong enough to hold off defenders and fast enough to deceive a goalkeeper. His natural agility and quick reactions were the envy of the League. And on a cold Monday evening in December they saved his life.

The day had begun like most Mondays during the football season with the Fulham first team having breakfast together in the canteen at Motspur Park training ground. As usual, the mood at the table was dictated by the result of their game at the weekend. That Sunday they had lost 1-0 away at Nottingham Forest and no one was in any doubt as to whose fault it was — as the scrappy, bad-tempered match was drawing to a close, Zac had missed an open goal.

Five minutes later, the final whistle had blown and the cold, frustrated travelling fans had jeered. Zac had dropped to his knees on the pitch, drained and disappointed.

"Star striker?" he heard one of his teammates mutter as they slouched into the dressing room. "Star striker, my — "

Zac had hung back so he didn't have to hear anymore but the reprieve had been temporary and it had been a long journey home from Nottingham. There was more of the same at breakfast — they called it banter but some of the jibes were razor sharp. He pushed his food around his plate and got up to leave as soon as he could.

It was a day of recovery and reckoning. A morning of light training and heavy post-match dissection taken by the coaches and analysts. The criticism was fairly evenly spread — for a top squad they had all underperformed — and Zac's glaring error was neither glossed over nor dwelt on. Just before lunch came the news that their playmaker, Antonio Perez Alvarez, who had injured his hamstring the previous week, would be out of action until after Christmas. The update did nothing to improve the mood of the group.

Zac's appetite hadn't returned so he spent most of lunchtime checking his social media. Which, of course, was a mistake.

Noticing his teammate was quiet and withdrawn, Leo Blake leaned across the table, his short plaits falling over eyes brimming with sympathy. "Don't beat yourself up about it, bro. From that angle ... "

But Zac shook his head. "Thanks, but it would've been easier to score than miss. That's what everyone else thinks anyway."

He turned his phone round so Leo could see a screen full of vitriol — tweets from Sunday night.

"Ignore it," said Leo. "They've got no clue. Come on, we've got to go."

Zac switched off his phone, appreciating the reassurance, but not the reminder that he was about to come face to face with the one person he couldn't ignore.

***

For Marko Maric, manager of Fulham Football Club, Monday had also started predictably. He had arrived at Motspur Park early and gone straight to the gym, pleased to find it empty. Just as he was finishing his session a few people started to drift in. The timing suited Marko perfectly; he liked his players to know he kept himself fit but he didn't want to share the gym with them while he did it.

He showered and went up to his office, his dark hair damp but his clothes immaculate. The office was clinically impersonal. There were no photos of his family, no reminders of home in Croatia. His one concession to comfort was a state-of-the-art coffee machine which he flicked on as he entered. The coffee in the canteen was tailored to the players' tastes for weak, milky creations. If Marko could drop someone from the first team for drinking a vanilla latte, he would.

He had a busy morning dealing with the least interesting parts of his job — mainly paperwork and the media — then after a hasty late lunch and a quick change of clothes, jogged downstairs to accompany the players on a short recovery run around the playing fields across the road from the training ground.

He spotted Zac Miller hovering on the edge of the group; Zac's height and old-gold hair gave him nowhere to hide. He needed to speak to his striker and the run was the perfect opportunity. On the way home from Nottingham, he wouldn't have been able to control his temper faced with the bright blue eyes, soft Texan drawl and reminder of failure.

Marko signalled to the fitness coach, his compatriot Dario Kovatic, to set off and fell into step with Zac. He didn't speak until they were on their way back, slowing down as they approached the road, and when he did, it was with uncompromising reproach. "You know you let me down?"

Zac stumbled and righted himself before saying, "Yes."

"Your job is to score goals."

"Yes," Zac said tightly, "and I do."

It was a fair comment. Zac's finishing ability was uncoachable and his scoring record impressive. But it just made the error even less forgivable. "I'd just like to know why you choked like that."

"So would I," Zac said with feeling.

Marko glanced at him, confused by the response. In pre-season, Marko had implemented a system which worked because every component player knew their job and obeyed every instruction to the letter. There was no room for mistakes or frailty. "Don't let it happen again."

Although they had started out in daylight, the early winter dusk was dropping fast but even in the fading light it was impossible to miss the intensity of Marko's gaze. The fact of the matter was that while Zac made scoring goals look easy, it wasn't as easy as Marko seemed to think and sometimes it wasn't easy at all. Watching the passing traffic, Zac said, "I don't want it to happen again either."

They were joined on the pavement by team captain and centre back Jamie Crawford. "Bringing up the rear, Jamie?" Marko said in a lighter tone than he had spoken to Zac.

"Just used to being at the back," Jamie replied. They had timed the return badly — not only was the light going but it was rush hour.

There was a gap in the traffic and they stepped out, Zac and Marko in the lead, Jamie just behind. The car seemed to come out of nowhere and Jamie realised why only later — it was a black car, unlit in the gathering darkness. The driver flicked the headlights on at the last moment. The beams caught the men in the car's path but the driver didn't swerve or slow, rather in the last few yards before almost certain impact, the car speeded up.

Jamie leapt back to safety but Zac and Marko were momentarily mesmerised by the searing headlights. Then Zac's reactions kicked in — he pushed Marko one way and dived the other. Marko hit the pavement and scrambled up while Zac's movement had taken him into the path of a Mini coming the other way. The Mini's brakes screeched, Zac rolled twice and crashed into the kerb.

He lay dazed for a few seconds listening to Jamie thanking the driver of the Mini while horns were already blaring from other vehicles. The black car had long gone.

Zac was sitting up when Jamie came over. "Are you OK?"

"Yeah, I think so. Just bruised."

When the road was clear they crossed over to Marko who was surreptitiously rubbing his knee. Jamie was about to speak but Marko jumped in first, "What the hell are you playing at?"

The question was addressed to Zac who looked shaken and nonplussed. "What were we just talking about?" Marko went on, anger making his accent stronger. "How are you going to score goals with a broken leg?"

"Boss —" Zac began indignantly but faced with Marko's furious expression ended by muttering, "Nothing's broken."

When they were inside the training ground, Jamie said, "We should tell the police."

"And say what?" Marko snapped, glancing at Zac, "That some people are attracted to trouble?"

"Well ... " Jamie thought Marko was being unreasonable but recognised that his acerbic tone was mainly a reaction to what had just happened. "I think I saw some letters on the car's number plate — VOR — like VAR. But I suppose that's not enough … that was too bloody close," he concluded.

Marko, who had survived a civil war, didn't dignify the statement with a response but he looked at Zac again, this time with a more concerned eye. He was about to ask "Are you all right?" but he realised that time was getting on and he had somewhere else to be. Instead he said, "Go and get showered. I'll see you tomorrow."

By the time Zac and Jamie got to the first team changing room it was nearly empty. From somewhere Zac heard the words " ... my mamma could have scored it," followed by another voice saying wearily, "Just shut it, Javi."

"Forget about the match, mate," Jamie said. "The result doesn't matter. We're still in the play-offs."

"And that black car? What just happened?" Zac said. "Forget about that, too?"

"What?"

In answer, Zac took his phone out of his locker and showed Jamie the extract from his Twitter timeline that Leo had seen earlier.

Jamie shook his head in disgust. "Ignore it. Most of them won't be fans. Just stupid kids hiding behind their screens. What just happened ... " he shook his head and started to strip off his training kit, adding it to the pile in the laundry bin. "I don't know. It was probably just an accident."

He looked at Zac and frowned. "Mate, you're shaking. Get in the shower, that'll warm you up."

Zac nodded, relieved that the conversation was over. But he wasn't shaking because he was cold.

Jamie, meanwhile, picking up stray socks and tossing them in the bin to make life easier for the cleaners, reflected that his team-mate was in a strange mood but that was hardly surprising. Zac had had two near-misses in as many days. That would be enough to put anyone off their stride, even without the Twitter abuse.

***

As he got ready for his trip to north London, Marko likewise reflected on what had just happened. Not the incident with the car but his conversation with Zac.

Fulham had crashed out of the Premier League back in May after several seasons of clinging onto 17th place. David Patterson, the owner, had sacked the manager the following day and appointed Marko a week after that. This was Marko's first management job in England after years of coaching on the continent. It wasn't exactly the role he had been looking for but he was pragmatic enough to know that he and Patterson had similar ambitions, at least in the short term. He had negotiated a good salary and an even better transfer budget and had shopped his way around the clubs of England and Europe assembling a group of players who could play his brand of football — fast, focused and furious — no questions asked, no quarter given.

He had picked those players to fit around Zac Miller because he knew that the striker was the key to Fulham's, and his own, success. Which meant he needed Zac to stay fit and sharp and not have any collisions with moving vehicles or miss any more open goals.

After some initial issues getting the new players to slot in with the old guard and some poor results as the squad adjusted to Marko's system, Fulham had climbed the Championship table. Promotion back to the Premier League at the first time of asking looked possible. Sunday's result had been disappointing but not disastrous and he wasn't overly worried about the team's performance on the pitch. He was aware, though, that they weren't so harmonious off it and that he needed to keep his eye on the wrangling.

Unlike his predecessor, who had famously lost the dressing room (and, frankly, the plot), Marko had no concerns about loyalty. He controlled every squad he managed with an iron glove and most realised eventually that it concealed a velvet fist. His Fulham team weren't at that stage yet.

When he was ready to leave, he glanced at his phone, intending to call his wife, Ivana, to let her know he would miss dinner but then had second thoughts. It was odd though, he thought, looking at his recent call list that, strained as their relationship was, he still seemed to phone her more than anyone else. He sent her a brief text and knew better than to wait for a reply.

He got in his car and selected a suitable playlist for the drive, musing that he had a long way to go to conduct an affair that was very close to home.

Sunday 15th December — Craven Cottage

Not everything in life could be black and white. It was too messy and dirty for that. Way too messy. David Patterson stood on his balcony, overlooking Old Father Thames, Putney Bridge in full view to his left, Hammersmith Bridge slightly further north up the river to his right, their softly lit outlines fuzzily traced in the dark. Early evening rowers glided through the river in front of him, the sounds of splashes and shouts from the boats drifted upwards but they passed by unregistered.

"It's not what I want to do but guess it's out of my hands," he said into the phone. He sounded resigned rather than angry. He stepped over to the edge of the balcony and lent on the sharp, cold metal railing, almost at shoulder height, his free hand palm open, imploring the gods.

"Yes, go ahead. Just eighteen stores now, no more. Let's just bloody hope that stops the rot," he couldn't believe he was saying all this. "But the Club's off limits — you know that. There'll be other ways to solve this."

The phone's screen went dark. He looked down at the river. He'd come out without a coat and he was starting to feel the cold, his thin cotton shirt offering no protection against the chilled wind breezing across the water. How had it come to this? His jaw clenched as he mulled that the writing had been on the wall for a long time. But selling wasn't in his make-up, he was too much of a hoarder at heart. Selling anything when your hand was forced felt like defeat but some of the poorer performing stores would have to go. His only chance of saving something from his retail empire.

David stepped back into his brightly lit apartment and took it in for a moment. This was the perfect living-above-the-shop arrangement, his very own football shop. The new Riverside Stand at the ground, with a small number of apartments at the top, was proving a great success. They were the ultimate pied-a-terre for many of the Club's directors. And there would be more to come with the development of the Putney End. His thoughts were interrupted by the door-bell. David checked his watch. It was Marko Maric, punctual as usual.

"Sit down, Marko. What's it to be? Beer? Vodka? What's your poison?"

Marko took a seat on the edge of the large cream sofa in the middle of the open-plan room. "A beer is good, thank you."

David went to grab the beers from the kitchen, talking as he went, giving Marko the opportunity to appraise the apartment and its river view. "Thanks for coming along with me to this dinner tonight, Marko. You don't have to stay too long. I know it's a busy time of the season, but I appreciate you coming, it's something we've just got to do."

"It is not a problem," Marko replied.

"Good to get a drink in first though, we've been meaning to do this for a while," David added.

Marko Maric, with his serious demeanour, didn't give the impression of being entirely relaxed in his boss's company. Their relationship was still in its infancy and it was a transactional one. But Patterson's state of affairs meant that Marko Maric had no reason to be worried, he was one of his boss's few current success stories.

Sitting back in an armchair opposite Marko, David lifted his glass, "Your good health." His manager raised his glass, quietly repeating the words.

David studied him for a moment. He'd had chapter and verse on Marko Maric's reputation, both on and off the field, before he'd made him an offer he couldn't refuse. Marko was too damn good-looking for his own good, even David could see that. But his record of footballing success meant that David was confident that if anyone could get his Club back into the Premier League it was this man sitting in front him.

"I've probably told you this before, Marko, but when I was a little boy, my dad used to take me to Craven Cottage. We lived in a block of flats up in Shepherd's Bush. Before a match, I wouldn't be able to sleep with excitement. My biggest regret in life was him not being here when I bought this Club. Nothing would have made him prouder."

Marko listened attentively. He paused to find the right words. "I understand. Football is not just a game. It is everything. I will try my best to honour your family."

"I knew you were right for us," David said chuckling under his breath. His smile fell away as he leaned forward in his chair. "You're my best shot, Marko. I need you to deliver for me — this season more than ever.

"Already, I can see how you're turning the team around — you've got us in the top six. But at the end of the season, Marko, it's not the play-offs I want. That's not good enough. It's got to be top two, we need to be in the automatics," David stopped. "You understand, don't you? There's got to be no leaving promotion to chance."

Marko's steely grey eyes met David Patterson's. His one-word answer was all the Club's owner wanted to hear. "Understood."

Kensington

As football dinners went, it was going to be a relatively intimate but informal affair, so no partners or black tie. There were twenty of so people from each of the three clubs and the rest made up from the Council and the Foundation.

It was only a short trip from Omar Hamarat's Knightsbridge home to the hotel on Kensington High Street where the dinner was taking place. No heads turned as he got into his chauffeur-driven Bentley — it was an unremarkable sight in this part of London. For that to happen you needed to be brashly revving the likes of metallic gold Lamborghinis and luminous orange Ferraris. The young male drivers (they always were) reaching top speeds of 15 mph on the congested streets.

The city was no stranger to inordinate wealth. It had always been a draw for the wealthy but now it was a high-strength magnet for the world's super-rich. The language, the access to Britain's rule of law and its leagues of accountants and lawyers but, especially, its crown jewels — the shopping, the culture and its sporting offer — all made London a natural destination for the elite.

Many of the moneyed people wanted to not just live in London but also own a piece of it, especially if it was on the Monopoly board or had a Royal connection. They ploughed their cash into world-famous trophy buildings, from Park Lane hotels to City towers, de-risking their wealth by converting it into tradeable investments and rich men's playthings (it usually was men) — like football clubs, such as the Diamond Blues.

Being one of an elite group of global billionaires, Omar Hamarat enjoyed all that his wealth could offer from private planes, yachts, fast cars and a second marriage to an ex-Miss Turkey beauty queen. Now in his 50s, he'd had a home in London for over twenty years. And for the last seven of them he'd owned the Diamonds, one of London's best known football clubs.

Hamarat would never confirm the rumour that he'd acquired the club for a bet, always saying it had been a considered business decision. The story went that a fellow Turk had bet him one night over a whisky-fuelled dinner that he couldn't buy a football club in a week — the winner got to take up the last judging place on the Miss Turkey beauty pageant. It was said that a few clubs nearly came within Hamarat's grasp but he managed to agree the Diamonds deal with only hours to go, to clinch the bet. In whatever circumstances it was acquired, he had ended up with a new football club and, shortly after, a new wife.

***

The Foundation's charity dinner presented the perfect opportunity for Hamarat to test the water and start making waves concerning a certain riverside football club.

Hamarat had been the one to seize the initiative, instigating the 'West London Clubs Together Football Foundation' — combining the charitable efforts of the three football clubs of the borough, the Diamond Blues, Fulham and Queens Park Rangers, for the good of the wider community. Individually, the clubs had been doing great things in Hammersmith and Fulham for decades, harnessing sport to improve education and health, but for some time they'd talked about joining forces. Now it was actually happening.

At the drinks reception before the dinner, there had been firm handshakes and slaps on backs between the clubs' owners and managers. The Leader of the Council and its Chief Executive looked to be in good spirits too, as did the Foundation's representatives and guests. All smiled widely for the official photographs. Hamarat had made sure that he'd arranged his post-dinner drink with Fulham's owner David Patterson, or Dudley Patterson as he was sometimes called behind his back. The resemblance to the actor Dudley Moore was uncanny.

Once the dinner and speeches were finished, David Patterson, with Marko Maric alongside him, made their way over to Hamarat, who was standing in the bar area with someone Patterson didn't recognise.

"Omar, great evening. We really should have done something like this sooner," David said.

"We should have. But now we have a good foundation for the Foundation," Hamarat chortled.

"Not sure if you know each other already but let me introduce you to Marko Maric. He's doing a fabulous job for us this season."

Marko Maric shrugged nonchalantly as he shook hands with Omar Hamarat.

"A pleasure to meet you, Marko. And can I introduce you both to my good friend and guest for the evening, Kerim Bayram. Kerim is from the world of property and an ally of the Foundation."

The four chatted about the evening, sharing some general football gossip. Marko Maric wasn't one for small talk but he was in the company of his boss, as well as the owner of the club that was currently top of the Premier League. He made an effort to join in.

"You're an ex-Diamonds man, are you not?" Hamarat enquired of Marko.

Marko smiled, replying, "In its previous form, yes."

"The Blues get in your veins. Many, many people make their way back. Who knows, you may do the same. Maybe you will be our manager one day?" Hamarat's eyes twinkled, making it hard to know if he was teasing or not.

Marko shook his head and mumbled an inaudible response while David Patterson coughed loudly, saying, "As if we at Fulham don't think the same! Anyway, Marko's a Fulham man now and he's got a job to do with us. Including getting us promoted so we can play you guys next season. Beating you at the Cottage, of course!"

Kerim Bayram was first to break from the group and Marko Maric used his departure as an opportunity to exit, leaving the two club owners together. Patterson and Hamarat headed towards a table in the corner of the lounge. Two glasses of single malt whisky were brought over.

They usually only saw each other at occasional dinners and events. Both members of the wealthy-enough-to-own a football-club group, they respected each other, but Hamarat and Patterson were not friends. Hamarat didn't want to draw the night out for any longer than needed.

He sat back in his chair, legs crossed. "David, I don't know what you propose to do long term, but I wanted to say this to you in person, owner to owner, so to speak. If ever you decide to sell that wonderful, quaint, historic football club of yours, you must let me know first."

David Patterson's eyes widened. He shook his head slowly before averting his gaze to the glass tumbler he was holding.

"Why would you think I'd ever want to sell?"

"It's just I heard that you might want to focus on your other business interests. Now is a good time to cash in, perhaps?"

"Well, you're not allowed to own two football clubs, Omar, you know that as well as I do," the politeness from Patterson's voice had gone. "So why on earth are you interested in mine?"

"I understand. I do. With football clubs, it's hard to make objective business decisions. But I agree, even if I could have more, one is plenty enough for anyone. I'm politely enquiring on behalf of a person who could take it off your hands — to take care of it — for the right price, of course."

Friday 3rd January — Motspur Park

Marko was in no hurry to leave the office. Christmas in the Maric household had been tense and the New Year fraught. Drinking coffee and going through his preparations for tomorrow's third round FA Cup match was a better option than rushing home.

The FA Cup, the oldest cup competition in the world, triggered good memories. Marko had enjoyed a lot of success in the Cup as a player and he was looking forward to his first attempt at it as a manager. In the back of his mind was his recent conversation with David Patterson in which the owner had made it clear that only automatic promotion would do — failure to go up was not an option. Marko knew that with his relatively small squad, the challenges of a Cup run could conflict with David's demands but Marko had fought against following orders all his life. He wasn't about to conform now. The adulation for a manager who did well in the FA Cup with a Championship team would exceed the plaudits for winning the Championship itself.

Perhaps, he mused, unconsciously straightening items on his already tidy desk, his own ambitions and Patterson's weren't as aligned as he had thought. But Marko wasn't perturbed at the idea of crossing an employer. It wouldn't be the first time.

Pleased with his team selection, he finished his coffee and looked at his emails. One was from a scout about a young Diamonds player he thought Marko might be interested in. Marko skimmed the text. He didn't need a so-called tricky winger who clearly wasn't tricky enough to break into the Diamonds first team but any mention of his old club jolted him back to his encounter with Omar Hamarat before Christmas.

"Maybe you will be our manager one day … " the Turk had said. Perhaps it had been just a throwaway line or, at most, a comment to rile David Patterson but Marko couldn't help dwelling on it. He wanted to find his way to a top six club sooner rather than later — and a long FA Cup run was exactly the way to attract the right sort of attention.

The next email informed him that the home stands at the Cottage were sold out for tomorrow's game. Marko couldn't care less. Some players performed better in front of a full house but Marko was indifferent to fan engagement. The beautiful game was wasted on people who had never played it.

Saturday 4th January — Craven Cottage
FA CUP THIRD ROUND — Fulham FC v Luton Town FC

Jack

January is a quiet time in the floristry business, a fact I welcomed after an eye-aching, finger-bleeding December making so many wreaths and table centres that by Christmas holly had become my nemesis.

The only problem with the lack of customers was that Saturday morning dragged in my Pimlico shop and there were no distractions from my standard pre-match cocktail of nerves, anticipation, excitement and fear.

My assistant, Fleur, noticed. "Who are Fulham playing today?"

"Luton," I said. "This is the third round of the FA Cup."

Fleur looked puzzled and I could see she was struggling to remember if I'd mentioned the first and second rounds, which I hadn't. But Fleur found everything about football puzzling including why a woman like me was completely obsessed with it. When I left for the match at 1.30 p.m., she wished me good luck, but not because she cared about the game. Like everyone else who worked or lived with a football fan, Fleur knew that my moods were inextricably linked with the ups and downs of my Club. If Fulham won, life was rosy; if Fulham lost, I was as prickly as a cactus.

It was a dry, cold day but I wore enough black-and-white accessories to keep me warm. By 2.15 p.m., Loz and I were walking down the Thames path from Hammersmith, drinking cappuccinos and discussing Marko Maric's team selection, which we'd checked on Twitter.

It was still early days for Marko as manager but we were cautiously optimistic, if not about an immediate return to the Premier League then at least about enjoying the attempt. Marko's football was fast, skilful and often enthralling to watch.

After an early exit from the League Cup, thanks to being drawn away at Man City, we were both pleased that Marko was taking the FA Cup seriously. The team he'd picked was, in our view (and we considered ourselves experts) the best available, taking into account Antonio Perez Alvarez's absence through injury. It was a strong line-up to face Championship strugglers Luton and we were hoping for a victorious afternoon.

Hoping but not expecting. We were Fulham fans and we knew it was the hope that kills you.

At the Cottage, we joined a dense, but orderly, queue, squeezed through the old turnstiles and scrambled up to our seats in the Hammersmith End, arriving just before kick-off. We exchanged New Year greetings with our neighbours — we had all sat together for several seasons and supported each other through the agonies (many) and ecstasies (few) of following Fulham. Even Moany Man who sometimes drove us to distraction with his criticism of the players, the tactics, the officials and football in general, was in a reasonable mood and up for the Cup.

The match started slowly. Luton put in a lot of effort but their football was unimaginative and one-dimensional. They defended well but had little idea of how to mount a successful attack against Fulham's experienced and organised back line. The first half was 45 minutes of stop-start football interspersed with some shots from Zac Miller and Leo Blake and some good work from the Luton goalkeeper. The two teams' contrasting styles did not blend into attractive football; it was turgid rather than edge-of-the-seat stuff. Luton fans would have been happy to reach half-time with the game goalless while we were feeling that familiar Fulham frustration.

Luton started the second half strongly with their first (and only) sustained attack on goal. The Fulham defence, led by Jamie Crawford, as vocal and commanding as ever, weathered the storm and Luton faded after their burst of effort. Eric Jovic, playing further forward than usual in Antonio's absence, was taking control of the midfield and Zac Miller, ominously for Luton, was moving forward — each foray faster and deeper than the last. The first goal, when it came, was a terrific one. Javier Herrera out-skilled his opponent and delivered a perfect cross. Zac leapt for the ball, collected it and directed it around the goalkeeper and into the net.

There are few things more exciting for a Fulham fan than watching a white-clad hoard attack the Hammy End at speed. And on that Saturday afternoon the speed was blistering. Zac, Leo, Eric and Javier were all racing forwards in wave after wave of bombardments.

The second goal was always coming. There was some delicious build-up play. Marko's team often seemed to tease the opposition, to tempt them into making mistakes with their quick and clever passes. On the 80th minute, Eric worked his way to the edge of the box and flicked the ball into Zac's feet. Zac's shot was so powerful that the flailing goalkeeper's hand did nothing except help it on its way.

In the stand, we were jumping up and down, screaming Zac's name. On the pitch, the Fulham players were all around him, Leo leaping on his back, Eric pounding his shoulder, Jamie running down the pitch to join in the celebrations. And Zac himself stared up into the stand, face alight, arms outstretched as if he was trying to draw in the energy and emotion of the crowd. As if he was trying, I thought for a fleeting moment, to feel something he didn't really feel.

Then the referee was blowing his whistle and waving everyone back for kick-off and the moment was over.

There were 10 minutes left to play but the game was already won and we watched the closing stages in a mixture of relief and anticipation. Fulham were on a Cup run and who knew where it might take us?

<u>Loz</u>

"That was sooo good," I said to Jack, as we glanced at each other grinning. We both had our hands up high, applauding our team. The show was over and the audience had been enraptured by a virtuoso second-half performance. The floodlit pitch had been the stage and the cast made their way towards us in the home stand, applauding us in turn and hugging and back-slapping each other. The Cottage was alive with super-charged, feel-good energy, despite the cold, windy weather. Even Moany Man looked happy. The crowd sang along to the tinny Andy Williams playing in the background, "*… you're just too good to be true, can't take my eyes off of you … de, de, de, de, de …*"

I looked for Zac Miller in the melee of players coming towards us. His height and blond hair made him easy to pick out. Typical

Zac, I thought, he's at the back, not hogging the limelight. He looked like he'd given his all on the pitch with his mud-streaked kit and his cheeks pink with exertion. He'd been the star of the show and his two goals had been sublime. There was no doubt that he was a firm fan favourite and, with the form he was in, he was heading towards Fulham legend status. As he got closer to the edge of the pitch, the roars and cheers from the crowd got louder as the singing changed. "*There's only one ... Zac Miller, one ... Zac Miller, there's only one Zac Mill-er ...*"

"Good to see Marko coming over, too," Jack commented. "He doesn't usually. Nice to see him appreciating us."

We certainly appreciated him, and not just for his good looks, although that added to our admiration, we had to admit. Since his appointment, we'd done much better in the League and he'd got us playing entertaining free-flowing football again.

"Right, Jack, bar time. Shall we head to the Riverside?"

Jack grinned, "Good idea."

By the time we got to the Riverside Bar, it was pretty crowded. The Club had done a good job with the new stand with its bars and restaurants and, after the win, the atmosphere was buzzing. I recognised the tall, dark-haired barman as he nodded to me, acknowledging I was up next.

"Hi, Will. Jack and I aren't doing dry January. And we've won. So, no house wine for us," I laughed. "Two large glasses of the Australian shiraz, please!"

"Gotcha," Will saluted. "And let me guess, no plastic glasses?"

We'd got to know Will, part-time barman at the Riverside and, as he told us, "general club dogsbody", not only as we were regular bar goers but also because of our wine deliberations. Will, on quieter nights, had indulged us by letting us try different wines from the bar's extensive list, talking us through them without using over-the-top descriptions. We'd told him one evening that one pub we used to go before the Cottage's Riverside Bar opened had started to serve wine in plastic glasses, which led to us immediately boycotting it — did two women in multiple fluffy football accessories look like we were going to start a fight?

I weaved my way through the tables of satisfied-looking fans and spotted Jack, with her short dark hair, bright stripey jumper and dangly earrings, sitting in the far corner, phone in hand checking the other scores.

"Well, that was a convincing-enough performance and a confidence boost for the League," Jack said as I sat down.

"We're into the last 32 now," I added, "and the next round draw's on Monday, so let's just hope we avoid the big guns." We clinked glasses and took our first sip.

"Mmm. This is nice," Jack said approvingly, "very full-bodied."

"Do you think Marko cares about the Cup?" I asked.

She paused. "Not sure," she said slowly. "You know what he's like, he's such a cold fish. I mean, he's doing a great job for us at the moment. He's certainly instilled some steel into the team, so we're not so easy to beat. Not sure what he'd think about the Cup though. I can't help wondering if we should just concentrate on the League seeing as we're doing so well?"

"The fans would like a Cup run though," I said, "I certainly would. You're right though — it's impossible to tell what Marko thinks."

In Marko's interviews, we'd seen no particular affection for the Club or appreciation of the fans. He was ambitious and ruthless and, although he was turning Fulham around, he wasn't winning hearts and minds along the way.

As a Fulham player, Marko had never been a fan favourite, partly because he never gave the impression he wanted to stay. He'd only been at the Club for a season following a hurried departure from West Ham and before a speedy transfer to Crystal Palace. He'd played the central defensive midfield role and played it well, heading off danger, thwarting attacks and interrupting the opposition's rhythm. But his overly tough tackles, arrogant attitude and pack of yellow cards didn't endear him to the Fulham Faithful who liked more finesse and fair play.

After a more successful period at Palace, he moved to Chelsea, now the Diamond Blues, where his uncompromising commitment, no-nonsense style and tendency for casual brutality had gone down rather well before his playing career had ended prematurely and abruptly due to injury.

Over our wine, we did our usual post-match dissection, chatting about individual players' performances and notable incidents. The action happens so quickly when you're watching it live, so it was sometimes hard to know who'd passed to who in build-up play and even who the goal scorers were. This meant we always delighted in poring over goal replays on social media and catching up on other fans' comments, as well as posting our own.

After our game analytics were exhausted, we got round to talking about things other than our favourite subject.

"Not sure if it's a sign of desperation but I got three Frank Best leaflets this week," Jack said. "Not very sustainable!"

After football, politics was always a regular topic of ours, especially with the forthcoming London mayoral election in May. Jack and I both agreed that we didn't want Frank Best, the current Labour mayor, to get re-elected as neither of us thought he was doing a good enough job. Best was going for a second four-year term and with London generally being a Labour city, we knew he was more than likely to win.

"This is going to be such a boring election. Best's a done deal," I complained, not realising how wrong I'd be.

Tuesday 7th January — St James's

On the afternoon of the interview, Hamarat was dropped off at his club by his driver half an hour before he was due to meet Julie Martinez, The Post's award-winning journalist. He liked leaving ample time to ensure he was entirely comfortable with the arrangements, which included being in position when she arrived. He aimed to watch her closely as she walked towards him, making sure she was aware of him doing so. He enjoyed subtly unnerving people, part of a gentle power play.

The top-hatted doorman greeted him as he arrived. Hamarat nodded and headed inside to the chequered floored hallway where he was escorted to his favoured seat in the club's Churchill Suite.

The two large oxblood leather chairs in the corner of the room would be Hamarat's lair. Sitting back, he took a second to enjoy the richness of his surroundings with the room's high ornate ceilings, thick claret drapes and gilded mirrors. He turned his chair slightly so that he could gaze diagonally across the room towards the entrance door. Playing with the wedding ring on his right hand, as he had a habit of doing, he waited for Julie Martinez.

Hamarat didn't need to wear a chunky gold watch or jewelled rings to indicate that he was an immensely affluent man — everything about him made that evident. His soft and finely woven, dark grey wool suit was tailored on Jermyn Street and his shoes were handmade Italian leather. He wore his crisp white shirt open at the neck — as the member profile had changed at the club, so had its tie policy. His well-cut, steel grey hair was slicked back, a style he hadn't altered for at least twenty years, even though he was increasingly receding at the temples. Last time he was at the barbers, he had thought about changing it but was told that it made him look distinguished.

This private members' club in St James's felt like home turf to Hamarat. He loved it, its history and tradition. To him, the club was the epitome of Britishness and it conjured up images of different James Bonds sitting in big leather chairs by open fires being waited on by attentive staff. In fact, it was pretty much still like that – aside from the membership which had changed significantly since Sean Connery's or Roger Moore's days. His fellow club members were less likely to be MI6 secret agents, senior British politicians or titans of UK industry and were now a cosmopolitan set from a range of backgrounds, albeit all monied ones. Wealth and exclusivity remained a constant, as did the gender balance.

He had agreed to do the interview with Julie Martinez on the basis of two strict conditions: firstly, he set the parameters for the questions and, secondly, he got to sign-off on the piece before publication. Hamarat guessed that a journalist of her experience would not be happy with this but as he rarely gave interviews it was too tempting an offer for her to turn down. For Hamarat, it was an opportunity to talk about the new football foundation he was spearheading. And doing some controlled media from time to time was the price to pay for owning a London football club. It would be, he thought, a piece that any journalist could have written — but that wasn't the point.

Julie Martinez arrived on time and was composed as she walked across the room. He looked at her intently, noting her dark green shift dress and black-heeled shoes, with a large black tote bag over her shoulder. Hamarat hated it when women wore flat shoes. In his opinion, she wasn't a head-turner but she was a reasonably attractive woman with her brunette hair and large brown eyes. She was much less glamorous than the sort of women he was used to — British women just didn't seem to pay as much attention to their looks as the Turkish women he knew. But he was pleased she was easy on the eye. It made it much less effort to be his charming best.

He stood up as she approached him. "Ms Martinez, a pleasure to meet you," he said in his deep voice, the accent of his home country still there. He shook her hand firmly and gestured for her to sit.

"Call me Julie, please," she replied and sat down, opening up her bag as she did so, pulling out a notepad and pen. She perched at the edge of her chair, clearly a lady of the lean-in variety, and after commenting on the splendour of the room, looked him straight in the eye.

"You're a busy man, Mr Hamarat, so let's make a start. So, firstly, what would you put your successful business career down to?" The implication behind Julie Martinez's first question was clear.

I like this woman, Hamarat thought, before choosing his answer. He smiled as he spoke. "Well, Ms Martinez ... apologies, Julie. I believe it is a combination of two principal factors. Number one, I had some luck, but more importantly, number two, I used it wisely. I was lucky to have had some good connections in Turkey.

"Let us say that my family were in the right place at the right time when the government wanted to privatise some state-owned assets. But I believe I was best placed to own and run the media operations that I acquired. And everything that has followed has been down to disciplined focus. Wealth and opportunities do not just land in front of you. Of course not, you must work hard for them."

Julie scribbled as he spoke. The slight purse of her lips gave away her awareness of him studying her. He kept his voice soft and tone comforting until soon her shoulders began to drop and she began to nod along to his responses. After a few more questions about his media empire, his Turkish newspapers, magazines and radio stations, as well as some probing into his niche PR company, where she managed to just brush the surface, given the pre-agreed nature of the interview, she got on to asking him about his UK interests.

"Tell me about buying the Diamond Blues. How did that come about?"

His hands together resting on his chin, Hamarat contemplated his answer. "It was a strange beginning."

"Oh yes? Why was that exactly?" Julie asked. She had obviously heard the rumours.

"The Club's previous owner just phoned me up out of the blue." Hamarat stopped and laughed at what he had said. "Out of the blue being very appropriate. You agree, Julie?"

She smiled and gestured for him to continue. "I was asked if I wanted to buy the Club. He had heard about me somehow, that I might be in the market, and after some deliberation, I thought why not? And I am pleased to say it has been one of my most satisfying business decisions."

"And the decision to change the name?" Julie asked.

"I understand that the old name was important to the legacy fans but I took the view that it needed refreshing to give the Club wider appeal. My Daily Diamond newspaper was my first in Ankara and so that was my inspiration."

"Did you expect the backlash that followed from the 'legacy fans'?"

He noticed she frowned as she asked the question. "People are resistant to change but without it, nothing progresses. And look at what my investment has reaped. I'm sure that that has won the fans around. We go forwards not backwards."

"You have sporting interests outside of the UK. Tell me about those in the US."

"Of course. Five years ago, I acquired my team in the North American Football league. It made good sense on a business and personal level, given the amount of time I spend in the US. My NFL team are very dear to me." Once again, he laughed at his pun, repeating, "Very dear!"

Julie smiled amiably. Hamarat was satisfied that his charm had eroded some of her initial edge.

"Well, Mr Hamarat, I'm here to ask you to comment on the new charity which I know you have been the driving force of ... " she checked her notes before continuing, " ... the West London Clubs Together Football Foundation. Can you talk me through how this came about?"

Hamarat gave her the spiel and was surprised to find that he had enjoyed talking to her — those brown eyes helped. She might be less polished than the women he was used to, he thought, noticing her nails could do with a manicure, something his wife would never be guilty of, but there was also something strangely alluring about that.

After it was clear that the questions were winding up, Hamarat brought the conversation round to the main purpose of this going-through-the-motions interview — her husband, Joe Martinez. Julie had no idea but it was Joe, a Labour politician with a position in the Shadow Cabinet, who was the real focus of Hamarat's attentions. If everything went to plan, her ambitious husband was the key to Hamarat bringing his grand plans for London to profitable fruition.

***

Hamarat sat alone following Julie Martinez's departure. He looked over his shoulder to check for eavesdroppers before picking up his phone and dialling.

"Angus, how are you, my friend? I wanted to call you in person to say thank you for the most kind invitation to your retirement dinner but I must say that surely you are too young, my friend, much too young."

He was speaking to Angus Lee, Julie Martinez's Editor-in-Chief at The Post, a role he'd had for over twenty years. He was a highly respected Fleet Street stalwart who had decided he was bowing out on his terms before his blood pressure or the digital onslaught got him first. Their paths had crossed many times over the years and Lee had been a guest of Hamarat's at the Diamond Arena for a few notable Champions League and Cup matches.

Wanting to get this over with, Hamarat quickly got to the point of the call. "Angus, really, I don't want to put you to any trouble and I know you will not be spending your precious time on a seating plan for your dinner like some new bride and groom, but I would greatly appreciate it if you could put Tabitha and me on the same table as your wonderful journalist Julie Martinez. I just wanted to follow up on a couple of things from our interview today. You know how it is."

That had been simple, he thought as he ended the call. The next one would require a little more thought. He took out two pieces of paper from his jacket pocket and unfolded them. The first displayed photos — they showed Frank Best, London mayor, shaking hands with another man in a high street cafe. The picture had been taken from the street and other photos showed Frank Best and the other man entering the café separately but leaving together. The second page was text headed 'Relevant Material'.

Hamarat placed the call, impressed that his people had managed to get his direct number, but then everything has a price. Hamarat didn't expect him to pick up but he did.

"Frank, so good to speak to you. It's Omar Hamarat."

There was a gruff reply and before the call could be terminated, Hamarat interjected, "I hear that you've not been well, Frank. I wanted to send you my best wishes and see if I could be of help. But let me tell you, I have also heard that there are about to be rumours spread about you Frank, nasty rumours."

He sensed Frank Best's hackles rise at the end of the line so Hamarat raced on. "Rumours of you awarding a huge TfL construction contract to an old friend of yours."

Hamarat could anticipate Best's reaction.

"You dirty bastard. What are you up to?" Frank Best spluttered. "Everything I've done has been by the book. And it's bloody rich coming from you. If you're threatening me ... "

"Frank, Frank. Calm down. Of course, I'm not threatening you. On the contrary, I'm trying to help. The last thing you need is any scandal, especially when your health is poor. You know what the public are like, they'll be thinking, no smoke without fire —"

Frank cut him off. "I don't need help, not from you or anybody else. And you're a bigger fool than I had you for if you think this call will help you on Wembley."

But Wembley wasn't the only football ground Hamarat had plans for, where he'd need the mayor to ease things along. "Well, I'm here if you need me, but I suggest you let me help you. It could get very messy otherwise," Hamarat replied.

He decided to leave it there. No need to overplay his hand.

PART 2

Wednesday 8th January

On the pitch, everything was perfect. The eleven players were a unit, thinking and playing as one. Every attacking player was eager for the ball, running into space, calling, signalling. At the back, the defence was disciplined and coordinated, each player knowing exactly where the others were.

I had watched Fulham play Preston North End at Craven Cottage and if you didn't know what I knew, you would believe this was a team in harmony, a club united, a group of players who supported each other off the pitch as well as on. But you'd be wrong.

The newspapers talked about tiki taka and total football and the Barcelona of the Championship. They hailed the footballing revolution that Marko Maric had brought to the banks of the Thames. They talked about the creativity of Antonio Perez Alvarez, the prowess of Zac Miller, the leadership of Jamie Crawford, the promise of Leo Blake. They talked about a club on the rise, a club which had found the recipe for success. But they only saw the pretty patterns on the pitch and the ascent of the table. They didn't witness the bickering, the rows and the open hostility. They didn't see what lay beneath the goals and the glory.

After the game, I made my way to the players' lounge and waited. I was essential but invisible. I saw everything, but nobody saw me.

The room was fluttering with WAGs, glamorous despite the chill of the January evening. Conversation was high pitched and loud and I kept alert, listening for any interesting information. At the centre of one group was the unsmiling ice queen, Ivana Maric; holding court in another was her victorious husband. The two ignored one another. As usual.

Fulham's owner, David Patterson, was absent — abroad trying to rescue one of his struggling businesses. Marko's right-hand man, Dario Kovatic, whose job title was fitness coach but whose remit went much further than sprinting and sit ups, was already in the lounge and, by the bar, a small group of middle-aged men in expensive but ill-fitting suits. One had a flashy tie pin; another, a diamond sparkling in his ear. These were the players' agents — snouts in the trough, ears to the ground and eyes peeled for the main chance. The January transfer window was open and they were poised for action.

The relationship between a player and his agent is symbiotic but weighted in the agent's favour. The player wanted his time at a club to be happy and fulfilling; the agent wanted it to come with a big transfer fee. Zac Miller's agent, a hefty dark-haired man with an enormous signet ring, guzzled his gin and tonic.

" ... Patterson's desperate for promotion," I heard one of the agents say. "It'll be a real test for this lot."

"Especially if they lose their star player," another replied.

The man with the signet ring kept quiet.

From across the room, a girl's voice said: " ... separate bedrooms, apparently."

"I'm not surprised," someone replied with a giggle.

The first player to emerge from the dressing room was Lucas Karlsson, blond hair still damp from the briefest of showers. Lucas, a passionate climate change campaigner, fell into conversation with the coaching staff and I could hear him, self-deprecating as ever, giving Marko credit for tonight's victory. Self-deprecating, or too clever by half?

The next arrival was Jamie Crawford, the team captain, scanning the room, as alert to trouble off the pitch as on it. Jamie was always the calming influence, the arbitrator, the captain everyone looked up to. Jamie was a great guy, just a shame that he'd never got over not being picked to play for England.

They were all coming in now, this team which was the Barcelona of the Championship, including the man who thought he was its Messi — Antonio Perez Alvarez, the most talented midfielder in the League, they said, except I knew he didn't want to be in this League anymore. If Fulham didn't get promoted then he would be off to the Premier League or back home to Spain. We would see how he matched up to Messi then.

Antonio joined his agent while his wife Pia detached herself from the group of WAGs competing for Marko's attention and went to take her husband's arm. Pia's place was taken by Marko's compatriot Eric Jovic who shook Marko's hand. Marko never showed any favouritism towards Eric. It was another Croatian whom he trusted above anyone else: Dario Kovatic, standing alone, watching the scene but not part of it. Just like me.

At one point, I saw Marko's eyes scan the room and linger on the back of his wife's platinum blonde head. As if she felt the attention, she flicked a strand of long hair impatiently over her shoulder. They were a stunning looking couple. Apart from the fact they were barely a couple at all, of course.

Everyone at the Club knew about Marko's wandering eye but not everyone knew that it wasn't just another relationship he might be open to. Marko had a reputation around Europe for making conquests and moving on quickly. That went for football clubs as well as girls' hearts. Marko wasn't going to commit his long-term future to a club as small as Fulham. He might have already decided that one season here was enough, promotion or no promotion. But Marko also had a reputation for success and I was beginning to see how he achieved it — it wasn't just the WAGs who hung on his every word.

Recently, I had overheard Marko talking about Zac Miller and a near-miss with a car that might not have been an accident. The usually blasé Marko had sounded perturbed. So many rumours, so many whispers echoing around the Club. The jolly goalkeeper Davy Walker liked a bet on the horses, so they said, Phil Philopoussis drank a bit more than a professional athlete should and as for 18 year old Leo Blake, there were rumours of a different kind about him ...

Of course, in some cases rumours weren't necessary because the truth was blatant. Here came Mitch Masters, who thought he was the best striker in the League when he wasn't even the best striker at Fulham. And behind him, Javier Herrera, who would supply Zac with perfect crosses on the pitch but despised and belittled him off it.

And here was the man himself. Last out of the dressing room but without any thought to the entrance he would make. Zac Miller's hair caught the light and his blue eyes swept the crowd searching for one person only, his wife Tammy. She quickly crossed to Zac's side. With her toffee-coloured curls tied back and her freckled face untouched by makeup, she was by far the most beautiful woman in the room. They kissed briefly but Zac's arrival had been noticed and they wouldn't be left alone. Zac was the star of the Fulham show. He had scored another goal tonight, taking his total to 21 for the season. If Fulham were to be promoted, if the FA Cup run was to be extended, if Marko Maric's ambitions were to be fulfilled, then it was Zac who had to deliver.

But Zac had been absent from training one day last week and tonight I saw the strain around his eyes and the artifice in his smile. It was hard to carry a team all the way to the top of the League and I wondered if he was about to falter. If Zac Miller was falling apart, then Fulham were in trouble.

Monday 13th January — Hammersmith

Loz

I took one last close-up look in the mirror. Good, no make-up streaks or unruly curls. I headed down the hallway stairs, stepped over the ever-present bikes and out into the bright but chilly morning. I loved that I could walk to work, not many people in London could do that.

As I passed the high street shops and local cafes, listening to the latest Fulham Focus podcast, I thought about the weekend. Fulham had won — a critical mood influencer — and Dom and I had enjoyed a long walk along the river in winter sunshine.

I arrived at the Council's tired-looking offices, scanned my security pass and headed up the stairs to the second floor rather than use the unreliable lifts. It was still early and so the office was quiet. As a planning officer at Hammersmith and Fulham Council, I enjoyed the variety of issues I dealt with and that I got to meet lots of interesting people. My latest case included a new riverside site in Fulham. The owners wanted to redevelop the office space for flats. You couldn't blame them — the values along the river were getting ridiculous. But they were trying to over-develop the site and I knew I would have to make them rein it in — that meant a drawn-out battle.

My coffee-making was purposefully delayed until mid-morning as I knew as soon as I moved from my desk the 'Monday Morning Football Weekend Round-up' would start. I'd already bumped into Anaisha, our team support, who wasn't particularly into football but claimed to follow Man United. We'd had a brief chat about our respective weekends, including the inevitable reference to the football results.

"Is your Dom a Fulham fan as well?" she'd asked me.

"Dom? He has no interest whatsoever. Cricket though, that's a different story. Must be something to do with him being an Aussie," I'd responded, with a look making it clear it didn't make any sense to me.

I headed into the kitchen. Already in there were Big Al — unironically a giant of a man and, more notably, an AFC Wimbledon supporter — and Matt, who took his Leeds support to ultimate levels. He really did have the tattoo and the duvet cover.

"You did OK then," Big Al said as soon as he saw me. Monday-morning conversation always kicked off this way.

"Yep. Zac Miller's in great form — his finishing's incredible," I said as I reached for my mug. "But I still don't know if we'll finish in the top six," I added. Doom was never far behind my happiness. "You happy with your one-all draw?"

"Guess so. Just happy MK Dons lost," Big Al smirked.

We already knew each others' results as that was part of the weekend ritual. We would scan for score lines and newsworthy action — like disallowed goals, missed penalties, sendings off and last-minute winners.

Like other fans, I would link whoever I knew, past and present, with certain teams, forever imprinted. That meant I always looked out for Crystal Palace's results as my Uncle John was a season ticket holder. Same for my cousins' teams, Millwall and Arsenal. London was a magnet for people from all over the place so friends and colleagues also supported a range of teams, such as Sheffield Wednesday, Everton, Bristol City and, of course, Leeds. That meant any notable result would be mentally clocked along with a prediction of how those fans would be feeling. Even Dom commented when Newcastle had a big win or major loss as his boss was an Alan Shearer-loving Geordie.

In the world of office politics (and workplaces beyond), supporting one of the 'top' teams was seen as a lazy choice — unless it was your birthright, in which case you were absolved from derision.

It wasn't controversial to think that increasingly the big clubs weren't about the match-going fans, their focus was on their commercial interests gained from TV rights, lucrative sponsorship deals and merchandise sales. These dictated everything from when games were played to which kits were worn. They even changed the names of clubs. Deep historical and cultural treasures wiped out by a billionaire's wave of the hand. For the most part, their fans accepted this Faustian pact as it lured many of the best players in the world to ply their trade in England. The huge commercial carrots made teams in the leagues below strive to break into the Premier League, despite the near-impossibility of the smaller clubs being able to realistically compete with the super-rich ones with their fantasy teams.

I caught up on some reports I'd been working on and when my stomach started grumbling, headed down to the ground-floor canteen, rebranded in neon green colours. For some inexplicable reason, it was trying to create an American diner vibe in a Hammersmith Council office. I spied Andy and Matt across the room as I queued for my lunch and soon joined them clutching my tray.

"Good weekend, Andy?" I asked. I'd already had the obligatory football de-brief from Matt in the kitchen and so was fully up to speed with Leeds United's victory.

Andy nodded, adding, "The kids were driving us mad but I managed to watch most of the Blues' game, on the telly at least. Good result for you, though. I wouldn't mind nabbing your striker, he'd slot in nicely to our style of play," he baited.

Andy was the case officer who was dealing with Fulham's new Putney Stand planning application — and him a Diamond Blues fan! Not that he ever called them the Diamonds — like a lot of their fans, he refused to — only ever 'the Blues'. It was a case I would have loved to have been assigned, even though I knew I'd never be able to assess it objectively. I'd seen the plans and thought what the Club was proposing looked good, the stand sitting graciously between the trademark Cottage in the corner of the ground and the Thames. The ground's riverside setting was something Fulham fans cherished and visiting fans admired. A rendition of London Calling at half-time allowed Fulham fans to sing heartily that we, " ... *live by the river* ... ". The already developed new Riverside Stand had been a success, so the fans were happy for the Putney End to be next, increasing the ground's capacity but without diminishing the intimacy that fans treasured.

Andy told me that most technical matters had been crossed off and suggested that the scheme had the support of the key local politicians including most of the ones on the planning committee. This was essential as they'd vote on whether to give permission or not. I was confident that the mayor wouldn't overrule a positive decision, as the GLA, London's governing body, had already made clear their support.

"Actually Loz, I found out something that might interest you. Bob, the guy leading the project from Fulham's end told me that your manager's not interested at all in the Club, and couldn't care less about the new stand. Says he's not in it for the long run, despite what he spouts in the press. In fact, he was saying even though you're flying in the League, he didn't think it was a particularly happy ship. Lots of money worries too."

I couldn't tell if Andy was just saying this to wind me up or not. He knew that I was desperate to get any second-hand gossip when I could. Marko Maric, the Club's manager, not being 100% committed was hardly newsworthy. Managers were on a perpetual merry-go-round, driven by a combination of owners wanting instant results, fans being impatient and fickle, and big sums of money being thrown about. But if the money worries were so bad that David Patterson might be forced to sell, that wouldn't be good for our promotion race and any Cup run we might put together.

I tried to put Fulham gossip out of my head, at least until I could discuss it with Jack when we next met, so we quickly moved on to chatting about the London mayoral elections. We all loved living and working in London but we were also acutely aware that it had its problems. My colleagues were in agreement that the current mayor, Frank Best, despite his campaign slogan, 'Frank. Best for London', hadn't been.

"For the first time in my life, I'm thinking of voting Green," Matt said. "That Sonia lady is making sense to me. We need something radical to sort out the planet and she looks like she means what she says."

"Well, let's see how she performs in the debate," I said.

Thursday 16th January
Pimlico

Jack

Within a week of Fulham's FA Cup third round win, Loz and I had made plans to go to the fourth round match — the glamour tie which was Barnsley away. I booked the train tickets and went back to helping Fleur prepare the day's deliveries. Murphy, my black and white cat, had deigned to descend from my upstairs flat and had taken up station on the shop counter, the only monochrome in a pallet of colour.

"Wow," said Fleur, "this is an expensive order."

I peered over her shoulder at the computer screen. The order was for an enormous hand-tied bouquet of pink, red and white roses which we would assemble from stems of All for Love, Red Naomi and Vendella still in bud. The effect was always spectacular both in appearance and scent but at a cost of over £350, we didn't supply this bouquet very often.

"What do you think," Fleur went on, "Guilt flowers?"

"You're so cynical!" I scolded her. "It's probably a birthday or anniversary."

I was turning away from the screen but then something caught my eye — the flowers had been ordered by a Mr M Maric. And as the song went, There's Only One Marko Maric …

I said quickly, "Do you mind if I do the deliveries today?"

Fleur looked at me in surprise — a morning in the shop with Murphy for company versus hours driving around South London and Surrey getting stuck in traffic and potentially lost. It was a no brainer. "Sure."

"Great," I said, reaching for the roses.

***

I had owned and run the flower shop in Pimlico for over five years. After I finished my fine art degree, I tried various jobs before realising that with a lot of hard graft and a bit of luck, I could be my own boss.

I had scoured west London for cheap, modern premises but had fallen in love with an old three-storey building which met none of my requirements. It was boarded up, full of mice, had the same toilets that had been installed when the place was built, no kitchen and a leaky roof. And, yet, despite all of that, it was still beyond my budget.

Within six weeks of finding the place Murphy and I had moved in. I opened Coming Up Roses three weeks later and hired Fleur a month after that. The flat took a lot longer to renovate and, for over a year, I was living off things you can cook in a microwave. Strangely, as his food comes out of a tin, the deprivations seemed to bother Murphy more than me but I suppose he was the one walking around on the splintery floorboards bare foot.

It was hard work running the business, not least because I was much better with flowers than I was with money, but my luck had continued. I had picked up some valuable corporate accounts over the years, my proudest achievement being that I was the official florist to Fulham Football Club.

So, before my trip to the Marics' house that morning, I first had a delivery to Craven Cottage, one of my favourite places. I was waved through reception with a large crate of Queen of the Night and Snow Star tulips and directed to the largest of the lounges in the Riverside Stand.

I was surprised but pleased to run into Will just beyond reception and coerced him into helping with the heavy crate. "What's the event?" I asked.

"New Year fundraiser for the Clubs Together Foundation," he replied. "Lots of people flashing their gold cards while drinking too much. It's a good cause though and close to Mr Patterson's heart."

"Do any of the players come to these events?" I asked, idly imagining Zac Miller admiring my work as much as I admired his.

"They do a lot of stuff for charity but not a dinner like this mid-season," he said.

"Are you here helping to set up?" I asked as we entered the lounge and set the crate down.

"No," said Will. "Leo Blake lost his wallet and thought he might have left it in the dressing room so I was sent to look. No joy though.

I'd better get going now." He nodded towards a suited man sitting at one of the window tables.

"Who's that?" I asked.

"Richard Green, Director of Communications."

"Is he your boss?"

"No but he's one of the powers behind the scenes at Motspur, sees and knows everything that goes on."

I was suitably impressed and started displaying the flowers. There were two huge bowls, one on each end of the bar, and lots of smaller vases, one for each table.

I left Richard Green's table until last in case he was about to leave and I wouldn't have to disturb him. When I made my way over to the windows, he was on the phone, saying loudly, " ... no, I won't confirm that."

And then, "There is no truth in the rumour that Mr Patterson is thinking of selling the Club."

I fumbled the vase I was holding but luckily it was only a tulip that fell to the floor. I rescued it as Richard snapped, "No, you can't quote me and I really do not appreciate this call. I suggest that you find another story to run."

He ended the call while I tried to slide the vase onto the table without him noticing I was there. I failed but he glanced at the flowers then at me and said, "They look nice," before getting up and striding away.

Will had gone so I couldn't query what I had overheard with him. Instead, I took a long look out of the windows over the panoramic view of the river, the Wetland Centre and west London beyond and prepared myself for the last delivery of the day.

Surrey

I didn't get lost in the leafy lanes of Surrey but it was a close-run thing. The Marics' house had a name rather than a number and was invisible from the road behind a pair of intimidatingly solid gates.

I pressed the buzzer on a discreet intercom. I was nervous. I knew Marko was unlikely to be at home because the Fulham first team usually trained in the mornings. But I couldn't help picture myself being so starstruck that I dropped the flowers, tripped over, couldn't speak or otherwise made a fool of myself. Probably, I was thinking, as I waited for the buzzer to be answered, Mrs Maric wouldn't be home either and I would have to leave the flowers with the cleaner and the trip would end in an anti-climax.

But the voice that answered through the intercom with a peremptory, “Yes?” was unmistakably accented. My heart started racing. It was her!

I stuttered slightly as I introduced myself — my state of nervous excitement at the thought of standing on Marko’s doorstep was increasing exponentially as the encounter with that doorstep drew closer. The disembodied voice snapped, “Come,” and in front of me the gates started swinging slowly open.

When it came into view at the end of a long drive, the house proved to be large and modern but designed in an Art Deco style — all smooth curves and clean lines — which made it look imposing but not unwelcoming.

I knew the woman who opened the front door was Ivana Maric because I had seen photos of her. She was supermodel slim with long, sleek blonde hair and perfect makeup. Her simple but elegant fitted dress made me feel scruffy in my work fleece and jeans. She barely glanced at either me or the flowers.

“Bring them in,” she ordered.

I stepped into the house and followed Ivana down a long corridor. I had a sense of minimalist style in the rooms I glanced into and the corridor itself was beautifully decorated in shades of vanilla and nutmeg. Ivana strutted in front of me like she was on a catwalk but I had to wonder why she was wearing three-inch stilettos when she was apparently home alone.

She led me into an enormous room at the back of the house — part kitchen, part breakfast room, part living room with a wall of floor-to-ceiling glass doors looking out over a huge, well-manicured garden. On the wall in front of me, three football shirts had been framed and hung, all with the name Maric at the top and a number 6 underneath. One was an old Chelsea shirt and another, with pride of place in the middle, was Marko’s Croatia shirt, probably the one he wore when Croatia came third in the 1998 World Cup. The third was a similar blue to the Chelsea shirt but I didn’t recognise it. The fact that the display read 666 was slightly disconcerting.

“Put them there,” Ivana gestured to the largest island unit I had ever seen and I turned, relieved to put the heavy bouquet down. But I caught my breath as I saw the opposite wall. Three more framed shirts were hanging there, again with the ominous 666 message but on this wall, between the claret and blue of West Ham and the red and blue of Crystal Palace, was the black and white of Fulham.

"Thank you," said Ivana. She didn't mean it as an expression of gratitude, she meant it as a signal to leave.

Emboldened by the sight of the Fulham shirt, I asked, "Is it your birthday?"

"No, nothing like that," she said dismissively while conducting me to the front door.

Back outside, I found that I was breathing like I had been exercising and not just because the flowers had been so heavy. I felt like a spy, sneaking into Marko Maric's house and snooping even though I hadn't seen anything I shouldn't have. But I knew I had discovered a secret today — either Marko adored his wife so much that he sent her very expensive flowers on a Thursday in January for no reason at all or Fleur had been right and the luxurious bouquet had been chosen for a very specific reason indeed.

Craven Cottage

Richard Green dressed with care on Thursday evening, giving his bow tie the attention it deserved and making sure his monogrammed gold cuff links were visible. Richard took pride in his appearance — never more so than when he had been invited for a drink by his boss.

Richard had been Director of Communications at Fulham for just over a year. It was a challenging role. When he had taken the job, Fulham were a Premier League club and he had built up a good working relationship with the old manager. Then suddenly, they weren't a Premier League club anymore and the manager had been replaced by the morose and arrogant Marko Maric who didn't seem to realise that his role was to cooperate with the media, not antagonise them.

And now there was a potential new problem; the phone call he'd received that morning from the journalist was disturbing. Football was an area where there most definitely could be smoke without fire but Richard needed to know if there was any substance behind the story put to him earlier. He had sent a vaguely worded text to David Patterson who had kindly invited Richard to his flat at the Cottage for a drink before the dinner they'd both be attending in the Riverside Lounge. Richard accepted immediately.

Richard enjoyed striding through the Cottage gates in his dinner suit, accepting the deference that was his due from everyone he passed. It wasn't always like this. The backroom staff at a football club were often overlooked, much to Richard's chagrin. He arrived at the flat exactly on time and David opened the door himself. Richard was disappointed to spot that his boss's bow tie was a pre-knotted one but David's greeting was cheerful. "Richard! Come in, come in. What's your poison? Beer?"

Beer wouldn't, in fact, have been Richard's choice but David was already handing a bottle over so he accepted it with thanks. He asked, "Is Mrs Patterson coming tonight?"

"No," said David. "She's in Aspen, skiing." He shrugged, indicating slithering around in the snow wasn't for him.

Richard guessed Harriet wasn't staying in a hotel. He couldn't keep track of the Pattersons' residences in the UK and around the world. The one he was really interested in was the Caribbean-based yacht. That's where he'd rather be having a drink tonight, not in cold and gloomy London.

Unlike Marko Maric, Richard excelled at small talk and managed a whole gamut of uncontroversial topics before bringing the conversation round to the critical one. "You saw my text earlier. I had a call from a journalist," he said. "He seemed to think you might be selling the Club. I put him right, of course, but … "

"Too bloody right I'm not selling!" David slammed his bottle onto the coffee table with a force that caused the beer to bubble out. "You can tell him that again and you can tell anyone else who asks the same thing. Fulham Football Club is not for sale. Not now, not ever."

"That's what I thought," Richard said smoothly. "But I could do my job better if I knew what might have given him the idea ... ?"

David picked up his beer again, "I'm selling some of my stores," he said. "It's a bad time for retail, everyone knows that. But that has nothing to do with the Club. It hasn't even crossed my mind to sell. On the contrary. I've told Marko and now I'm telling you — it's nothing less than automatic promotion for us this year. I've made it clear to Marko and he's going to deliver. That's the story you need to be putting out there — the Whites are going up!"

Richard nodded earnestly but his mind was pondering interesting possibilities. He wanted Fulham to get back to the Premier League almost as much as David did — there was a lot more prestige, not to mention money, involved in working for a top-flight club. But there were 24 teams in the Championship and there was still nearly half of the season to play. If Marko Maric had promised that Fulham would finish in the top two then he might well have overreached himself. And the consequences of that could be rather amusing.

Friday 17th January — Park Lane

After the interview with Julie Martinez, Omar Hamarat had arranged for flowers, from an upmarket florist, of course, to be sent to her at her office — he couldn't send them to her home as that would have given away that he knew where she lived. The message on the thick embossed card inside the cellophane had said, '*Julie, a pleasure to be interviewed by you. Collaboration is the key. Look forward to our paths crossing again. Omar*'.

From her questioning that afternoon and the slight sideways scrunch of her mouth, he could tell she was at times frustrated by the nature of the interview. Whenever she tried to go off-piste, Hamarat politely got her back to what he had agreed to talk about.

Underestimating people was not one of Hamarat's weaknesses and as a journalist with a certain reputation, he expected Julie to have done her research. She would have been desperate to delve into the origins of his wealth and to uncover any hint of ill-gotten means.

He recalled her reaction at the end of their veneer of an interview, with as much information gathered as he had pre-orchestrated. Hamarat had engaged Julie in some family chit-chat about her children and asked how she managed juggling a challenging job, especially with her husband doing the same. Julie had slowly smiled, made aware that, unsurprisingly, Hamarat knew that her husband was a politician in the Shadow Cabinet.

Joe Martinez had a reasonably high profile for those interested in politics and while they weren't quite regulars on London's social scene, they were occasional participants and sometimes referred to in media articles as a 'power couple'.

Hamarat had offered up his views on national politics to her, espousing that the government was stale because it had been in power for too long. He had wagged his finger vigorously, telling her that Labour's current leader was never going to win that power back. Hamarat had held her gaze as he suggested that Joe would be a much better leader.

He could see in her uncertain eyes and from her quick laugh that she wasn't sure whether he was just being mischievous.

***

The Park Lane retirement dinner for The Post's editor, Angus Lee, was attended by many of the UK's movers and shakers.

Hamarat and his wife Tabitha weaved their way through the tables spread around the large dining room to take their places. As they neared their destination, Hamarat could see Joe Martinez chatting to some other guests seated alongside him, while his wife Julie had her head down, consulting the menu.

Hamarat's smile was already in place when, clearly sensing someone beside her, Julie looked up. He did a mini-step back, lifting his hands in the air.

"What a surprise and pleasure this is," he said, before introducing her to Tabitha.

After the fun and frivolity of the after-dinner charity auction — Hamarat had donated one of the lots, VIP tickets to a Diamond Blues match and guided tour of the Diamond Arena — most people got up from the table. Hamarat moved to sit alongside Joe.

It had been straightforward to find out the basics. The initial bio he'd received on Joe was short:

MP for Hampstead and Kilburn for over 10 years, majority of over 11,000. Currently in Labour Shadow Cabinet (Business). Good public recognition/popular. Proud of working-class background. State-educated. Scholarship to Oxford to read Politics, Philosophy and Economics. Head of Labour Group at University. Post-university, went into management consultancy before entering politics, working for 12 years, one of youngest to reach partnership. Married with three children. Wife, Julie, a journalist for The Post. Lives in a recently renovated Victorian-semi in Primrose Hill — large mortgage. Numerous other loan facilities. Declared Arsenal fan. Polished, intelligent, articulate and highly ambitious.

Hamarat had taken an interest in UK politics from when he first landed in the country. After all, you needed to understand the place where you'd decided to set up shop, how it worked, how it was run and, of course, how it could be influenced. He enjoyed the ease of doing business. But the very things he liked were also the things that frustrated him — why weren't more people open to oiling the wheels if it meant you could get things done better and faster? There was always someone, somewhere, willing to bend or even break the rules for the right incentive, you just had to find them.

It had been Joe's appearance on the BBC's Question Time last year that had first got Hamarat's attention. Joe had come across as likeable, with a sense of humour even. He was that metaphorical politician you could imagine having a drink down the pub with. But Hamarat sensed untapped potential, hints of traits not dissimilar to his own lurking just below the surface. Behind Joe's smiling eyes, Hamarat could detect something else, more than just an ambitious ego. Maybe a certain need to prove himself.

Joe's answers had been delivered with consummate charm but they had been straightforward, unambiguous even. He had declared, "You do what it takes. You do whatever you have to."

It was more than just a hollow statement. Hamarat believed this could be Joe's inner motto. The time had come to test him.

Frank Best had been London's Labour mayor for over three years. In that time, Hamarat had come across him on several occasions, most recently in his bid to buy Wembley Stadium. Their relationship was poor — as an old-style conviction politician and ex-union head from his Dagenham car plant days, oligarchs were not Frank Best's natural allies.

When Best was first elected, he was well regarded. But his subsequent strong support for striking transport unions and his stringent policies to curtail City excesses were blamed for some companies, and therefore jobs, leaving London for Frankfurt, Amsterdam and Singapore.

Rumours swirled of Frank Best being burnt out. There'd also been talk of two mini-heart attacks. Hamarat's source had advised him that it might not take much to topple Best, and in the end, a gentle nudge from him was all it took. Just a few days after their recent call Hamarat had received confirmation that Best had decided to stand down. It had been easier than Hamarat could have dared hope. Best's health issues must have been even worse than they thought.

The huge headache for the Labour party was that the incumbent mayor had already been reselected as their candidate for the election less than four months away. For the moment, only a handful of people knew of Best's decision and Hamarat amused himself with thoughts of the party being in full-scale panic mode. They'd be trying to keep it under wraps, he had mused, until they could announce a replacement. But Hamarat had the knowledge and the power.

***

Hamarat, port glass in hand, settled into easy conversation with Joe even though this was their first meeting, laughing about the evening's auction before switching to football chat. Meeting new people was something they were both used to and Joe assumed that the conversation would stay light. But there was a change in tone when Hamarat said to him, "Joe, you seem a clever man. How would you describe it … switched on?"

Joe smiled almost coyly at the description.

"You will know that doing business is not easy. In Turkey, I needed my friends in business. There is still so much corruption in my mother country, but I have learnt that you must play them at their own game even if you use different rules. I have many politicians who are my friends, not just in Turkey but elsewhere as well."

Hamarat went on. "I have grown to feel that London is very much my home. Every man needs a base, somewhere to come back to. I want to see London continue to prosper and I have many wonderful ideas for investing in this city. It is sad that I cannot do this without having the assurance that I will get the support I need. Frank Best has not been good for London. He has not been good for me."

Joe was normally guarded in his views but the meal and wine had relaxed him and Hamarat was proving interesting company.

"Yes, not Best for London," Joe replied. "Bloody bad for London."

At this point, Hamarat moved his chair slightly and leaned towards him.

"Do you think you could do a better job? Because I think you could."

"I'll get my application in for the election in just over four years' time then," Joe laughed, clearly flattered by the vote of confidence.

Hamarat continued. "What if I was to say there is an opening coming up, sooner than you think? A mayor who was able to work in a collaborative way with me would have my backing and support in whatever way he needed."

Joe stopped smiling. With a raised eyebrow he asked, "What have you heard exactly? Is Frank stepping down or something? I haven't heard anything."

Hamarat paused before responding, "I understand so, yes."

He took a sip of his port. "As an experienced politician, you know, of course, that being London mayor is a great stepping-stone to the future leadership of your party. That means possibly the future Prime Minister. I have been following your career for some time and if my intuition is right, you have what it takes. If you grasp this opportunity, I can help you. You know I have the influence and the funds for a mayoral campaign."

Joe was taken back. He couldn't understand why Omar Hamarat, a man he had never spoken to before that evening, had taken so much interest in him and his career. A moment ago, he had felt the mellowing effects of the port flowing through him, now he began to tingle with excitement.

Joe hadn't given much thought to this mayoral race; it was Frank's so there was nothing to think about. If there was an opening though, that was massive news. His mind raced. There was no doubt that being London mayor would be impressive. As for raising his profile, well, that would be without question. And anything that could alleviate his increasingly financially precarious state was an opportunity that he'd run towards. Standing for mayor was something he had privately entertained but not until Frank retired, which he assumed wouldn't be until after his next term. As Hamarat had pointed out, it could just be the launchpad for even bigger and better things. Lucrative things.

Joe thought bitterly, all my life I've come face to face with people in business and in politics who have got there because of their connections, mocking the self-congratulatory notion of the meritocratic UK. Why shouldn't I get the support I need to turbo-charge my career with the help of new powerful friends?

Looking Hamarat in the eye, he said, "If I did put myself forward, I'd be doing this for London, OK?"

"Of course," responded Hamarat.

"And my family." He dared not look across at his wife, Julie.

"Yes, your family would be so proud, I am sure."

Joe gazed up to the room's ornate chandeliers to buy some time before committing. He took a deep breath before looking squarely at Hamarat. "OK," he said, "So what's the plan?"

With a wide smile, Hamarat raised his glass and Joe lifted his in turn. With a clink they downed the rest of their ports.

Wednesday 22nd January — Surrey

Managing a football team is more than a full-time job. It's an every-waking-moment job and even then, there weren't enough hours in the day to accomplish everything. You could delegate to an extent, but Marko had never been one of those managers who relied too much on coaches and backroom staff. There were no shortcuts, not much glory and a lot of thankless tasks which meant it was a bit like playing defensive midfielder. Which was partly why Marko was so good at it.

Because he had a few extracurricular activities to manage as well, it was inevitable that minor matters sometimes fell through the cracks. He realised on the morning of Fulham's home match against Reading that his suit needed cleaning. As it was an evening kick-off, Ivana would have plenty of time to get it to the dry cleaners and back during the day.

She was uncooperative. "Wear another suit," she said, "You've got plenty. Or wear a tracksuit. Other managers do."

"Well, I don't," said Marko. "And I want to wear this suit. Please."

Later, he took a light pre-match training session which confirmed his choices for the starting eleven. The frost was beginning to melt and the players left bright green footprints as they ran through it, their breath filling the air with clouds. Marko's phone buzzed with confirmation from Ivana that the mission had been accomplished but, she seemed to imply, at vast inconvenience and discomfort to herself.

On his way to his office, he was struck with what seemed like a good idea and summoned the young club assistant. Marko couldn't remember the lad's name — Will or Bill or something — but he looked eager to please when he arrived.

Marko held out two £50 notes, "Go to the shops and buy some flowers for my wife."

Will/Bill gaped at the enormity of this task. He was used to dealing with the petty demands of footballers. Flowers were outside of his experience. He stammered, "What kind of flowers does she like?"

"Expensive ones," said Marko.

***

Despite Will/Bill's self-doubt, Marko was satisfied with the bouquet of purple and white blooms delivered to him early that afternoon. When he arrived home to change before heading to the match, his suit was hanging on the kitchen door in its pristine plastic wrapping and Ivana was drinking coffee at the table.

He laid the flowers down with a heartfelt, "Thank you."

Ivana looked at the flowers and then at Marko. Even for a trip to the cleaners she was exquisitely dressed in a leather jacket and designer jeans. "What are these for?"

"For helping me out."

"Really. And what were the last flowers for?"

He was getting impatient. And defensive. "Nothing. Why did they have to be for something?"

"Because I know you, Marko." She pushed her chair back, the legs scraping excruciatingly on the tiled floor. She stood up. "You sending me flowers makes me think the worst of you, not the best. It reminds me of … " she bit off the sentence.

Marko shook his head. "You've got it all wrong. The last flowers were for nothing, just for ... "

" … for putting up with you?"

"Yes, because I'm so hard to put up with, aren't I?"

Like all midfielders and, indeed, all beleaguered husbands, Marko knew that the best form of defence was attack. He gestured around the vast kitchen. "All of this, all the holidays, all your clothes."

He touched the sleeve of her jacket. The leather was so soft it felt like silk. "This is new, isn't it?"

"No," snapped Ivana. "I've had this for years."

"And what about these?" Marko swept on, catching her left hand and holding her rings up to the light. The marquise-cut diamond on her middle finger flashed. "These must be really hard to put up with."

Rows with Ivana only went in one direction and Marko was thinking that it would be a good idea to move out of a room full of sharp objects and that he should let someone know he might arrive late at the Cottage. But then his phone rang, and the spell was broken.

Ivana snatched her fingers away. Marko would have refused the call but he saw it was from the one person he could not ignore — David Patterson.

"Hello, David."

It was usual for Fulham's owner to call before a match to check on the line-up and wish everyone good luck. He said, "Are you all right? You sound out of breath."

"I've been running," Marko improvised.

"Oh, OK. I just wanted to check that Ivana's coming tonight. Harriet's in LA and I'd really like Ivana's company in my box."

"I ... um ... don't know. I'll ask her," Marko said. He knew he sounded hesitant but he found himself caught between his she-devil of a wife and the stormy blue sea of a disappointed boss. He told David he would phone back and ended the call.

He had heard Ivana's heels clip-clopping away as he was speaking and found her in the formal drawing room. She had thrown the new/

old leather jacket over the back of a chair and was standing in front of the fireplace, arms folded.

Their eyes met in the mirror on the chimney piece. He said, "That was David Patterson. He wants to know if you're going to the game. He wants you to join him in his box."

She was silent for a long time but whether that was because she was angry or indecisive, he couldn't tell. Eventually she asked, "What time is kick-off?"

"7.45 p.m."

"I'll see."

***

Marko's day improved rapidly after that. Fulham beat Reading 2-1 with goals from Zac Miller and Leo Blake. He strode into the players' lounge after the final whistle feeling pleased with himself and felt even better when he saw David Patterson and Ivana drinking champagne by the window. At once something struck him as odd about Ivana and then he realised she was wearing flat heeled boots so as not to tower over David.

The owner wrung Marko's hand. "What a match! That goal from Zac was something else." He carried on effusively for some minutes. " ... up to third, Marko, we can do this!"

Marko accepted the gratitude as his due, conscious of a group of WAGs watching them from the other side of the room.

Eventually, David concluded, "Right, I've got some calls to make before they shut up shop in New York. Thank you for your company, my dear," he said to Ivana who stooped subtly so he could kiss both her cheeks.

Marko waited for Ivana to congratulate him but when it became clear she wasn't going to, he said, "If the boots are new then that was money well spent."

"Don't start this again."

"I'm not starting anything."

She scooped up the new/old leather jacket and put it on. "What are you doing?" Marko asked.

"Going home. I only came because David asked me to."

Marko caught her hand for the second time that day. "You are the most infuriating woman in the world."

Again, she pulled her fingers away, the marquise diamond scratching his palm. "If I am," she said, flinging a look at the WAGs, "then, I have good reason to be."

Saturday 25th January — Barnsley
FA CUP FOURTH ROUND — Barnsley FC v Fulham FC

Jack

On the last Saturday morning of January, I left the shop in Fleur's capable green fingers and met Loz at Kings Cross for the journey to Barnsley and Fulham's fourth round FA Cup match. Over cappuccinos on the way, we chatted about my delivery to the Marics' house, including the 666 shirts and Ivana's frostiness. We speculated about the reasons behind Marko's gesture but got no further than the obvious conclusion.

As we walked out of the station, Loz told me that an architect called Will Alsop had once proposed redesigning Barnsley as the Tuscany of the north, modelling it on the walled town of Lucca. Loz was always coming out with this sort of stuff. Once, when we were walking through Watford on our way to Vicarage Road, she pointed out a car park designed by her favourite car park designer. Favourite car park designer! I could barely decide who my favourite Fulham player was.

Unfortunately (or otherwise), Alsop's plans were shelved and the only traces of Italy I noticed in the Yorkshire town were pizzerias.

Oakwell is a traditional stadium where away fans aren't shoved in an inhospitable corner but are given an excellent view of the pitch from the North Stand. Despite the fact Barnsley had become a bogey team for Fulham in recent years, the stand was noisy and busy.

The first half was disappointing from a Fulham perspective. Antonio Perez Alvarez, in his first start since returning from injury, was particularly off the pace. Fulham were slow, placid and in some disarray. Eric Jovic kept passing to the invisible man. This wasn't as bad as Sunday Oyetoro who kept passing to Barnsley players.

Barnsley started the game quickly and aggressively and instead of toughening up and meeting them halfway, we met them at the edge of the18-yard box with some nervous last-ditch defending. Marko Maric, dark-clad and angry, paced the technical area, shouting instructions that no one seemed to heed.

However, having staggered to half-time with the score at 0-0, a different Fulham emerged after the break with no one improving as much as Antonio. Everything went through him — short passes, long passes, perfectly weighted ground skimming forward passes which set the wingers free. The first goal came from one of those — a long curving ball down the left wing which Lucas Karlsson sprinted onto.

He crossed the ball into the box where Zac Miller was arriving to tap it into the goal.

Barnsley fought back for a while but Antonio was just as adept at defence as attack and the ball hardly crossed the half way line. Zac's second goal was the result of another team effort — 18 passes featuring everyone except Davy Walker, our goalie, culminated in a cross from Javier Herrera which found Zac in just the right place at just the right time.

Now, on the touchline, Marko looked calm, even arrogant. This is what his team was capable of — every player on the pitch performed his role perfectly. We weren't watching random moves, we were watching a carefully choreographed and rehearsed routine in which eleven men thought and played as one. The beautiful game.

We were celebrating in the stands — Fulham's name was surely in the hat for the fifth round draw. We even started checking scores from other fourth round matches to see who we might play next.

"Right," I said, as the final whistle blew, "have we got time for a drink before we get the train?"

Loz

Away days were always more intense. That level of commitment, that concentration of fandom, somehow made you feel extra loyal, hard-core even — part of an elite group, the SAS of football fans. If truth be told, Jack and I didn't go to that many away matches but we did try to go to at least one non-London game a season. Fulham being a London club meant that there were lots of away matches you could go to without leaving your own city. Depending on which division we were in, we could go to away games at Charlton, Millwall, Crystal Palace, Brentford, Spurs, Arsenal and West Ham, never mind the ones we could do without actually leaving the borough.

Our selection for which away matches we'd go to depended on several informal criteria, some weighted heavier than others, such as did it clash with other (often neglected) commitments, was it a place we hadn't been to before or wanted to go again, or was it a crucial match.

The Barnsley away match had passed our mini-assessment so we'd been proud witnesses to our important win. There'd been about 1,500 of us there, not bad for a wintery day in January, and the atmosphere had been upbeat from the off. At half-time, I had a good look around me in the stands to take it all in and registered something we knew already, that Jack and I weren't your typical away fans, as two women, not part of a bigger group. Though I saw plenty of older men, couples and some small family groups, many of the Fulham fans were young guys in their late teens or early 20s, probably free of other social and family commitments. The number of recognisable faces increased with each game we went to. We were part of this footballing family, this Fulham tribe, and the bonds were strong.

We'd already made a change at Doncaster and the London-bound train was bursting with white-shirted Fulham fans. The warmth inside the train felt especially good after our afternoon outside in the biting wind. Black-and-white scarves were draped over seats and the empty beer cans were evidence of the post-win celebrations. A group of fans further along the carriage were in full singing mode.

Jack and I had already talked a lot about the match on the way back to the station, but our de-brief continued on the train.

"It's brilliant we're through to the next round," I said. "Zac's in such good form. You can see why so many struggling Prem teams are trying to nab him before the transfer window shuts at the end of the month."

"We'd never agree to let him go. It would be stupid if we did," said Jack.

It wasn't until about an hour into the journey from Doncaster that the singing Fulham fans began to quieten down, the euphoria simmering to a mellower mix of post-match chatter.

"Did you know that Laura, in her first year in England, went to see Luton play Barnsley with the guy she was going out with at the time?" I asked Jack. Laura was an American friend of ours who'd lived in London for about ten years and occasionally came to see matches with us at the Cottage. She loved it that Fulham FC had a strong history of having American players in the team.

"Was that the notorious guacamole incident?" asked Jack, smiling. I nodded.

Apparently, Laura's Luton-supporting boyfriend had taken her to a Barnsley chippy following the match and, after scanning what someone else had just been served, she asked the server, in a bright American accent, for chips with guacamole.

He looked confused. "Gwoka-what?" He replied, in a broad Yorkshire accent.

She pointed to the guy beside her, busy putting lashings of salt and vinegar on his food.

"That's mooshy peas, luv."

She told us some time afterwards that she'd also asked for a mint tea at half-time — she'd probably called it an interval — and that didn't go down well, either. The boyfriend ended up presenting her with a Bovril. "A meat drink?" Laura exclaimed. To this day, she shakes her head in disgust whenever it's brought up in conversation.

Jack and I had lots of similar stories about friends who tried to take an interest in football for our sakes but didn't quite get it. From one asking me in all seriousness, "Will they still be playing if it's raining?" (we were talking light rain at the time, not tropical storms) to a good Australian friend insisting on calling the ref an umpire. Another mate told us the score of a match we'd not managed to follow, and we were both elated when she advised us we'd won two-nil. Turns out we'd been playing away and she'd got the score the wrong way round. We'd actually lost. That's why Jack and I tended to keep our footie chat for each other and kindred spirits.

The intermittent train wi-fi gave us a chance to catch up on all of the other football scores and the day's news.

"Did you read that Frank Best's standing down as mayor?" Jack asked, showing me her phone.

"Yep, that was a shock," I said. "But Labour's announced they're going with Joe Martinez instead, which I think's a smart move — he comes across OK. Not that the other candidates are up to much."

Still looking at her phone, Jack said, "He's supposedly an avid Gooner but I've seen tweets from Arsenal fans saying they've never seen him at matches. It's funny when politicians try and get street cred from supporting a football team."

"We should try and get tickets for the election debate at City Hall in a couple of weeks," I suggested and Jack agreed readily.

Over the train's tannoy, the guard announced we were shortly coming into King's Cross. As we gathered our things, I remembered something I needed to tell Jack. "Oh, I spoke to my colleague Andy about the Putney Stand application last week and he's hoping to get it to committee next month."

"It'll get through OK, won't it?"

"Hopefully. But there's always a risk. Just hope the objectors don't get too vocal and spook the politicians into not supporting it," I replied.

We filed off the train along with the other fans who'd recommenced their singing, filling up the station's concourse. The Barnsley journey may have ended but our Fulham FA Cup journey was still motoring.

Wednesday 5th February — City Hall

Joe Martinez shut his front door and walked over the railway bridge and down the hill towards Chalk Farm tube station. He was a little short for time; he'd been deliberating which tie to put on, red seemed a bit too obvious, overtly tribal. In the end, Joe settled on a greenish paisley one. He checked himself in the hall mirror, grimaced and pulled off the tie plaster-quick, stuffing it in his pocket on his way out. Sure, he wanted to look authoritative and, of course, assured, but he didn't want to look stuffy and out of touch. The trouble was he didn't know what a modern mayor looked like. Not that he'd won — yet.

Joe was heading to the first of two scheduled debates for the candidates before the May election. With Frank standing down, the press's view was this mayoral race was a simple baton change: it was Joe's to lose.

The day after his conversation with Hamarat, Joe had gone to the shadow leader's chief of staff, the real person with the power, and offered himself up for the mayoral role. Hamarat had made it clear that Joe had to be on the offensive. There had been a couple of other possible contenders with ambitions of their own, but the party had pushed them aside, not worried about it looking like a coronation. Time was tight and Labour just needed to get this election out of the way. Besides, Joe Martinez was the best known, most relatable and least left-leaning of the bunch and was seen as capable of putting right some of Frank's policies.

To receive the backing of a person like Hamarat, with his funds, was pure serendipity. What he wanted from Joe in return wasn't that bad, Joe told himself. He was content he was now on the right path and was more than happy to leave his second-rate shadow cabinet colleagues behind. Even better, he'd done it without the connections of the establishment types with their incredible networks forged at exclusive public schools.

***

The Channel 4 TV presenter, Vanessa Capaldi, stood at the lectern. "This evening, ladies and gentle-men, in front of our live audience at City Hall, we'll be hearing from the four highest-rated candidates in recent polls, who think they're best placed to be the next mayor of London."

The seated candidates looked out from the stage towards the gathered audience arranged in arched tiers before them.

Vanessa went on, "With Mayor Best standing down," all eyes in the room went to Frank Best, sitting conspicuously in the front row of the auditorium as Vanessa gestured towards him smiling warmly, "there will be a fresh figurehead for London. In this evening's debate, we will hear from Londoners here at City Hall and we'll be engaging with those of you watching at home and on social media using the hashtag MayoralDebate."

Behind her, a large screen showed images of the candidates and details of how people could comment via various social media platforms.

"What are the issues that matter to people? How will the new mayor tackle London's economy and its need for housing? Will our candidates offer a fresh approach beyond party politics, beyond soundbites, and convince you that they're the right person for the job? Let's see."

Pimlico

<u>Loz</u>

"Here we go then, let's see what they're made of. It would've been good to be there but the vibe's quite fun here," said Jack.

We were in a wine bar, a regular Pimlico haunt near Jack's flat, and it was full of people clustered around small tables looking towards the large TV screen on the back wall.

"I'm interested how Arjun will do," commented Fleur. She'd been persuaded to come along at the last minute even though it wouldn't have been her natural inclination to watch the debate. "He was great on The Apprentice and I think he should've won it."

Even though the others in the group hadn't watched the programme, we knew exactly who Arjun Shah was, running as the Conservative candidate. Arjun, all of 32 years old, good looking, with the whitest perfect teeth, confident, extravagantly-dressed, immaculately coiffured, thought he was the answer to run London and the Tories thought he might have the 'X-factor' needed to break through Labour's red ceiling.

Arjun definitely wasn't like other politicians, and that wasn't just because he was openly pan-sexual and frequently pictured in gossip pages coming out of nightclubs with different partners. He was popular, especially with younger people, and had over two million Instagram followers who hung on his every word and action. He'd decided not to go into his wealthy west London family's Indian food production business and instead had had moderate success with his own on-line fashion company and had been the runner-up in the reality TV show, The Apprentice. Some of his comments were insightful and amusing and resonated with people, but some of his put-downs were seen to over-step the mark. Most commentators didn't consider him to be a serious candidate but everyone agreed that he made the election much more interesting.

"Let's see if people on Twitter like him as much as you then, Fleur," Dom said, looking at his phone. We all started scrolling to see what other debate watchers thought and were tweeting.

At City Hall, each of the candidates set out the basics of their campaigns. The Lib Dem contender, the tall and wiry Reuben Bailey, usually seen in his hi-viz jacket and bike helmet either on his Brompton or with it folded up by his side, was stressing the need for more cycle lanes.

Arjun Shah wanted to make London the start-up capital of the world, supporting new businesses, creative hubs and free enterprise.

The Green candidate, Sonia Smith, laid out that she wanted Londoners to have healthier lifestyles — cutting down on waste, promoting veganism and the sharing economy. Many of these ideas resonated with the public but it was her delivery which was left wanting — it was bordering on sanctimonious. Photos of her from previous Extinction Rebellion campaigns disrupting public transport started to circulate on social media.

Last up was Joe Martinez. His pitch was smooth, almost matching Arjun Shah on charisma, but beating the others on gravitas and statesman-like quality. As they all did, he talked about tackling the persistent challenges — crime, housing, air quality — but he also declared his 'grass roots' campaign to intensify the use of community and leisure assets, like schools' sporting facilities and the capital's football grounds, to the benefit of local people. Surplus public land, he said, could be sold for housing development to help pay for better public services.

I gave my view. "Arjun's pitch was quite good, I thought. Better than I expected, really. But he's just too young to be mayor. I mean running London isn't quite the same as a reality TV show."

Jack looked at her phone, "I think that's what most people on Twitter think too, Loz. A lot liked what he was saying but there's loads of tweets going on about how many buttons he had undone on his shirt and him not wearing socks in February!"

"Well, I'd vote for him *because* of what he was wearing," replied Fleur.

We turned our attention back to City Hall for the Q&A session. Most of the questions put to the candidates and their answers were fairly predictable. But Arjun was getting the most laughs. The Twittersphere was proving more entertaining than the debate itself.

"I don't really know much about her but Lydia Edwards is posting some really good tweets," said Jack.

"Who's she?" asked Fleur.

"She's that business woman, wears bright block colours, short blonde hair, distinctive black-framed glasses. Often on TV. I quite like her," I replied.

Fleur furrowed her brow, still unsure so I looked at my phone for help. "Her Twitter handle says, Lydia Edwards — social entrepreneur, free-thinker, Londoner. Striving for a better planet."

"She's clearly not a fan of Joe Martinez," Jack commented reading some tweets, "nor Sonia Smith. She thinks she's pretty rubbish. Listen to this:

@LydiaEdwards — JM needs to stop thinking London is his for the taking. London needs a reboot NOT based on old style political allegiances #MayoralDebate

@LydiaEdwards — good ideas from SS esp promoting sharing economy. Great to have female candidate BUT please don't lecture people, it won't work #MayoralDebate

@LydiaEdwards replying to @Sue_rubixcube — what would I do if I was running? Aim to make London world's most liveable city, a kinder city, link business with caring and sharing economy #MayoralDebate."

Vanessa Capaldi was drawing the debate to a conclusion. The audience applauded the candidates. There were no knock-out punches but the truth remained that Joe Martinez was the favourite and it would take something to go disastrously wrong for him not to be anointed London mayor in May.

The Pimlico wine bar was beginning to empty out and people were finishing off their drinks. "Have you seen what's trending on

Twitter now?" Dom asked. "#Lydia4London, #L4L, #Londydia. Everyone's saying Lydia Edwards should run, especially if we want a female mayor for a change. No one thinks Sonia Smith has a chance. Wonder if she'd go for it?"

St James's

In his club in St James's Square, the TV was still on in the lounge but the sound had been turned down low. Hamarat nodded to the waiter for the bill. He'd met with a business associate earlier on in the evening and had stayed on to watch the debate rather than head back home, wanting to watch it in real time. Joe Martinez had done well, he thought. He looked and sounded convincing, not hard when your competition was poor. Good choice, he thought to himself.

The waiter fetched Hamarat's coat and helped him put it on. Hamarat wrapped his scarf around his neck and walked into the adjacent bar on the way through to the entrance hall. The bar looked warm and inviting on a winter's evening with its rich claret colours and low-level lighting. He looked to see if he recognised any faces. At one of the tables near the far wall, a woman caught his eye, sitting with a stubbly, casually dressed man he didn't know. They were engaged in an animated conversation. Well, if it's not Lydia Edwards, he thought, unaware that she'd been trending on Twitter that evening.

Hamarat stepped into his waiting car. The journey from St James's to Knightsbridge was short but long enough for him to gaze out the window and remember a Lydia Edwards well before the trade-mark pixie haircut and black-rimmed glasses. Their joint venture hadn't reaped rewards, in fact, had been one to forget. But he never forgot anything.

PART 3

Monday 2nd March — Motspur Park

On Monday morning, the first team ate breakfast in the canteen together as usual. The mood was fractious. On Saturday, they had lost away at Derby in a lacklustre performance which had left them dispirited and at the mercy of Marko Maric's acerbic tongue. The players were conscious they had let their manager down but reluctant to take responsibility.

Jamie sat at the table, silent as recriminations raged around him. " … hadn't scored all season and we give him two!" " … it wasn't me who did the suicidal back pass!" "… if Mr Super Striker had passed to me instead of going for glory, I would've scored."

The last comment was from Javier Herrera and Jamie had had enough. "Just give it a rest, will you? You're worse than my kids!"

It was, he thought, testament to the squad's ambitions that they were feeling so frustrated about an uncharacteristic loss that hadn't even threatened their third place in the League. He just wished they could be ambitious but not fight as much.

Jamie caught Phil Philopoussis's eye across the table. Phil had joined the Club last summer and was the biggest and oldest outfield player. He was used to being a team's enforcer but he had told Jamie he had never had to play the role as often in his own dressing room as he had this season. Phil was pulling his hair into its topknot signalling he was ready for training.

"Let's get going," Jamie said across the table. "What's up, Leo?"

Leo had stood up and was frantically patting his pockets. "I've lost my phone!"

Phil shook his head but Jamie was pleased with the diversion. "Do we fine people for losing their phones?" he asked.

Lucas Karlsson, who ran the squad's system of fines with the assiduousness of a forensic accountant said, "No, not usually. We might make an exception though. This is the second time in two weeks."

"Oh, come on!" Leo protested.

"What's he owe now?" Phil asked.

"£140," Lucas replied without needing to check. "£20 for each time he left his water bottle on the training pitch last week, £50 for forgetting his phone charger when we went to Barnsley and £50 for the stupid goal celebration at QPR."

"Wasn't that stupid," Leo muttered.

"How much for not coming to training?" Javier asked.

There was an empty chair at the table and they all glanced at it, some deliberately, some subconsciously.

"That's for the Club to deal with, not us," said Lucas.

"But what d'you think?" Javier continued. "When does someone who keeps missing training get dropped from the team?"

Lucas rose and started sorting food waste from recycling. Jamie stood up as well, "Come on," he said. "We're here to train, not chat." He found Lucas waiting for him outside the canteen.

"Zac's a no-show again," Lucas said quietly.

"Maybe the gaffer gave him the day off?" Jamie suggested hopefully.

Lucas shook his head. "Marko never gives anyone the day off. Remember when Phil had been playing in Australia and Marko made him come straight to training from Heathrow even though he'd just got off a 24-hour flight. And it's not just missing training. He's been very quiet recently. I sat next to him on the way to Derby and he hardly spoke. Then he went apeshit when he got that yellow card. He was about to punch the ref's lights out before you stepped in."

Jamie frowned at the memory. "He didn't deserve the card but it was a massive overreaction."

"This is how it started last time," Lucas said, "with stuff like this. You know he deleted his Twitter account? I thought that might have helped."

"Guess, we better look out for him," Jamie said.

"Yes," Lucas agreed. "And you better speak to Marko."

Jamie sighed. He always approached meetings with Marko with trepidation. Marko was difficult to read and you never knew quite where you stood with him.

Jamie had worked with a lot of managers in his career. Some had been better than others. Some made the mistake of being too friendly — Marko went too far the other way. Some left too much work to the coaches whereas Marko was very hands-on. Some hugged you when you came off the pitch and deluged you with praise. From Marko you might, if you were lucky, get a handshake and a few words of constructive criticism.

Jamie found visiting Marko's office like going to see the headmaster at school, particularly when he had a delicate subject to raise.

Earlier in the season, he had tried to convey Antonio Perez Alvarez's concerns about his wife not settling into English life, but Marko had just stared at him incredulously. Jamie shuddered to remember the embarrassing encounter. Frankly, he would rather mark Lionel Messi for 90 minutes in a must-win match than talk to Marko Maric about issues around mental health.

***

Marko had been told soon after the horror tackle in a Cup match that his footballing career was over. He had fought against the knowledge in the months which followed but, even for someone as determined as him, there was no way back from the catastrophic injury.

Eventually, he could run and kick a football again but the doctors and physios had been clear — as a professional footballer, he was finished.

The bitterness had taken even longer to get over than the injury. His career had been shot down at its zenith. Just as his name was being mentioned along with the very best of his era, as doors were being opened for him all over Europe, his dreams had been shattered and his contract quietly terminated. He was yesterday's news.

It didn't help that the old injury still troubled him sometimes. He pushed himself hard — to keep up with the players on a run, to pass the ball around so people said, "Marko's still the best player at the Club." When he overdid it, his knee would ache and, because he didn't like anyone to see him limping, he would avoid training and catch up on paperwork.

Today was one of those days and the timing was bad — it was two days before the fifth round FA Cup tie against Brighton and Marko wanted to motivate as well as drill the team following Saturday's error-strewn performance. It was frustrating to be stuck behind his desk.

Before the injury, he had never considered going into management. While he was recuperating, it didn't feel like a serious possibility until a Croatian club approached him. Even then, his acceptance of their offer was half-hearted, motivated in part by the instinct of a wounded creature to crawl home.

But the inauspicious start had rapidly turned into an unexpected success. Marko worked harder at management than he had needed to as player and he applied every positive technique he had learnt from coaches in the past. But it wasn't all about work ethic and borrowed tricks of the trade. Marko knew how to win and, despite what had happened on Saturday, he knew his Fulham team were beginning to understand his formula for success.

The poor result at Derby had left Marko feeling more disappointed than angry. But that had changed when he'd received a call from David Patterson yesterday. Patterson was not an unreasonable boss and he hadn't used emotional or coercive language, but his message was clear — fighting on two fronts wasn't working and

Fulham needed to bow out gracefully from the Cup and focus fully on automatic promotion.

Marko had listened in silence, grateful Patterson couldn't see the disdain on his face. He knew what his team was capable of and neither a rare defeat nor the views of his boss would convince him otherwise. Besides, subtle exits of any kind weren't Marko's style.

At noon, he stood up and stretched, then hobbled out onto the balcony overlooking the pitches. As he expected, Charlie Paxton, to whom he had entrusted training, was just finishing off and the players were straggling back to the changing rooms. Charlie and Jamie Crawford were last to come in. Jamie was helping to put the equipment away while Charlie was doing keepie uppies. Not particularly well, Marko noted.

On the pitch, Marko liked Jamie Crawford. He was exactly the sort of no-nonsense defender he had preferred to play with in his heyday: strong, vocal and decisive.

Off the pitch, in contrast, Jamie wasn't strong, vocal and decisive. He was gentle, softy spoken and thoughtful. He had a kind word for everyone in the Club, he knew everyone's name, he asked after their wives and children. If players were visiting a school or hospice, Jamie was always one of the group. He would mentor the academy players, help out the ground staff and compliment the caterers.

Jamie and Charlie walked towards the building passing a ball between them and chatting. Talking about the weather, Marko thought cynically, as the English did. He was about to turn away when Jamie looked up at him hopefully and raised a hand in an interrogative gesture. Clearly, he wanted to talk. Marko would rather not but it was Jamie's prerogative as captain so Marko nodded and stepped back inside.

A few minutes later, Jamie knocked on the door and entered. "Hi, Boss. How are you?"

"Fine," said Marko, although it wasn't true.

"How's Ivana?"

"Fine," said Marko, which might or might not have been true. Although they lived in the same house, he hardly seemed to see Ivana these days.

Jamie said, "Training was good. The lads are really up for the match."

One of the things Marko grudgingly admired about Jamie was the fact he didn't brood or dwell on mistakes. Jamie had been part of a defence which had conceded two goals on Saturday, but he had moved on and Marko knew he had to as well, especially if he was going to defy David Patterson.

He couldn't quite hide his impatience when he said, "What can I do for you, Jamie?"

"I'm worried about Zac," Jamie said, then stopped.

It wasn't what Marko had been expecting to hear and perhaps it was the surprise on his face which made Jamie hesitate. "Umm ... "

Marko repeated, "Worried about Zac?" Somewhere in the back of his mind, a memory twitched.

"Yes. He wasn't at training today."

"Oh," Marko said. "He left a message saying he had sore throat but should be better tomorrow. You obviously weren't told."

His tone was dismissive but one of the other things Marko admired about Jamie was that the captain didn't take the easy way out when it was offered.

"I'm not sure it's just a sore throat," Jamie said.

"What? Are you a doctor now?"

"No. I think ... " he tried to pick his words carefully "I think Zac might have some issues."

Marko sat back in his chair and narrowed his eyes. He said, "Zac's scored 27 goals this season. You're worrying about nothing."

"I don't think I am," Jamie said stubbornly. "Something like this happened before — about three years ago. I think we need to keep an eye on him."

This time, it was Marko who had an easy way out and because his knee was still hurting and he wanted to be left in peace, he took it. "And we will," he said. "I'll keep an eye on him. Of course. Now get off home, Jamie, and thanks for mentioning this."

When Jamie had gone, Marko made an espresso and contemplated what the captain had said. Yes, Zac had missed training today and it wasn't the first time. But Marko preferred people with coughs and colds (not that he was susceptible to these things himself of course) to stay at home rather than spread them around the team.

He sipped the dark, aromatic coffee and stared out of the window. In many ways, Fulham Football Club was too small, too old fashioned and too quirky for him but the facilities were good. Motspur Park was picturesque in the early spring sunshine. Of course, the facilities at a bigger club would be better.

He thought fondly of the Blues' training ground and then, less fondly, of his most recent visit to the Diamond Arena the previous week. Brighton had played the Diamond Blues in the League and Marko had invited himself along to watch — it was no problem for an ex-player to secure a seat. The Diamond Blues had won and Marko had picked up a few tips about Brighton's strengths and weaknesses but his ulterior motive for attending the game had been foiled. He had hoped to engineer another encounter with Omar Hamarat but the owner had been too busy with other people to even look Marko's way.

But the disappointment hadn't changed anything. Marko had ambitious plans for the rest of this season and beyond. And Zac Miller, although he didn't know it yet, was a part of those plans.

Jamie's words had taken Marko back to the incident with the car in December. Marko couldn't afford for his star striker to be out of action. He would claim to know little of mental health problems — any form of weakness was anathema to Marko, even his own — but he realised he might have a problem on his hands.

He had a sudden idea and picked up the phone, dialling the internal number for the Club secretary. "Is the doctor here? Good. Send him up to my office."

***

Andrew Brown has been the Fulham Club doctor for nearly two seasons. It was a prestigious post but not a particularly interesting one. The players were the fittest and healthiest human specimens he had ever come across and most of their ailments were minor and usually needed treatment from a physiotherapist, not a doctor.

Dr Brown had had a good relationship with the previous manager. He had had little contact with Marko Maric since his arrival although the doctor's diagnosis was arrogance bordering on rudeness, with a bad case of egoism thrown in.

He was surprised by the call from the secretary, but an urgent summons wasn't something any doctor could ignore. He arrived at Marko's office at a jog with his medical bag.

"What's the problem?" He asked.

"Problem?" Marko repeated, frowning.

"I was asked to come urgently. I thought you were having a heart attack or something."

"No," said Marko brusquely, "Of course not. I'm fine. Sit down." He waited until the doctor had obeyed before going on, "Were you here three seasons ago?"

"No. I've been here two years."

"But when you arrived there were records of the players?"

"Medical records? Yes, of course."

"And you read them?"

"Of course," said Dr Brown, wondering where this was going.

"Was there anything ... " Marko paused and the doctor waited expectantly. He had noticed that Marko did this sometimes — appeared to be translating words in his mind but Brown guessed it was a technique Marko used to give himself time to think. He went on, " ... unusual in Zac Miller's records?"

"Not that I recall," the doctor said. "What sort of thing did you have in mind?"

But Marko shook his head. "Nothing in particular. I was just wondering. But keep an eye on Zac for me."

Dr Brown scooped up his bag and left, mystified. Back in his own office he sat at the computer and called up the medical notes headed "Zachary Miller" and skimmed through them. As he had remembered, there was very little there, just records of the usual sprains and torn muscles.

But when he scrolled back to April three years ago, he thought he might have found what Marko was referring to. The entry was brief and fairly cryptic: insomnia, for which Zac had been signed off for the rest of the season.

Dr Brown scrolled up and down again but there was nothing else in the notes which was out of the ordinary. Insomnia. He wondered if this job was about to become interesting after all.

Wednesday 4th March — Craven Cottage
FA CUP FIFTH ROUND — Fulham FC v Brighton & Hove Albion FC

Jack

One of the best things about a Cup run is playing teams in different leagues, especially teams from a league above. The Luton and Barnsley ties had been good matches but Fulham had been favourites in them both. Brighton, however, were another matter.

Now that Fleur had developed a new interest in politics, I suggested she broaden her horizons to football as well and booked the seat next to ours for the evening match. She had been hesitant at first but words like "men" and "shorts" had convinced her to give it a go.

As expected, Brighton were business-like and efficient. They passed the ball quickly and accurately, they attacked fast and they counter-attacked even faster. At the back, Jamie Crawford and Phil Philopoussis had their work cut out while up front Zac Miller existed on very slim pickings. Our busiest player by far was our goalie, Davy Walker, whose experience and judgment were vital, but even he couldn't deal with the curling cross and powerful header which led to a Brighton goal.

At half-time, the atmosphere in the stands was flat. We couldn't see Marko Maric's face from H7 but, judging by his body language as he stalked across the pitch to the Cottage, he wasn't happy. Marko was famously immune to the elements but as it was a cold evening, he had added a black scarf to his usual dark suit and flicked one end of it angrily over his shoulder as he walked. I guessed his words in the dressing room would be a lot warmer than the temperature outside.

But Marko wasn't just a man of words. When the team jogged out onto the pitch 15 minutes later as London Calling blasted round the ground, we saw that Leo Blake had been replaced with the more physically robust Mitch Masters, which would hopefully make for a lively second half. We were down, but not out.

Before I could say, "We need to score an early goal," we had scored an early goal — an unstoppable rocket of a shot from Mitch from just outside the area. And, suddenly, Fulham were back in the game and Brighton were in disarray. They hadn't been expecting the combination of Zac's subtlety and Mitch's brute force.

Zac got the second quite soon after, a header from one of Antonio's precise corner deliveries. Despite chaos raging in the box, Zac followed the flight of the ball and timed his leap to perfection, meeting it with his head when all around him were losing theirs.

During the last twenty minutes, Davy Walker and the defence fought frantically to keep the score at 2-1 under an ever-increasing Brighton bombardment. In the stands, we were singing to the Brighton fans, "Who are you? Who are you?" Fleur joined in wholeheartedly but, like the novice fan that she was, put the emphasis on the chant's last word rather than the second.

When the final whistle went and the players ran towards us, we were relieved as well as delighted that Fulham's FA Cup adventures would continue.

"Bar?" suggested Loz as we applauded.

"Bar," I concurred.

***

I got a round in and joined Loz and Fleur at a table. Both were looking at their phones. "So, we're in the last eight of the Cup," Loz said. "Guess who the other seven are?"

"Tell me."

"Liverpool, Man City, Man United, Spurs, Arsenal, the Diamonds and Leicester."

"Oh God! That really takes the shine off the win!"

"Why?" Fleur asked.

"Those are the top seven teams in the Premier League," Loz explained. "Who would you prefer?"

"None of them," I said. "I suppose Leicester are the most beatable team at the moment but they'll want to make up for losing the League Cup Final."

That Final had taken place the previous weekend. The Diamond Blues had won courtesy of what was widely acknowledged to be a soft penalty but, on balance, it sounded like they'd deserved the victory.

Fleur, who had recently started following Arjun Shah on Twitter, said, "Here's something you two will be interested in — Lydia Edwards has just announced she's going to stand for mayor, as an independent candidate."

"Wow," said Loz, "she'll really shake up the campaign."

I was pleased. "It's about time we had a woman as mayor."

"I still like Arjun," said Fleur resolutely.

"Of course, you do," I said. "But I can't vote for him. Lydia's going to give people a lot to think about."

We toasted Fulham's win and Loz admired the big display of tulips on the bar and the matching smaller ones on all the tables which Fleur and I had arranged and delivered to the Club that afternoon. "Black and white," she said. "Very appropriate."

I was about to explain the black ones were in fact a very dark red when Will appeared and took the seat next to Fleur's.

I said, "Have you been working tonight?"

"Yes," he replied, "but not behind the bar. And now I'm having a well-earned drink. Can I get you ladies another?"

Loz and I declined on the basis we had to go to work the next day. Fleur, who also had to go to work the next day and was in the presence of her boss, accepted. "Generation Z," I muttered. Loz grimaced sympathetically.

On the other side of the table, flirting was in full swing so Loz and I talked about the match, the election campaign and the planning permission for the new Putney Stand until Will interrupted.

"What did you think of the match, then?"

"Great," I said. "Zac and Mitch played really well together. I suppose they're good friends, both being American."

Will chuckled drunkenly. "You'd think so, wouldn't you? But you'd be wrong. I'm not sure any of this lot are really friends. The stuff they say sometimes. It's supposed to be banter but it sounds like bullying to me."

"What sort of stuff?" I asked. "Doesn't Marko try and manage it?"

"Yeah, well, the rumour is Marko's got something else on his mind."

"Like what?" I asked, glancing first at Loz who nodded and then at Fleur, who appeared to have fallen asleep.

"Not that Marko'll be here for much longer," Will pronounced. "I heard him on the phone the other day. He was saying, 'It's not a long move but it's a big one.'"

He looked pleased with himself at revealing this cryptic statement and went on. "It might be for the best."

"I think we'd better get Fleur home," Loz suggested.

We shook Fleur awake, wrapped her in her coat and steered her outside to a taxi. I told the driver her address and told her not to come to the shop until tomorrow lunchtime.

We watched the cab drive away then walked towards the tube. "What was Will on about?" Loz asked. "All that stuff about Zac and Mitch, and Marko?"

"God knows. I suppose he might have overheard things, but I think we should take most of that with a pinch of salt. It was just the drink talking. Anyway, it's the quarter-final draw tomorrow night. Who do we want? Or who do we really not want?"

"Liverpool away," Loz said immediately. "That would be impossible. We'd never win that."

***

The following night Fulham were drawn away to Liverpool in the quarter-finals of the FA Cup.

Wednesday 18th March — Craven Cottage

<u>Loz</u>

I met Jack after work at Hammersmith Tube station as we'd planned to walk down to the ground together. I spotted her easily as she came out of the District Line exit into the shopping mall in her fuchsia pink coat and matching earrings; a smile spreading across her face when she saw me.

She gave me hug and giggled as she said, "Loz, this is brilliant. Thank you. Thank you. Thank you for sorting this out."

We were both excited to be heading down to the Cottage for an evening of mingling with some of Fulham's great and good — facilitated by a Diamond Blues fan! We were off to celebrate the Club's latest success, but not on the football field.

Everyone who knew me appreciated my excitement about Fulham's Putney Stand planning application. The proposals were, in my humble professional and personal opinion, a work of art. The architectural design with its sleek frame and gently curving roofline would look both in-keeping with the historic ground's listed elements and would complement the recently completed Riverside Stand. Luckily, it wasn't just me who thought that and despite local objections, the Council's planning committee had approved the application at their February meeting.

I had attended that meeting, watching nervously from the public gallery, as my colleague Andy presented the scheme. Andy had been happy to celebrate the approval with me in the pub afterwards and I congratulated him on his good work — even though he was a Blues fan who wanted to poach our best player. We'd only had a quick drink but it was long enough for him to gloat about the Diamond Blues' League Cup win and how well they were doing in the League.

When he'd stopped though, he told me that Fulham were going to be having a celebration at the Cottage to mark the new stand's permission and if I was nice to him, he could get me on the guest list. Without hesitation, I told him I'd make him coffee for a month if he could get my friend Jack on it too.

***

We chatted non-stop as we walked along by the river towards the ground.

"So, who exactly is going to be there? Any of the players?" Jack asked excitedly.

"Well I asked Andy again today and he said he thinks it'll be a bit of a mix. Obviously, there's Fulham people, so maybe David Patterson if he's in the country, Bob, the project manager, but Marko Maric should be there too, hopefully. He wasn't sure about any players.

They'll also be people from their associated charity and some bigwigs from the Council. "

"We need to get talking to Bob," said Jack. "Find out any gossip. But, thinking about it, not knowing us from Adam, he's hardly going to tell us whether it's a happy ship or if Patterson's intentions are to sell, is he?"

"Well, no harm in trying," I said. "If we talk to him, we can see what he says and then ask Will next time we see him what he thinks."

"I'd love it if some of the players were there — it would be embarrassing but I'd have to get a selfie," Jack said.

For a brief second, I did wonder to myself, maybe our non-footballing friends were right to think that two seemingly mature women being this excited about a football club was really not healthy.

***

We knew we were in the right place because Billy the Badger, the Club's mascot, all six foot two of him, was standing at the entrance to the Riverside Lounge.

"Hello Billy," we shouted almost in unison and he gave us a friendly furry wave.

"We should have asked for his autograph," I joked as we headed inside and gave our names to the young woman with the clipboard.

We made our way over to the bar, looking out to see if Will was working. A smiling waiter handed us each a glass of chilled white wine. We paused to take in the scene — being at the Cottage on a non-match day felt extra-special, a real privilege. As we looked around the room to see who we recognised, I noticed a roving Club photographer taking pictures of different groups of people.

"See anyone interesting?" I asked Jack as we tried to blend in — it was a prestigious event and we were supposed to be participants rather than spectators.

"Over there near the edge of the bar. I can see Jamie Crawford, looking well turned out, and he's with Marko."

"Wow. Marko really is very good looking — don't tell Dom I said that! Is that his wife with him?"

Jack nodded, "Yep, he's definitely handsome," she said appreciatively, "and yes, that's Mrs Maric."

We knew there'd be speeches and, apart from the charity partner, thankfully they didn't go on and on. It must have been the Club's head of communications or marketing, a Richard someone, who did the introductions. First up was the Council's Leader who talked of the fruitful working partnership with the Club. We were pleased to see that Fulham's owner was indeed at the event, as he walked up to the (now lowered) microphone, taking over from the Leader.

David Patterson only took a few minutes and seemed sincere when he said how special the Club was to him and his family, and how he wanted to ensure that the investment he was ploughing into it benefited as many people as possible. You had to mean it if you'd spent hundreds of millions of pounds. We listened carefully for any hint of business woes or wanting out.

With the speeches finished, we went to the bar to pick up another glass of wine and doing the same was the new stand's architect — I recognised him by the signature flowery shirt that he'd also worn for his appearance at the planning committee. I introduced myself and Jack to him and was vaguely conscious that I was probably being a little too gushing about his design. As we were chatting, behind his shoulder, I noticed Ivana Maric approaching the bar. I gently nudged Jack and could tell she had clocked her too.

Jack had described Ivana to me as glamorous but a cold fish. Her long blonde hair swished as she strode over in an elegant fitted navy pin-striped trouser suit and spiky navy patent heels. I knew that Jack and Fleur felt that the flowers had signalled that her husband was guilty of something. Ivana hadn't looked overjoyed to receive them but I was more sceptical. Why did romance have to be dead?

Ivana took a glass of white wine from the bar and spotted us. Well, she spotted Jack to be exact.

"It is you. The Flower Woman," she said to Jack without smiling, choosing to ignore both me and the architect.

She thought for a moment before saying, "I want you to do something for me."

I nearly spilt my drink — I was so thrilled that we, well Jack, was chatting with Marko's wife. I turned towards the architect so Jack could continue the conversation and pretended to listen to what he had to say while desperately trying to eavesdrop on them. Ivana moved Jack towards the end of the bar which meant they were now beyond my strained hearing reach.

Andy joined me and the architect, together with Bob, the project manager and gossip provider. At this stage, my priority wasn't to find out anything from Bob — it wasn't the right opportunity anyway — but to keep an eye on Jack. I managed to position myself so I could see her and her new BFF and, all the while, fake my participation in the conversation. But it was impossible to hold back a laugh when I saw the roving photographer take a photo of Jack with Ivana. One for the album, I thought.

People had started to drift off. Jack made her way over to Andy and me and it took a lot to curb my desire to quiz her until we were by ourselves.

As the three of us headed towards the exit, we saw that Billy the Badger was still there and he took us by surprise by flinging his furry arms around Jack and me in a badger sandwich. Without hesitation, Andy beckoned the nearby photographer who lifted his camera. With any self-consciousness having evaporated away with the evening's wine, we smiled cheesily as he took the shot.

"This better be on the Fulham website," I said.

***

"OK, Jack. Out with it," I demanded. We were walking at pace back along the river towards Hammersmith Bridge.

"That was surreal," said Jack. "Ivana … "

"Your new best friend?"

"Yes, her. Well, she wants me to deliver flowers … "

"I don't understand. What? To her?"

"No, no. To some hotel in Wembley. I've been given quite strict instructions. I have to deliver them to a room — not leave them at reception — around 5 p.m. tomorrow evening and I have to make sure I give them to the woman staying in the room.

"When I hand them over I have to try and memorise what she looks like — hair colour, length, height, shape, eye colour, God knows what."

"Blimey," I said. "That's mad. Did she say why?"

"No, I didn't ask, to be honest," Jack said. "She wasn't inviting questions, just giving me directions. When she first started talking to me she just asked if I'd be willing to help her. I guess she might already know who this woman is and just wants confirmation, but who knows?"

We arrived at Hammersmith Tube station where we'd be going our separate ways. Our walk had given us both the chance to ponder on the night's events and I sensed we'd both come to the same conclusion.

"You were right about the Guilt Flowers, Jack. Marko … well … he must be playing away."

She nodded in agreement.

"And now you are going to be instrumental in helping Ivana Maric in her Wagatha Christie quest. How bloody exciting is that?!"

Thursday 19th March
Motspur Park

At Motspur Park, the players were practising corners while Charlie, the first team coach, and Marko watched, the former encouragingly, the latter menacingly.

The weather was cold and damp and the mood in the squad was irritable. They had lost away at Stoke at the weekend. The inquisition into whose fault it was had started on the way home and continued ever since. Aidan Rafferty had fouled a Stoke player in the box and, unsurprisingly, Davy Walker hadn't saved the resulting penalty and the forwards had produced nothing. It was the first poor result since the loss to Derby at the start of the month. But in the race for the League title, Sheffield Wednesday had won at home and extended their lead at the top of the table.

Corner practice was going badly, despite Antonio's deliveries being good. An hour in and the battle of attackers versus defenders turned into a shoving match and then a tussle on the ground. Most players emerged muddy and cursing while Zac crawled out with a cut along his forearm.

Leo tried to peer at it sympathetically but Zac snatched his arm away and swore with uncharacteristic vehemence.

Charlie jogged over and said matter of factly, "You'll have to get that seen to. The doctor's in this morning. Go and see him."

Zac, torn between reluctance at seeing the doctor and relief at avoiding another brawl, trudged towards the building, his arm hurting and the cold catching up with him. Alex McKenna, the reserve goalie, and the academy goalkeepers were training on another pitch. One of the boys called, "Come and practise some penalties, Zac!" but he didn't reply.

Long ago, in Texas, he had wanted to be a goalkeeper. He had played almost exclusively in goal until he was in his teens when a coach, desperate at the no-show of his striker one Sunday morning, had told Zac to "give it a go" up front. Zac had scored a hat trick and never played in goal again.

Watching the youngsters now, he missed his old position but, although he had the reactions and the agility of a goalkeeper, he didn't have the big, intimidating physique.

He wasn't sure, he thought walking on, if he had the nerve either, and shuddered slightly.

***

Andrew Brown had tried to obey Marko's instruction to keep an eye on Zac but it hadn't been easy. From the bench at recent matches he had seen only what he expected to see — an athlete who combined power and grace, a striker who played with intelligence and commitment. Zac always came off the pitch looking shattered but that wasn't surprising given the hard graft he put into the game. In the players' lounge after a recent home match, Dr Brown had watched Zac greet the lovely young wife who obviously adored him and wondered if he was wasting his time.

Zac turning up at his office looking chilly and dejected was therefore fortuitous.

Dr Brown's bedside manner was more suited to his elderly private patients than young footballers but he deployed it now and, if it didn't exactly put Zac at ease, it did at least entice him into the office.

"Oh dear. What caused this? A stud? I thought you played football with your feet. Well, not where you're from of course. I've never understood that — playing 'football' with your hands."

He directed Zac to sit down where the cut could be inspected under the light.

"Doesn't look too bad but there's some mud in there." Dr Brown watched Zac's right knee jigging up and down then glanced at his patient's face. The bright blue eyes avoided his. He asked, "Are you hurt anywhere else?"

"No, just this."

"You seem a bit agitated."

"I prefer being outside, that's all."

The answers were a little too pat, but the doctor concentrated on cleaning the cut then tried another tactic.

"I'll just look at your notes to check your tetanus jabs are up to date."

He moved over to the computer leaving Zac to look around the room at posters showing various human body parts.

The doctor turned back. "All fine," he said. "But there is something interesting. I see my predecessor diagnosed you with insomnia a few years ago. How's that these days?"

He had hoped to catch Zac off guard but realised that was no more likely to happen in his office than it was on the pitch.

The movement of Zac's knee increased in velocity as he said, "It comes and goes. Are we finished?"

"Nearly," said the doctor, producing a tube of cream. "This is antiseptic, so it'll sting a bit. Have you been feeling stressed or anxious? Anything like that?"

Zac flinched but whether it was a reaction to the antiseptic or to the words Brown couldn't tell. "No," he said.

"When's your next match? Saturday? This'll be fine by then. I'll find a dressing." He got up and rummaged in a drawer saying over his shoulder. "If you ever want to talk about anything you know where I am."

For the first time, Zac's blue eyes didn't skitter away when he tried to catch them. "Thank you," he said, as polite as always. "But I doubt I will."

Wembley

Jack

On the day after the Putney Stand party, I left Fleur to supervise the shop and made up the bouquet Ivana Maric had instructed me to take to the Wembley Astra Grand Hotel. I had proposed a budget of £200 which she had accepted without batting an eye so I wished I'd suggested more. However, the price was more than enough to cover the bouquet of China Pink and West Point yellow tulips I was assembling and the cost of the trip to Wembley.

Thankfully, the hotel was easy to find — a modern monolith of glass, steel and brick which looked sleek if unimaginative. Inside, though, the decor was a stylish and subtle blend of blues and purples and there were hints of luxury in every discreet corner.

I had delivered flowers to hotel guests before although I didn't normally feel nervous when I did so. I strode up to the front desk and peered around the bouquet at the receptionist. Her name badge read, "Melissa".

"What gorgeous flowers!" Melissa said.

"Thanks. They're for room 207. OK if I pop up with them?"

"207." Melissa tapped at her keyboard. "Hmm. That's not his usual room. But, yes, go on up. You'll need a pass to operate the lift but I can let you have a spare one for a few minutes."

She handed over the credit card-sized pass and pointed to her right.

'His usual room', Melissa had said. Ivana had been evasive when giving me directions but I had always suspected what this was about and Melissa's words had confirmed my thoughts — I was about to knock on Marko Maric's hotel room door.

The lift was slow which made my nerves harder to contain. It was similar to when I had made the delivery to Ivana at home but this time coming face to face with Fulham's manager was a lot more likely.

From the second floor lift lobby I followed the sign to rooms 201 to 210. Outside room 207 I paused for a moment then knocked twice and waited. There were sounds of movement behind the door then it opened.

The person who stood in the doorway wasn't Marko Maric.

I held out the bouquet, "Delivery for you."

I have seen every possible reaction to an unexpected flower delivery: surprise, elation, laughter, indifference, rudeness, anger, sobbing; on one occasion I'd had a door slammed in my face. The woman in room 207 was a little confused but still gracious, "Are you sure?"

"Room 207," I said. "Yes, I'm sure."

"But who are they from?"

I thought quickly. "From the hotel," I lied, "Because your usual room wasn't available.

"Thank you, then," and she accepted the big bouquet with a small smile and stepped back into the room.

I let out the breath I had been holding and walked away.

***

My Wembley adventure wasn't quite over because when I gave the pass back to Melissa she said, "I'm getting married in the summer and I'd absolutely love a bouquet like that. Have you got a card?"

"Sure," I said and handed it to her with the pass. We made arrangements to speak the following week and I left the hotel silently thanking Ivana Maric for putting more business my way.

Surrey

I set off in the van not for Pimlico but for Surrey. It was a long journey with a difficult conversation at the end of it. I wasn't looking forward to confirming to Ivana that her husband was having an affair. I drove up to her big fancy gates with trepidation.

Ivana buzzed me through and, once again, answered the door herself, smartly dressed and coiffured with a lot of gold jewellery on display. "Come in," she ordered.

I followed her obediently down her pale and airy corridor to the kitchen with its island unit the size of Mallorca, and the 666 shirts.

Without preamble, Ivana picked up her phone. "Did a woman answer the door?"

"Yes."

"What did she look like?"

"Long dark hair, brown eyes, about my height."

Ivana started swiping through her picture library and holding up photos for me to look at. Judging by the glamorous appearance of the various women, I guessed they were probably WAGs.

"Her?"

"No. More olive skin."

"Her?"

"No. Not Oriental."

"This one?"

"No. More — " I cut myself off. I had been about to say, "more beautiful" but that would have been a hideous mistake. "More curly hair," I said quickly.

A few more swipes and another photo appeared. I nodded. "Yes, that's her."

Ivana nodded. "Thank you," she said and the words were a dismissal. But as I turned away, she said, "Jack. Isn't that a man's name?"

"It's short for Jacqueline," I explained.

"Oh, like Jacqueline Kennedy," she managed to make it sound like a criticism. Frankly, if we were to compare the US presidents our names could be linked with, I'd win hands down.

***

As soon as the Flower Woman left, Ivana took a bottle of wine from the fridge and poured herself a large glass. Developing her plan so suddenly and seeing it come to fruition so quickly was disconcerting.

There had been dalliances before of course, she had always known it. But she had turned a blind eye. Because of the lifestyle, the money, the house, the jewellery — the possessions that Marko had taunted her with in their row a few weeks ago. And because of the shame of admitting to her family and friends that her husband was cheating on her.

But things were different now. For one thing, her daughters were grown up and no longer living at home. Both girls were studying abroad — one in Paris, the other in New York.

She put her glass down and snatched up her phone, scrolling through the pictures again to the one of Marko's latest conquest. She was just his type — young, pretty, pliable. As bored and lonely in damp and unwelcoming England as Ivana herself was.

It had started towards the beginning of the season, Ivana estimated. The beginning of the season, that said it all! For so many years her life had had to fit into the football calendar — no family Christmases, no trips to Croatia at Easter, birthdays and anniversaries missed if they clashed with a match.

She had gone into investigation mode — checking credit card statements and eavesdropping on phone calls. At Christmas, she had moved up a level and started answering Marko's phone if it rang when he left it lying around. For weeks she had learnt nothing — all the calls were about football.

Then yesterday, the breakthrough had come.

While Marko was in the shower, she answered a call from a hotel in Wembley with the news that they had mixed up Mr Maric's booking. His usual room, 606, wasn't available so they had allocated him suite 207 instead at no extra cost and assumed he would be checking in around 3 p.m. as usual.

Room 606, she thought bitterly, looking at the stupid football shirts he insisted had pride of place in every house they lived in. She had mulled over the information all day, wondering how best to make use of it. Running into the Flower Woman at the party had felt like an amazing stroke of providence and Ivana had acted immediately.

But now that she had acquired the information, she had to decide what to do with it. She leaned her elbows on the counter, putting her head in her hands, careful not to spoil her expensively styled hair.

Should she confront him? Have it out with him? Or store the knowledge away for future use? Would she be brave enough to leave him? To go out on her own for the first time in her life, in her 40s?

She had met Marko when she was 20. She was an aspiring actress. He was a footballing legend already. He had had a bad time in the civil war — his grandparents had been killed and his home destroyed. He never spoke of that period nor of his part in the Yugoslavia team which won the 1987 World Youth Championship.

Their first few years had been blissful, travelling to London and setting up home together as Marko's playing career thrived. The girls had come along in quick succession and she had enjoyed motherhood. Marko hadn't been a hands-on father but that hadn't mattered, he adored the girls and despite his transgressions as a husband he had always been a devoted parent.

They had both wanted, quite desperately, another baby, a little boy to complete the family and for Marko to be extra proud of. That had ended in disappointment and misery, but the anguish had brought them very close for a while and even now, fifteen turbulent years later, the shared hurt would occasionally catch them unawares and strengthen rather than weaken the marriage.

Instead, the real damage to the relationship had been caused by Marko's injury. He had lived for football and it had been snatched away from him. She had tried to be sympathetic but he had taken his vile temper out on her and she had reciprocated. Although they patched things up, Marko had changed, his ambitions all consuming, his charisma buried deep and morosity his default mood. Only his inclination towards infidelity remained the same.

It didn't help that travelling around Europe had become tedious rather than glamorous. Being uprooted every time a better career opportunity came along for Marko was unsettling and, of course, he expected every house they moved into to be furnished and decorated to perfection within days.

What should she do? Surely it was time to put an end to this moribund marriage? The evidence she had now would get her the financial settlement she deserved. She could get out of this grim country and go home to Croatia and start a new life on her own, with Marko where he deserved to be — in her past.

As she was picturing the sunlit streets of Zagreb, she heard the front door open. Immediately she raised her head, smoothed her hair and straightened her blouse.

She heard his footsteps in the hall and her heartbeat quickened even before she saw him. She watched him walk into the kitchen, into her kitchen, looking immaculate in dark trousers and a black shirt, his silver-flecked hair neat, his frozen grey eyes boring into her.

Marko put his keys on the table and looked at her wine glass. "I'll have some of that," he said, in the dialect of their childhood.

She complied, but sighed to herself as she reached for another glass and unscrewed the bottle. Marko had this way of making everything in her life difficult, including the decision of whether or not to leave him.

PART 4

Saturday 21st March — Liverpool
FA CUP QUARTER-FINAL — Liverpool FC v Fulham FC

Fulham's FA Cup quarter-final against Liverpool would kick off at 12.30 p.m. on the Sunday of a busy footballing weekend. The squad travelled north by train on Saturday morning, their excitement palpable. Brighton has been just the warm-up act; they were about to play one of the best teams in Europe.

They arrived in Liverpool at lunchtime and checked into their hotel, an old and imposing building, a regular haunt for travelling football teams. After lunch, they took a series of minibuses to Everton's training ground at Finch Farm.

Training was light and was run by Charlie Paxton, the first team coach. At the end, Marko called the players over and they gathered around quickly, jostling for the places closest to the manager, drinking in his words.

"First the team," Marko said. "Unchanged from last week. Bench as well."

The players nodded.

"It's going to be tough out there. Even if Liverpool don't play their best team, it will still be the toughest game you've had this season. They'll be expecting to win. Prove them wrong. Most of you have played at Anfield before and you know what the atmosphere will be like. But you have to get past that. Don't let it get to you. We've trained for this. You know what to do."

Marko stopped and the players began to shift on their feet, but he hadn't finished. "Make me proud," he added.

He had never said it before, and more than one player looked surprised as Marko walked away.

Charlie said, "Let's get back to the hotel," and the group began to jog or stroll to the car park.

Zac, who was checking his phone for messages from Tammy, found Marko next to him, always a daunting experience. The manager was the most important person at any football club and if he spoke to you, you gave him your full attention whether he was handing out praise or criticism. With the unpredictable Marko, there was an added element of trepidation, particularly if you were feeling off balance, as Zac was at the moment.

Marko asked, "How are you feeling about the game?"

It was an innocuous question, but Zac couldn't reply honestly with "terrified."

"Good," he responded.

Marko nodded. "Score me a goal," he said, "I know you can."

No doubt it was meant as a confidence boost but tomorrow Zac had to try to score a goal in one of the most hostile footballing territories in Europe and Marko's expectations had just added to the pressure.

***

Marko and Zac climbed into the last minibus. Lucas Karlsson and Charlie were already sitting in the rear seats discussing the London mayoral election. At the front, Leo Blake was chatting to Jamie Crawford but turned round to speak to Zac, his braids flicking across his face.

"I think you'll score tomorrow, mate. Think about it. Silencing the Kop. That would be sick. I'll chip it in from the edge of the box and you'll smash it top bins! Just imagine it!"

Zac closed his eyes and tipped his head back. "Yeah, maybe," he said, his off-hand tone silencing Leo, an achievement of sorts.

The journey was short. The six men jumped down from the minibus, Zac and Marko in the lead. The hotel was a vast red brick building covered with ornate decorations, pediments and balconies, the largest of which was at first-floor level, jutting out above the main door.

As they strode towards the entrance, a tiny movement in Marko's peripheral vision made him glance up at the balcony. "Govno!" he cried.

Zac didn't understand the word, but he heard the alarm in the manager's voice. He looked round but saw nothing, then felt Marko slam into him with a force that sent him flying through the air before hitting the ground a few feet away. As he smacked down onto the tarmac, there was an explosion behind him and then a cacophony of voices and shouting.

***

From further back, Charlie Paxton had a better view of the enormous terracotta flowerpot wobbling on the edge of the balcony then beginning to tip. The pot missed Zac and Marko by inches, smashing into the pavement and shattering into smithereens, soil and terracotta chunks scattering like shrapnel. Echoing Marko, Charlie cried, "Shit!"

Leo rushed at once to the spreadeagled Zac while Lucas pointed upwards and said to Charlie, "There's someone on that balcony!"

"Come on!" Charlie said, pulling Lucas's sleeve.

They leapt over the heap of soil, plants and broken terracotta and dashed through the hotel reception to the stairs. On the way up, they passed Antonio Perez Alvarez coming down, followed by the fitness coach, Dario Kovatic. Antonio was asking questions to which Charlie shouted vague answers then he and Lucas crashed through a fire door onto the balcony.

There was no one there. Charlie looked around wildly. It was obvious where the flowerpot had been moved from because there was a round mark on the floor next to two similarly sized undamaged pots. "Don't touch anything! The police need to see this."

"Shit, Charlie. Who would do this? What the hell is going on?"

Charlie, who was remembering the strange incident with the car at Motspur Park, which he but not the players had been told about, was even more alarmed than Lucas. He tried not to show it, but his answer revealed his concern anyway.

"Let's go and see how Zac is," he said.

***

Zac was used to being shoved around by defenders, but when you were knocked to the ground on a football pitch you met soft, forgiving grass. He wasn't used to face planting on tarmac and was conscious of pain in his hands and ribs. Leo Blake was bending over him, full of concern and urgency.

Zac said, "I'm OK." He looked as his palms, which were grazed, and his tracksuit, which was ripped across the knees.

He became aware of what Leo was saying and it showed an unexpected presence of mind. "Let's get inside in case anything else happens."

Leo and Zac went in through the hotel's revolving door, just as Dario was going out. Jamie Crawford was already inside trying to calm Antonio, who was talking non-stop in Spanish.

Leo said, "Shut up and let Zac sit down."

Zac registered Jamie's surprise at the sudden role reversal then accepted the chair which Leo pulled out for him.

Leo said, "Are you sure you're OK?"

Zac leant forward and inspected his knees. "Yes, just some cuts."

He held out his grazed palms in reassurance.

Leo said, "Your face is hurt as well," and, with a tenderness Zac found at odds with Leo's command of the situation, reached out and touched Zac's cheek just under the cut.

Charlie and Lucas leapt down the stairs, the former saying, "Someone needs to call the police."

"Call them then," snapped Leo. "And you call Dr Brown," he ordered Lucas.

By this time, the hotel staff were milling around, anxious about their important and high-paying guests. Antonio, who was kneeling by Zac and still speaking excitedly in Spanish, finally found enough English to say, "Oh God. Zac."

"Hang about," said Leo suddenly. "Where's the gaffer?"

***

Andrew Brown arrived in reception. He was looking at Zac's hands when Dario and Marko came in through the hotel entrance, the latter waving away the former's assistance.

In his playing days, Marko hadn't been above diving to win a penalty or a free kick. After he had shoved Zac out of the path of the flowerpot, he had dived like he was in the box in the last minute of a World Cup final which Croatia were losing. He avoided the flowerpot and the debris, but the movement twisted his bad knee and the pain was both familiar and agonising.

" … a bit of grit in there but nothing serious," Dr Brown said. "Go to your room and I'll be up in a few minutes."

The entire group, plus the ten or so hovering hotel staff, turned to look at Marko and Dario.

Leo said to the doctor, "I'll take Zac upstairs. You see to him."

Then to his teammates: "Show's over. Let's get out of the way."

***

Dr Brown had tried to turn his ministrations to Marko but had been sharply dismissed. He went up to Zac's room where he found the striker pacing around restlessly, still wearing his training kit. "Why's it always you who gets hurt?"

"If you ever find out, let me know." Zac sounded cynical.

Brown said, "Come and sit down," and Zac perched reluctantly on the edge of the bed. Around him, the room was neat and tidy, his bag unpacked, all his trainers arranged in pairs and lined up against the wall.

The doctor looked at the latest cut, just over an inch long above a day or so's growth of golden stubble. "This isn't too bad. I can close it up with steri-strips, no need for stitches."

Zac bore the treatment impatiently, blue eyes closed. They opened when Brown stepped away saying, "That'll do for now. I'll look at it again in the morning. How are you otherwise?"

He asked the question lightly, but Zac looked away as he answered it. "I'm fine."

"Then you'd be the only person in the world to be fine after they've nearly been decapitated."

"Maybe I'm tougher than you think."

The doctor was packing up his medical bag but paused. "Oh, I know you're tough. And I'd say a touch intransigent too."

***

By the time Dr Brown entered Marko's room after being summoned, the evening was drawing in. The only light came from the laptop screen on the paper-strewn desk where Marko was working.

It must have suited Marko but to the doctor it felt like he was meeting with a vampire — craving darkness and contemplating iniquity.

"Strange business," Brown commented.

"Yes."

Marko rubbed his knee and Brown said, "Do you want me to take a look at that?"

"No. It's fine."

The doctor raised his eyebrows at the answer, so similar to Zac's; Marko missed the reaction in the dark.

"How's Zac?" Marko asked.

"Other than a nasty cut on his cheek, pretty much unscathed."

"So, he can play tomorrow?"

"Yes, he can play tomorrow."

"And what we spoke about before. Is there anything to worry about?"

The doctor's eyes had grown used to the dimness. Other than the desk, the room was fastidiously neat; another trait Zac and Marko apparently shared.

He said, "There may be. It looks like my predecessor had similar suspicions. I'd say he's suffering from some form of anxiety. Probably mild and never properly diagnosed, at least not over here. He's good at hiding it. Or at least, denying it. Certainly, we need to keep an eye on him, as you've already suggested."

Marko nodded. "Zac's very important," he said. "Both now and for the future."

The doctor was about to answer when there was a knock at the door and Charlie Paxton's disembodied head appeared. "The police are here," he said, then acknowledging Brown's presence asked Marko, "Are you all right?"

Brown had guessed that Marko's fitness wasn't quite as perfect as he liked everyone to think it was. He wondered if this thought had also crossed Charlie's mind.

But Marko reacted to the sympathetic enquiry in a tone even colder than usual. "Of course."

"You had a close shave … " Charlie persisted.

"Zac had a close shave, as you put it," Marko corrected. "I just happened to be there."

"Lucky you were," the doctor said.

***

The police wanted to speak to everyone involved in the incident, threatening to derail the team's quiet dinner and early night. Marko didn't emerge from his room all evening but Charlie Paxton, who was almost as good in a crisis as Leo Blake, made sure the disruption was kept to a minimum.

The officers interviewed Marko, who was rude and dismissive, Dario Kovatic, who was offhand and unhelpful, and Leo, who was cooperative and voluble but had nothing useful to say. Charlie and Lucas Karlsson were told off for potentially contaminating a crime scene, which neither appreciated.

The police found Zac Miller more gracious, helpful and polite than any of the others, but he said nothing of substance. They weren't to know that Zac dealt with them in the same way as he handled journalists asking unwelcome questions. As they were leaving, the sergeant, an Everton fan, told Zac, "I've got a tenner on you to score tomorrow."

For once, the Texan wasn't gracious, helpful or polite enough to reply.

***

A football manager's workload didn't change on away trips and Marko kept up his usual frantic pace, sustained by a club sandwich and an espresso from room service. He was tempted to order something stronger, but this wasn't a weekend for clouding his judgment.

Making footballing decisions was as easy for Marko as playing the game had been. He enjoyed the subtlety and inventiveness of the tactical side of the sport — utilising his players' strengths, studying the opposition and devising a strategy to outwit other managers.

Although he rarely showed it, he loved being a hands-on coach; he was at his happiest with a whistle in his hand on the training pitch. He was interested in the stats and the soccernomics but less so than some managers. Marko knew instinctively how to put a team together, who to hire, who to play and who to drop to get results.

Beyond football, though, things weren't so easy; dealing with what had happened that afternoon being his latest problem. The near-miss with the car outside Motspur Park in December had seemed serious at the time but its importance had faded. Instead of being a deliberate attempt to run Zac over, Marko had begun to think that it was probably just a case of careless driving.

Now though, he was paying for his complacency. What had happened this afternoon couldn't have been an accident and Zac was again the target. To compound matters, the police were involved and he had had to order the communications director, Richard Green, to ensure the press didn't follow suit. He had played things down with the police and instructed Charlie and the others to do the same. The car incident wasn't to be mentioned and the flowerpot episode was to be referred to as a prank. He had double-checked the meaning of the English word just to be sure.

Fortunately, the Merseyside police were busier with bigger cases. Richard would be able to buy any inquisitive journalist's silence with the offer of an exclusive interview. ("Not with Zac," Marko had stressed. "Anyone but Zac.") He was confident that the hotel staff, keen to keep the business of travelling teams, would be discreet.

He had reported the incident to David Patterson, but casually, when the owner phoned from New York to ask about tomorrow's line-up. A recent run of victories in the Championship had moved Fulham up to second place in the table and Marko felt that Patterson was finally catching the Cup fever already consuming the fans.

He ordered another espresso and sipped it standing by the window. Management was lonely. Marko never made the mistake of getting friendly with anyone at a club although his apparent coldness meant that no one wanted to get close anyway. He carried the burdens of the job alone. He trusted Charlie Paxton but not to the point of sharing his innermost thoughts; he trusted Dario Kovatic but the intricacies of this situation would be lost on his strong, silent henchman. For a moment, he contemplated phoning Ivana, but he would get no sympathy from her, either for his aching knee or his management dilemmas. There was another number he might have called, of course, but that relationship wasn't about trust or support. Or even friendship.

It was at times like this, when events had slipped out of his control, that he questioned if management had been the right choice. He could be in another Liverpool hotel now enjoying a few beers before offering some easy punditry in a warm, comfortable studio tomorrow. Instead, he was drinking coffee at ten at night, gripping the cup too hard and feeling his heart beat too fast.

What he had said to the doctor was true: Zac was key to Marko's plans. He wasn't sure what was more concerning — the doctor's opinion that Zac's mental health was fragile or the fact that his striker's physical health was clearly under threat.

***

After the police left, Zac stayed in his room, lights turned down and curtains open. The television was off, but music was coming softly from the speakers. He was standing at the window when he heard the first knock on the door, his reflection superimposed on the lights of the city. His normally old-gold hair was muted to tawny in the dimness. The row of butterfly stitches on his face was neat but incongruous.

His visitor knocked again, and Zac reluctantly opened the door. His captain stood in the hallway.

"You missed dinner," said Jamie. "I came to see how you are."

Zac shrugged. "OK, I guess."

In truth, he was tired and he couldn't face either food or company. He didn't want to let Jamie in but he didn't want to have a conversation in the corridor either. He opened the door wider and hoped Jamie wouldn't stay long.

Jamie glanced at the phone lying on the bed. "Have you been talking to Tammy?"

"No," Zac replied impatiently, "I don't want to worry her."

That was true but it also meant he felt guilty as he would usually phone Tammy regularly when he was away. Still, over the years, he had developed a ritual of sending her a text full of heart emojis a few hours before every game. As long as he did that tomorrow, she would assume he was all right.

"Zac … what's going on?" Jamie asked. "Should I be worried about you?"

Zac guessed that the open-ended question wasn't intended to

refer only to the incidents with the car and the flowerpot but that was all he was prepared to talk about.

"I don't know," he said, his voice rough and unfamiliar. "Should you be? First someone tried to run me over and now someone tried to knock my head off. So, yeah, maybe y'all should be worried."

"But who?" Jamie asked. "Who would do that?"

"Who would do that?" Zac repeated with a harsh laugh. "Well, that's easy. Javier hates me because he wants to play up front. Mitch hates me because he wants my place on the US team."

"Yes, but … "

Zac watched Jamie struggle for a response. Jamie was a good team captain, but he was out of his depth here. Zac was more touched by the concern than he wanted to show so he offered a way out.

"Yeah, I know," he said. "Javier and Mitch don't want to kill me. Especially not now, when everyone thinks I'm going to score tomorrow." He laughed ironically.

"What about those fans?" Jamie asked. "The ones who were trolling you on Twitter."

Zac shrugged, "That was months ago."

"Maybe it's all just coincidence," Jamie suggested.

Zac said, "I've got a headache, Jamie."

Headaches, he had discovered, were useful because no one could prove you didn't have one. But tonight, he wasn't faking.

"I'll go," Jamie said, "I'll see you at breakfast. Try to get some sleep."

Zac responded to that sentence with a grimace. Jamie didn't know that "try" was the operative word.

And tomorrow they had to play Liverpool.

<u>Jack</u>

Loz and I travelled up to Liverpool by train on Saturday morning. We had hoped we would be on the same train as the players but no such luck.

We sipped cappuccinos while the world raced by and Loz asked, "How was your week?"

"Good," I said. "Yesterday I had to make an emergency flower delivery."

"What?" said Loz, "Are florists the fourth emergency service now?"

"Pretty much. I had a call from Gemma, my contact at the Club in a complete panic. She'd forgotten there was a do at the Cottage last night and hadn't ordered any flowers. Luckily, I was able to oblige. They were a funny mix and not in Club colours, but they looked OK. She was massively grateful."

"I bet she was. She owes you one!"

***

We had a great time exploring the Liverpool waterfront on Saturday afternoon and roaming around the Cavern District that night. On Sunday morning, we checked out of the hotel, cured our hangovers with a large brunch and squeezed onto a bus full of Liverpool fans, destination Anfield.

Anfield is a word synonymous with football but the stadium is big and unattractive having been extended and amended piecemeal over the years. Before going in, we visited the Hillsborough Memorial, which was understated and bedecked with flowers as fans arriving for the game paid their respects.

Liverpool had become well known over recent seasons for not playing their full-strength team in Cup ties, a strategy that had almost backfired more than once. Their celebrated manager had picked a hybrid team for this match: Champions League defence, reserve midfield and bit-part attack. This meant that, instead of watching football, we were watching chess, a game I suspected the coldly analytical Marko Maric was rather good at.

I glanced at the touchline as I thought of him — a black-clad, isolated figure on the edge of the technical area. Marko Maric, playing away in more ways than one.

While this was an edge-of-the-seat game (or it would have been if we hadn't been standing up) it wasn't a thriller. The two sides cancelled each other out. Davy Walker was in great form, catching any ball which came his way but Zac Miller was having a difficult time of it up front. The Liverpool defenders were used to quicksilver skills and lightning pace and Zac was having to think and shoot from outside the box. Leo Blake was buzzing around as usual, but he was an irritant not a threat and, as the second half wore on, Marko replaced him with Mitch Masters. Yet again, Mitch burst onto the pitch full of energy and ambition, but the defenders thwarted him with effortless efficiency.

Antonio had the best chance of both sides when his free kick curled close to the top corner of the goal, but the Liverpool goalie saw it just in time and tipped the ball over the bar. Lucas and Javier tried to capitalise on the resulting corner by taking it short and fast, but the experienced defenders were wise to the trick and the opportunity was wasted.

Although the game wasn't an enthralling one, with ten minutes to go the excitement was building amongst the away fans — could we hold on and force the replay?

The answer, after a stressful few minutes when the Liverpool players suddenly and belatedly realised what was happening, was a resounding yes.

It felt odd celebrating a 0-0 draw. The players must have felt it too because although they all came over to the away section, there was no prolonged applause or chest baring and shirt throwing. Marko had disappeared rather stiffly down the tunnel immediately after the final whistle and the players soon followed.

We all knew that although this was a good result and it put our name in the hat for the semi-final draw, it also meant an extra game in a busy run-in when automatic promotion still wasn't guaranteed. But it set up a tantalising and terrifying tie at the Cottage — this time, there would be no bit-part players for Liverpool.

Wednesday 25th March — Hammersmith Apollo

Joe Martinez's team made sure he got regular updates on the frenetic mayoral election newsfeed as Londoners' interest became more intense. Sonia Smith, the Green candidate, was getting attention for her past Extinction Rebellion protests and Arjun Shah, the Conservative candidate, had been mixing with the wrong people. He'd been photographed at a glamorous birthday party given by a wealthy business tycoon, beaming widely alongside him in a brotherly embrace. The trouble for Arjun was that it had recently come to light that this tycoon had been part of a large-scale tax evasion scheme. Arjun wasn't guilty of anything but, by association, he'd been getting a pasting in the press. Joe Martinez, on the other hand, hadn't put a foot wrong.

After the first debate in February, Joe had come out best in the polls, although Arjun hadn't been far behind. As for the Greens, they weren't going to win but they were polling better than they ever had before. The biggest turn of events since then had been Lydia Edwards, social entrepreneur, announcing her intention to stand via a video on Instagram to her growing number of followers.

It was inevitable that with Lydia now in the mix running as an independent, some votes would be siphoned away from the other candidates. Joe could only hope that most of them wouldn't be his.

Since entering the race, there had been a media buzz around Lydia. Earlier that week Joe had read the flattering piece about her in London's Evening Standard:

> Lydia Edwards, 43, is a successful self-made business woman who doesn't do boring. She is easily recognisable with her short blonde hair, cool glasses and colourful dress sense. She is more often in trainers than heels, but she wears both very well. She is intelligent and insightful and likes to do things differently.
>
> She made her mark developing her own beauty product lines after spending time in South America and since then Lydia's has established herself as a savvy business woman. She arose in the public consciousness through BBC2's short series, 'Crisis Management', where she embedded herself within companies as a trouble-shooter. With the combination of her calm almost, dare we say it, motherly manner and striking appearance, she lit up stuffy male-dominated boardrooms, making for entertaining TV and begging the question, where are the other female entrepreneurs?
>
> Many think it's time that London had a female mayor, and turned its back on outdated tribal politics, and Lydia Edwards is seen as having the best chance of shattering that ceiling, with or without heels.

Joe was confident but not naïve. London was a Labour city, and Lydia and Arjun were both longshots. But he couldn't allow them to gain any ground. The attention they were getting was useful — it would provide him with the extra adrenalin nudge to put in a performance. The public also sensed that the race wasn't quite a done deal. Demand for tickets for the second debate had been so strong that the event was moved to a larger venue, the Hammersmith Apollo, more commonly associated with stand-up comedy than political sparring.

Loz

The Council had an allocation of tickets so Dom, Jack, Fleur — with her new-found interest in politics, aka Arjun Shah — and I headed to the Apollo. My work mates Andy and Matt were also going. The crowd outside the Apollo would have been similar for a Jack Dee performance but the atmosphere was not. There was a feeling of anticipation but little light-heartedness.

The candidates took their places on the stage. Once again it was Vanessa Capaldi, the TV presenter, who was hosting. Pacing the stage, she said, "Welcome to everybody here and those watching at home and using social media, to the second London Mayor's Debate. We'd like you to join in with the discussion using the hashtag MayoralDebate." She was small in stature but had a powerful, authoritative voice and commanded the arena. Behind her stood five mayoral hopefuls at transparent lecterns.

Jack dug Fleur in the ribs. "Have you seen what Arjun's wearing this time?"

I could see that Fleur wasn't put off as she looked on admiringly at Arjun Shah's expensive ensemble of lime green jacket, yellow shirt — still with many buttons undone — and checked dark green three-quarter length trousers.

"Since the last debate we have a new entrant to the contest, Lydia Edwards, running as an independent candidate and so welcome to you."

Vanessa Capaldi pointed towards Lydia, while the other four candidates looked over in her direction, smiling weakly before turning back to the audience.

All of the candidates were asked to set out their visions for London. The audience listened politely to Reuben Bailey, the Lib Deb, and also to Sonia Smith for the Greens. But it noticeably perked up when it came to Lydia Edwards delivering hers — even Fleur, who hadn't previously been paying much attention, sat up in her seat.

Lydia explained, "My vision is simple. To make London the most thriving, liveable city in the world. To link business with a caring, sharing way of life by introducing financial and social incentives, where credits can be accumulated — 'karma kredits' — with rewards provided by philanthropic companies and institutions."

The audience reacted immediately and any groans were drowned out with cheers and whistles. Within minutes, I could see #karmakredits and #londydia trending on Twitter. The other candidates tried to look unruffled.

To the delight of Fleur, and plenty of others in the crowd, Arjun was up next. "My vision? I'd get people ... " pausing and looking directly at the bike-clip wearing Lib Dem candidate, " ... to wear better clothes." The audience laughed. "I'd ban sportswear, especially football tops … how shall I say this politely … " and looking like he had a bad smell up his nose, he said " … on un-sporty body types. London would look so much better."

He then attempted to give a more serious answer but the audience was laughing so much that he didn't get the chance.

Joe followed. "I think we have to embrace change in this great city of ours. Don't be frightened if development happens in your area. London needs to grow and evolve. Love it. Don't frustrate it."

After a few more rounds like this — including the obligatory light-hearted I-support-Arsenal comment from Joe (to which one red-shirted punter shouted, "Never seen you at the Emirates, mate") — the candidates were asked by an audience member, what was the best thing about London. Arjun's answer got the biggest laugh from the audience when he said, it was London Fashion Week, adding "I LOVE IT — especially if I'm sitting in the front row and anywhere near Posh!"

One audience member who'd had their hand up almost since the debate started, eventually caught Vanessa's attention and asked, "How would you change how London was governed?"

Lydia answered first. "Politics is just too parochial. I suggest that like the TV series, 'Wife Swap', there should be 'Councillor Swap' between boroughs." I tilted forward and looked down the row at Andy and Matt, knowing what we were all thinking, interesting but mad! "That would mean councillors from Westminster might go to Newham to understand their issues and decide their policies and planning decisions, Newham's would go to Richmond, Richmond to Hackney, Hackney to Hillingdon and so on. Why not? Everyone would have their eyes opened."

Arjun took his turn. "If Sonia and her Extinction Rebellion friends didn't disrupt public transport maybe London could function a lot better than it does!" People laughed. "It has to be about freeing up enterprise and encouraging start-ups with mayoral support. We need more Silicon Roundabouts, we need Enfield Enterprise Villages, Hackney Hubs, Brixton Unions, a Croydon Circus. You get the picture?" He waved at the audience and most people were cheering him on.

Sonia's reply was curt. "London doesn't need gimmicks. It needs less of the traditional parties and the *grand projets* such as cable cars, airports and garden bridges. It needs more allotments! And more bees."

No one really listened to Reuben's answer, the audience was getting more rowdy and Arjun looked at over him and quipped, "You might wear hi-viz but to Londoners you're invisible!"

It's was Joe's turn to answer. "I think we need City Hall to be able to work more closely with the boroughs, especially when reusing public land. It would be sensible for City Hall to have more powers for when they're needed."

In response, Arjun retorted, "Typical power-grab from our estate agent looking Labour friend here," whilst looking contemptuously at Joe in his suit and tie.

There was no stopping the audience now, hands were up all over the auditorium. Crime was a topic that many wanted addressed. How could you cut London's crime rate? Joe thought football clubs should get much more involved in contributing financially and socially to community initiatives. Arjun thought that those convicted should do more meaningful and effective community service. Sonia's idea was making young people join choirs and dance groups. At this Lydia, threw up her hands and commented that you can't make people do anything and instead you need to encourage and incentivise. Her idea was about getting employers to work with schools, offering more sponsorships. Arjun glanced over at Lydia before pointedly saying, "You might find that people of my generation see things differently."

This comment was the trigger for Vanessa Capaldi to draw things to a close.

I looked at my phone, #Londydia was still trending but there were favourable comments about pretty much all of the candidates, especially Arjun's put-downs. Everyone in the audience gave one last round of applause before we started to make our way out.

"I thought Joe was quite impressive, actually," I said to our group as we gathered outside, "but I'm not sure whether he's a friend or foe of football clubs."

"Well, I vote for us heading to the pub before everyone else gets there," said Dom.

Knightsbridge

Hamarat had watched the debate alone — his wife had no interest — in the comfort of his home, red wine by his side. He was surprised that the election was proving so stimulating.

Joe Martinez as London mayor couldn't happen soon enough — his Wembley proposals just couldn't sit in some bureaucrat's in-tray indefinitely. Hamarat's NFL team were perfectly poised to take advantage of an expanded presence in London, possibly becoming its own permanent team. The plans for the intensification around the stadium were also pressing.

Getting Joe Martinez in place was important to Hamarat on a more basic level. To demonstrate to his friends, like Bayram, his reach and influence, to impress them still after all these years, was a matter of personal pride.

It amused Hamarat to hear the discussions in the media about corruption in other countries when he knew that in the UK democracy was for sale as much as anywhere else. He was aware of the undercurrents ready to wage war on clean government. At least, he thought, his intent was clear — for good old-fashioned, personal financial gain — whereas many of these invisible donors using 'dark money' on the web to support political parties and campaigns, had anarchic, wicked ambitions, focused on eroding trust and institutions. He felt he was one of the good guys.

Having Lydia Edwards in the mix wasn't necessarily a problem. He could deal with her if he had to. But he didn't want her derailing his plans. Joe Martinez was his man, with his useful political network and party behind him.

Wednesday 1st April — Craven Cottage
FA CUP QUARTER-FINAL REPLAY — Fulham FC v Liverpool FC

In its long history, Craven Cottage had seen good days, bad days and almost the end of days. That April, the glory days came back to the Cottage and I was there to see them.

The squad returned from Liverpool, mainly in good spirits, with the dubious trophy of a 0-0 draw and a replay. I noticed, as I roamed the corridors of Motspur Park eyes wide open and ears tilted to doorways, that the exceptions to this were Marko Maric, who was more aloof and irascible than ever, and Zac Miller, who refused to elucidate on the so-called 'training ground incident' that had left a cut on his face and scrapes on his hands and knees. Last time I looked, footballers trained on grass. Not that whatever happened had caused any lasting damage. Zac was scoring for fun in the League and it looked like Fulham were going to secure automatic promotion, which would be a major achievement for a club that, frankly, didn't have a well-stocked trophy cabinet.

The Liverpool replay was scheduled for the first Wednesday evening in early April. After the draw at Anfield, Liverpool's manager didn't make the same mistake twice. The team that came to town for the replay was the line-up that had beaten Manchester City on the Saturday and narrowly lost to Benfica the previous week in the Champions League. This was a team of internationals, a team of superstars.

But although the cards were stacked in Liverpool's favour, Fulham had the trump: we were playing at Craven Cottage under the flood-lights. The old, proud ground comes alive on nights like this. The crowd creates a solid wall of noise right up against the pitch to envelop the Fulham players and overwhelm the opposition.

Liverpool scored early on, somewhat against the run of play, but the fact of the matter is you only have to give a glimmer of a chance to players of that calibre and they'll take it and you'll be one goal down.

The crowd responded with a collective groan. It really felt like the game, and the FA Cup run with it, was over. Even a non-believer like me couldn't help feeling disappointed.

On the pitch, however, the sentiment was different. Rather than being disheartened, the Fulham team, directed by Jamie Crawford and led from the front by Zac Miller at his very best, were galvanised. The way they battled against slick, sophisticated Liverpool was fantastic: the focus and the fight. The players never stopped believing they could win and they never stopped fighting for the victory.

Marko had prepared the team well not just tactically or in terms of physical fitness but mentally, too — if you can't out-skill your opponent, you can still out-think him. His ability might be better than yours but his will to win won't be.

When Zac scored just before half-time, Fulham were back in the game and the Liverpool players were desperate to get to the break to regroup and recover. But Liverpool walked out for the second half into a maelstrom of noise to kick off against a team even more determined, confident and battle-ready than before.

The solidity of the defence, which let in only one goal against a team that had just beaten Arsenal, Spurs and Man City, cannot be overstated. Yes, there were individual mistakes — Phil Philopoussis put the ball out for a corner when there was no attacker anywhere near him, Aidan Rafferty lived dangerously by passing the ball across the face of the goal and sometimes Davy Walker couldn't decide whether to catch or punch. But Sunday Oyetoro kept Fulham in the game with an athletic and dramatic goal-line clearance in the 80th minute. Overall, this was an assured performance, led by Jamie Crawford who made no mistakes at all.

During the course of the match, Liverpool went from complacent to rattled to desperate as their usually composed manager screamed instructions from the sidelines and their usually prolific strikers found themselves thwarted again and again.

At the other end, Zac was getting closer and closer to scoring the winner, but time was running out. The Fulham players had given everything to the match and the crowd knew that going into extra time would only benefit Liverpool.

In the 89th minute, Leo Blake won a corner with some sleight-of-foot trickery in front of goal. Antonio ran to take it, roared on by the Hammersmith End. No silly short corner this time; Antonio lofted the ball straight and true into the penalty area where Zac leapt like a stag to head it past the flailing goalkeeper into the back of the net.

Of course, Liverpool were allowed eight minutes of added time to redress the balance. And, of course, Fulham made the extra time feel twice that, with fans growing more stressed as the defence became more stretched. When the whistle blew, I don't mind admitting that I shared the mixture of jubilation and relief along with the rest of the crowd.

It gets to you sometimes, this funny little Club.

Loz

"I can't believe it, Jack! I can't bloody believe it! We've only just gone and beaten Liverpool!"

Jack and I turned to each other wide-eyed, our faces beaming, and gave each other a bear hug. Similar scenes were replicated all around the ground. In the row in front of us, the two septuagenarian brothers who'd been going to the Cottage for decades shook off their advanced years and danced a little jig, next to us, Moany Man nearly transformed into a Butlins Red Coat as he enthusiastically punched the air, and our neighbours behind us had given up their usual, clinical post-match analysis and instead wrapped their arms around each other and roared their full-throated joy.

The Cottage was as charged as I had ever seen or felt it. It was on nights like this that football fans got their reward for their loyalty and dedication. This is why this night, and the small handful of others like it, were so special and meaningful. The elusiveness of such highs meant that they were religiously savoured, every aspect of them committed to memory. After all, they had to sustain a fan's raison d'etre, possibly for the rest of their lives.

There were plenty of Fulham fans around the country, and around the world, who followed the team on TV screens in pubs and bars, as well as at home or on the move, who would have been jubilant at the win, but there was absolutely no substitute for being there. Every fan in the Cottage that night knew that they could say with pride that they were there. That first-hand witnessing of an historic win over a mighty side, with a sublime late goal, was as intense and as satisfying an experience as any fan could get.

Evening matches at the Cottage were the best ones for fans — the dark skies and tall floodlights concentrated the intensity — it was a communion of the committed. The match played out as a piece of theatre — the players' faces dramatically more visible, expressions exaggerated and easier to read.

This performance had been a thriller, the audience on tenterhooks until the last minute and pretty much the last kick of the match. Too tense to sit, the fans had stood as one, willing on the team, not for the first time and definitely not the last. The twelfth man had, in our minds, been responsible for the winning goal.

***

The Riverside was packed, as we'd expected. Jack and I ordered two large glasses of Australian riesling. I looked down the bar and before turning away asked the barman, "Will not working tonight?"

"He popped in earlier but, no, not tonight," he replied.

We headed into the middle of the room where there was some space. The bar felt as energised as a Dublin pub on St Patrick's night — almost as good as it had been in the stadium. Music and laughter filled the room. Jack and I knew we had just witnessed a match that went straight into a Fulham Top 10, if not a Top 5.

In the bar, our phones buzzed with friends and family messaging us their congratulations. They knew how important this was for the Club and so, by association, us.

"Crazy we're in the last four now and Arsenal are up next," I said, having seen the draw earlier.

"Yep. And if, IF, we can beat Arsenal, we'll have Spurs or the Diamonds in the Final. How hard can it be?" Jack said, eyebrows raised.

We were like giddy schoolgirls stoked with adrenalin. I had no urge to pull myself away and I knew Dom wouldn't be expecting me back early after that win — he knew exactly what a big deal this was.

When Jack went to the bar to get the next round, I caught up on some of the match comments on Twitter and the three-word match reviews for the *Fulhamish* podcast — MILLER MAGIC

MAESTRO — ZAC ATTACKS REDS — LAST GASP WIN — WHITES BLEED REDS.

After a few minutes, I looked up to check if she'd managed to get served. As I did, I noticed something going on at the far end of room — people were standing and had started to applaud. It was the players coming in to celebrate with the fans. Jack had noticed them, too, on her way back with the drinks and was as excited as me by their arrival.

"Looks like most of them are there. Quite a few of their wives and girlfriends, too," Jack said.

"Can't see the man of the moment, Zac, though. Can you?"

"No. He must have thought he'd get mobbed or something. Guess, he's right. It's selfie city over there now!" she laughed. "No Marko, either."

The players were dressed in black Fulham team track suits and looked a lot cleaner than when we'd last seen them on the pitch. Most of the women who accompanied them looked far more glamorously attired.

"Hey, Jack … " I said as I looked across at the group, " … is she there? The woman from the hotel?"

Jack shook her head. "Not that I can see. There's a couple with dark hair but they're not her. I can't see my New BFF, Ivana, either though."

"Maybe they've killed each other?"

Jack let out a snort.

We hadn't noticed him at first, which you would have thought would have been impossible given his size, but mingling in the bar was the Club's furry mascot, Billy the Badger.

"We've already had a selfie with him," I said, "not quite got the T-shirt yet, but there's always your birthday."

"I really like Billy the Badger," Jack said, looking at me seriously. "I mean, for a start, he looks like what he's supposed to, a black-and-white badger. Some mascots are really random, like QPR's Jude the Cat. What's all that about, then?"

We both laughed. Billy passed nearby and gave us a big wave. "He must remember us being his super-fans," I said.

We finished off our drinks and headed for the door.

"Can't wait to see Andy tomorrow at work," I laughed. "He's been gloating about the Diamond Blues' season but now I can taunt him about us getting in the way of their FA Cup glory. We can live in hope."

Thursday 9th April
Southwark

Lydia Edwards gazed out of her window, captivated by the iridescent dappling of the River Thames. The view from her 23rd floor penthouse apartment on a sunny evening was why she loved living here, with the added bonus of being able to pop into the adjacent Tate Modern. A bang from the kitchen startled her, making her turn away.

"Mum?" A girl's voice shouted, sounding agitated. "Where's the bottle opener? It's not here."

Lydia walked through the sleekly furnished living room, prominent Warhol and Lichtenstein pictures on the wall, into the wide open-plan kitchen, reached into a drawer and handed the opener to her daughter.

"Maybe you were just looking in the wrong place," she said.

Lydia and Skye were similar heights and builds but in contrast to her mother, Skye's hair was long, straight and dark, almost black. She had Lydia's good skin and their eyes were a similar colour, bluey-grey, or dishwater, as Skye would say. Her small tanzanite crystal nose stud matched her eyes. Skye was preparing for a night in with her boyfriend of six months, planned as her mother was going out.

"You seeing Jonathan later?" Skye asked.

"The talk will finish about 8.30 p.m. so, yes, meeting Jonathan after for dinner," Lydia replied. "I take it you're not cooking for Tom?"

Skye shook her head, eyes downward, as she concentrated on opening a bottle of wine.

Lydia studied her daughter as she proceeded to take out two wine glasses from the cupboard.

"Ellie should be here any minute to run through my diary and then we're heading over to Shoreditch for my talk. I'm quite pleased with the title — the Kindness Contagion," Lydia said, in a rare moment of self-congratulation.

Ellie, Lydia's campaign director, arrived promptly and when they'd finished their catch-up they called out a goodbye to Skye.

Lydia and Ellie made their way along Southwark Bridge Road to the bus stop. Now Lydia was a woman of the people, their plan was to get the 344 towards Old Street, being seen by and greeting voters en route, rather than using her car to get around town. She had to walk the walk, so to speak and so that definitely meant for the time being heels were out.

Since she started her mayoral campaign, having time to herself — to think — had almost disappeared. Last week, Lydia had got up earlier than usual and with her coffee in hand, had stood at her favoured vantage point in her living room, staring at the river, meditating on its movements on a particularly wet and windy day. It seemed like the first time she'd had a chance to ask herself if she was really doing the right thing. Rather than choosing to spend more time with her daughter, to help her get her directionless life on track, Lydia was instead competing for the highest profile job in London. One that would be nothing less than a 24/7 role. But Lydia couldn't change who she was. In her world, she'd succeeded on her own without a helping hand. I just don't know how to equip my daughter to do the same, she thought.

Lydia had flirted with the idea of politics in the past but not in any tangible way. The social media surge had taken her by surprise, carrying her along a path that felt natural, like it was meant to be.

Mental images of the other candidates had flashed into Lydia's mind. When she'd been publicly critical of them, she hadn't anticipated she'd soon be putting her blonde head above the parapet too, but — here she was. Remarkably, despite a late start, recent polls showed she wasn't a total outsider. Lydia knew that Arjun Shah came across as young, naïve and flippant but he was clever, interesting and different, which made him popular with new voters. She shuddered at the thought of coming third to someone who couldn't combine socks with shoes. Joe Martinez was clearly her main threat. But she'd been advised that if he didn't win outright in the first round of voting, it wasn't out of the question that she had a chance of coming through on the second preference vote.

Lydia had the self-belief to think she really could make London a better place. In business, she'd been a success, always able to read the room. Being kinder was the zeitgeist and the message that resonated, and individualism was beyond resuscitation. The support for her Karma Kredits proposal had been overwhelming, and not just with London's citizens. It was also hitting the spot with businesses, either because they genuinely wanted to give back or at least be seen to. She didn't much care which.

She was thrilled when some of her ideas from the last mayoral election debate had exploded on social media. She was reaching audiences the other politicians couldn't. The media had initially dismissed the trending of #londydia as a flash in the pan, as had Lydia herself, but the depth and sustained nature of the positive comments and support had been impossible to ignore. The history-making if she won — London's first female mayor, the female Dick Whittington — was a badge she now coveted.

But having elegantly skimmed her hat into the electoral ring, it had brought uncomfortable, almost immodest, levels of personal scrutiny. One junior journalist at The Post was tenaciously tracking her every move. Lydia had suspicions that Joe Martinez's wife might have something to do with it. They'd printed some articles about her, much of the content supposition or invention, alluding to some of her previous South American business dealings having a bad smell about them. It had given her some pause for thought.

Just ignore the white noise, she told herself. After all, her life and business interests in South America were a long time ago.

Shoreditch

Lydia looked out at the crowd, a sea of eager, youthful faces staring back. The 'Kindness Contagion' theme with these tech entrepreneurs had evidently proved alluring. Lydia stood there, hands clutched in front of her white T-shirt with its large black letters spelling out 'HOPE', Katherine Hamnett-style.

The applause, accompanied by whoops and whistles, took a long time to subside once her talk had ended. She smiled from the platform, energised by the reaction. They'd been an attentive audience, seemingly devoted to her cause, looking for something and someone to believe in. Lydia wasn't unnerved. Maybe being mayor was her ultimate vocation.

***

He was already at the restaurant when she arrived. He always knew which table to get, tucked away in a discreet corner. He stood up as she walked across the room; she couldn't help but feel a flutter when she saw how he looked at her, and she took in his casual elegance. He placed his hand on her hip and kissed her on the lips, his handsome face smiling as he drew away.

"Well, how was it?" he asked as he swept back his sandy-coloured hair.

Jonathan had been the best thing to come into her life in a long while. He wasn't cowed by a successful woman, he had nothing to prove. She knew she'd get an easier ride in the press and it would be more publicly agreeable if her partner had been the male equivalent of Amal Clooney, a human rights lawyer, but life's seldom that simple, Lydia thought, so he's under wraps, at least for now.

Friday 10th April — Central London

Brian Stanley, Zac Miller's agent, had arranged to meet his client at 3.30 p.m. in a Mayfair hotel bar. The timing suited Brian because he could celebrate the end of the working week with a large gin and tonic and it suited Zac because Tammy had gone to a spa for the day with Antonio's wife Pia and he never had enough to do in the afternoons anyway.

Brian had represented Zac since his arrival in England four years before. He wasn't Brian's best client, but he was undemanding and appreciative which set him apart. In fact, Brian thought as he hustled through the hotel reception, battered briefcase in one hand and buzzing phone in the other, Zac was unusual in several ways. For one thing, he was intelligent and for another, he was … Brian searched for the word … sensitive. You wouldn't think that someone so polite and charming could be forceful enough to score so many goals.

Brian was slightly overweight, slightly crumpled and slightly out of breath. He found his client sitting at the bar, head bent over his phone, a spotlight above him picking out the golden tones in his hair and the new scar on his cheek. He was wearing jeans and a checked shirt and although there was no sign of cowboy boots or a Stetson, something about him hinted at his home state. Don't mess with … Zac.

The two men shook hands and Brian ordered his G&T. Zac was going to have a coke but the barman talked him into a non-alcoholic botanical that arrived in a tall glass with lots of foliage and proved rather pleasant but was not, Zac reflected, something to mention to the folks back home in Texas or, indeed, at Motspur Park.

Brian had the previous Thursday's newspapers with him and laid them on the bar. The back pages were dominated by photos of Zac celebrating the winner in the quarter-final replay. Zac looked away modestly, but Brian tapped the newsprint.

"Well done," he said. "The man who scored two against Liverpool. People are talking about you, Zacky."

Zac disliked being called "Zacky" but they'd had that conversation before and it would be a waste of breath to mention it again.

"That's nice," he said. "Kind of."

"It's more than nice," said Brian. His huge signet ring flashed in the light as he clinked his glass against Zac's. "It's profitable. And it's timely. I was going to talk to you soon about what to do in the summer, but this puts us in pole position. A lot of clubs are going to be interested. I've already had an approach from … "

"Wait, wait, wait!" Zac put his glass down. "I don't want to go anywhere in the summer. I've got a year left on my contract and I just want a new one."

Brian sighed. "That's not how it works."

"Look, it's really flattering but … "

"It's not about flattery," said Brian. "You're 25 now. The next move has got to be the right one. After the way you've been playing recently, we could be looking at somewhere like Newcastle. Even Everton."

A move to Everton was very hard to argue against but Zac pressed on. "Fulham are going to get promoted. I know it's not guaranteed but we've got a good chance. I appreciate you looking out for me, Brian, but I just want to stay where I am."

Brian was used to this kind of thing from footballers even if they didn't always put it so courteously. He tapped the newspapers again, this time indicating a small photo of Marko Maric, staring moodily at the camera. "Is it because of him?"

"Partly," Zac agreed.

Brian nodded. "He's been the making of you. All those fancy passes and then you put the ball away. He's had as good a year as you, but do you think he's going to hang around if something else comes up?"

"If we get promoted … " Zac began but Brian overrode him.

"And something very big might be coming up. The rumour is Lorenzo Verdi's off to Madrid so the Diamond Blues are looking for a new manager. Ex-player who's had a good season in the Championship — they've gone down that route before. So, if Marko leaves Fulham, where does that leave you?"

"I don't know," said Zac. "But it all sounds very hypothetical." Which was not a word Brian heard every day.

"Listen, Zacky. This is what we're going to do. I'm going to put out some feelers and I'm also going to drop some hints to the press. You're hot property right now and there're a lot of options out there. Even if we do decide you stay at Fulham, we need to negotiate a new contract and we'll get a much better deal if you're in demand. You do see that?"

"I do," said Zac reluctantly. "But … "

"You've got to play the game, Zacky."

"There's only one game I'm interested in playing," Zac said, in a different tone, and Brian suddenly understood how Zac scored all those goals after all.

***

Zac didn't want to be cooped up on the Tube or in a cab so he walked to Waterloo. One of the things he liked about London was the anonymity. Last week, his face had been all over the newspapers. Today, he could walk through Mayfair and no one gave him a second glance. OK, he didn't walk around with the number 9 on his back in black and white, but he had a feeling that he would get a lot less freedom in Liverpool or Newcastle.

Brian was just doing his job. But Zac tried to avoid thinking about the wheeling and dealing side of the game. He knew he was a commodity in a marketplace — something to be bought and sold for a price to be agreed. It was the way of the football world, but he didn't like it.

He wondered, running the gauntlet across Piccadilly, if he should be more careful. He had had two near misses already and if someone wanted a third try then he was making it easy for them by sauntering around. By the Ritz, he heard the blast of a horn behind him and he spun on the spot, but it was nothing — just the sound of London in the long Friday rush hour.

The idea that he was under threat felt bizarre. Sometimes, when he lay awake at night, he relived the terror of anticipating the car's impact or the panic when he heard the flowerpot shatter. But out here on a warm spring day, the incidents seemed unreal. Marko was surely correct when he called what happened in Liverpool a prank.

Marko who might be off to the Diamond Blues, apparently. Zac knew about Marko's reputation for never staying at a club for long, of course, but, at the moment, his focus on Fulham's success seemed unwavering. Still, as Zac knew very well, it was easy to hide things. People saw what they wanted to see. For example, if you scored two goals against Liverpool, everyone assumed you were perfectly OK.

As he cut across St James Park, a football landed at his feet. He flicked it up and chipped it back to the small boy who had kicked it then walked on, pulling out his phone to check train times. The screen was full of group chat and, as usual on the day before a match, the baiting was particularly vicious. Zac wondered for the first time if a move away from Fulham wasn't an entirely bad idea.

***

The concourse at Waterloo was busy and he had to run for his train. It was like a fitness session: dodge the people, jink around the coffee stand, jump the luggage, sidestep the snarling Alsatian, glide past the ticket machines, swerve away from the ticket inspector, slide through the barrier and sprint down the platform.

He jumped off the train at Wimbledon and walked home, looking forward to seeing Tammy, who should be back from the spa by now. As he reached their driveway, a black car was pulling out and Tammy was waving it off from the porch.

Usually, even after a short separation, he would have eyes only for his wife, but the sight of the car made him pause and stare. He stood gazing into space for so long after it drove away that Tammy came down the steps to meet him. "Are you alright?" she asked, taking his hand.

"Who was that?"

"Pia, of course. What's the problem?"

"Nothing," he said. But he had glimpsed the car's number plate as it pulled away and he knew where he'd seen it before.

PART 5

Sunday 19th April
FA CUP SEMI-FINAL — Arsenal FC v Fulham FC
Olympic Park

Loz

I'd arranged to meet Jack at Victoria Station so we could travel to the game together. At Hammersmith Broadway my excitement levels climbed as I spotted clusters of white-topped Fulham fans scattered along the length of the platform. It made it seem more real somehow. That morning when I'd woken up, even before I could remember exactly why, I'd had an anxious feeling, a tightness in the pit of my stomach. It was a typical pre-match sensation, the intensity correlating with how critical the match was. That Sunday's game was huge on any scale — an FA Cup semi-final.

The neutral venue for the match was a great choice for both sets of fans. It was coincidental that the four semi-finalists were all London clubs — albeit not all from the Premier League, for this season anyway. The Diamond Blues had, unsurprisingly given their form, beaten Spurs on the Saturday at Villa Park and so here we were, playing Arsenal for a place in the FA Cup Final. The Fulham and Arsenal match-going fans would have travelled pretty much anywhere that Sunday but as it happened, we didn't even have to leave London.

When we hopped off the Tube at Stratford, we found the interchange packed with eager fans and followed the signs to the Queen Elizabeth Olympic Park. On the train, Jack had presented me with a fetching white trilby hat with black trim, matching the one she was wearing with her white Fulham top. I donned it immediately, tilting it for extra jauntiness. In our sunglasses, we looked like a Fulham version of the Blues Brothers — the *Whites Sisters*.

We hadn't yet managed to see a game at the London Stadium, West Ham's new home since 2016.

"So, Jack, ready for the planning seminar before the match?" For a split-second she looked confused by my question.

"Of course," she said enthusiastically. Jack knew we couldn't be in such a transformed part of the city without me saying something plannery on the matter, FA Cup or no FA Cup. She was always a polite audience, giving the impression at least, of finding what I said interesting.

"Well, the London Legacy Development Corporation was established in 2012 and has its own planning policies ... " I checked that she was paying attention before carrying on, " … and its main purpose is to promote regeneration around the Olympic Park."

"Must be working," Jack said, looking around her and seeing all of the new buildings that had sprung up around the Park's edges.

"The Park's been a big success with its green spaces, amazing landscaping and waterways." I continued, "but the focus of the vision has been around the sports venues left over from the Olympics so they've been working hard to make it an emerging cultural district, too."

"Oh, I didn't know that," Jack said.

Encouraged to go on, I said, "The big challenge for the GLA though is getting the benefits to radiate out to the local communities."

I looked back at Jack. I knew she was thinking I was probably being too enthusiastic for my own good.

"Any questions?" I asked, folding my arms and trying to hold back a smile.

Jack put her finger on her chin and, after a short pause replied, "Yep. Who's going to score first today, d'ya think?"

West Ham's move from their tired and cramped but wonderfully atmospheric Boleyn Ground (Upton Park, to most people) — their home since 1904 — had been a major change. The Olympic Stadium, now named the London Stadium, couldn't have been more different. I couldn't imagine ever leaving Craven Cottage — it would be like the ravens leaving the Tower of London — even though previous owners had thought about it with the aim of cashing in on its riverside location. It was unquestionably irreplaceable.

The footballing world couldn't fail to be impressed that, since their move, the Hammers had seen big crowds and could boast the cheapest season ticket in the Premier League. They also now had one of the highest home attendances in Europe. The Club was rightly proud of having opened up football in an affordable and accessible way to fans and especially to children — the lifeblood for generations to come. For some fans though, this could never make up for the loss of their old home and its gritty atmosphere.

We were almost at the edge of the Stadium after our walk through the Queen Elizabeth Park so we stopped to look around us and take it in.

Today is going to be special, I thought. As underdogs, Fulham fans were here to enjoy the day come what may — but who knew what could happen? Having beaten Liverpool, we were just one match away from an FA Cup Final place.

Measure for measure, a win for Fulham would mean so much more to the average Fulham fan than to an Arsenal one, I told myself.

Jack

The first time I went to the London Stadium was on a balmy summer's night in 2012 when the American women's 4x100 relay team set a new world record of 40.82 seconds. I was mesmerised by the Olympic flame and deafened by the tremendous atmosphere. Returning a few weeks later for the Paralympics, I watched Oscar Pistorius race and was impressed and inspired by his determination and courage — there was no foreshadowing of what was to come.

I was hoping that my third trip to the stadium for Fulham's first FA Cup semi-final since 1975 would be as entertaining and uplifting as my previous two.

And, somewhat to my surprise, it was.

We entered the huge arena with trepidation. Arsenal were, of course, favourites to win the match. Despite the fact Fulham had beaten Liverpool to get here, the view of the press was that the result had been a fluke and the semi-final would be a match too far for a Championship team.

Arsenal supporters had travelled across London in numbers and their end of the stadium, like ours, was full. The atmosphere was good, as 60,000 expectant fans took their seats. The Arsenal fans would probably have said it was excellent but when you're used to a small, historic, compact ground, a large, modern stadium just can't compete in terms of looks or feel.

Looking down at the faraway pitch, I honed in on Zac Miller as he waited to kick off the match. There had been a lot of stories linking him with other clubs recently which was always unsettling for fans, never mind the player concerned, but Zac looked alert and composed. Then the referee (or, more likely, the TV producer) decided it was time to start. The whistle blew, Zac passed the ball backwards, and it was game on.

It was nerve-racking watching the match from the stands but a neutral following on television would have enjoyed it. They would have been astonished at the quality of Championship football. For us, it was fantastic to watch Marko's Fulham play another team with a similar style — all about passing, possession and perfection. It was like a carefully choreographed ballroom dance performed at dizzying speed — touching and moving, spinning through space, controlling the tempo, gliding into attack, then pivoting to defend.

Once again, Marko had prepared his team well. This wasn't a grim, edgy fight to the death like the Liverpool replay. This was a balanced contest between two evenly matched sides. Arsenal were everything a top team should be — they defended confidently, they tackled competitively and they attacked like, well, Gunners. As the football pundits were fond of saying, they asked a lot of questions. Just how good was Davy Walker? How strong was the centre-back partnership? Could the Fulham forwards score from distance because they weren't getting any chances in the box? And, as the match wore on, the biggest question of all: where was a goal going to come from?

The problem with football is that, unlike ballroom dancing, you don't win just by being better than the competition. You have to score goals. During the second half, we knew that Fulham could be caught out. We had Arsenal pegged back but we couldn't break through their defence. If the game went into extra time their greater experience and, well, arsenal would begin to tell. Their manager had already brought yet another international striker off the bench and there were more superstars eager to enter the fray. Marko Maric, meanwhile, had subbed off the anonymous Antonio Perez Alvarez in favour of the more dynamic Mitch Masters.

As the clock ticked down, it became inevitable that there was only going to be one goal in the game and that the breakthrough was likely to be sudden and controversial.

In the 85th minute, Sunday Oyetoro raced down the wing with the ball and cut inside. He passed to Mitch who drove forwards into the box. The sudden danger panicked the Arsenal defenders and one leapt into Mitch's path. There was nothing in the challenge — just a tired defender timing his tackle badly but instead of taking the ball he caught Mitch's ankle. Even before Mitch landed head first on the pitch, the referee was blowing his whistle and pointing at the penalty spot.

I was immediately gripped by terror rather than hope. Fulham had a long history of generosity to opponents, including penalty misses.

There was bedlam in the stands around us and chaos on the pitch. Fans jostled to get the best view. The Arsenal players had run to the referee begging and pleading while the Fulham players were already forming a semi-circle outside the box.

There were only two people in the stadium who were motionless. In front of the goal, Zac Miller had scooped up the ball and stood holding it, his head bowed, tuning out noise and emotion; and on the edge of the technical area, Marko Maric, a dark and haunting figure, stood with his arms folded, impassively watching the action.

The referee tired of the Arsenal players' protestations and waved them away. The goalkeeper muttered something to Zac on his way back to the goal, but Zac didn't react.

Our seats were behind the goal, but we were too far away to read Zac's expression. We had to wait to watch the replays for that and I was surprised at how tense and grim he looked. Then the ref blew the whistle, Zac struck the ball, the keeper dived the wrong way and the game was as good as over. The Fulham players piled on top of Zac and, in the stands, we proved the atmosphere in big, new stadiums could be excellent after all.

Which was a good thing as that goal booked our place in the FA Cup Final in the biggest stadium in England. We were going to Wembley.

Loz

Along with every other Fulham fan, we had been in no hurry to leave the stadium. The atmosphere was one that we not only wanted to savour, we wanted to bottle it up and take it home with us.

What we had just witnessed was what the FA Cup was supposed to be all about — the potential for teams from lower divisions to beat teams above them in a classic Cupset. This is what football pundits and TV channels longed for, giving them plenty of newsworthy material to fill their column inches and sports programmes. To Jack and me though, this hadn't been an upset, it had been thoroughly deserved.

We left the ground, our voices hoarse, in a dreamlike euphoric state — exactly as we'd felt last time Jack and I were here, at the Paralympic games. Groups of Fulham fans looked similarly punch-drunk.

We were stunned by the improbability of our team getting to the FA Cup Final for the first time in decades. My legs were feeling shaky, my adrenalin levels dropping, as we started to walk along the path back towards the Tube.

"What do you think, Jack?" I paused to take a couple of deep breaths, feeing like that match had physically aged me. "One quick drink here while it's still sunny?"

The bars were all overflowing and so we decided to get a couple of mini proseccos from a supermarket and found some stone blocks to sit on at the edge of the park.

"This is one of the best moments of my life," said Jack.

"Well, not for long, if we go on to win the Cup," I said, before adding, "Just the small matter of having to beat the Diamonds, the best team in the universe right now."

"You could see what that meant to the players. They looked absolutely ecstatic," Jack said. "Not sure what it means to Marko though."

"He did disappear quicker than anyone else, I noted, which is just bad manners! Billy the Badger was funny though. He was literally breakdancing at the end. Who knew badgers could do that?"

We both let out a loud sigh, taking in this rare moment of total footballing satisfaction.

The match's highlights were tumbling round in my head. After a while I said, "It was good before kick-off when the cameras went around the stands picking out famous people, making them give a wave to the big screen. Think we matched them on the celeb stakes."

"Definitely," Jack agreed. "Always good to see Hugh Grant there supporting Fulham. And the mighty Mucklowes, of course."

We both lifted our mini-bottles up, silently toasted our celeb supporters and took a mouthful of the warming prosecco.

"But seeing Joe Martinez was funny. I'd seen some stuff on Twitter with Arsenal fans complaining he was a phoney fan because he was asked in some interview about his favourite match this season and he couldn't think of an answer. Pretty pathetic if you badge yourself as a fan to make yourself more electable."

"Not good for your image either, is it, being linked to a losing team?" Jack said dryly.

I looked across at Jack and she'd taken off her hat and had her face tilted to the sun, lapping up the rays, and I decided to do the same. I felt the glow of the sun on my skin and was starting to feel the effects of the bubbly prosecco. Life felt amazing.

Surrey

It was a long time before Marko left the stadium.

At the final whistle, he strode down the tunnel leaving the players to celebrate with the fans if they wanted to. When they straggled jubilantly into the dressing room, he was waiting for them, looking forbidding. The group gradually fell silent, leaving Leo's last statement " … bloody brilliant!" hanging awkwardly in the air.

Marko said, "Do you think you've won something?"

His tone made it clear that he wasn't expecting a reply. They had two league matches that week and Marko needed them to forget about the Cup for a while. It was tight at the top of the Championship and if things went wrong, Fulham could end up finishing third and in the play-offs — the situation he had assured David Patterson months ago that he would avoid. Glory was so close — promotion and the FA Cup Final. But lose the next three matches and they would be back where they started — in the Championship next season, tainted with disappointment and failure.

He gave the press the same message: he was pleased with the performance but now he was focusing on the League.

The reporters, looking for a more interesting angle than sensible game management, asked how he felt about playing his old club in the biggest match in English football.

"It will be a great occasion, of course," Marko said. "But I played for several English clubs. Including Fulham."

"But surely," one reporter persisted, unable to see past his top six bias, "You must feel a lot of affection for the Diamonds? You spent several seasons there. It was where you made your name in England."

"The old one, maybe," said Marko. "I am Fulham's manager and I am focusing on Fulham."

Another reporter asked, "Are you thinking about Europe yet?"

If Fulham won the FA Cup, it was likely that they would also win a place in next season's Europa League competition.

"No," Marko lied.

Eventually, after another visit to the dressing room to order his players to calm down, he escaped to the car. The driver opened the back door for him, and he found Ivana, her legs elegantly crossed, waiting for him. He liked the way her perfume filled the air.

"Sorry it took so long."

"The players were very rowdy today," she said. "I thought they'd never let you get away."

In truth, as far as the players were concerned, it was a double celebration because Sunday Oyetoro's wife had given birth to a baby boy the previous day. Marko had felt a pang at the news and he knew Ivana would, too — even after all these years a reminder of what they didn't have could upset her. Instead, he said, "They're excited, but they shouldn't be."

He spent most of the journey on the phone, first to David Patterson in New York. He said again, "We haven't won anything yet," although more politely than he had to the players, and reassured David of his focus on the Championship. Later, Richard Green phoned to say The Post wanted to do an in-depth interview with Zac the next day.

"Not Zac," said Marko.

"Why not?"

Marko pictured Zac shattered when he was subbed off just after scoring the penalty.

"Because I say so," he answered, ending the call.

Ivana looked across at him, "Why don't you turn it off?"

He nodded and followed her suggestion then turned to stare out of the window. Ivana, who recognised his moods as easily as her own, knew better than to expect him to talk.

***

At home Ivana opened a bottle of wine and said, "I spoke to Dario earlier."

"Oh yes?" Marko was hanging up his jacket. Under it, his dark shirt was slightly crumpled; his hair ruffled at the end of a long and busy day.

"He told me what happened in Liverpool. When you got back to the hotel."

"He shouldn't have told you that."

"Why didn't YOU tell me?"

He sighed and watched her pouring the wine. "It was just a prank."

"He said you'd say that."

She pushed one of the glasses towards him.

"But, Marko, in this country, with their stupid sense of humour, they think a prank is pulling your chair away before you sit down or letting the air out of your tyres, not trying to kill someone."

"No one got killed," Marko muttered into his glass.

"Dario said Zac might have been. Or you!"

He tried to work out if her tone was angry or concerned. "Not really," he said.

"He said you saved Zac's life."

"Well, we were playing Liverpool the next day. Who else was going to play up front?"

Ivana slammed the wine bottle back into the fridge. "This isn't a joking matter."

"No, but Dario's exaggerating everything."

He smiled at her over his glass and, disconcerted by this unusual display of amusement, she looked away.

"I can't believe anyone would try to hurt Zac."

She slipped off her leather jacket — he still hadn't worked out if it was old or new — revealing a white jumper and black trousers. He wondered if her choice of Fulham colours had been deliberate or subconscious. David Patterson hadn't been around today so she was wearing stilettos.

"I know, but someone did try and it wasn't the first time. He was nearly run over before Christmas."

"What? You didn't tell me about that either. I suppose you saved his life then, too?"

"Well ... " began Marko, but then he frowned and continued in his usual surly tone. "I have to watch the replay of the match."

He snatched up his glass and walked out of the kitchen without another word.

***

There were analysts at the Club who were paid to watch match replays but Marko liked to study a game in detail and make notes before talking to the players. It was comfortable in his home office with the wine and the big screen but, despite the powerful performance of his team today, he found it hard to concentrate on watching them.

He kept thinking back to the near miss outside Motspur Park in the December dusk. In the intervening months he had created a version of events in which he had, if not saved Zac's life as Ivana had so poetically put it, at least been the hero of the piece. But, of course, it hadn't happened like that at all and the reality made him shudder. If the car and the flowerpot hadn't been aimed at Zac, then there was only one other possible target.

But then, who was the perpetrator? From the kitchen, he could hear Ivana attacking vegetables with a knife. If he was going to think about who might be murderously angry with him then he didn't have to look very far from home. But, of course, that was ridiculous.

***

It was typical of Marko, Ivana thought: the untimely reminder of humour and warmth and then the almost immediate reversion to his normal discontented self. She wondered what he was brooding about this time — it certainly wasn't winning an FA Cup semi-final. He was unhappy about something and as usual doing nothing to hide it.

And here she was cooking his dinner after trailing around East London all day watching yet another football match. She could get out of here, she reminded herself, pack her bags and fly to Croatia and not look back.

But that bloody smile of his. Over 20 years of him and she still couldn't resist the charm he took such care to conceal. The situation was impossible because he was impossible. What was the point, she thought, of contemplating leaving Marko, of imagining life without him when, in spite of it all, she still loved him?

Thursday 24th April — St James's

Hamarat sat back in his grand leather chair in the corner of the lounge, his manicured hands together, satisfaction etched across his face. Unconsciously twisting his wedding ring, he thought, what a remarkable year this is turning out to be, even better than expected.

His reverie was interrupted by his friend, a relaxed-looking Kerim Bayram walking towards him, dressed in jeans and a shiny buttoned navy blazer over his white shirt.

"Omar, you look like the cat who has had the cream and is expecting some more," Bayram said on greeting his friend and gesturing for him to stay seated.

It had been a few months since they had met up in person, what with business trips taking them both out of the country and holidays to fit in.

With drinks ordered, Bayram asked, "So Omar, tell me, how is that beautiful wife of yours?"

"Still beautiful. Still costing me a small fortune. But for me, spoiling her is a pleasure, that is why it works," Hamarat replied with a shrug of his shoulder.

"Well you look in good health. She must be worth it. But I know you. It cannot just be Tabitha. I guess that west London football club of yours must have something to do with it?" Bayram teased, knowing that the Diamond Blues were already guaranteed the Premier League title.

There were still four league matches to go before the end of the season but with the Diamonds 14 points clear of second place Manchester United, they were uncatchable. This had the football press salivating over their ability to win matches even if the team wasn't always playing beautiful football.

"So, I hear you are on course for the treble," Bayram remarked. "You must be very proud?"

"Treble? Treble?" Hamarat played at sounding confused. "We are going for the quadruple, Kerim. Just the Champions League and the small matter of the domestic FA Cup to go. This would be a first in English football and I intend for the Club, *my* Club, to go down in history. It will make it the biggest club in European football. This west London football club has proven a very worthwhile investment. Much like Tabitha," he smiled.

Hamarat had reason to be bullish. The Diamonds were having a remarkable season, by anyone's standards. Their earlier League Cup win beating Leicester City 1–0, had been efficient, perfunctory even. The football commentators had considered them worthy winners, even though the Diamonds' goal had come as a result of a fairly soft penalty.

On the back of their Premier League performance, the press had been rapturous over the Diamonds' win over Tottenham Hotspur in their FA Cup semi-final on the previous Saturday, a convincing 3–1 victory at Villa Park. This meant that, once again, they would be in the FA Cup Final, scheduled for Saturday 30th May, a little later than usual.

Footballing calendars across the world were being shifted. That year, the World Cup was to take place in winter rather than summer. Not coincidentally, it was being hosted by a small but extremely rich Middle Eastern nation. Playing football matches in their summer, with temperatures of 50-plus °C, would have been impossible for the players and unthinkable for the supporters. It wasn't a popular choice for fans, but money talked, especially in football.

The knock-on implications of a winter World Cup meant UEFA having to change the scheduling of the Champions League Final in Porto to Saturday 23rd May, a week earlier than usual, with many countries' domestic cup competitions having to follow.

"Well done on reaching the FA Cup Final, Omar. You must be pleased. Who is it you play? I'm afraid I did not follow the other semi-final on Sunday."

"We play Fulham, our close neighbours. I know you like their riverside ground very much," Hamarat said, touching the end of his nose with his finger. "And I am doing my best to line up their current home for you Kerim."

His companion gave a shallow nod. Hamarat carried on.

“But Kerim, they are not even a Premier League club — not as yet. But it is favourable that they have beaten Arsenal, it means the Diamonds do not have to meet them in the Final.”

Bayram pondered. “So, putting the Cup to one side, if Fulham gets promoted, does that mean Patterson will want to cash in now? Sure, it will inflate the price I have to pay but if he needs money as badly as everyone is saying, this could be the trigger for him to let the Club go. What do you think, Omar?”

Hamarat pursed his lips. “I spoke to Patterson earlier this week, about a Foundation event. He sounded in good spirits. Said the sale of some of his stores has steadied his retail ship but I doubt that, Kerim, very much. He won’t be able to get out of trouble that easily. It’s just bravado.”

“And not wanting to look like a forced seller,” said Bayram.

“Of course,” agreed Hamarat.

Sitting back, with his arms along both armrests, Bayram muttered, “So, I will wait.”

After their teacups were refilled, their conversation resumed.

“And so the FA Cup has the Diamonds’ name on it?” Bayram asked.

Hamarat, leaning forward in his chair, said, “I don’t want to be overly complacent, Kerim. Fulham must have something if they can reach the Final but we will be too good for them. But you know me, my success has not come about by leaving things to chance. I have leverage I can use if need be.”

Lowering his voice, Hamarat added, “If we can win the Champions League, we will be able to achieve what no one else has — the legendary quadruple. The football holy grail. Can you imagine, Kerim? This team, this Club, will go down in history.”

He shook his head, taking in the enormity of the prospect.

“But the English newspapers think that is impossible. I admire your spirit,” Bayram replied.

“The English psyche is unattractively negative, they lack self-belief,” Hamarat pouted. “They talk themselves into defeat, happy just to have done well rather than actually winning! But we are so close, Kerim, and this team is special. I saw how we brushed aside Borussia Dortmund in our quarter-final legs. Now we are in the last four and we have to see off Real Madrid next Tuesday.”

Smiling, he added, “I am confident we can reach that Final.”

“I think you owe me for encouraging you to buy a football club in the first place,” joked Bayram. “What a smart move.”

It wasn't just the papers that were saying that to win the quadruple would be almost impossible but the Diamond Blues' Italian manager joined in, evidently trying to manage the fans' expectations, those of the media and, of course, his boss — Hamarat's. The manager, Lorenzo Verdi, who was now footballing's hottest property, reiterated to the press that while they still *theoretically* could become the first English club to win all four trophies in one campaign, it was a most unlikely outcome and he was taking it "one game at a time".

The Times' football correspondent that morning had reported on the "almost impossible" expectation management with regard to the quadruple clean sweep but commented:

> Like the national lottery, you have to be in it to win it, and the Diamond Blues remain firmly on course for making footballing history. For understandable reasons, the four trophy haul has remained out of reach of all the great English sides. It is a test of endurance and consistency that requires quality, resilience and plenty of good fortune along the way. All the pieces must be in place for almost all of the campaign. It would be an exceptional achievement and the odds are not in the Blues' favour — yet those same odds are reducing game by game so why bet against them?

"I am pleased for you, Omar. I want to be at any party you have to celebrate! And what of the other matter, the election for London mayor and sorting out your grand plans for Wembley? And, of course, my future plans for Fulham's ground. Is this proceeding to plan?" Bayram enquired.

"I am content," Hamarat responded. "If you watched the election debate earlier this month you will have seen that Joe Martinez did well. He is sure to win. The Conservative person is popular with young people but not a real threat. There is a lady, a Lydia Edwards, who recently entered the race, running as an independent. As it happens, I know her, our paths have crossed in the past in a joint business venture. She is quite formidable. Impressive, even. My advisers say she will take votes from all of the parties, but this will work in our favour, she will split the Tory share. London is a Labour city — all these liberal elites and its young population.

"We will have our man in City Hall, Kerim, and he knows what is expected of him. With the Diamonds making European footballing history, it is even more vital our commercial interests are supported. In fact, my friend, stay — Joe Martinez is coming here very soon to see me. You could meet him."

Bayram shook his head, he preferred to steer clear of politicians. As Bayram was leaving, putting on his trench coat and turning up his collar, he spotted Joe Martinez striding into the reception area. He looks an open, honest man, Bayram thought; quite perfect, in fact.

***

Hamarat was on his third Earl Grey of the afternoon when he greeted Joe Martinez. Their handshake was that of business partners, not friends. Joe relaxed back into the chair, crossing his legs. Hamarat studied him. Joe looked mayoral, he thought, poised and polished, but the creases under his eyes told of late nights and some recent hard graft. He recalled Joe's attractive wife and what an asset she'd be to her husband in front of the cameras.

"Good afternoon, Joe. You look well."

"I'm feeling good. The campaign is going well, and I have a great team behind me."

His manner was confident and he looked a man in control of his destiny.

"The polls are positive, too," he continued. "I'm still favourite, even if the gap between me and Arjun Shah and Lydia Edwards is narrowing a little."

"Hmm, Lydia Edwards," Hamarat said, his hand to his chin, "she has many popular ideas, some of them good. You will need to take a few of these for your campaign. I see her as your main threat so please do not underestimate her."

Joe was listening intently as Hamarat continued, "You are only two short weeks away from being the next mayor of London. I have told you what I expect from you — there is no room for misunderstandings as I will need you to execute the plan from the outset."

Joe's expression didn't give anything away.

"For you, Joe, this is your path to even bigger and better things. I look forward to the day when you can be leading not just your party but this wonderful country of yours, or should I say *ours*?" Hamarat smiled.

"I've been delighted to support your successful campaign and to provide you with some, what shall we call them … " Hamarat glanced upwards as if searching for the right words in the air, " … *bonus* payments that I assume have been gratefully received," he nodded expectantly at Joe. Hamarat's smug smile hinted at his knowledge of the financial precariousness of Joe's over-extended lifestyle.

Hamarat's voice was soft but his message was focused, "Joe, I am counting on you to win. I've made clear my need for more *relaxed* development policies. Not for the benefit of everyone, of course. You can wave away the inevitable objections from the local councils to our proposals. I know you share my ambitions for this great city."

Joe was composed. "I know you believe in London. I also know that London needs investment, from many sources, including you, Omar."

"I have great plans for Wembley Stadium, Joe, and I need my scheme signed off — a sensible return on my investment," Hamarat said, his smile stretching out his thin lips.

Subtly, Joe nodded to convey he understood.

"As for the Diamond Arena, with the status and profile the Diamonds now have, these plans are even bigger than they were before. A wonderful new leisure and pleasure complex — restaurants, nightclubs, who knows?

"And for my associates, like Kerim Bayram, he has some creative ideas to free up land for the housing that London needs — consolidating some football stadia, such a sensible thing to do in this crowded city. The mayor can overcome the sensitivities that get in the way of making things happen."

Joe smiled by way of acknowledgement. Hamarat put his cup down to indicate the meeting was coming to a close.

"It was good to see you again, Joe. I look forward to celebrating your win in a couple of weeks. It's a shame for you that that team of yours doesn't have what it takes to win. I thought we'd be meeting Arsenal in the FA Cup Final, but you couldn't beat a Championship side," he teased. "So sad."

Hamarat stood up to shake Joe's hand. "Good luck, my friend," he said patting him on the back, "not that you will need it with all my help."

On the other side of the room, a man sat forward in his seat and, with a quizzical look, turned to his companion.

"Isn't that Joe Martinez with Mr Blues himself, Omar Hamarat? Think I might need to have a little chat with Julie next time I see her."

Saturday 2nd May — Motspur Park

The Championship fixtures computer had excelled itself by picking Fulham's last game of the League season to be at home to Sheffield Wednesday, the team Fulham had been stalking at the top of the table for the last few months. Fulham had drawn away at Millwall during the week and Wednesday were now only two points in front.

Wednesday had the advantage: win or draw, they would finish first. To win the League, Fulham had to win the match.

On the day before the game, the final training session was run by Charlie Paxton because Marko Maric was busy with the press. Richard Green was in his element making sure Fulham were all over the back pages. An outsider would be forgiven for thinking that Richard's role was more important than Marko's at the moment.

Richard did his job well though and David Patterson and the fans were delighted to see their Club get the coverage it deserved for a change. Sports journalists tended forget that football happened outside of the top six, never mind outside of the Premier League but they had belatedly realised that Fulham could be on the verge of an historic double: winning the Championship and the FA Cup. They did not, of course, find this anywhere near as exciting as the fact that the Diamond Blues were aiming for an historic quadruple. But they had column inches and webpages to fill and Fulham's training ground at Motspur Park was only a short trip from London.

The training session was a technical one involving taking and defending free kicks and corners. At the top levels of football, where teams tended to be closely matched, a game could be decided on set pieces so it was essential that a squad was well-drilled.

It was a glorious late spring day full of warmth, birdsong and promise. The kind of day that made a professional footballer feel even luckier than usual — to be outside, playing the game they loved with their teammates in a spirit of camaraderie and anticipation. Unless you were in the Fulham team, of course, where the spirit was one of envy and mistrust.

At Millwall, Zac had had a goal disallowed for offside by the narrowest possible margin. His angry reaction had earned him another yellow card and some snide remarks from his teammates. "All he needs to do," he overheard while he was in the shower, "is shut up, stay on side and put the ball in the net. How hard is that?"

But everything was hard because Zac was more distracted than usual — he couldn't get the sight of Pia's car out of his head. A black Mercedes with the initials VOR in the number plate. The same car he had seen speeding towards him out of the dark last December. But it couldn't be the same car. Pia couldn't have been trying to run him over. It didn't make any sense.

Antonio's usually reliable free kicks had become wayward so they were practising with Javier taking them instead. The ball sailed over the defensive wall and Zac saw it too late, mistiming his jump so the ball swept past him and around the post. "Sorry!" He called, raising a hand to Javier.

It wasn't the first one he had missed and Javier lost his temper.

"Sorry!" He mimicked, marching around the wall. "Lo siento, he says, Mr Star Striker, Senor Dorado Bota. Sorry isn't good enough. Do you want to win the League or not?"

With one heavily tattooed hand, he pushed Zac sharply in the chest, awaiting a reaction, which he got but not the one he expected. "Lo siento," Zac repeated but in recognition, not apology.

Jamie was about to intervene, but Phil grabbed his arm and shook his head.

"Leave them to it," he said wearily.

Jamie knew Phil had a point, but Phil didn't know what he knew. Zac, overtly so successful and popular, was an odd choice for Javier's enmity. But Javier was a bully and, like all bullies, he sensed weakness like a shark senses blood in the water.

"So, you keep saying but just try and head the ball," Javier sneered at Zac.

"I will," said Zac and added, as Javier began to turn away, "and never push me like that again."

Javier spun back but before he could speak or, more likely, push Zac like that again a voice shouted from the touch line. "What the hell are you two playing at? You're supposed to be taking free kicks!"

Javier and Zac both looked over. Marko Maric had finished with the press and had come to see how his team were doing.

Javier snarled at Zac and ran back around the wall to collect another ball. Zac stalked into the six-yard box where Jamie was waiting to mark him.

Jamie said quietly, "Are you OK?"

"I need to talk to you," Zac replied.

"We can go to the canteen … "

"Not here," Zac said with another glance at Marko.

At that moment, Javier struck a delivery of perfect line and length. Zac leapt for it, heading it into the back of the net.

***

Jamie invited Zac to his house after training so they could talk. Zac accepted with a terse nod rather than his usual politeness and without expanding on what he wanted to talk about. Leo had already invited himself over and Jamie thought about putting him off. But if Zac was in a dark place, a bit of Leo's hero worship might help.

When Jamie arrived home with Leo in tow, he scooped up the latest felled forest of election leaflets from the mat and dumped them on the breakfast bar. Leo grabbed the remote and flicked on the TV. It was already tuned to a sports channel and highlights of a Premier League match between the Diamond Blues and Manchester United were playing. Like most footballers, Jamie and Leo spent a lot of the time when they weren't actually playing football or at football training, either watching football, playing football-related computer games or talking about football.

Jamie sorted out drinks while Leo scanned through the election literature. "Are you going to vote?" He asked.

"God knows," said Jamie.

"I quite like Arjun."

"What?" Jamie was horrified. "You grew up in a council flat. You can't vote Tory!"

"Ex-council flat," corrected Leo, "My mum bought it. Thanks to Mrs Thatcher."

Jamie rolled his eyes, "Arjun isn't a serious contender. I remember him from The Apprentice. He's just a joker."

"No he isn't," said Leo. "He's got good ideas about getting young people to start up businesses. Plus, he's got a big personality, just what you need for a big job."

At that moment the doorbell rang and Jamie didn't have to reply.

***

Jamie returned to the kitchen with Zac. Leo offered him a fist pump while Jamie asked, "Coffee?"

"Do you have decaf?"

Jamie frowned. "I'm not running a cafe, mate."

"Then no thanks. Just water."

As he filled a glass, Jamie took the plunge. "So how are you, Zac? You haven't missed training for a while. We get worried when you miss training and stuff."

"Y'all … " Zac cleared his throat. "I'm fine. Stop worrying. This isn't about me. It's something else."

He drank some of the water and said seriously, in his soft, southern drawl, "I'm pretty certain that Marko's having an affair with Pia Alvarez, Antonio's wife."

This announcement, so baldly put, stunned his listeners. Eventually, Jamie said, "What?"

Zac nodded and explained it all — the car with VOR in the number plate at Motspur Park and seeing it again with Pia driving. Antonio had been injured and absent from training back in December, but he knew all about the run from the training schedules and WhatsApp.

"And then there's what happened in Liverpool," Zac went on. "This morning, when Javier said 'lo siento' I remembered Antonio saying it over and over in the lobby of the hotel. He was apologising for hurting me. You hear Spanish all the time in Texas but not over here. I didn't make the connection until now."

"Oh yeah," Leo said. It wasn't the first time he had relived the scene. He looked over at Zac, at the scar, which was slowly fading. "Antonio was rambling in Spanish the whole time."

"Yeah, he was," Jamie remembered. "But you're saying Antonio aimed that pot at Marko. Are you sure about this, Zac?"

"Pretty much," said Zac, and he sounded angry now. "Marko has a reputation for this sort of thing, doesn't he?"

"For what?" Leo asked.

Jamie sighed and said, "He had to leave West Ham because of one of the other players' wives and I've heard something happened at Palace as well. But this stuff goes on in football, Zac, you know that. Football and fidelity don't always go together."

On the screen, the Diamonds' striker, Robert Ludwig, smashed the ball into the goal from twenty yards out. All three Fulham players grimaced.

"Shit, this is all we need," said Jamie.

***

At that moment, Jamie's wife, Sarah and the children came home, the latter running noisily into the kitchen where they were thrilled to find Zac. Sarah shooed them out into the garden.

Zac rose to greet her and she felt herself beginning to blush as he kissed both her cheeks. More than any of the other players, Zac had star quality. And what was that shade of blue? Bluebell? Or forget-me-not?

Hoping she appeared calmer than she felt Sarah said, "Lovely to see you," and managed to include Leo in the statement. "I've got things to do, Jamie. Keep an eye on the kids, won't you?"

After this interlude, Jamie said, rather impatiently, "So, what are you saying, Zac? Marko and Pia are having an affair. I can believe that. But that Antonio wants to what ... ? Kill Marko?"

"I don't think so. Frighten him probably. But that's not the point. The point is Marko."

Zac knew that Jamie's comments about footballers' infidelities were correct. Temptation was often thrown their way, and some found it hard to resist. But a player having a fling with a girl he met at a party was very different to the manager getting involved with a player's wife.

"This could stop us winning the League and the Cup," Zac pointed out. "Antonio's been off his game recently. No wonder. He did nothing against Arsenal and he was all over the place the other night. This morning he couldn't even kick the ball straight. And what if he tries to do something stupid again? And Marko or someone gets badly hurt this time?"

"But what can we do?" Jamie asked.

Zac looked at him as if the answer was obvious. "You have to talk to Antonio."

***

The back door opened and Jamie's daughter Zadie appeared. "Will you come and play with us, Leo? You can go in goal," she added as if this was the most generous offer in the world.

Leo looked from Zac to Jamie, intrigued by the tension between them. But he was 18 and as compelling as this 'grown up' discussion was, he found the prospect of football in the garden more enticing.

"Sure," he answered. "But if you want a goalkeeper, it's Zac you need."

Without looking away from Jamie, Zac said, "I'll be out in a bit."

Zadie beamed and Leo followed her outside.

Jamie said, "How the hell am I going to talk to Antonio about this? What do I say? What good will it do?"

"You can stop him doing something he'll regret. Reassure him," Zac said, in a tone that emphasised it wasn't his problem.

Zac wasn't done. "I'm so pissed with Marko. I was just starting to like him. I used to think he was all about results and the stuff about him changing clubs too often was true, but I've seen a different side to him. Like, results aren't all he cares about but now … "

Zac trailed off and Jamie signed, half-irritated at being lumbered with the problem, half-resigned to solving it.

Being Fulham captain was the culmination of Jamie's long and successful career. Sometimes it still rankled that he had never been picked to play for England when in another generation of centre-backs, he surely would have been. But being where he was now — captain of a team about to be promoted, about to play its first FA Cup Final in five decades — more or less made up for any disappointments.

He had always known that being club captain was more than setting an example, more than organising the team on the pitch and acting as ambassador off it. But no one could have predicted that it would involve his current predicament.

"You're not the only one Marko's won over," Jamie said grudgingly.

Then, intrigued, he asked, "Why did Leo say you should play in goal?"

"Because that's what I used to do. Back home. Leo and I practice pens sometimes. That's how he knows."

"Any good?" Jamie asked, still trying to picture Zac as a goalkeeper.

"Yeah, not bad. In goal you always get the benefit of the doubt. People don't expect you to make every save but when you make a good one, you're a hero. If I miss an easy shot or I'm an inch offside I get slated. Last season, I had to score goals to keep us up, now I've got to score goals to get us promoted."

He didn't want to continue the conversation, so he slid off his stool and joined Leo and the kids in the garden. Jamie watched him go, his mind turning back, with resentment, to the problem Zac had landed him with.

They all idolise him, Jamie thought, Leo, my kids, even my wife, but it's me who's got to do the dirty work while he gets all the attention.

Just like on the pitch.

Sunday 3rd May
Primrose Hill

The journalist and cameraman were expected at any moment. At least it's not raining, Joe thought, I don't want to have to do this inside the house.

Julie came into the bedroom, arms stretching out as she got close. "I like that tie," she said as she straightened the knot. "The dark stripes match the suit. Looks good."

Joe's laugh made it clear that his appearance had not been at the forefront of his mind.

"You all set?" she asked as they made their way down the stairs.

The reckoning had started the previous evening when Joe had got home after a long day on the campaign trail.

As soon as he'd shut the front door behind him, the house had felt different. He instantly sensed the children's absence. At this time of day, they'd normally be sprawled on the living room floor watching TV or playing games. Julie was in the kitchen sitting down at a bare table, alone, waiting for him. Julie, the investigative journalist.

There was no build-up. She spoke plainly. She'd bumped into an ex-colleague in her office the previous week. He told her he was currently researching a book on London's richest residents, investigating how people like Omar Hamarat had accumulated their vast wealth.

Her old colleague had told her about spotting Joe with Omar at a private members' club, adding he hadn't realised that they were friends and half-joked that he might need to investigate their relationship, too. This had been news to her — Joe hadn't mentioned a recent meeting with Hamarat. Straight away she knew that the omission hadn't just been an oversight as she recalled they'd gone out for dinner — something they'd both been too busy to do for a while — the same evening he'd been seen at the club. The dinner was meant to have been a rare time to catch up, but there had been no mention of any such encounter. The more she thought about it, she couldn't help picturing how matey Joe and Hamarat had seemed, chatting away at her editor's retirement dinner, earlier on in the year.

She had meant to follow it up with Joe, eager to find out what he and Hamarat had talked about and how it had come about, but a combination of her work and his demanding campaign meant that it hadn't happened and she had put it to the back of her mind.

That Saturday, however, Julie had had the luxury of a few hours to herself and, feeling virtuous, decided to review their finances. She'd checked online first but then had to call the building society for confirmation. When she eventually got through to a human, a chirpy-sounding girl brightly dropped a bombshell. "Yes, Mrs Martinez, your mortgage has been paid off in its entirety, that is £803,000. That was done two weeks ago."

It was enough to make Julie's head explode. She knew they'd stretched themselves financially but didn't realise the lengths Joe was prepared to go to ease the burden. That huge sum had come from someone and she had a very good idea from whom.

Their kitchen had been the interrogation room. Joe had protested that he was going to tell her about the money, almost casually admitting that it was from Omar Hamarat. At first, he tried to explain away his relationship with Hamarat — it was helpful to have a wealthy benefactor, he said, someone to collaborate with, a person of influence on his side. Joe cringed at how hollow it sounded. It forced him to admit that the cash would guarantee his support for Hamarat's investments and his development projects. Like in London football clubs — and Wembley Stadium. The look on Julie's face made him turn away. His own burned with shame.

Julie had arranged for the children to stay over at her parents, leaving them able to talk late into the night. She had convinced him that it was best to jump before some journalist down the line pushed him in front of a press juggernaut. Joe might be 'doing the right thing' but the price was reneging on a deal with Hamarat and inevitable public humiliation. Julie's threat to take the kids and leave had been the turning point.

Together they'd worked out a plan. He called Kelly, his campaign manager, and she'd picked up straightaway despite the late hour, worried that something had happened. As instructed, she'd set in motion the TV announcement, in time for the Sunday morning political bulletins. He didn't tell her what it was all about; he preferred to tell her face to face.

From his living room he could see there was activity in front of his house. Outside, the cameraman was getting his equipment prepared and the journalist with him was on the phone. They both looked like they'd had late nights, too.

Before he opened the front door, he picked up his phone and texted Hamarat. *I'm sorry but I'm out. Turn on TV.* Such simple words. He lifted his head and pushed his shoulders back. Julie approached and touched his cheek.

"You're doing the right thing," she said.

After polite but brief introductions, Joe stood with his back to his front door, clutching a single piece of paper as the camera began to roll.

"It has been an enormous privilege to have had so much support from so many people for my campaign to be the next mayor of London. I am both grateful and humbled by the response I have had.

"After much deliberation, however, and with much regret, I have taken the decision that for the sake of my family and for personal reasons, as from this morning, I am stepping away from the race."

The two TV people looked astonished.

"I know people will question my decision given the late timing but I ask that you respect it and allow my family and me some privacy. Thank you."

With a half-smile, he turned and re-entered his house. The camera continued to roll as the young journalist made a statement just in front of Joe's hastily shut front door.

"The news that Joe Martinez has dropped out of the race for mayor for London, a contest that he was widely predicted to win, has come as a total shock. It leaves many questions as to the real reasons behind his surprise decision and we anticipate that speculation will mount if these remain unanswered."

***

Looking at his TV from his breakfast stool in his highly polished kitchen, coffee in hand, Hamarat's eyes narrowed as small beads of sweat appeared on his brow. He placed his cup carefully on the counter, his hand shaking almost imperceptibly. Memories of their last meeting flashed through his mind — there had been no hint of Joe getting weak-kneed. Not getting his own way was unfamiliar territory but composure and a clear head was what Hamarat needed right now. His rage could be harnessed and released at a time of his choosing.

His investment of time and money had evaporated with Joe's closing of his front door but the fundamentals hadn't changed — the need for him to have influence at the top of London's power tree so as to see out his Wembley and Diamond Arena plans. Breathing deeply to calm himself down, he told himself not to act in haste.

There was always a Plan B.

Craven Cottage

Jack

You would have thought that football fans on their way to the final match of the season — a match which could result in their team winning the Championship — would have talked only about football and the enthralling contest in front of them.

Instead, Loz and I walked along the river path under a blazing hot sun, dodging runners and cyclists, talking about Joe Martinez.

"I really can't believe it," Loz said, "He was the favourite. He's had lots of publicity this last week and he would have probably won."

"He said it was for 'personal reasons'," I commented.

Loz virtually snorted. "That old chestnut!"

"Maybe he's having an affair as well," I said, glancing over my shoulder to check no one was in earshot. "Like Marko."

"Maybe," said Loz, "But he doesn't seem the type."

"They don't always," I said darkly.

"It's so weird to think of the election taking place without a Labour party candidate," Loz said. "The party must be furious with him. It sounds like he hadn't told anyone he was pulling out before he made the public announcement."

"It blows the race wide open," I said. "I suppose some people won't bother to vote now but others will switch."

"Have you made up your mind?" Loz asked

"I think so, and Joe's decision doesn't make any difference. It was always between Sonia and Lydia for me and Lydia's just so full of ideas and energy. I really do think she's what London needs right now."

***

As we neared Craven Cottage, we stopped talking about politics and started talking about football. The game would be an unusual one in that there could almost be no losers. Both teams were going to get promoted whatever happened and while there was kudos in winning the League the real prize was promotion itself.

At our seats, we greeted our neighbours, all of whom were as excited as we were. Except maybe Moany Man, who was muttering about the latest rumours linking Zac Miller with half the clubs in the Premier League.

There was a carefree element to both sets of fans, safe in the knowledge that this would be a Premier League fixture next season. Unfortunately, though, the game itself felt more like something from the bottom of League 1.

The problem was Sheffield Wednesday had come to play for the draw. They started with a tactic used by our cleverest and most desperate opponents: making Fulham attack the home end in the first half, thus depriving the team of an edge, should they need one, at the end of the game.

"I hate it when teams do this," said Loz.

The other tactic Wednesday adopted, which was obvious and much used but rarely successful, was to try to mark Zac Miller out of the game. Wednesday were better at it than most but it made for a stilted, stop-start match, almost a series of vignettes involving set pieces and goal kicks. In the first half, no one came close to scoring and Wednesday were halfway to the point they needed to secure the title.

Things went wrong early in the second half with an injury to Javier Herrera. It was too early for Marko to start making defensive subs so he brought on Mitch Masters and moved Leo Blake to the right wing. This proved to be a master stroke, with Wednesday struggling to deal with an extra attacker. Mitch hit the post and Leo nearly scored from a corner but if anyone's name was going to be on the scoresheet, it was always going to be Zac Miller's, looking to score his 35th league goal of the season.

In the 71st minute, Leo put in a cross that curved up and over the defence and seemed to hover in the air just above the goal. Mitch moved, drawing the defenders with him, leaving Zac free to jump for the header with just the goalkeeper to beat. The goalie leapt, flapped, flailed and missed. The ball flew into the net, the Putney End went mad and Fulham went top of the League.

But the match was far from over. For one thing, Wednesday were worthy of more than the draw their manager had been aiming for. For another, Leo Blake offered a lot less defensively than Javier Herrera — he was a lion running forward but a headless chicken scampering back. Marko swiftly made two defensive subs. But in the Hammersmith End, we were on the edge of our seats with our hearts in our mouths and our hands almost over our eyes as Davy Walker's goal came under constant bombardment.

And in the 86th minute, it all went horribly, Fulhamishly wrong.

Davy Walker was an experienced goalkeeper and usually a cool presence in a crisis. No one watching the match had any idea what possessed him. Why did he come for the ball? Sunday Oyetoro looked to have it covered.

But, perhaps in some misplaced sense of heroism, as the ball spun forwards and bounced high, Davy didn't just leave his line, he left the 18-yard box. And he didn't just misjudge the flight of the ball, he somehow managed to collect it on his arm instead of his chest.

The entire Fulham crowd immediately went silent. We could hear the Sheffield Wednesday fans singing in the void but even some of them looked aghast at the mistake.

The referee blew his whistle. Straight red card, no defence, no point arguing. Ten men on the pitch, all subs used, four minutes to play and the Championship to lose. Suddenly, the second place which we would have settled for earlier in the season and even earlier in the day felt like failure. We wanted very much to win the League. We were desperate to hold on.

***

On the pitch, Jamie watched Davy start the long, lonely walk to the tunnel. The Sheffield Wednesday captain tried to offer Davy a handshake but the goalie brushed him away.

Jamie felt the other nine Fulham players gravitate towards him while the Wednesday players retreated respectfully. Aidan and Leo were talking, of course, but Jamie ignored them. Mitch was swearing and Sunday shaking his head.

Jamie looked along the touchline to the technical area where some kind of argument was going on. Marko was objecting vociferously to the decision while Charlie was trying to calm things down — managers had been sent to the stands for outbursts like this. All the officials and both benches were milling around either joining in or watching the scene. Jamie knew he couldn't afford to be distracted by the side show and was relieved to see Barry, the kit man, emerge from the melee and jog over holding a spare orange goalie shirt and a pair of gloves.

When he reached them, Jamie asked, "Any instructions?"

Barry shook his head. "No chance. I've never seen him this furious before."

"Great," Jamie said and took the small bundle from Barry's hands. As he did so, the silence of the crowd dissolved. From the back of the Hammy End a chant began and quickly spread until it was filling the ground. "*Come on Fulham! Come on Fulham! Come on Fulham!*"

Aidan said quickly, "I'll go in goal. I've played Gaelic football. Good with my hands."

Phil Philopoussis tightened his topknot and said, "I'll do it, mate."

But Jamie shook his head. These were both generous offers and Phil certainly had the impressive build and intimating appearance of a goalkeeper. But Jamie had already made up his mind. "Zac's going in goal," he said.

Everyone looked surprised except Zac himself, although whether the lack of reaction was genuine or conditioned Jamie didn't know.

He went on, "Leo, wait on the halfway line. Everyone else, stay back and defend. Get the ball to Leo. Then, Leo, take it to the corner and keep it there as long as you can."

As a plan, he reflected, it was neither original nor subtle. But they had four minutes plus injury time to survive with their backs against the wall and it was the best chance they had.

Leo was nodding and bouncing on the spot. The others were looking at each other, testing resilience and resolve. The referee stepped into Jamie's line of vision and tapped his watch.

"Let's go," Jamie said and proffered the shirt and gloves to Zac.

Zac stepped away and stripped off his white number 9 shirt. The reaction from the crowd was immediate: a collective indrawn breath and then the song changed. *"There's only one Zac Mill-er! One Zac Mill-er! One Zac Mill-er!"*

He pulled on the orange shirt and fumbled with the gloves. He was surprised to find it was Mitch who came up to help him fasten the Velcro and even more surprised when Mitch offered his bare knuckles to pump against Zac's gloved ones.

"You got this, buddy," Mitch said.

Zac walked slowly towards the Hammersmith End goal. How many goals, he wondered, had he scored here? It suddenly seemed important to know. How many goals had he prevented here? None. Yet.

He reached the six-yard box and drank in the noise of the crowd, all on their feet, all chanting his name. He raised his hand to them then turned his back. Time to get down to business.

The clock on the scoreboard above the Putney End said 89 minutes but this was false reassurance: all the time the Fulham players had huddled by the touch line and all the time he had spent swapping shirts and fiddling with his gloves would be added on. But he had other things to worry about.

The Sheffield Wednesday free kick specialist was lining up a kick from the position where Davy Walker had handled the ball. This was exactly the scenario they had been practising yesterday but Zac hadn't been paying attention to what the attackers were meant to be doing, never mind the defenders.

In front of him, Phil was organising the wall and looked round to check with Zac that it was in the right place. Zac wasn't sure but Phil knew what he was doing so Zac gave him a thumbs-up and took up station in the centre of the goal mouth. He had a second to feel nervous then the ref blew his whistle. All thought and all feeling were swept from Zac's mind as he focused only on the ball curving towards him.

The wall jumped as one and Phil's head caught the ball but sent it upwards rather than back down the pitch. In the box, the players jostled, desperate to get the first touch. The ball fell to Jamie, poised by the goal line. He took it on his chest, intending to hoof it away but the attackers were on him at once and his options were limited. Ordinarily, he would have put the ball out for a corner but could Zac defend a corner? The moment's hesitation cost him. The Wednesday striker trapped the ball, spun and struck.

Without thought or consideration, Zac flung himself on the ball as if he was smothering fire. He felt someone leap his prone body and land close to his ribs then the tide of men retreated until there was just Jamie standing over him saying, "Stay down, stay down."

He lay prone for as long as he could, until the ref angrily blew the whistle again. "Kick it to Leo," Jamie said, jogging away.

The clock said 90 minutes and the fourth official was holding up a board displaying the number 6 as Zac put the ball down for the goal kick. But then he made his first mistake: he could make the ball swerve and spin and find the goal from ten yards, but he couldn't kick it straight and true for 50.

Leo was holding off two big defenders on the halfway line but the kick fell short and he had to come back for it. One of the defenders shouldered Leo aside and got to the ball first, passing it out wide. The shot came in before any Fulham player could stop it. But Zac felt his old goalkeeping instincts coming back — he knew without thinking that the shot was going over the bar.

Ninety-two minutes, and another goal kick. "You take it," he said to Jamie. This was a dangerous tactic because you were immediately playing everyone onside but his kick was a good one — soaring forwards over the halfway line. Leo ripped himself away from his markers and sprang for the ball.

Behind Zac, the crowd was screaming, drowning out Jamie yelling, "Take it to the corner! Take it to the corner!"

But, of course, Leo didn't take it to the corner. He had the ball free and clear in the Wednesday half and he sensed glory. Another goal now would finish the match. At the edge of the box, he could hear the defenders pounding behind him, but he had only the goalkeeper to beat. Without breaking stride, he took the ball on his right foot and smashed it towards goal …

… and straight into the goalie's hands.

The goalie played the ball out short. It was a good idea because the extra man could play with impunity while the Fulham players had to race back and defend. Like the inexorable assault of the incoming tide, the ball was coming Zac's way again and he knew he was going to have to deal with it.

Phil blocked a shot 20 yards out and there was chaos on the edge of the box — all the outfield players pushing and shoving and hacking at the ball. The ref looked like he was officiating at rugby, peering into the scrum, waiting for an infringement. When it came, he awarded the foul against Fulham and Wednesday had another free kick, this time just outside the box.

Zac found he was out of breath although he shouldn't have been. In the corner of his eye, he saw a blur of scarlet — the Wednesday 'keeper had been waved forward. They knew this was their last chance.

Wednesday's striker lined up the kick. He had scored numerous free kicks from this sort of position all season. In fact, if it wasn't for a certain Zac Miller, he would be the League's top scorer.

Behind the wall, Zac couldn't see the ball or the player. All he could do was wait for the whistle and anticipate the shot.

The striker knew, as soon as he struck the ball, that the shot was perfect; that it would clear the wall and curl down towards the top corner of the goal. He watched its soaring flight, he watched Phil Philopoussis leap for it and miss, he watched it dip and dive and dance ...

And then he watched an out-flung orange arm enter the orbit of the ball and a white fingertip brush it.

Zac hit the ground painfully and the ball tipped over the bar for a corner.

The first person to get to him was the Wednesday 'keeper who hauled him to his feet. "Respect man, respect," he said.

Zac realised he had been admitted to the goalkeepers' union. He said, "Thanks," quickly and looked round wildly to see where the ball was.

Wednesday were organising themselves for the corner. Jamie had run to the referee and was tapping his wrist. The ref dismissed him with a wave of the hand but signalled urgently to the corner taker. The message was clear: the six minutes of extra time were up; Wednesday could take the corner but then the final whistle would blow.

Jamie ran back into the box. There was no time to give directions, no time for anything but instinct. The Wednesday goalkeeper was still up but Mitch was marking him like a seasoned defender. Leo had attached himself to Wednesday's scrawny goal poacher and the two of them were racing around snapping at each other like dogs in the park. Lucas was on the edge of the box ensuring the ball wouldn't come in low and lethal while Jamie had Zac's back on the goal line. But where was the spare man? Where would the danger come from … ?

The whistle blew and the ball floated in and Jamie saw him too late: the runner from the edge of the box whom no one was free to pick up. It was Wednesday's left back, capable of a deadly shot. He connected well with the ball and it sliced forwards, taking a deflection on its journey and diverting just out of Aidan's reach. Jamie tried to jump, desperate and hopeless because the ball had already passed him.

He needn't have worried. Zac leapt, hands high above his head and caught the ball solidly then clutched it to his chest like a child.

Jamie pounded Zac's shoulder, Phil wrapped him in a bear hug, Aidan jumped on his back and Leo had tears in his eyes as he said, "I love you, Zac, I love you."

Then the ref blew the whistle three times and all hell broke loose.

Thursday 7th May — Southwark

It was going to be a long 24 hours. There was now nothing more Lydia could do. It was only midday and she'd already had four cups of coffee. It was too early for lunch and, although tempting, definitely too early for a glass of wine — but it felt like it should be evening already.

She'd got up early and taken a long hot shower. She had a swarm of things going round in her head, something she wasn't used to as she prided herself on being a clear thinker. She laughed to herself when she thought, this could be the ultimate power shower transforming her from a business woman into a city mayor.

Skye had agreed to accompany her to the polling station so they could vote together despite the inevitable presence of cameras. She normally preferred to keep out of the limelight, but her mother had been persuasive and while not always the most empathetic, Skye understood that Lydia needed her.

The cameras had caught mother and daughter smiling as they entered the school building being used for the day as the local voting venue. Outside there were lots of people milling about, some with rosettes and signs signifying their allegiances, as well as voters who had stopped to see one of the candidates casting their own vote.

Reporters jostled for attention, shouting out a string of questions that they hardly expected to be answered: *How would it feel to be the first female mayor, Lydia? Were you surprised when Joe Martinez dropped out? What are your plans for the rest of the day, Lydia?*

Lydia smiled and waved. "I've answered all the questions I can and so my only comment for now is to tell everyone who is able to in this great city of ours to get out and vote, whoever they support."

Lydia could not have anticipated the turn of events. She hadn't had the TV on last Sunday morning but Ellie had called instructing her to switch it on immediately. She had seen Joe Martinez give his statement many times now having watched the news every hour that day to see if there was any credible explanation. In his delivery, he appeared calm and collected and it was only as he was coming to the end that she detected the faintest hint of a quiver in his voice as if he went on any longer it would break. He hadn't said very much but what he'd said was game-changing.

Up to the weekend, the polls had Joe Martinez as favourite, even though the gap had narrowed as the election got closer. All commentators predicted that with the vote split across the three strongest candidates — Joe, Arjun and Lydia — there was pretty much no chance of a candidate winning over 50% of the vote. It would almost certainly go to the second preference vote. With Joe now out of the race, journalists and commentators had said that it was possible that either she or Arjun could get through after the first round.

Joe dropping out hadn't made any sense to her at all. Lydia guessed there must be some skeleton in his closet that the papers had threatened to unveil, or just maybe, she thought, he couldn't stand the extra pressure, the additional scrutiny, and the impact that would have on his young family. Somehow that didn't seem as likely — to her mind, he would have known what he was getting into.

Lydia had always thought she had an outside chance but deep down hadn't really believed becoming mayor would be a reality. But now it could be.

Lydia had the flat to herself. Jonathan had business meetings that he had tried really hard, but unsuccessfully, to move so he could spend the day with her. She couldn't help but wonder if that really was the case but quickly put the thought away. Lydia didn't know what else to do so she sat back on her sofa and pulled her legs up, tucking her feet under her and reached for the remote control. Flicking between channels she saw one news report showing Arjun Shah at his local polling station looking like a Jermyn Street dandy in his royal blue silk cravat, tight pale blue shirt and matching striped blazer. He had two attractive and equally flamboyantly dressed friends, a young man and a young woman, one on either arm, to accompany him. Before heading inside to vote, he responded to some of the assembled press pack.

A reporter asked him for his message to voters. "London needs a Conservative mayor after the inadequacies of the last Labour one. I believe I can inject new life into this wonderful city. I'm also the right person to harness its incredible cultural platform to make London really buzz."

He turned away from the reporters as if finished, before turning back adding, "At this time, London needs a youthful, energetic and dynamic mayor — and one who knows how to have fun," he flashed a dazzlingly white toothy smile, "supported by an established political party. It won't be kindness and karma that make this city tick."

Lydia had been wounded by what he'd said, clearly directed at her. *She wasn't that old, and she knew how to have fun!* She felt a mixture of hurt and irritation, demonstrating to herself that she wasn't as thick-skinned as she thought — a vital attribute if she was going to succeed in the dirty world of politics.

She stared at Arjun Shah with an undisguised look of scorn, not quite believing that he was now her principal opposition. But there was no doubting his popularity — he had a huge and growing following on social media. Voting wasn't going to finish until 10 p.m. and she couldn't stop herself looking at the large clock.

The results, depending on whether it would go to second round votes, might not be announced until sometime tomorrow. She flicked off the TV and picked up a glossy magazine to test its power of distraction.

Friday 8th May — City Hall

Lydia had got to bed late but still had a fitful night's sleep. She had awoken perspiring, flashes of dreams coming to her — Lydia, in her late teens, telling her father she was going off travelling to South America. In another fuzzy scene, she was frantically trying to scramble up the muddy banks of a river but kept slipping back. She quickly put her dreams aside. She had to prepare herself for whatever today brought.

Her team had arranged for her to be in City Hall for the declaration that evening. There was no certainty over what time the results would be called but it was likely to be late — exit polls had predicted the count would have to go to the second round. Jonathan had come over for lunch and he was thankfully sticking around until she got back later. They agreed they'd have champagne whatever the result. This time, she was whisked away by car rather than public transport.

At City Hall, Ellie was taking control of everything from arranging coffees to making sure she had the media contacts in hand. The team of people who swarmed around her were the helpful worker bees and Lydia looked on, impressed with Ellie's organisation. Around the auditorium Lydia could see the other candidates with their entourages busily buzzing around them — it all felt surreal.

At 11.25 p.m., the huddled heads of officials and some arm waving across the room indicated that the results were imminent and a few minutes later one came over to Lydia and asked her to take the stage, along with the other candidates. Ellie gave Lydia a hug. Lydia's stomach was churning. She wondered why she was putting herself through this — she felt as if she was about to go before a firing squad.

It was 11.38 p.m., and the Greater London Returning Officer responsible for overseeing the election announced that she was able to declare the results. In a loud, clear voice, after some preamble, she said, "The results of this year's Greater London Council Mayoral elections are as follows:

"Lydia Edwards — Independent — 1,276,490"

The Returning Officer didn't pause even though the room let out an audible gasp. Lydia had clearly done well but her total meant it was almost guaranteed that it would require second choice votes being counted.

"Arjun Shah — Conservative and Unionist Party — 1,110,286"

Again, there was a loud noise from the crowd that had gathered in front of the stage. Arjun smiled the smile he used when he came second on The Apprentice.

The other candidates' totals were read out; none anywhere near Arjun's and Lydia's tallies. Noise levels began to rise in the room. The Returning Officer coughed into the microphone to get people's attention before carrying on.

"In accordance with the electoral regulations, under the Supplementary Vote system, as no candidate has received more than 50% of the first-choice votes, all except the top two candidates are eliminated.

"Those whose first-choice candidate has been eliminated, their second choices if for one of the top two, have been counted and the results are as follows:

> "Lydia Edwards — Independent — second round votes — 307,511 — giving a total of 1,584,001
>
> "Arjun Shah — Conservative and Unionist Party — second round votes — 241,617 — giving a total of 1,351,903

"I declare the winner of the mayor for London contest to be the independent candidate, Lydia Edwards."

Lydia looked out at the crowd in disbelief and then in a semi-trance made her way to the lectern to give her pre-prepared speech. Almost instantly, #londydia started trending on Twitter.

PART 6

Early May

Marko gave the players two days off training when they won the League. He didn't take a break himself, of course, but carried on working at his usual frantic pace. It was as if he had ticked the Championship title off a list and simply moved on to his next target: the FA Cup.

I heard that during those two days, despite their achievement, the players' bickering continued via WhatsApp. Davy Walker was so vilified that he left the group. Davy had been whisked away from Craven Cottage before the final whistle and had not been seen since. His red card meant he was banned for Fulham's next game. And, of course, that game was only the FA Cup Final against Fulham's long-time neighbours and some-time rivals, the Diamond Blues.

The problem with the squad was that each man had been hand-picked for his footballing skills with no thought to his temperament or personality. What everyone had in common was a determination to compete for Marko's attention and sparingly given praise. Comrades on the pitch and a team of rivals off it.

When Marko took training, his mood was aloof and impatient but the players had learned how to deal with his criticism — as the season went on and the victories mounted, they had seen that the caustic comments and nit-picking corrections were for their own good. They had even seen that, under the arrogance, he enjoyed training them. They had begun — and I noticed it more every day — not just to respect the man who had coached them to the Championship title, but to like him.

Marko's work with the players was broken up with press conferences in which, while he didn't overtly take credit for the unexpected success of Zac Miller in goal, he didn't deflect praise towards Zac or Jamie Crawford either. As far as the wider world was aware, there was only one genius at Fulham and that was Marko.

Jamie, who was also interviewed by the press, was too modest to take any credit for something that wasn't much more than a whim. He was also preoccupied these days. There seemed to be some tension between Jamie and Zac. I passed them in the corridor one day and Zac was saying, "Have you done it yet?" in nothing like his usual soft and polite manner. Jamie replied tersely, "No. I'll do it when the time's right."

Zac was kept well away from the press other than for some obligatory photos with his Golden Boot trophy. Despite that accolade and his revelatory goalkeeping, he looked more strained than ever, the shadows under his eyes as dark as bruises. While the rest of the team was excited about an FA Cup Final in front of 90,000 people, I wondered if Zac was dreading it.

As for the other members of the squad, the young Scottish reserve 'keeper Alex McKenna had been thrust, quaking slightly, into the spotlight. He had only played one first-team game this season — a loss to Manchester City in the League Cup. While this didn't bode well, Alex looked fit and focused in training, if a little in awe of the approaching occasion and the man who had briefly worn his orange shirt. I suggested to several colleagues that Zac should play in goal for the Final but they all ignored me. Meanwhile, Antonio Perez Alvarez was permanently furious and on an hourly basis switched between openly talking about a transfer to Spain and not talking at all.

It was a kind of silly season at Motspur in those early days of May. Dusk came later and blossom blew across the training pitches but it felt like the limbo between Christmas and New Year. The League had finished but the team had another game still to play — the biggest game of all.

One day, the squad trained at Craven Cottage and there was a photo shoot with the Championship trophy. Tempers frayed as players jostled to get the best places in the group photo. Rumour swirled wherever Marko walked and his players watched him with the same intensity as I did. Jamie brooded, Zac fretted and Antonio plotted. This was not a team which was ready for the challenge that lay ahead.

The only question was whether it would implode before the FA Cup Final or during it.

Monday 11th May
Hammersmith and Fulham Council

<u>Loz</u>

"Oh my God," I put my hand to my forehead. "First of all, she was horribly late, looking like she'd just got out of bed, and then she agreed with them that the tower could be acceptable if they use their other site in the Borough for affordable housing." I looked down at my lunch, stabbing at my lukewarm penne. "Fourteen storeys on that site is just mad — even if there is a housing crisis."

"You look like you've had a good morning," Andy said, nodding at me as he joined us, putting down his tray.

"She just had a meeting with our esteemed team leader," said Matt.

"Got it," Andy said. "It's amazing how people like her can somehow get these senior jobs. Anyway, there's more important matters to discuss — football."

Matt sighed. While his team, Leeds, hadn't had a bad season — being safely (or, in reality, boringly) mid-table, that didn't mean he wanted to hear about ours.

"I wonder why the Diamonds supporter … " and then looking at me, " ... and the Fulham supporter might be happy to talk about football, huh?"

"Well Matt, I've never known a time when you didn't want talk about football, so I don't see why you'd start now," I said.

Matt sat forward, "Did you know some woman from some management institute said recently that people shouldn't talk about football in offices as it could lead to others feeling excluded. Especially women. She thought banter about VAR and stuff should be banned."

We all laughed at the notion.

"Fair dues, though," Matt said, "the Diamond Blues being on for the quadruple. I mean, I would've thought that it was virtually impossible but, bloody hell, looks like it's not."

Andy's provocatively smug smile compelled me to intervene.

"Excuse me," I said, as I climbed up on to my soap box. "One, they still have to beat Monaco in the Champions League Final on the 23rd. And, two, they have the small matter of meeting us in the FA Cup Final a week later. Even if the Diamonds can beat Monaco, which I grant you, they could well do as everyone knows that they've been lucky to get to the Final, we are *definitely* going to be more than happy to upset the quadruple party."

"All the pundits say it's the Blues' time," Andy said, folding his arms across his chest.

"That's what the FA Cup's about," I said defiantly. "The underdog. And on the day, anything could happen. Our team's had a phenomenal season as well and if Zac Miller's on form and our defence plays like they have done, then who knows?"

"We'll agree to disagree then, Loz," said Andy, smiling. "But on the subject of Fulham Football Club, there's something you should hear. I was contacted by Bob, Fulham's development guy last week."

"Yeah, I remember you talking about him. I saw him at the Putney Stand event down at the Cottage although I didn't really get a chance to talk to him," I said.

"He wanted my opinion on ground sharing in the Borough."

This statement was met with a collective raised eyebrow. Andy continued. "And, get this — he wanted to know if there were any circumstances where the Council would consider the *sympathetic* development of Craven Cottage, in the same way as Highbury was redeveloped for housing, for instance."

We all knew that the Council had policies to protect its football grounds, but it didn't stop us being taken back by the audacity of the enquiry. I needed to know more.

"Did you ask what was behind him wanting to know?"

Andy nodded, "Of course. He said, totally off the record, a Turkish guy, a chap called Bayram, think he said his first name was Kerim, contacted him because he thinks the Cottage will be up for sale before too long and he wants it. This bloke wanted to know what Bob's opinion was on the *opportunity.* Bob said he thought there'd be no chance and so he just wanted to double check with me that he hadn't been barking up the wrong tree."

"Bloody cheek," I said. "David Patterson must really be in financial dire straits. But you shouldn't be able to just buy a football club if it comes up for sale," I continued. "The football authorities, the FA or whoever need to get a grip. Clubs need proper governance and to be owned by fit and proper people. Look what happened to Wigan not long ago."

"There's too much money involved in football — no wonder things get corrupt," Matt said. "I heard that if Joe Martinez had won the election that he might have been a bit of a soft touch for developers."

"Where did you hear that?" Andy asked.

"I've seen some tweets along those lines," Matt said. "None of them substantiated, but something to do with him meeting lots of developers in the run-up to the election."

"Well, we'll soon see if Lydia Edwards is all talk and no action. She says she wants to break up the status quo."

At that, we all started to sing with added air guitar, "*And here we go, and here we go, oh, oh, rockin' all over the world. And I like it, I like it, oh, oh, oh ...* "

Laughing, we picked up our trays and headed out of the neon green diner to the dowdy offices above.

"You busy this afternoon, Loz?" Andy asked by the stairwell.

"You bet. I need to Google Kerim Bayram."

Motspur Park

Jamie was getting tired of Zac's raised eyebrows and searching looks. There was enough tension in the squad without Zac creating friction when normally he counted the striker as a friend. He was aware though, as both friend and team captain, that Zac wasn't in the best frame of mind and that the Final hung heavily over him.

"Last season, I had to score goals to keep us up, now I've got to score goals to get us promoted," Zac had said and the pressure of being expected to score in the Final was clearly getting to him. There had been more missed training sessions and more random excuses, and when he did come to training, he was either withdrawn or argumentative.

Jamie knew he was putting off the conversation with Antonio but it would be so excruciating that he could hardly bear to contemplate it. He was even hoping that Zac's theory was wrong and sounded out a few others, starting with his wife, Sarah.

Just after breakfast he asked, "Have you heard any rumours about Marko?"

His tone was more contrived than he had intended but Sarah was getting the children ready for school so she didn't give Jamie her full attention.

"What sort of rumours?" She asked.

"About his personal life."

"You mean Ivana?" said Sarah, checking through the children's bags and looking for their water bottles. "No, I haven't heard anything. I've always thought they had a bit of an odd relationship, to be honest."

"In what way?"

"Oh, I don't know," said Sarah now looking for sweatshirts and shoes. "I don't think they're very supportive of each other. The opposite really, like they're in competition."

Certainly, Ivana wasn't easy to get on with and it wasn't because of any language barrier. She was cold and offhand most of the time, her polished beauty intimidating rather than enviable. Sarah guessed that being married to the broodingly handsome but breathtakingly arrogant Marko would be hard work.

"But you haven't heard … anything about them?" Jamie asked vaguely.

"Like what? Oh, you mean like an affair? No, nothing specific but there are always whispers at a football club, you know what it's like." She shouted, "Come on kids, time to go!"

Jamie tried again later, this time with Phil Philopoussis in the car park as they were leaving training. Again, he opened with, "Have you heard any rumours about Marko?"

His tone sounded more genuine this time, but Phil took the question the wrong way.

"Only the same ones you have," he said, throwing his bag into the back of his Audi. "That he might be leaving even though we've been promoted." He shrugged. "If he goes, Mr Patterson will get a new guy in, someone with Prem experience."

"Well, yes ... " said Jamie trying to divert the conversation to the non-football aspects of Marko's life but Phil wasn't listening.

"Next season could be great. Marko or no Marko. We'll have to get a few new faces, especially in midfield if Antonio goes."

"Oh yes, Antonio … " Jamie saw a new way to seize the initiative. "Any idea what's up with him?"

"Nah," Phil said, "he's been so grumpy I've hardly spoken to him." He looked at his watch. "Gotta go, mate. I said I'd pick up the kids today."

Jamie raised a hand in farewell. This was going nowhere.

***

Antonio was at the point of wishing Fulham had lost the semi-final to Arsenal so that the season was over. He couldn't take much more of the bickering on WhatsApp or the quarrelling at training. Most of all, he couldn't take much more of Marko Maric.

Antonio and Pia had arrived in England in August when Antonio signed for Fulham as part of a grand plan by his agent to get some experience of the English game before a move to a Premier League club.

The couple were recently married and Pia was initially excited by playing house in glamorous London and performing the role of a footballer's wife. But the idea of being married to a footballer was a lot more exotic than the reality, which involved spending many hours alone in a foreign country with no job or family to occupy her. Pia was bored and lonely. By September, she was already talking about hating life in England and wanting to go home. Antonio, who was a devoted if old-fashioned husband, was worried and upset.

But in October, when 3 p.m. kick-offs were finishing in darkness and there was a crispness in the air, Antonio had noticed a change in Pia. She was suddenly enthusiastic about coming to matches and sitting on the chilly Cottage balcony. She was not just willing but happy to linger in the players' lounge over drinks afterwards. At first, Antonio had been pleased. Pia was sparkling company and he hoped that she would make friends.

But after one match, he had intercepted a glance between Marko and Pia. It was only fleeting but Antonio was jealous enough and insecure enough to jump to conclusions. After that, he was on high alert. There were more meaningful looks in the lounge, some unexplained text messages and phone calls that ended as soon as he entered a room.

In December, Antonio had torn his hamstring and spent a frustrating few weeks on the sidelines of the game and, he felt, on the sidelines of his marriage. He was at home most of the time and Pia had had nowhere to hide.

Determined to find out what was going on, Antonio followed her to a hotel in north London. He didn't see Marko but his car with its number plate MM6 was parked shamelessly in the car park.

After that, he stewed for a while, imagining all kinds of painful revenge. Antonio recognised that this wasn't entirely Marko's fault but he would deal with Pia later. The fact that it took two to tango and a third to be neglectful escaped Antonio's consciousness.

While recovering from his injury he switched to following Marko, unsure of what he wanted to prove but unable to stop himself. All he learnt though, was that Marko worked very hard. He was at Motspur Park at all hours, either in his office or in the gym when he wasn't taking training. Twice he went north again, first to London Colney. Antonio lost him in the village, but he knew from Lucas, who had been in the academy, that this was where Arsenal's training ground was located so Marko must have gone there on business. The second time, he went to Vicarage Road stadium where Watford's academy were playing Newcastle. So, Marko was looking out for young talent, not recruiting a harem.

Gradually, Antonio's plans simmered down from violent death, through crippling injury and agonising torture to scaring Marko off. Antonio knew about the group run in December and he knew Pia's new car (ordered as a present before Antonio had any inkling of her duplicity) wouldn't be recognised.

He had felt, driving away with adrenaline flooding his veins, that the near miss with the car had gone well but it soon turned out that it hadn't worked — Marko didn't back off. Antonio didn't have the nerve to try again until they were in Liverpool. That had been a spur-of-the-moment decision. Antonio had wandered onto the balcony when exploring the hotel and had seen the big flowerpots just as the minibus from Finch Farm was depositing Marko and the others on the pavement.

He had been terrified initially that he had injured Zac, whom he liked, along with his wife Tammy, who had done her best to befriend

Pia. Since Liverpool, the mysterious phone calls and messages had tailed off but Pia was miserable and evasive, and Antonio just wanted to go home to Spain and forget all about Fulham Football Club and Marko Maric.

***

Summer had come early to England. The grass was lush and warm, and the air was thick and heavy under a cloudless blue bowl of sky. It was getting too hot for football, but the Fulham first team were training at full throttle, breaking for drinks when Charlie reminded Marko to allow them to and seeking shade whenever they could. It was the kind of weather in which tempers could fray but that was no excuse for what happened on Monday afternoon — the two protagonists in this most domestic of dramas came from international climes far hotter than Surrey.

Marko was in a difficult mood — aloof and distant all through training. He had come home the night before to find a large box on the kitchen table wrapped in pale blue paper and decorated with bows and ribbons. Ivana was sitting with her back to it, at the breakfast bar.

His heart stumbled in its rhythm but he felt he had no choice other than to say, "What's this?"

"A present for Sunday's baby," Ivana said, in a tone so deliberately offhand that it would have fooled no one. "You can take it in tomorrow."

He crossed the kitchen towards her and as he paused behind her, she said, "You didn't tell me. I should have got something before."

"I didn't want to ... " he reached out to touch her arm. A strand of soft blonde hair got caught in his fingers and he smoothed it into place. She didn't respond to either the words or the gesture.

In a tone even less convincing than hers, he said, "I'll put it in the car now. So I don't forget in the morning."

Javier Herrera's injured ankle was better. Marko had kept him, Zac and Antonio back to practise a new short corner routine. It was a good idea, in theory, but Antonio was weary and distracted and his dead ball deliveries, once so reliable, were wayward at best.

When Antonio sent the fifth ball in a row swerving out of play, Marko swore and strode towards him gesticulating.

"For Christ's sake, Antonio! You have to do better than this!"

Zac and Javier watched in horror as Antonio leapt at Marko like an animal, his face contorted with fury, a snarl emitting from his mouth. His outstretched hands seized Marko by the throat and began to crush together.

Shouting, the others ran to intervene. But they weren't needed. Instead of trying to prise Antonio's hands away, Marko reacted with a ferocious uppercut to Antonio's chin which not only released his grip but sent him staggering to the ground.

Marko rasped, "Get him out of my sight."

Zac said quietly to Javier, "He needs to see the doctor. That was … " he glanced over his shoulder but Marko was out of earshot "savage."

Javier looked unusually shaken. "I think it will need both of us," he said and between them, they got Antonio on his feet and helped him walk to the building, Javier reassuring him in Spanish all the way.

Zac explained what had happened to Dr Brown, managing to make it sound like an accident and without mentioning any names. Antonio hadn't spoken since the punch and there were tears in his eyes. He put an exploratory hand to his swelling jaw and winced. Javier said something which was clearly meant to be fortifying and the doctor said, "Thank you for your assistance, Javier."

"Assisting is what Javier does best," Zac said.

Javier glared at him but seemed to accept that the statement was an easy exit line from the doctor's office rather than an insult. When they were outside, he said, "Cristo. First Davy, now this. Do you think Marko will drop him?"

Zac shrugged. "He'll have to, won't he?" He shuddered, reliving the violence in Marko's punch.

He guessed Javier was doing the same when the Argentinian said, "I think we should keep quiet about this."

"I agree," said Zac. This was how they usually communicated on the pitch, not off it.

In the changing room, Javier stripped off his shirt and flung it into the laundry bin. His entire upper body was covered in tattoos which came to life as he moved.

"Thanks for assisting me for a change," Javier said, as he walked to the showers.

***

Zac didn't emerge from the shower until Javier had gone. He was under no illusions about his teammate. They played together well and he admired Javier's quick thinking; it wasn't just Antonio and Marko who would benefit from the fracas being kept quiet. If it became public knowledge, Marko would know who spread the story and would deal with them accordingly. But Javier was a schoolyard bully on a bigger stage, he had picked out Zac as a target long ago and that wasn't going to change just because of their cooperation today.

As he dressed, Zac contemplated what to do — he couldn't break his agreement with Javier and tell Jamie what had happened. But if Jamie spoke to Antonio now it would exacerbate the situation. He took out his phone and fired off a text: "Too late. Don't speak to Antonio. Damage is done."

Then, not wanting to deal with a reply, he turned his phone off and drove home.

City Hall

Lydia was well aware of the history that came with the job, having learnt the dates in case she was tested by some smart-ass journalist and made to look stupid: *1397 — Dick Whittington becomes Lord Mayor of London — serving four terms between 1397 and 1420.*

Now she had made history, for lots of reasons, and she needed time to take it all in. Not that she'd have any of that now, her time wouldn't be her own again for at least four years.

The day after the election result was called, Lydia had made a statement to the press outside City Hall, with Tower Bridge her iconic backdrop. She'd prepped herself well — it was a speech that could define her tenure and she was at pains to avoid any hint of triumphalism. Looking confidently at the cameras, she said, "In electing me, the people of London have entrusted me to lead the greatest, most cosmopolitan, multi-cultural and generous-hearted city in the world.

"I am certainly stunned and very excited to be elected and to be London's first female mayor. For those who didn't vote for me, I promise you that I will work flat out to win your trust — we need to be a united city, to come together. I want to speak for the whole of London — in times of joy, of course, but also when we are challenged, as inevitably we will be from time to time.

"I want to take this opportunity to pay credit to the other candidates who all had London and its people at the heart of their campaigns. I would like to think we can continue our discussions in my new capacity as mayor.

"I believe that London has now been transformed into a truly independent city — not beholden to narrow party politics.

"Londoners have elected me because of my determination to do things differently. We will be working with businesses across the city to help them provide social capital through my 'Karma Kredits' initiative. With the right incentives, we can all live a cleaner, leaner, greener way of life."

Lydia finished off her speech thanking her team and the friends and family that had supported her. She agreed to answer some questions from the journalists who had gathered, not just from the UK, but from around the world.

One journalist asked, "When did you realise you could win?"

She answered after a moment of thought, allowing herself a slight smile, "I guess just in the last couple of weeks — the winds of change were blowing."

The next question was one she'd been expecting, when someone asked, "Do you think things would have been different if Joe Martinez hadn't dropped out?"

Shrugging her shoulders, she replied, "Guess, we'll never know."

After a few more questions, she told the pack, "That's all for now," and turned to enter City Hall, her new fiefdom.

***

On the Sunday morning, Lydia had been up early and while still in her dressing gown, had waded through the pile of newspapers on her kitchen counter. The Post had run the following article:

> Lydia Edwards — whose management experience is limited to small and medium sized companies and TV's 'Crisis Management' reality business show — will now be in charge of an annual budget of over £19bn. She will wield more executive power than any other politician outside of central government.
>
> The Prime Minister offered his congratulations, emphasising the need for collaboration. The Labour leader, also congratulated the new mayor, as he moved to placate the party for their 'no show' in the election that has left them reeling. A source said that he told members that Joe Martinez had behaved with 'great dignity' during a difficult time but declined to comment further on what led to his stepping down. There will no doubt be recriminations when the inquest into the debacle starts today.
>
> Arjun Shah, the Conservative candidate, is said to blame the PM's chief of staff and a small coterie of Tory insiders for not taking his campaign seriously enough and undermining him.

Lydia Edwards, notoriously guarded about her personal life, celebrated her win with friends and family in a local Italian restaurant.

Lydia knew she was now legitimate political fodder — fair game. Everything she had ever done would be under the spotlight and if they couldn't find stuff, they'd probably make it up. She knew it wasn't going to be plain sailing.

***

The Monday was her first full day at City Hall. Lydia had been working with her campaign director, Ellie, to agree her team — she wanted to hit the ground running. There would need to be fresh faces in the chief roles but the GLA officers would be treated more carefully, with just some pruning where necessary.

She looked around her new office and made a mental note to personalise it with some plants and some photos of Skye. Jonathan wasn't for public consumption.

Some newspapers had been right, annoyingly, about her having reached out to the other candidates and Arjun Shah had accepted her invitation to be part of her team, as had Sonia Smith, both seemingly taken back by her collegiateness. Reuben Bailey for undisclosed reasons, had declined.

She set about considering and appointing trusted people to the many roles she had to fill. She worked through her key political advisers, strategists, PR and marketing team appointments, making Ellie, who'd been doing a fabulous job, her chief of staff.

She chose senior people to lead the police and fire authorities, several deputy mayors with responsibility for a range of roles — policing, culture, crime, young people. She also needed to appoint the mayor's senior adviser for housing and planning. Usually they were ex-political leaders of councils along party allegiances but as an independent she felt less confined. Lydia was confident there were plenty of possible candidates for the role, but she needed someone who understood development pressures and someone she could trust.

That afternoon, she addressed the City Hall staff in the central auditorium. She looked across at them and saw the expectation in their eyes. They saw a mayor who looked like none of her predecessors.

"I know that many of you would have enjoyed working under the previous mayor, Frank Best. He did what he thought was in London's best interests and I will do the same. And that means there will be some changes."

Some staff crossed their arms or glanced nervously at their colleagues.

"I know some of you will feel uncertain about your futures having worked with Mayor Best for four years. However, now is the time for us to work together, to find common ground. I see before me a huge reservoir of talent that I want to harness, to use you to the best of your abilities. You will all be instrumental in helping me achieve the goals and aspirations I have been voted in on."

In her office after her talk, she sat back in her chair, a mug of bad instant coffee in hand — a new coffee machine had to go on her list — and allowed herself some time to scroll through her phone. The congratulation messages had been endless since Friday night. Jonathan had just sent a text — *dinner at yours tonight. I'm cooking. OK?! Xx*. She replied with a thumbs up and a kiss. She continued to scroll and, without thinking, opened up a message from just a number: *'Congratulations Lydia, aka mayor Edwards! An impressive performance. I insist on you joining me for dinner at my club sometime very soon to talk over old times. I will be in touch to arrange. Omar'*.

At that moment, after a cursory brief knock, Ellie entered her office. Lydia looked up, her hand clasped over her mouth.

"Lydia, you OK? You look like you've seen a ghost."

Thursday 14th May — Surrey

Marko had been relieved that Ivana had left for Paris to visit their daughter Julia on the day of his scrap with Antonio. No immediate need, then, to explain the marks on his neck or the bruises on his hand. He had gone home, showered and heated up the lasagna their Italian housekeeper had left for him. He felt too tired to do anything other than sit at the table and scroll through his phone. When he came to Ivana's name, he had a sudden idea of ringing her which he quickly dismissed. When he came to Pia's name, he pushed his phone away as impatiently as he had his plate.

He was working harder than ever: taking training, rehearsing tactics, studying recordings, talking to the press. Antonio's foolishness had added a new dilemma. The Cup Final was a huge opportunity for Marko, his ticket to the big time. The match could make his name as a manager and blast him from the obscurity of the Championship onto the back page of every newspaper in Europe. He had to pick his best team to play on the pitch, regardless of their behaviour off it.

He wasn't used to being home alone in the evenings and although he wasn't much of a drinker, he found the company of the vodka bottle reassuring. The days of enjoying a relaxed evening with Ivana were long gone but he had got used to telling her about his footballing day while she cooked and her advice, although often half-hearted, was sometimes surprisingly useful.

On the afternoon of Ivana's return, Marko had a meeting with David Patterson and an interview with the BBC. After some experimentation, he wore a shirt and tie for both — it wasn't his usual style and the tie made him feel like he was being strangled again. But he thought that the slick, formal look was just right for a successful, ambitious manager and the BBC makeup girl had seemed convinced.

When he arrived home, he knew at once that Ivana was there — there was a trace of rich, floral scent in the pale, airy hall — and he unconsciously loosened his tie in anticipation of seeing her.

For her part, Ivana had enjoyed her visit to Paris. She and Julia had explored the city, alternating shopping therapy with cafe society. As a rehearsal for the new, single life she was beginning to imagine, the trip had been promising. She could picture herself flitting between the capitals of Europe, dressed to impress, drinking in culture and cocktails in all the best places. Art in Paris, opera in Rome, watching the moon rise over the Acropolis. She was aware that London was rather better connected than Zagreb, but money would remove most of the inconveniences of travel.

She heard the front door shut and checked her reflection in the mirror above the fireplace.

Marko threw down his keys and his tie. He didn't come closer than the island unit but he asked about Julia and the trip as if he was genuinely interested.

Ivana studied his smooth, arrogant face as she answered. He looked tired, she thought, which was unusual. "Julia is well. The trip was good, thank you."

"Great." He undid the top button of his shirt with a grimace of relief and added, "Perhaps we could go to Paris together in the summer."

Despite the fact that she had pictured herself enjoying cocktails and culture alone she was on the point of saying "yes" or at least "maybe" when she saw the mark on his neck revealed by his now open collar.

"Or perhaps not," she said coldly. "I know what you get up to in North London, Marko."

He turned to her, horrified. How could she possibly know about that? His deepest secret which he had taken every precaution to protect her from? He was floundering for an explanation when she went on.

"Little Pia, so sweet and pretty. Or have you moved on to someone else now?"

He stopped scrabbling for words and realised where her gaze was directed. He spun abruptly to the mirror and pulled his collar down.

"Oh, this!" The relief in his voice was so extreme she might have found it suspicious, but he rushed on. "This happened in training."

"Really," Ivana said flatly.

"Yes, really." Marko wasn't used to defending himself by telling the truth (or at least an approximation of it) and it didn't seem to be working. He held up his bruised fingers in support of his story.

"This was all just an accident. And as for Pia," he shook his head, "That was over months ago. Look, I'm sorry but it was nothing."

"How many times have I heard that before?" Ivana wrapped her arms around herself as if she was cold although the breeze that wafted through the open glass doors was warm.

Marko was about to reply when his phone started ringing with his blaring choice of ringtone.

"Christ! I've got to take this." He stabbed the phone harder than necessary and Ivana heard him greet Richard Green.

Rather than listen to Marko speak English, she stepped outside and looked down the garden. She had no great interest in plants, but the gardener did a good job. Everything was pristine.

She wondered how Marko would feel if she turned the tables on him and had an affair with one of the players. Jamie Crawford perhaps with his mocha skin and kind smile or Javier Herrera with his smouldering eyes and all those tattoos to explore. Of course, her first choice would be Zac Miller with his golden good looks and intense blue gaze. But when Marko finished his call and came out onto the terrace the image of Zac paled beside the reality of Marko.

"What was that about?"

"I was interviewed by the BBC today. It's Sky tomorrow." He went on: "Ivana, this could be a really good time for me, for us. If we win the Cup then my career will take off. Bigger clubs will come calling — "

"Bigger clubs in England?" She interrupted.

"Well, yes. The Premier League is the best the world. You know that — "

"I hate this country," Ivana said. "I hate this house. I hate the people here. I hate the weather. I hate the way they drive on the wrong side of the road."

"And you like how much I get paid here," Marko said harshly. He watched her as she turned away. He wasn't ashamed of his words but he wasn't proud of his behaviour. Long before Pia, infidelity had become a habit, although most of his dalliances had been short lived and begun more out of a desire for attention than a desire for the girls concerned.

Ivana was infuriatingly good at concealment and so he was never sure what she knew or what she felt about it. Her sudden anger worried him. He went on, more softly, "Look, I'm going away next weekend, to Porto for the Champions League final. We can talk again after that. But then it's my Final," he emphasised the word "my" as if he had got Fulham to Wembley all by himself. "I would appreciate it if you were there with me."

Ivana didn't answer at once. She had noticed that one of the rose bushes was getting too big and overblown and made a mental note to mention it to the gardener.

Eventually she said, "I'll come to Wembley with you but after that I don't know. I don't know if I can stay with you."

She was still looking down the garden so she missed the emotion which flickered across his face as he said, "What if I promised it wouldn't happen again?"

"Then I'd like to believe you," she replied.

"Well, I mean it — " he began but she cut him off.

"I'll decide after Wembley, Marko," she said and stepped past him into the house.

Friday 15th May — Central London

Bayram looked around him before glancing down at the menu and gave his verdict, "I approve."

"I thought you'd enjoy it here," said Hamarat.

They were sitting at a table in the corner of a large, opulently decorated Mayfair restaurant. Chandeliers hung from the ceiling and large mirrors encased in elaborate ironwork adorned the walls. At one end of the room, an open plan kitchen was a hive of activity with chefs pan-frying over flashes of flames, others were sharpening knives and some had their heads down, concentrating as if defusing a bomb.

They ordered their food from the surly waiter and got down to business. "Omar, tell me what happened? What went wrong?"

They had already spoken on the phone to arrange the lunch. The call had been short, both cautious as to what was said until they were face to face, but Hamarat knew exactly what Bayram was referring to.

"It took me by surprise. I will admit that. We do not have 'our man in City Hall', as we had hoped. Like you, I am very disappointed." Hamarat shook his head, with a look more of distain than disappointment.

"I know it causes you a great problem, Omar, especially now. You need to be … what is the English phrase … making hay when the sun is shining? With the Diamond Blues creating footballing history, you need to capitalise on it. Right now. Not in a few years' time. And, of course, you have your big plans for Wembley."

Omar Hamarat paused as the waiter poured a small amount of white wine in his thin-stemmed glass. He swirled the golden liquid around the bowl before sniffing its aroma and taking a sip. He let the wine wash over his tongue before slowly swallowing.

"The Montrachet to your liking, sir?"

He nodded and the waiter poured each of them a glass and left the bottle beside the table in an ornate silver wine stand.

"You know I have my plans also, Omar? If I'm to buy the Fulham ground for my next development project, I will need the mayor to support me." Bayram paused to take some of his wine, his face not registering pleasure or displeasure at the taste.

"I spoke to someone who knows the Club well last week. He has no allegiance to them — he has been working as a consultant to the Club. I know he'll work for anyone who will pay his wage."

Hamarat was listening attentively, twisting his simple gold wedding band as he did so.

"This man, Bob … whatever … has been dealing with the local council recently over a new stand. So I asked him what he thought they would think of the Borough's football clubs combining grounds so this pretty riverside site could instead be better used for housing. Every paper in this country talks about needing more housing, so surely this is a good idea?"

Bayram was working himself up as he talked, his speech quickening and tone becoming more frustrated.

"Ground sharing with the other local clubs would make perfect sense."

He drank some more wine. "This man, Bob, I know would like to work on such an ambitious project with me — wants to be on my payroll. Do you know what he said?"

Hamarat shook his head.

"He said, 'I'm sorry Kerim, but I don't think there's much chance at all. It could only happen if the mayor intervened and overrode the council but in this case that would never happen."

Bayram slapped his open palm on the table; the wine glasses shook gently. "Your man, Joe Martinez, was supposed to be that person. Without him, there is no way I can do anything."

Hamarat had anticipated this reaction and the necessity of saving face. He placed both wrists against the table, the cuffs of his starched shirt with their plain gold disc cufflinks on show and clasped his hands together.

"Kerim, I understand. You can have my assurance that I am already looking into other avenues for us. We need to overcome these hurdles because you are right, with the Diamonds about to win the historic quadruple, I need to invest in the Arena beyond anything that has been planned before as we can be one of — no — *the* biggest club in the world. And of course, my plans for Wembley cannot wait for long drawn-out planning battles with no guarantee of success."

Bayram nodded, his outburst having simmered to a sulk.

"The new mayor, Lydia Edwards, will also have to be pragmatic over investment, yes? Let's just say that like everybody, she has weak spots. And I might happen to know what they are, following our previous dealings from some time ago. In fact, Kerim, this outcome could be very favourable."

This was unexpected news and Bayram allowed himself a smile, coinciding with the arrival of their food, the presentation and descriptions by the waiter taking longer than either diner would have liked. As soon as the waiter had finished, they continued their conversation.

"I've read lots about David Patterson's empire in the media this week," Hamarat said.

"Yes, I've seen those articles. They said he has more department stores up for sale, three in London even, including maybe the one on Oxford Street. He reported that other parts of his business are doing well and he will never sell his football club. But surely he still needs the money?"

"I read the same," Hamarat replied. "As we were in Turkey, we just need to be patient, Kerim. But always be ready to pounce." Hamarat said, lifting his hands and mimicking a cat's claws.

They finished the main courses and the waiter took their plates. They chose their desserts without needing to look at the menu — Hamarat knew the restaurant was renowned for its excellent syrniki.

"So, you think the quadruple is yours, Omar? That's what I admire about you — your self-belief. You still have two big football matches to win." Bayram smiled at his friend. "And thank you for the invitation to the Final next week. Porto will be nice at this time of year and I would not miss it for the world. I hear that you should beat Monaco."

Hamarat looked happy with that assessment and they both picked up their glasses and nodded before taking simultaneous mouthfuls.

"You're right, Kerim, I'm not worried about Monaco. They do not have the strength and depth of our team, and Lorenzo has done his homework on them. He is the best manager we have ever had. Alas, we will lose him after this season. I understand, what more can he achieve with us? After this season, it would only be downhill. The big Spanish clubs are after him. He won't want to stay in England."

Bayram wiped his mouth vigorously with his napkin, his dessert plate left only with a few morsels.

"You must have someone lined up for the job. I know you. You don't leave things to chance."

"I know a few managers who are very keen. That's good for me, Kerim. It means I can make them dance to my tune for a while," Hamarat laughed.

"And the FA Cup? A formality?"

"I know, of course, our dear close neighbour, Fulham, would be delighted to stop us attaining the quadruple but that cannot happen — I won't let it. I told you before that they were only a Championship team but next season they will be in the Premier League — and they were League winners. They also beat Liverpool and Arsenal to get to the FA Cup Final."

The waiter interrupted them again, carefully placing coffee cups down, moving the handles towards them, with a wooden box of petit fours.

"This country loves an underdog. Which other country has an Eddie the Eagle as a sporting hero?" Hamarat raised an eyebrow. "The media will be torn between wanting the Diamonds to do something no other club has done and wanting the smaller underdog to cause an upset."

Hamarat drained his coffee cup and gestured across the room for the bill.

"What options do you have to, aahh, *manage* your success?" Bayram asked.

"It's a shame that they won't now have their first-choice goalie — frustrating — as he could have been an asset to me."

Bayram looked unsure of what his friend meant but said nothing.

"I have instead invited their manager, Marko Maric, to watch the Champions League Final with us. He used to play for the Club, you know. He has done well for Fulham, especially so with the players he has available to him. I wonder what he would be prepared to do for the promise of the Diamonds job?"

"I never doubted you, Omar, for a minute," Bayram said, evidently impressed.

Hamarat shrugged his shoulders, happy with his reaction.

"Of course, Kerim, I'm not involving anyone else at the Club in my plans. I know they'd find it somewhat … unsporting. But I am of the view that the end more than justifies the means."

Saturday 23rd May
Pimlico

Jack

I wouldn't normally make an effort to watch the Diamond Blues play football. But when Loz suggested we got together to watch the Champions League Final I agreed because it felt like ages since we'd seen Fulham play and any football is better than no football. Also, we could study our FA Cup Final opponents.

The Saturday evening match would be shown live in the wine bar opposite my shop. During the week, I had casually mentioned the arrangement to Fleur and had been surprised when she said, "D'you mind if I tag along? I might ask Will."

I had glanced up from the lilies I was arranging and said, "I didn't know you were seeing him."

"Oh well, you know," said Fleur which didn't make any sense, but the upshot was that Will would be joining us.

The wine bar was always busy on a Saturday evening and the crowd was bigger than usual because of the game. About an hour before kick-off we saw the team line-ups. As expected, the Diamonds team looked expensive and strong. Their German striker Robert

Ludwig, winner of the Premier League Golden Boot, was expected to be the difference in the match. A picture of Ludwig appeared on the screen — he was a smug, blond, somewhat porcine-looking individual although his speed and agility belied his looks.

I started to wonder how Jamie Crawford and Phil Philopoussis would cope with Ludwig next week then remembered there was some news I hadn't told Loz.

"I meant to tell you, I heard from my contact in hospitality at the Club — Gemma, who orders the flowers — she's done us an amazing favour in return for me having helped her out. There's a VIP area at Wembley and she's got us two tickets. We can go there before and after the match."

Loz actually squealed. Dom looked around in alarm but Loz was hugging me and saying, "Oh my God that's amazing, Jack!"

"It is amazing," I agreed. "And it'll also be interesting because the girl with the long dark hair will probably be there: Marko's mistress."

"Oh yes," said Loz. "And your friend Ivana will be there, too."

I nodded. "So, we might end up watching fireworks as well as football."

<u>Loz</u>

Estadio do Dragao, the home of FC Porto, was hosting the Diamonds' match against Monaco. They'd put on a spectacular show with a stunning opening ceremony. The TV cameras panned the enthralled crowd in the 50,000-seater stadium, giving a few faces their five seconds of fame before focusing on the footballing royalty in attendance: the UEFA and FIFA presidents; previous Champions League Final winners; and former Diamonds and Monaco players.

"The Diamonds' owner looks happy with himself," I said when Omar Hamarat appeared on screen, smiling widely. He was sitting next to an attractive woman I assumed to be his wife, in one of the stadium's boxes. To his other side was a wealthy-looking man in a blazer and shirt, slightly younger than Hamarat. I knew I knew him; then it came to me.

"That bloke is Kerim Bayram." I made a face.

Jack looked quizzical, "Who's he?"

After Andy had told me that Fulham's project manager had contacted him following Bayram's approach, I had spent that afternoon finding out what I could about the guy. I knew you couldn't believe everything you read online but I felt I'd got enough to know what he was about. I had sent Jack a message that evening:

L – Think Patterson might want to sell. Turkish money man sniffing around. Wants Cottage for flats!

J – Who wouldn't want the Cottage — for football! Will never happen. Couldn't could it??!!

L – No. Ne fret pas. Council wld never allow it. Nor mayor if they ever said yes …

J – Phew!!

I answered Jack's question. "He's the Turkish guy I texted you about a couple of weeks ago. The guy who wants to buy the Cottage. He's an ex-banker, turned property developer. Looks like he's got his sights on our ground being his next project. Must be mates with Hamarat."

Jack and I both looked daggers at the screen.

"And look who else is there," Dom said.

Jack and I were delighted to see our handsome manager, Marko Maric.

"Good he's doing his homework. Hope he'll be taking some detailed notes," Jack said.

"Sure he's not lining himself up for the Diamonds job?" Dom asked. While Dom said he didn't follow football, he made sure he knew enough to humour me.

"You might have a point," said Jack. "Everyone's been saying that Lorenzo Verdi will be off to Real Madrid. They're desperate for him — they've had a rubbish season by their standards. Ironically, Verdi's team beating them in the semi-finals might have clinched the job for him."

"How could Marko abandon us when he's just got us promoted?" I asked.

"I was only joking," Dom said. He was always a calming influence when Jack and I had histrionics over injuries, fixtures, results, draws, you name it. "Anyway, I didn't think you liked him that much."

"Of course, we do. We've just won the League with him and got promoted. What's not to like?"

As I said it, I wasn't sure I believed it. Jack and I were never convinced Fulham ran through Marko's veins as much as it should.

Will had been quiet throughout this conversation. "What do you think then, Will?" Jack asked. "Any rumours about Marko at the Cottage?"

"Well," he said softly, before sighing deeply, "there's always rumours about something or other, goes with the territory, but when you think about it, it sort of makes sense that Marko would fancy the Diamonds job. Guess he's … " he hesitated, "a focused kind of guy."

"Very diplomatic, Will." I remembered he wasn't actually a Fulham fan; the Club was just where he worked. "But I'd say 'ruthless' rather than focused."

Before I could say anything else, a 'ping' distracted me. It was a message from Andy:

A – Wish I could be there but kids don't look after themselves apparently. Am confident we can do this. Bet you can't wait to take on the European Champions next week at Wembley!

L – Careful. Pride comes before a fall…hope none of your players get injured or anything!

On screen, the teams had assembled into their positions and the Italian referee in the centre of the pitch put the whistle in his mouth and blew.

Jack

The match was a good one for a neutral, although a better one for Diamonds fans because, as all the pundits had predicted, the Blues controlled the game and ended up winning 3-1. Robert Ludwig scored twice, once from the penalty spot. His other goal was an immensely skilful strike from the edge of the box that seemed to swerve first one way then the other to skim past the defenders and over the line.

I'll admit that even through the pleasant fuzziness of good wine and good company, I was worried. The Diamonds were clinical, cynical and ruthless. They had made beating Monaco look easy. The FA Cup Final was going to be nerve-racking. I said as much to Loz, who nodded her agreement.

"They so want to win the quadruple," I said. "It would be brilliant to be the team that stops them."

I meant it but the sentiment was one of hope rather than expectation: the Diamonds looked unstoppable.

"Look, there's Marko again," said Loz.

The camera had focused on Omar Hamarat looking pleased with himself as he accepted the congratulations of those around him, the man Loz had identified as Kerim Bayram amongst them. Marko Maric was approaching and Hamarat not only spoke to him but reached out to grab his forearm. Marko's face was rarely animated but as Hamarat spoke, we saw him frown and start to say something. But Hamarat ignored him, stepping back and turning away to accept yet more fawning and felicitations.

“What was all that about?" I asked. "Marko's got a face like thunder.”

“Probably Hamarat describing how easily the Diamonds are going to win next week,” Loz suggested, frowning almost as darkly as Marko.

To add arrogance to insult, the screen switched to a shot of Robert Ludwig looking pink and sweaty as he was interviewed by an ex-player Sky had rescued from obscurity. Ludwig spoke eloquently about tactics, objectives and targets and concluded that the win was well deserved, mainly due to his own efforts.

The ex-player asked, "And what about your next game? How do you fancy your chances of winning the FA Cup — for the quadru — the quadru — the quad?”

Ludwig smiled. “Oh, very good," he said. “I don't think our little neighbours are going to be too hard to beat.”

I slammed my glass down so hard that people on nearby tables glanced up. “What a horrible man! I hope we wipe the smile off his ugly face next week!”

Loz clashed her glass against mine. “Cheers to that!”

<u>Loz</u>

We turned away from the screens before the presentation ceremony; we'd seen enough.

“I guess we have to give the Diamonds their dues — they've had a phenomenal season,” I paused, unable to contain my unease, “but just when we get to the FA Cup Final for the first time in a zillion years, why do we have to meet the bloody European Champions?”

“Don't tell me, it's ‘un … fair’?” Dom gently mocked me.

“It is! We don't even have our first-choice goalie for the match! We need the whole team to be in top form but we're already at a disadvantage.” The others were looking at the debate between us and smiling. “Dom, you just don't understand football. Why it matters so much.”

“What about all this stuff you've been telling me about that in a final, especially in the FA Cup, anyone can beat anyone and if you're the underdog, the pressure's actually all on the other side?” Dom asked.

I took a quick sip of my wine before responding.

"That is totally true. And I do believe it. With the Fulham faithful behind the team, there's no reason we can't do it."

I looked over and grinned at Jack. "And I CANNOT wait to experience the Final in style. You getting those VIP lounge tickets for us is the best thing to happen to me in ages."

Dom put on his best hurt face.

"Poor Dom," Fleur said. "I really don't know how you put up with these two."

My phone on the table buzzed — predictably, it was a message from Andy. "*We r the champions, we r the champions …* "

I replied quickly, "*very happy for you*". I didn't add a smiley face.

Craven Cottage

David Patterson flicked off the TV in his Riverside apartment. The balcony doors were open and the breeze flowed through from the river. He turned his head to look towards the water where he could see the last of the day's dusty light.

The Diamond Blues had been worthy winners of the match. The win had been expected and so it had come to pass that Fulham would be playing the European Champions for the FA Cup in a week's time.

"You OK, darling?" asked Harriet. He'd had his bent finger in his mouth in a soft bite, obviously deep in thought.

"You worried about playing them next week?" she asked.

David didn't immediately answer so she followed up with, "At least Marko was there to find out as much as he can about them."

David had known that Marko was going to Porto and he also knew that he'd inevitably cross paths with Hamarat. When Marko had told him earlier that week that he was attending in person, David had been impressed with his thoroughness and commitment to the cause. In fact, he could find no fault with the man. He'd asked for automatic promotion from Marko, recalling the conversation in the apartment back in December. He'd not only delivered on that, but he'd done it by winning the League. The FA Cup had not even been a consideration and, in fact, if David had had his way, he would have given up on the Cup a long time ago to concentrate on the Championship — the focus was on getting back to the Premier League, nothing else. But Marko Maric had kept going and had now got the team to the Final and against the juiciest opposition going.

David looked at his wife. “Harriet, now we’ve got to the Final of the Cup, I want to win it. I don’t think I’ve ever wanted anything this much in my life!”

Harriet moved towards him, resting her hand on his leg. “For your dad?” she asked softly.

His eyes welled. “Yes, for dad. He took me to the Final in ‘75 against West Ham. It wasn’t to be then, but I want to do this for him, for us, too — never mind for the Club and all the fans.”

“I get it,” she said.

David tried his best to hide his pressures from his wife, but they’d been together for too long for him to carry it off. He could detect in her concerned eyes that Harriet was worried about him. He was sleeping so poorly that it was almost not worth going to bed. The pressure was relentless, with journalists and media outlets following his every move. Just a few days ago he’d had to issue a press release stressing that he was not selling off his entire retail empire and definitely not his football club.

David would have been disturbed to know that earlier that week Harriet had sought some advice that was a touch too close to home for comfort. She had agreed to meet her husband at Motspur Park on the Thursday so they could go straight out to dinner; Harriet was coming directly from Heathrow following a trip to New York. David occasionally used his office at Motspur when he wanted the distraction of looking out over the training fields.

She’d arrived at Motspur in good time and was about to go up the stairs, sunglasses on top of her wavy blonde hair, when she ran into Dr Brown.

“Hello Mrs Patterson,” he said politely. “Hope you’re well?”

She nodded. “I am, apart from a little jetlag,” she said, her accent having been refreshed even from just a few days in the States. As she looked at him, she decided she might as well ask for his opinion, it was opportune.

“Actually, doctor, do you have ten minutes? I’d like your advice on something.”

Dr Andrew Brown had been about to check on a youth team player who had some sprain or other but in order of priorities, apart from David Patterson, there was no one else, not even Marko Maric, who could trump the owner’s wife. “Of course,” he replied, gesturing towards his door a little way along the corridor.

Harriet had been careful not to divulge any business confidences but had told the doctor that she was worried her husband might be overdoing it. As a man in his 50s, slightly overweight and with high stress levels, she wondered what he should do and how she could help. Dr Brown had found the whole situation somewhat delicate, recommending regular blood pressure checks, a healthy diet, exercise and a sensible sleeping regime, but couldn't prescribe a magic miracle cure. Her visit had made him reflect on the multi-faceted nature of a football club.

David Patterson did, indeed, have a lot on his plate. The previous morning, he'd had a meeting at his office in town with his most senior lawyer and his team of accountants trying to work out a plan to cut their losses. Not only were his stores not performing, but the banks were becoming impatient. None of his advisers had wanted to be the one to tell him that along with more stores, his Oxford Street branch would have to go. Reports of his online businesses, including a couple of fashion brand labels, run by his son, doing well was the only bit of good news.

This puts the focus on Fulham Football Club, David had reflected once all the advisers had left. If only we can stay in the Premier League for a few seasons, he thought, it would mean a lot of money. The trouble was it would mean having to spend money — money he didn't have — to stay up. Winning the FA Cup wouldn't just be for his dad; beating the Diamonds and stopping them getting the quadruple would mean every football fan in Europe, if not the world, would hear of little old Fulham and that had to be good for the bottom line.

He had opened his office window and, looking down onto Oxford Street, bellowed, "Anyone sniffing around the Cottage can bloody well bugger off!"

Sunday 24th May — Porto

Marko Maric flew from Portugal to London on Sunday afternoon. His head hurt, then his knee started aching in sympathy, which made for an uncomfortable flight, even in business class. More unpleasant though was the mental turmoil he had been grappling with ever since his conversation with Omar Hamarat the night before.

He had enjoyed the Champions League Final as he enjoyed watching any football match. He appreciated the moments of skill, the tactical battles and the pace and physicality of the game. He'd also enjoyed the excitement of the big occasion, the quality of the hospitality and the excellent view from the VIP seats. He knew some of the other guests and felt proud when they congratulated him on winning the League and reaching the FA Cup Final.

"You've done great things at little Fulham," said one of his former adversaries.

He smiled and said, "Not so little now," and found that he meant it.

But this wasn't just a big occasion for the footballing fraternity; it felt like a big occasion for him personally and a crucial point in his career. He was watching the side his own team would face in the Final next weekend. Even more significantly, he was here as the guest of Omar Hamarat, a man who might well have a part to play in his future far beyond the next seven days.

He had been flattered and intrigued when Hamarat invited him to Porto. He hadn't been entirely surprised, but this recognition was more than he had dared hope. He had only managed to meet Hamarat on one occasion and that was fleetingly at the Foundation charity event before Christmas. The man had lived up to his reputation: charming but brash, pleasant but menacing. Marko knew how to deal with powerful men and, over drinks before kick-off, adopted an obsequious manner.

At the final whistle he congratulated Hamarat, who said, "Three steps towards winning the quadruple completed, Mr Maric. The fourth will be just a formality."

"I'll have to see what I can do about that."

"No, Mr Maric, you misunderstand me," Hamarat had gripped Marko's arm in a friendly looking gesture but squeezed it with an unfriendly force. "There will only be one winner next week. You will make sure of that for me."

Marko was frowning but other people were surrounding them now. Hamarat released Marko's arm but, before he turned away, added, "Come and see me later in the hotel. I will send for you."

Marko watched as Hamarat was absorbed by the loud, lionising group. It was a warm evening but he felt cold and shaken.

He looked down at the pitch where the Diamonds players were still celebrating. He hadn't felt like this since the last time he had worn a similar kit himself and collapsed on the grass in agony, his future and his dreams suddenly in doubt.

***

Marko went back to his room in the hotel where the Diamonds contingent were staying. He didn't know what to do or what to think so he stood at the window watching the moon rise over the twinkling lights of the city.

At some point, he ordered a room service meal, which he picked at then abandoned. He flicked on the TV and was bombarded with highlights of the match he had just attended. He watched Robert Ludwig take his penalty from ten different angles, some of which showed his expressionless face and dead eyes. The striker was exactly the sort of player Marko wanted to manage — an automaton. Ludwig was Zac Miller without the human flaws.

The Diamond Blues, he told himself, was exactly the sort of club he wanted to manage — successful, ambitious, ruthless.

As he switched off the TV, the phone rang.

***

A man with a strong accent told Marko to come to room 1201. He took the stairs to give himself time to prepare. Having waited half the night for the summons, he was suddenly nervous now he'd received it.

He had been waiting for months for the Diamond Blues to show some interest in him and it seemed that his patience was paying off. It was an open secret that Lorenzo Verdi was going to Real Madrid at the end of the season and that the Diamonds were looking for a long-term replacement. A young, up-and-coming manager might be more attractive than one of the tried and tested old guard who'd been on the managerial merry-go-round for too long.

As Fulham had climbed the Championship table, Marko's name had climbed the list of candidates for the Diamonds job. He had guessed, on receipt of the invite to Porto, that the long list had been whittled down, quite possibly to a shortlist of one.

When he reached the 12th floor, an unsmiling, black-suited man was waiting for him. Incredibly, Marko found himself being patted down and asked to hand over his phone. He complied, his nerves turning to fear.

He had thought that the trip to Porto might be some sort of interview, a test of his suitability off the pitch when he had already proved what he could make a team do on it. But in his wildest imaginings he hadn't expected this: a midnight summons, a clandestine meeting and the feeling, as the door opened to room 1201, that he was walking into danger.

***

Hamarat's greeting was initially reassuring. He shook Marko's hand and introduced his companion, a man Marko had seen at the match earlier and at the charity dinner as, "My associate, Kerim Bayram."

Bayram was holding a bottle of vodka and poured out a generous measure. Marko accepted the glass, raised it to them and drank. In his teens, he had drunk cheap vodka imported into Yugoslavia but this was a much finer version of the spirit, better even than the bottle he had worked his way through while Ivana was away.

Hamarat settled down in an armchair in a dimly lit corner of the room, gesturing for Marko to sit opposite him. "So, Mr Maric — may I call you Marko? — what did you think of the match?"

This was an easy question and Marko answered it fluently with his thoughts on the Diamonds' impressive squad. He kept the analysis positive which wasn't difficult — weaknesses were few and wouldn't be easy to exploit.

Hamarat, who was used to praise and positivity, nodded encouragingly and indicated that Bayram should top up Marko's glass.

Marko almost demurred — he didn't want to cloud his thoughts with alcohol, but he knew these men would take it as rudeness if he couldn't match them drink for drink.

"A very good team," said Hamarat. "The best team in Europe." He smiled as he said it and looked at Marko over the rim of his glass. "And do you think this team can be beaten?"

"Possibly," Marko said carefully.

"Well, I would like to make it impossible," Hamarat said. "I'll be honest with you, Marko. I want the Diamond Blues to win the quadruple and I don't want to leave it to chance. There's too much riding on it. I had a plan but your wretched goalkeeper ruined it. Now I need a new plan. I'm not wasting my time approaching another player. I'm coming straight to you."

Marko's heart began to beat in double time and his hands, gripping the crystal tumbler, became damp with sweat. He thought he had seen so much, done so much that nothing could faze him. He had grown up in a communist state and come of age in a war zone. In his playing career he had been known for uncompromising aggression that sometimes went too far — there had been red cards, injuries, fines and disciplinary proceedings. There had been incidents off the pitch, too — his scrap with Antonio hadn't been the first of its kind. As a manager, he had tempered his street fighting tendencies with cold calculation and created a brand of fast, forceful football which had led to his success.

He had thought that this would be enough to enhance his career prospects. He had encountered corruption in football before, of course, the dark side of a sport controlled by men with too much money. He knew results were sometimes manipulated and there had been occasions when matches were thrown (although he hadn't known his own goalkeeper had been approached to do it, for God's sake!) but he had never expected this. He had never thought that he would be asked to betray the sport he had loved all his life. To betray himself.

But he swirled the vodka around his glass and said, "And why would I get involved?"

Hamarat gestured expansively. "For the job of the Diamonds manager, of course. At a salary you can name and with a transfer budget bigger than the game has ever seen. That's the deal. Make sure Fulham lose the cup and the Diamonds, the quadruple-winning Diamonds, are all yours."

Marko accidentally swallowed the contents of his glass in one gulp and Bayram was immediately at his side topping it up. "That seems harsh on Fulham," Marko said.

This time it was Bayram who answered. "Fulham will soon be very different. That pretty little ground will be gone for one thing, covered in apartments. Make no mistake, Mr Maric, this is a once-in-a-lifetime opportunity. Accept Omar's offer and there will be no end to your success. Refuse it and, well, who knows?"

They had talked long into the night with Marko making objections, which the two men dismissed. It could be done, they said, in a way that raised no suspicions at all. "I hear there is a very good striker," Hamarat said, "Jack Miller, is that his name?"

"Zac," Marko corrected.

"He scores all your goals. Get him out of the way and there won't be any goals. Simple."

"How do I get him out of the way?" Marko asked, incredulous at the suggestion.

Hamarat shrugged. "That's your problem. I'm not going to think of everything for you. Now. Do we have a deal?" He held his hand out.

And almost against his will, Marko's hand reached out to shake it. A limitless salary and a transfer budget so large that success, fame and adulation were guaranteed.

"I agree," he said.

"Excellent," Hamarat said. "My man will return your phone and I don't have to tell you not to mention this conversation to anyone else, do I? I know you're good at keeping secrets from your wife."

Marko stood up and felt the alcohol flood into his brain. He almost staggered, either at the sensation or at what Hamarat's words conveyed. He thought about them again sitting wearily on the plane.

He was no longer his own man. He had made a deal with the devil and part of him regretted it already.

Monday 25th May — Surrey

He arrived home after midnight — almost exactly 24 hours after he had taken that fateful walk up the stairs to the 12th floor — and found the house in darkness, Ivana asleep upstairs. He didn't want to disturb her so he flopped down onto the sofa beneath the display of his old shirts, thought about getting up again to find something to drink, decided he couldn't be bothered and unexpectedly fell asleep.

The next thing he knew, light was flooding through the bifold doors and Ivana was gasping, having stumbled across him as she came in to put the coffee machine on.

"What are you doing in here? What time did you get back?"

"Late," he mumbled.

Ivana was wearing a white silk gown, her blonde hair drifting over it. She looked a bit like an angel, he thought vaguely.

She took pity on him. "Go and have a shower, I'll make coffee."

"And breakfast?" He said hopefully.

"I suppose so. What do you want?"

"You know how they do eggs and bacon here … ?"

"You mean fried?" She sounded horrified.

"Yeah. Like that. Please."

"If I must. This must have been a very hard trip, Marko. I thought you only went to watch a football match."

"So, did I," he said.

***

The combination of the shower, the coffee and the fried breakfast ("disgusting" said Ivana as she presented it to him) revived Marko in body if not in spirit before he left for Motspur Park.

On the journey, he thought about upgrading the Aston. He had discovered on the flight home that thinking about how he might spend the riches he would soon be coming into was a lot easier than thinking about how he was going to earn them.

He arrived during a break in training. Antonio was back with the group, but Marko ignored him. Antonio's injury had been, somewhat ironically, widely accepted to be an accident. Marko hadn't heard any rumours that it had been anything else and he hadn't spoken to Zac or Javier about what had happened. It seemed he hadn't needed to.

"Hi," said Charlie coming over. Something about Marko's appearance made him ask, "Are you all right?"

"Yes, of course," said Marko. "I got home very late, that's all. Carry on."

Marko watched the session with interest and pride. This was his team, a team he had used his knowledge to put together and his skill to mould from a group of individuals to a balanced, flexible and dangerous unit. He had brought Phil Philopoussis to Fulham knowing he would be the perfect counterpoint to Jamie Crawford; he had plucked Leo Blake out of the academy because he could see the young striker was ready for the Championship; he had known how to turn Zac Miller into a 35 goal a season —

"Where's Zac?" He snapped at Charlie.

"He phoned in sick," said Charlie, and then added quietly, "Again. How was the trip? I saw you with Omar Hamarat on TV."

Marko waved a dismissive hand at the association. "He was there, of course." He went on swiftly, "What did you think of the Blues?"

"They'll be hard to beat," Charlie said frankly. "We won't beat them at set pieces, we won't beat them on the counter, we won't get in behind. And if Ludwig gets the ball in the box, then he'll score."

"So, what's your plan," Marko sneered. "Play for the draw and try to win on penalties?"

Charlie replied, "No, of course not." But he stopped, trying to explain what he felt in a way that Marko, who never seemed interested in feelings, would understand. He gave it a go.

"There's something about our team," he said. "They're capable of magic and the Diamonds won't be expecting it. That's our strength and their confidence could be their undoing."

Marko smiled cynically. There was some truth in what Charlie said. This team could produce magic. But only when Zac Miller was part of it.

***

Marko walked back to his office. It was a stunning day. He and Ivana moaned about the British weather, but these early summer days of warmth and brightness and every shade of green made the winter weeks of cold and dampness almost worthwhile.

He liked working at Motspur Park but the facilities just down the road at the Diamonds' training ground were even better and the setting every bit as attractive. It would be an easy commute, too, in his new car. But it wasn't just the car he could trade up. He couldn't deal with all the issues Ivana had raised a fortnight ago but there were material compensations that could make her forget her threat of leaving after Wembley — new house, new car, new wardrobe, new jewellery.

When he overlooked the darker details of his conversation with Hamarat, he felt very positive about the new role. This could be the start of better times for him outside of work, too — he hadn't always been a good husband and he knew that none of his children would say he was an exemplary father. But he would improve.

He understood what he was risking in agreeing to Hamarat's plan. It would be a case of instant dismissal if David Patterson and the Board ever discovered his betrayal. Not to mention the fact that the FA would throw the book at him. He was contemplating the unpleasant consequences of being found out as he climbed the stairs to his office and suffered a jolt when he found Jamie Crawford and Phil Philopoussis standing outside his door. The two big centre-backs seemed to fill the corridor. Phil had released his long hair from its topknot so it fell messily around his shoulders, somehow making him look more threatening.

Marko had no idea why they were there unless, he thought irrationally, they suspected something. Although neither had a reputation for violence or even misconduct, their mere physical presence intimidated others on the pitch and he suddenly felt like an opposition player coming up against them.

But Phil, glancing in Marko's direction, gave Jamie a fist pump, said, "See you tomorrow, mate," and sauntered off while Jamie turned to Marko smiling. Marko got a grip on his paranoia and managed to say, "Come in," in almost his normal voice.

"Thanks, Boss," said Jamie. "How's Ivana? How was your trip to Porto?"

Marko had a sudden distracting vision of the angelic-looking Ivana bending over him earlier but said, "Ivana's fine. Porto was … interesting."

"That's kind of what I wanted to talk about," said Jamie.

"Oh yes?"

"I'm worried about Zac again. You know he wasn't here today.

Said he'd been for a really long run in the sun and was feeling shit. But I think it's more than that. I know I've mentioned this before and I'm sorry but … "

Jamie's concerns were exacerbated by the fact that he and Zac had barely spoken since Zac's terse text instructing him not to speak to Antonio. Zac was more detached than ever and Jamie felt powerless to help. And now, ironically, he was turning to the person who was the cause of the friction.

"That's OK ," said Marko. The beginnings of an idea were coming together in his mind. "You're right to worry. Make sure he comes to training tomorrow and I'll talk to him."

"Thanks Boss," Jamie said, relieved at Marko's reaction.

"So, what do you think about Saturday?" Marko asked.

"I think we can do it," Jamie replied at once.

Marko shook his head. "Really? With a striker who can't even face coming to training?" He laughed derisively. "Against this Diamonds team? You're going to mark Robert Ludwig out of the game, are you?"

He meant it as a challenge and Jamie took it as one. "Yes, I am."

Jamie didn't look away and Marko realised that he wasn't talking to the off pitch gentle giant anymore. This was the man who was in command on the pitch and in control of the dressing room, the team captain.

"I know we're the underdogs," Jamie continued. "But people have written us off before and we've proved them wrong. We won the League. We can win the Cup."

"So, you say," Marko replied. "But Fulham don't win major finals, they lose them. There's too much underdog in this Club and not enough winning mentality."

"I know it'll be hard," Jamie said, "I know we'll have to play the game of our lives, but we can do it!"

Marko glanced out across the training pitches, trying not to be impressed. There was something about this team.

He dropped his confrontational tone. "You really believe we can win?"

"Yes," said Jamie quickly, "Do you?"

Marko didn't respond immediately, partly because he wanted his reply to sound considered and partly because he was reluctant to speak the truth.

"Yes," he said, eventually. "Yes, I do."

Tuesday 26th May — Motspur Park

Marko studied Zac in training. He was quiet, but then he was always quiet in a team with Leo chatting and Lucas questioning and Javier moaning. When they practiced penalties, Zac took his without qualms and scored them all. When the attackers took on the defenders, he gave as good as he got.

At the end of the session, Marko said, "Come and see me when you've got changed," and Zac nodded.

Zac had been expecting some sort of reckoning from Marko ever since he'd witnessed that brief burst of violence on the training pitch. His sympathy towards Antonio had waned but, even before that display of savagery, his respect for Marko had been destroyed by the knowledge of his duplicity and its threat to the team. He didn't rush his shower or the walk to Marko's office.

The dark circles were prominent under Zac's eyes and Marko, who had just discovered the torment of sleepless nights caused by anxiety, wondered how Zac managed to live with it.

"Coffee?" Marko offered.

"No thanks," Zac said, then went on. "I'm sorry about yesterday. I was really dumb. I went for a long run on Sunday. It was hot and I got dehydrated. I'm a professional athlete and I should've known better. I won't do it again."

"I'm glad to hear it," Marko said. He watched Zac's knee jerking up and down like a jack hammer and said, "I know you're tired. I know what it's like to play a full League season and a Cup run as well. We rely on you a lot. Too much maybe. But there's one more game. Are you ready for it?"

The empathetic tone took Zac by surprise. He bit his lip before answering. "I thought I was, but ... "

"But?" Marko prompted.

"We were messaging each other during the game on Saturday — me and the guys. They're all really positive. They think we can beat the Diamonds but ... "

After a long pause, Marko almost prompted him again but then thought better of it.

"Sorry," Zac said eventually, "It's hard to talk about. I don't want to worry Tammy."

"No, of course," Marko said.

"But they were all like — *"Zac's gotta score," "it's all down to Zac,"* that kind of thing. I watched Robert Ludwig and I'm not that guy. I'm not some clockwork striker. But what if I don't score? What if I let them down?"

Marko shook his head. "You won't let them down. You can't. Jamie leads them but you inspire them. Whatever happens on Saturday — that won't change. I don't know how the match will go. The lads are confident, Charlie's confident, I spoke to Mr Patterson earlier and he's confident, too."

"And you?" Zac asked.

Marko's views were so ambivalent that he couldn't explain them in Croatian, never mind English. Instead, he said, "We have to give it our best shot."

"Sure," said Zac. "And I'm not your best shot at the moment — "

"Yes, you are," Marko interrupted quickly. He hadn't realised Zac was so close to breaking. He almost reconsidered his plan but he couldn't afford to leave anything to chance.

"You are my best shot — but not like this," he said. "I've had an idea. There's a hotel I know in Wembley. Close to the stadium, spa, gym, pool, great food. Instead of you staying with the rest of the guys the night before the game, why don't I book you a room there? You can chill, get your head in the game. No Leo talking non-stop, no Lucas asking endless questions. No fans and media outside. You can go there on Friday morning, have some time and space to yourself. How does that sound?"

Zac looked like a drowning man who had been thrown a lifeline. "That sounds awesome," he said. "Thanks, Boss."

Even in *extremis* Zac was still polite and thoughtful. "That's really great. Sometimes people think you're all about tactics and mechanics, so it means a lot that you're reaching out."

"I'll make the arrangements," Marko said. "And don't worry. We can do this."

He reflected, after Zac left and he was typing an email to his contact at the hotel, that his plan was going to be hard on his beleaguered striker. But it was a means to an end for Zac as much as himself, even if only one of them knew it.

***

After he sent the email, Marko looked out over the training ground. Only three people were visible. Alex McKenna and the goalkeeping coach were training on the Arena Pitch and, in the distance, Dario Kovatic was working out alone.

Marko headed out. Unlike the pitches, the offices were buzzing with frantic activity in these days before the Club's biggest match for years. Marko nodded at the people he passed in the corridor — he didn't know most of their names — and, once he was outside, raised a hand to Alex. He was impressed with Alex's skill as well as his work ethic and wished he had given him the opportunity to step up earlier. Just what the hell had Davy Walker been up to? It occurred to him that the red card against Sheffield Wednesday might not have been a matter of bad luck but belated good judgment instead. Easy to get out of throwing a game if you'd been banned from playing it. Had Davy changed his mind about helping Omar Hamarat?

It had crossed Marko's thoughts as they had raced in all directions during the long hours of the night to tell Hamarat the deal was off. Marko had sailed close to the wind before but to influence the result of the FA Cup Final was cheating on a biblical scale, which he would never have contemplated before his midnight meeting in Porto.

It had also occurred to him that there was an easier way out: let the match run its course, let Fulham take on the Diamonds at Wembley and see what happened. The result almost wasn't in doubt. What was the point in removing Zac Miller from the equation when the striker was in no state to play anyway?

And yet. There was that magic that Charlie had spoken about — the possibility that Fulham's hard graft, unity and a flash of inspiration could combine to be the Diamonds' undoing. He knew it could happen, so he had to stop it. He couldn't pass up the opportunity Hamarat was offering. And he couldn't face the future Bayram had hinted at if he let his new Turkish friends down — these men had a wide circle of influence and it wouldn't just be the Diamond Blues that closed its doors to him if he failed.

So he walked on, past the Arena Pitch and over to the far side of the ground where Dario was combining sprinting with sit-ups and press-ups. He was topless, sweat running over his hyper-toned body.

Marko had met his compatriot when they had played together at Dynamo Zagreb. Dario's extreme fitness made up for a lack of technical skill. They had kept in touch after Marko moved to England and had then come together again during Marko's managerial stint back in Croatia — he couldn't think of a better fitness coach. They still worked together all these years later while other assistants, coaches, advisers and scouts had come and gone. There was no one Marko trusted more.

“Join me,” Dario said, barely breathless after his 20th sprint.

“I can’t,” Marko said, “My knee’s playing up.” He wouldn’t have admitted it to anyone else.

“OK,” said Dario, grabbing his drink. “What brings you over here then?”

Marko looked back over the pitches to the long, white building, familiar and majestic in the sunshine, as if seeing it for the last time. One more chance to back out, to change his mind, to let fate decide his future. But he didn’t take it.

“I need your help with something,” Marko said, “Something big.”

PART 7

Friday 29th May
Wembley Astra Grand

The car came for Zac on Friday morning. He gave the driver his bag then turned to say goodbye to Tammy. Although he was used to leaving her behind when he went off to play football, he knew that this time she was worried about him but trying to hide it. She hugged him as if he was going away for a month rather than a day.

"I'll see you after the match," he said, and the driver looked away as he kissed her.

Like Ivana Maric, Zac didn't like driving in England. Besides driving on the "wrong" side, the London roads couldn't be more different than the wide, straight highways of Texas. Zac found the narrow lanes of London difficult to navigate, especially when they were packed with traffic.

Being driven was a much better experience. He found himself enjoying the journey to Wembley when all he had to do was sit on the comfortable back seat, stretch out his legs and watch the world go by.

The car dropped him outside the hotel and he was met in the lobby by Dario Kovatic who was holding a room pass. Dario didn't waste any time on preamble.

"You will have lunch at 1 p.m., the pool is reserved for your exclusive use between 2 and 3. We will meet in the gym at 3, then you're booked into the spa at 5."

Zac was used to structure and timetables, so this plan suited him well enough. He was less sure about what Dario said next, however.

"Your phone," he said, holding out his hand.

Zac hesitated but Dario went on. "Boss's orders. You don't need all that group chat today."

This was a good point and without further reluctance, Zac pulled out his phone, turned it off and handed it over.

"And your watch," said Dario. But then he looked at Zac's wrist, sneered and said, "Oh, it's not a smart watch. You can keep it. See you at 3." He gave Zac a room pass and strode away.

Zac looked at the pass. Room 606. Must be Marko's choice, he thought as he went up in the lift. He should be in room 909. But he didn't want to think about being number 9 at the moment.

He liked the room anyway. It was huge with an enormous bed, a TV more like a cinema screen and a fridge full of juices and bottled water. The bathroom was even better, with a bath the size of a shark tank and a shower that could host a small party.

Zac dropped his bag on the bed, threw himself onto the pile of puffy pillows and channel-surfed until his lunch arrived. When he clicked onto Sky Sports News and heard the words " ... *Cup Final tomorrow* ... ", he felt an unpleasant flood of adrenaline and flicked onto a film channel.

It was going to be a stressful 24 hours. But, he reflected, sinking further into the feathery duvet and reaching for his freshly squeezed orange and mango juice, there were far worse places to be stressed.

***

The basement swimming pool was small and softly lit. The warm water made for lazy stokes rather than serious swimming, but Zac was happy to float and drift. He met Dario in the gym at precisely 3 p.m., feeling refreshed and alert.

The session was easier than usual and included some yoga as well as weights and cardio. Both men found small talk an effort, so they barely spoke.

At 4.45 p.m., Dario gave him his orders. "You should get ready for the spa. I'll see you in the morning."

Zac thanked him and, for the first time, thought about the rest of the squad. They would be training together. He missed the camaraderie of the group but not the endless banter and baiting, even when it was good-humoured. As Dario had suggested earlier, it was bad enough in a constant stream of WhatsApp messages, but it could be even worse in person when you couldn't ignore it.

Up in his room, he stepped into the shower, which blasted him from all directions like a series of fire hoses. After five minutes, he turned off the torrent and wished he could turn off his thoughts just as easily.

***

Tammy had tried on many occasions to entice Zac to visit a spa with her. He would like it, she said. They could have a couple's massage and wallow in the jacuzzi, and he would leave feeling calm and relaxed.

Zac had always declined. He knew about massages — you had them in the physio room after training and they were often brutal and, as a soap-and-water man, he hated the thought of smelling of lavender or rosemary or vanilla.

It was with some trepidation then, that he wrapped himself in a luxurious white towelling robe and made his way to the spa. It would be an experience to tell Tammy about, if nothing else. He wondered what she was doing this afternoon. He missed her already, but he didn't miss the constant effort of pretending to her that he was OK.

The spa was part of the same complex as the gym but a world apart from its slick functionality. There were white tiles, brass fittings, trailing plants and piles of towels. Soft music was playing, and the air was filled with a scent that might have been lavender, rosemary or vanilla.

A girl in a white tunic and trousers appeared from a doorway. "Hiya! You must be Zac. I'm Jade. I'll be giving you your massage today."

She had what he recognised as a northern English accent and a cheerful smile he couldn't help returning.

He followed her into a small room lit by candles. Jade busied herself with a strange device in the corner. "Hop onto the table," she said. "I'm just heating the stones."

"Okaaaaaay," Zac said uncertainly.

Jade glanced over her shoulder, "It says on my form you're a footballer. That must be exciting."

"It has its moments," Zac said, concerned about how stones came into this.

"And you're in the FA Cup Final tomorrow. That's amazing! How do you feel about that?"

"Worried," said Zac honestly.

"Oh, the stones will help with that," said Jade confidently. "Right, they're ready. Slip your robe off and lie on your tummy."

Still deeply suspicious of what was going on, Zac complied.

"Where are you from?" She asked.

"Austin, Texas," said Zac as he felt a warm, tingling sensation down his spine and suddenly realised what the stones were for.

"What's it like there?" Jade asked and, as more of the smooth, warm, basalt stones were placed on his skin, Zac found himself telling her all about growing up in Texas and playing with his brothers and discovering soccer. And then discovering he was good at it.

"You didn't want to play American football then? With the funny shoulder pads and helmets?"

"God, no," he said. Or he might not have said it because he felt like he was floating and didn't need to talk.

All he needed to do was close his eyes and listen to the music and breathe in the air with its delicious scent of lavender or rosemary or vanilla while the stones enveloped his body with warmth and languor.

Eventually, and disappointingly, it seemed to be over and he came to his senses like he was coming round from unconsciousness. "You just lie there for a bit," Jade said. "I have to wash the stones."

"Those stones are magic. What's this smell, by the way — is it lavender or rosemary?"

"No. It's ylang-ylang with a touch of bergamot."

Zac sat up slowly. "That was awesome," he said. "Thank you."

"No worries, just doing my job. Although I don't often get to work on someone in such good shape." She glanced round at him approvingly. "You must be very strong."

"Hopefully strong enough," said Zac.

Hammersmith to Pimlico

Loz

The office was almost empty when I decided to call it a day. I started to tidy up my papers — I still hadn't mastered the paperless office. It had been my boss's birthday and we'd enjoyed handing over an office-sized birthday card, emblazoned with a large '5-0', that had been doing the rounds all week. It was followed by a neon pink helium balloon, also with a huge '50', brought out from under a nearby desk.

She looked suitably embarrassed as the ten or so of us there gathered round, looking down on her as she remained seated, making sure she couldn't escape. Someone mumbled *speech,* so she obliged with some unenthusiastic words of thanks and suggested we joined her in the pub after work for drinks. Andy was next to me.

"You going to the pub, Loz?"

I shook my head. "I've got some stuff to finish off here and then I'm heading over to see Jack in Pimlico. We've got to discuss our Cupset Day tomorrow."

I arched my eyebrows to indicate the hatching of a cunning plan.

He chuckled, "I love your optimism, I really do. You and Jack are true, dedicated, fans. To support a club that you *know* has no chance of winning is admirable."

"At least you can use the kids as an excuse to avoid watching us lift the Cup," I replied.

I knew Andy would be watching the match at home, or would be trying to at least, with his two young boys wrestling for his attention. I didn't want to admit it, but my bluff and bluster was pure bravado — it was part of a football fan's DNA. Our 'banter' was interrupted by Big Al coming over.

"Can't guess what you two are talking about," he said, munching on chocolate cake. "And, hate to say it, Loz, but the Diamonds' name's written all over that FA Cup and the quad."

Big Al looked at the cake in his hand, almost apologetically. "This is my third slice. You'd better get in there quick."

***

Jack was already ensconced in a corner of the wine bar with Fleur when I arrived. She immediately poured me a glass of white from the bottle sitting in the ice bucket.

"I've just gone for the cheap pinot grigio," Jack said, "thought we'd save the expensive wine for tomorrow's celebrations."

"Do you really think you're going to win then?" Fleur asked, clearly not sure what we thought.

"Of course," Jack responded in a blink, before adding, "You've got to believe, Fleur. It's all about believing."

We clinked our glasses and got straight to the main reason for meeting up. Fleur took on the role of responsible adult as Jack and I played the parts of excitable kids waiting for Christmas Day to arrive.

"So, have you got your outfits prepared?" Fleur asked.

I turned to Jack. "You up for wearing our jaunty black-and-white hats again? I think mine's still intact."

"Yep, definitely. With our white tops, of course. We'll be like two bricks in the White Wall."

"What about banners?" continued Fleur. "Flags or anything like that?"

"Hmmm," I said as if giving this serious thought. "Not sure we'd be allowed them in the VIP lounge."

Jack agreed, laughing, "We're going to be conspicuous enough in there already without waving banners and flags around."

The tickets to the Fulham VIP lounge were the ultimate cherry on the Cup-cake. Jack had received two embossed invitations, which looked similar to a formal wedding invite:

The FA CUP FINAL BETWEEN THE DIAMOND BLUES FC and FULHAM FC
5 p.m. Saturday 30th May
FULHAM FOOTBALL CLUB IS DELIGHTED TO INVITE YOU TO JOIN US IN OUR WEMBLEY VIP LOUNGE
Drinks and canapes will be served from 2.30 p.m.
The bar will be open after the match from 7.00 p.m.

Directions to the entrances and which level to get to were provided alongside the invitation. As luck would have it, our seats weren't too far away from the lounge so getting to and from them wouldn't be a problem.

I was making my way to the bar to get another bottle of wine and order some food when I saw Will arrive and head to our table. I caught Jack's eye and her wry smile told me that Will and Fleur were obviously becoming an item. I felt some satisfaction that Jack and I had helped get them together, even if it was inadvertent.

As I arrived back, Jack said, "I've already started the interrogation, Loz. Will's assured me that the team's fighting fit and raring to go."

"Good to hear," I said. "And Marko Maric? Is he behaving himself?"

"Marko's Marko," Will said.

"Will's going to be busy tomorrow, too, running around after the players," Fleur said proudly. "The team love him."

"I'm sure they do," Jack said. But keen not to stray off topic, she followed up with, "Any other Club gossip we should know about? Is Marko about to leave? Is the team really up for this? Come on, give us your insider view!"

We looked at him, hungry for any scraps of information we could feed off before the match.

"Well … " he seemed unsure what to tell us. "The team were happy going off in their coach to the Grove Hotel when I last saw them this afternoon."

"And?" said Jack, clearly not sated. "Anything else to report?"

Will looked like a man put on the spot. Maybe just to end the third degree, he replied, "I'm not really sure what's going on with Zac Miller."

Jack and I looked at each other and then turned back to Will. We could sense that he didn't like telling tales out of school and neither of us wanted to make him feel disloyal, but we were desperate to know more. It was a delicate balance, push too hard and he might clam up.

"Oh. Is he not getting on with the rest of the team or something?" I asked, trying to sound casual.

"It's just that … " he stopped.

"What?" Jack interjected. "What is it?" Her voice was slightly raised.

Will drank back what was left in his glass. "Oh, it's nothing. Just that he seems to be getting singled out for special treatment."

"Well he is our star striker, so he does need looking after," I said. Jack nodded enthusiastically in agreement.

"That must be it," Will commented. "Lots of special cotton wool wrapping for him."

Saturday 30th May
FA Cup Final — Diamond Blues FC v Fulham FC

Now is the time for the sinister goings-on to come to a head.

In football clubs up and down the country, anyone in my position would have also witnessed their fair share of bust-ups on and off the pitch. I guess that's inevitable when football players are driven by the need to compete. Not just with football, but also with cars, women, training, video games — you name it. Rivalries were unavoidable. The job of a manager was straightforward but not necessarily easy — to funnel their competitive natures, harness them, manipulate them and release them in an orchestrated way against the opposition — not each other.

But do other clubs have players linked to 'influencing' matches, like Davy Walker? Who knows? How about trying to kill their manager? Or at least looking like they'd really like to? I can't imagine they do.

The car accident was — thankfully — a near miss but without Zac's split-second reaction, it could have been a different story. Pots being thrown over balconies — not accidentally — was headline-making and yet, and yet, it got swept under the carpet. These incidents, serious incidents, made Antonio's attack on the manager and Marko's retaliation at Motspur Park look like schoolboy scrapes.

Journalists had been buzzing around the Club all week interviewing and photographing everyone — the owner, the players, WAGs and Marko Maric, even I had a cameo appearance — and none of them picked up the dark undercurrents. They demanded pictures of the players in all attires — in their kit, their civvies and, of course, their FA Cup Final tailor-made suits — smiling, looking serious, kicking a ball, holding a ball. I don't know how they put up with up it. In fact, the players seemed to like it.

At last, Final day had arrived. All the necessary preparation had been done. Now was the time to savour the experience. The team had left Motspur Park the previous evening to travel together to their hotel by coach. The cars left behind at the ground were those of a car lover's dreams. For once, the players all looked happy and excited. The exception was Marko Maric, of course, but that was nothing out of the ordinary. Everyone was there except two people, Davy Walker … and Zac Miller.

Things were definitely coming to a head.

Wembley Astra Grand

Zac slept fairly well under the huge downy duvet. He had woken around 4 a.m., as usual, to worry about the day ahead and a tangle of other problems, most of which he had no control over. But he had gone back to sleep and when he woke in daylight the dread had dissipated and he felt more energised than agitated.

Today, Fulham would play the champions of Europe in front of 92,000 people at Wembley Stadium. It was the biggest game of his career and he had been nervous about it for weeks. He was expected to score a goal and whether he did or he didn't, he would be compared to Robert Ludwig, the best striker in Europe.

But he wasn't on his own. There were eleven of them and they were in the form of their lives. They would go out there together and fight together and win or lose together. If — and he acknowledged it was a big if — there was to be a Fulham victory, it would come from teamwork, not individual effort.

He didn't feel sick yet so he raided the fridge for more juice — orange and raspberry this time — on his way to the shower. He wiped the steam from the mirror and looked into his china blue eyes, bright above the dark shadows.

"Bring it on," he said out loud.

***

His breakfast arrived shortly afterwards, and he ate it wrapped in the robe that still smelt of ylang-ylang and bergamot. On the tray was a typed timetable — *12 swim, 1 lunch, 2.30 gym, 3.30 depart for stadium* — embellished with a scrawled note. In what he assumed was Dario's handwriting, it said "See you at 2.30".

He was slightly disappointed that the spa didn't feature in today's timetable but not surprised. After Jade's ministrations last night, he couldn't have played tiddlywinks, never mind football.

He finished the one cup of coffee he allowed himself and folded up the timetable, willing himself to enjoy his quiet morning. He knew that he wouldn't be able to hold off his anxiety later, as kick-off drew nearer, but at the moment he was coping.

Marko booking him into this luxurious hideaway had been an inspired idea. Zac made a mental note to thank the manager as soon as they met at the stadium.

***

At 11.55 a.m. Zac left his room to go down to the pool. The lifts were all busy so he jogged down the stairs to the foyer. The reception area was empty except for one family waiting by the desk, looking out of place in their white football shirts in the plush surroundings.

Zac thought he could sneak past them unseen, but the smallest child noticed his approach, did a double-take and then stared at him open-mouthed. He grabbed his brother's arm and pointed, "Look!"

The other boy was older and reacted quickly, pulling out his phone and snapping a picture.

"Mum! Dad!" said the little one urgently. "Look who it is!"

But Zac was past the group now and almost at the entrance down to the Fitness Complex. He glanced round and saw the boys bouncing with excitement, still trying to convince their parents who they had seen. For the first time, he saw the name and number on the back of the smallest boy's shirt: Miller 9.

He smiled to himself because it felt like a good omen.

Surrey

Ivana dressed with particular care on Saturday morning. During the week, she had heard that the Fulham fans were intending to create a White Wall at Wembley and this had triggered a number of ideas in Ivana's mind. She issued a decree that all the Fulham WAGs were to wear white too.

Saturday was forecast to be hot and sunny so a pale outfit was ideal. More importantly, white suited her. An unforgiving colour, it looked better skimming over her angular body than it would on anyone with curves. And, of course, it was unforgiving in other ways too, ways that she might just exploit in the VIP lounge later.

Finally, the edict was an excuse to spend some of Marko's money on a new outfit. On Wednesday, she'd visited her favourite King's Road boutique and come home with a fabulous new trouser suit, the jacket flatteringly fitted, the trousers of weapons-grade skinniness.

Marko had been in an odd mood since his return from Portugal, uncommonly attentive and yet easily distracted as well. She had heard him on the phone to Dario several times and there had been other calls, too, in which he'd spoken in reassuring but subservient English.

He drank every evening, which was unusual, even when they were on holiday. For the last few days, he had got into the habit of opening a bottle of wine with dinner and he sometimes finished the evening off with vodka. He didn't get drunk, but he consumed just enough to take the edge off whatever was occupying his thoughts.

One night after dinner, he took his wine onto the terrace and she paused while clearing the table to watch him staring out into the darkness. Drawn to him despite herself, she picked up her own glass and stepped outside.

At her approach, he looked round and in the half light from the kitchen, she registered the familiarity of his features and the unfamiliar uncertainty of his expression.

"What is it?" she dared ask.

He looked away again and she thought at first he wasn't going to answer. She waited, feeling a breath of cool air on her skin.

At last he spoke. "I've been offered something I thought I wanted. Now I'm not sure."

She stared at him intently but he didn't go on. She asked, "Did something happen in Porto?"

He flicked a glance her way and a half smile as if in acknowledgement that she had read him well, but he didn't answer the question.

"It's nothing," he said, "I'm nervous about the match, that's all."

She knew an evasion when she heard one but just as she was about to press him, he said, "You're cold. Let's go in," and the moment passed.

That had been Thursday evening. On Friday, he had been business-like and peremptory as he departed for the team hotel with the brusque assurance that he would "See you at Wembley" which had been at odds with a kiss goodbye that she hadn't been expecting.

Now, she thought of him as she applied her subtle but effective make-up and carefully chosen jewellery. She slipped on a pair of stilettos with heels so high and thin that walking in them could have been an Olympic event and selected a tiny handbag from her extensive collection. She inspected herself in the mirror. She could pass for 30 easily — maybe less from a distance, she thought — and added a touch more lipgloss.

She had promised Marko she would stay with him until Wembley, until today. Tomorrow, she would have to decide what to do next.

Hammersmith

<u>Loz</u>

I woke up before the alarm, something I rarely do, the sunshine creeping into the room around the blurred edges of the blinds. It wasn't a gradual coming to, my mind was instantaneously switched to ON, enough to make me leap out of bed. It was Cup Final day and Fulham were in the Final, now that was the rarest thing of all.

I put on the kettle and pulled out my well-worn Fulham FC mug from the cupboard. The underlying sensation of nervous tension had already set in. Clutching my cereal bowl in one hand, mug of tea in the other, I headed into the living room. I switched on the TV and flicked through the channels as I ate. I was hoping to come across something on the Final and to immerse myself in the pre-match build-up.

After some trawling, I found a news channel showing the Diamond Blues team at their training ground. There was an interview with their manager, Verdi, and then another with their striker, Robert Ludwig. His serious demeanour and intense gaze were slightly unnerving. Interspersed with his interview were clips of some of his season's goals, many of which could safely be termed *worldies*. The piece ended with the interviewer, all but salivating, summing up the Diamonds' "*amazing*" season and finishing with an image of the FA Cup.

I must have missed the Fulham bit, I thought, it was probably at the beginning of the piece. I flicked channels again and managed to find another one covering the match. There were interviews with Omar Hamarat, the Diamonds' owner, the manager yet again and then other Diamonds players, including a long piece on Ludwig. At last, after the focus on the Diamonds, the programme showed some footage of the Fulham team training earlier in the week and then a short clip of them arriving at their hotel the previous day.

"Is that it?" I said out loud, just as Dom walked into the room looking sleepy.

"You talking to yourself now?" he said.

Pointing the remote in the direction of the TV, I replied, "Anyone would think there was only one team in this Final! Everyone's going on about the Diamonds and how bloody *amazing* they are. They're practically calling them quadruple winners already! They don't seem to remember that there's another team in this Final. We're not just making up the numbers, you know."

"Underestimating Fulham may be their undoing," said Dom before disappearing into the kitchen.

I put the TV on mute and picked up my mobile phone. A few good luck messages were coming in already from friends and family.

I messaged Jack: *The biased TV coverage has started — so annoying! DO NOT forget VIP tix today!! So excited. C U Victoria 1.30.*

She messaged me straight back. *I know!!! CANNOT WAIT. Outfit already on.*

She followed up almost immediately: *Meant to say, we need to talk about what Will said on way. Very interesting!*

I looked up and on the screen was Lydia Edwards, the new mayor of London. I unmuted the TV and heard them say that she'd be at the Final between the two London clubs. The interviewer asked who she'd be supporting today.

She smiled as she replied, "I'll be happy whoever wins."

I wondered if she even liked football.

Grove Hotel, Watford

The Fulham squad trained in the grounds of the Grove Hotel near Watford on Saturday morning. It was a short, light session, which no one got much out of. The younger players were too excited to do anything except chat and fool around and even the old hands like Jamie and Phil were grinning and joking.

"Calm down, all of you!" Charlie, whom Marko had wisely put in charge, shouted more than once.

They weren't listening but he was happy to see them burn off some excess energy before the long hours they would spend impatiently waiting for kick-off.

When Marko strolled up in his slim, dark match day suit, it was time to blow the whistle and call the players over. The manager looked crisp and smart, but a fresh haircut had revealed more silver at his temples than Charlie had noticed before. Marko's cold grey eyes were hidden by dark glasses although they were standing in the shadows.

When the group was assembled, Marko spoke without preamble: "First, the team: Alex, Sunday, Phil, Jamie, Aidan, Eric, Javier, Antonio, Lucas, Leo."

He nodded to each of them in turn, neither skimming over Antonio nor emphasising his name. "And Zac will be joining us later, of course."

He looked over the squad again before going on, his voice gruffer than usual, his accent more pronounced.

"You've been my team for nearly a year now. I put you together. I've played you to your strengths. I've tried to eliminate weaknesses. But any mistakes left are mine. We've come a long way this season. All the way to the top of the League and all the way to the Final of the FA Cup. Back in August, who would have thought this was possible? You should be proud of yourselves. I'm very proud of you."

He cleared his throat and the players, already hanging on his every word, seemed to draw closer to him.

"But this isn't about me anymore," he continued. "It's all over to you now. This will be the hardest game of your lives. But don't write off your chances. We've trained for this. You know how to deal with their attack, you know how to get past their defence. You're ready. Charlie said it best in the week. Sometimes, when you play together, when you play for each other, you create magic. That's what you need to do this afternoon. Don't play for me, play for each other."

He stopped and turned away abruptly, leaving the players still and silent in his wake.

Jamie was the first to break the tableau, jogging to catch up with Marko. "Great speech, Boss," he said.

Marko didn't answer so Jamie tried again with, "How's Zac?"

"He's fine. Dario is with him."

"And how are you?"

"I'm OK . Why shouldn't I be?" Marko snapped, the familiar irritation returning to his tone.

Because I've never heard you speak like that before, thought Jamie, because now you've shown us what this team means to you I find I'm surprised at the depth of your feelings.

He let Marko stride on ahead. He turned as Phil asked, "What did you say to him?"

"I asked him how Zac was and he said he's fine."

"Good, what else?"

"Nothing really," said Jamie. "You know, I used to think he could be a bit half-hearted about it all — about the Club, about us. But now I think I was wrong. He really thinks we can win today."

Victoria Station to Wembley Stadium

<u>Jack</u>

On the Tube on the way to Wembley Park, I said, "That was interesting last night with Will, especially what he said about Zac being wrapped in cotton wool."

"I'm glad they're looking after him properly," Loz said. "Without his goals, we wouldn't have got to the Final. Or won the League. We really need him to be at his best today. Just think, Jack, if we win this, we're in the Europa League!"

We fell into a detailed discussion about our chances in the Final until the train surfaced just before Finchley Road. Both our phones started beeping and trilling.

"I'm getting lots of good luck messages," said Loz. "Everyone I know wants us to stop the Diamonds winning the quadruple."

"Same," I said. "I've just had a text from Melissa, you know, the receptionist at the Wembley Astra Grand Hotel. I'm doing her wedding flowers next month."

I read the message out loud: "*Hiya Jack. Just wanted to say good luck for final and have a fab day!! Not working today but lots of Fulham fans staying at hotel last night. Btw, club booked room 606 again & guy who checked in is really fit! Mel xxx*"

Loz said, "Must be a special guest. Maybe an ex-player?"

Just as she said that, the Tube pulled into Wembley Park station.

Knightsbridge to Wembley Stadium

Hamarat looked over at his wife, Tabitha, as she walked into their living room.

"Do I look ready for a football match?" she laughed, striking a pose.

He'd almost got to the point where he took her beauty for granted but every now and then it caught him. She really was exquisite, he thought, quite mesmerising. He took a deep breath in, content that she was his. She is what money can buy he thought, understanding that without it she'd be with someone else.

The drive went by quickly, the traffic building up as they neared Wembley. As their driver approached the stadium, Hamarat and Tabitha surveyed throngs of fans through the car's darkened windows. The supporters, clad in white and in blue, mixed happily together, their scarves and flags held aloft.

Hamarat's last few weeks had been busy as he did his fair share of TV and newspaper interviews. He'd actually enjoyed the media frenzy that his Club had created, not for the personal attention or glory — it was good for the share price.

They made their way to the Diamond Blues club lounge, aware of the attention they received along the way. When they arrived, it wasn't yet 3 p.m. but many of the guests were already there — most of the board members, some local dignitaries, a handful of revered old players and, of course, the WAGs.

Hamarat spotted Kerim Bayram and, after some initial back

slapping, left Tabitha with him and excused himself, saying he would be back shortly.

***

The security guys opened the door to the Fulham lounge and Hamarat walked straight over to David Patterson and his wife, Harriet, who'd been talking to a small group of people.

"David," Hamarat shook his hand firmly before turning to his wife, "and the beautiful Harriet."

He lifted her hand and kissed it gently. She feigned a weak smile.

"I wanted to wish you well, but not too much luck, of course," Hamarat chuckled.

Both David and Harriet laughed politely.

As Hamarat was exchanging pleasantries with them, he could see Marko Maric over David's shoulder, standing alongside a well made-up blonde who he guessed was his wife, although he knew it was best not to assume anything, given Marko's reputation.

Hamarat left the Pattersons and headed Marko's way, happy to be seen with him in plain sight.

The Marics paused their conversation. Hamarat took Ivana's hand first, pretending to ignore Marko, and didn't let it go. He looked at her intently and, without averting his gaze, said, "Marko, why have you been hiding this goddess from me?"

Ivana pulled her hand away, letting it drop. From her, there was no feigned smile.

Hamarat turned to Marko. "I am impressed with what you have achieved with your club. The Championship … it's a tough league so to win it shows you have a good team and you know how to use them. You will give us some strong opposition today. I hope it will be a truly memorable Final."

"I hope so, too," Marko replied, his voice flat.

Ivana studied Marko as he spoke; she detected a slight deference in his demeanour, something she'd never seen before. Marko could be respectful, polite even, but he was never timorous. The steeliness in Marko's cold grey eyes seemed somehow dulled.

Hamarat paused and looked around him, smiling towards the clusters of people in the lounge. Ivana sensed he wanted her to move away to leave him to talk to Marko on his own. She had no intention of doing that.

"David Patterson has just said that he is sure your in-form striker will score today. You will appreciate that I hope that will not be the case," Hamarat said, head tilting a little to one side. "Do you agree with him, Marko?"

There was a slight purse to his lips before Marko replied tautly, "Well, I wouldn't put money on it."

Marko then turned quickly to Ivana and kissed her cheek. "I'm sorry. I must go. I need to be with the team for match preparations."

With that, he gave a nod to Hamarat and strode away.

Ivana was grateful that Hamarat's departure followed almost immediately. She remained standing in the same place, one leg elegantly in front of the other, allowing a waiter to top up her champagne glass, the rim branded with her shimmering lipgloss.

Marko was behaving oddly, and it wasn't just the public display of affection which had taken her back. She wondered if it was wrapped up in the Premier League club move he'd talked about before his Porto trip; she had now guessed that the Diamond Blues was the club involved.

Being around footballers for as long as she had, Ivana had often come across men like Hamarat, thinking money could buy everything. But she wasn't a fool — she could sense something wasn't right.

She took out her phone and texted Marko, *we will talk about that man later.* She hesitated before sending and, against her better judgement, added *good luck x* and quickly pressed send.

Southwark to Wembley Stadium

Her feet hadn't touched the ground since she was elected mayor only three short weeks ago. Lydia had expected the role to be life-changing but hadn't guessed how much so. She had never been a person to blend into the background and, in recent years in particular, had had a reasonably high public profile. But being London mayor was something else entirely — there was a lack of anonymity and total lack of diary control.

Lydia stoically accepted the scrutiny that came with her new role — even the fact that keeping her relationship with Jonathan under wraps would be all but impossible — but she was determined that she wasn't going to let every minute of her day be directed by someone else. But today was the FA Cup Final at Wembley Stadium and she had to attend whether she wanted to or not.

Ellie had briefed her on the event in the kitchen that morning. Another thing that had changed — even Saturday mornings were no longer her own.

“Here’s the guest list. There’s a mix of business people, some who call themselves social investors or creatives, but we’ve also got a few senior people from other parts of the GLA, the development corporations and the like. Arjun will be there, too.”

“OK,” Lydia said, scanning the list.

“The young Royals and some government ministers are in the nearby Royal Box if you fancy saying hello,” Ellie said smiling. “Oh, by the way, Lydia. Not sure what you’re planning on wearing today but I suggest you avoid royal blue or white.”

“So my Diamond Blues top’s out of the question?” Lydia asked without looking up.

Ellie was going to meet her at the stadium later, which meant Lydia had the luxury of being by herself in the back of her unadorned mayoral car, giving her precious downtime as she was driven through the streets of London.

“Looking forward to the game, Lydia?” her driver asked, peering into his rearview mirror, snapping her out of her deep reflections.

She gathered her thoughts. “I think I am, Mo. I know nothing about football apart from lots of people love it.” She paused before adding, “It will be fun, I’m sure.”

Apart from its popularity, Lydia also knew that football involved vast sums of money, which was why it attracted people like Omar Hamarat. She’d been told he would be there today and wondered if there would be any way of getting out of meeting him but guessed not, especially as his team were likely to win. That meant having to be seen offering her congratulations for the cameras. She vowed to keep the encounter as short as possible. And to suppress the haunting memories of their previous dealings in South America.

Before the game, she would make a short speech to her guests. It would be along the lines of it being a match between two historic and valued London clubs and that she wasn’t partisan, being the mayor for all of London. Lydia didn’t want to ramble on, but she was determined to get in a message about football and ‘grass-roots’ somehow.

The trip to Wembley may not have been Lydia’s preferred way to spend her Saturday afternoon but at least it was useful for her to see it in person — an informal site visit. Lydia’s predecessor must have given up the ghost well before quitting because Frank Best had left plenty of unfinished business, particularly the future of Wembley Stadium. It was already her biggest headache as mayor.

Best had had ample time to deal with it but the political curveball was now coming for Lydia. As mayor, she had the power but she wasn't sure how best to use it.

Despite a public outcry as to the ethics of selling the national silverware, Wembley Stadium's owners, the Football Association — the governing body of English football — had offered it up to the market and its fate was now going to be decided by her. The FA had agreed a sale price much higher than they could have hoped for but it was conditional on its preferred bidder, one Omar Hamarat, being able to secure planning permission for lots more events, including for his NFL team, and significant new development around the stadium. If permission was granted by the mayor, then the deal could complete.

Some time back, Frank Best had used his powers to 'call-in' the scheme, having been lobbied by the local council, Brent — it was too hot for them to handle with so many residents against it, as well as most football fans around the country. If it was simply a case of over-development, then the easy decision for the mayor would be for her to refuse it and the FA would have to start again. Trying to find a new buyer with a different approach would likely result in years of delay and less money.

For the decision makers, it wasn't that simple. Not only did the proposals create lots of much-needed jobs in the borough, but as part of the deal a new school had been promised nearby. With a chronic shortage of local school places and an underfunded council and GLA, it was an offer that was hard to ignore and unlikely to be repeated.

***

Lydia had opted for a primrose yellow shift dress with a chunky green necklace and earrings, feeling she was on safe ground with those colours. She wasn't sure her white trainers went that well, making a mental note to order some green ones later that evening. I bet most mayors never gave as much thought to sartorial choices, she wondered.

Getting out of the car into the warm sunshine, she smoothed her dress down and looked around. There were fans everywhere and she could hear laughter and singing coming from all directions. She was ushered through by the Wembley staff to the VIP area set aside for her and her guests. She checked her watch, it was just after 3 p.m., in-keeping with her schedule. Ellie saw her straightaway, came over and escorted her to the middle of the room.

"Nice dress," she whispered.

Fulham FC VIP Lounge

Loz

We stood at the top of the steps of Wembley Park station and took a moment to appreciate the famous stadium with its iconic arch, the home of football and where our hearts would be today. The sunny weather and late kick-off meant that fans had decided to get to the stadium early to make the most of the day and the crowds were already building.

We weaved our way through the melee. The stadium's well-oiled machine meant we were channelled smoothly through the security and ticket checks, and were soon outside the lounge. We looked up at the sign: *FULHAM FC VIP LOUNGE.*

"We've arrived, Loz … ," Jack beamed, " ... literally!"

We'd decided to get to the pre-match party at around 3 p.m. so we could make good use of it before the game. We knew we'd want to be in our seats to soak up the atmosphere well before the 5 p.m. kick-off. The door opened, and we stepped into the inner sanctum.

There were already a hundred or so people there and most of them were gathered on the far side nearest the windows looking out onto the pitch. Jack and I glanced at each other to signal we should move in that direction.

Our aim was to find a spot where we could see the pitch, people watch within the room and have maximum access to the circulating food and drink. We selected our vantage point quickly and, within a few minutes, each of us had a glass of chilled champagne in hand and were on our third canape.

"If Marko ever wants advice on tactics, he could do worse than consult us," Jack said.

We were trying to not resemble gate-crashers but everyone else was so smartly dressed, whereas we looked like … fans. The invitation hadn't said 'no jeans' but apart from us, no one else was wearing them. They all looked like they were going to a wedding rather than a football match, albeit an unusual wedding where the bride had told all the female guests that they positively *should* wear white. We scoured the room for any familiar faces.

"I can see Marko's wife, Ivana, over there," Jack said. "Oh, wow."

"What?" I said impatiently.

"Did you see what Ivana just did?"

"I can see she's talking into the ear of that waiter," I replied.

"Well, I just saw her slip him some money, looked like it could have been a £50 note," Jack said.

"Blimey, that's generous. Her champagne glass is guaranteed to stay topped up then!"

We continued to scan the room and turned our attention to another group of women standing around one of the white-clothed tall bar tables. Jack looked pleased with herself.

"Do you see that group of women there?" Jack moved her glass in their vague direction. "The smaller woman with the long wavy brown hair who's facing towards the pitch, she's the one I gave the flowers to — at the hotel."

We both stared in her direction.

"Well, she's young and pretty," I said.

"If I was Ivana, I would not be happy," Jack replied, adding, "and if she's here, she must be with one of the players. Marko is a *very* naughty boy."

We decided to move. With our glasses topped up, we went outside onto the terrace to look at the crowds arriving. At one end, we could see the Fulham fans gathering, a White Wall in formation. I could feel my nerves tingling. Neither of us spoke for a while.

"This is such a special place," Jack said reverentially.

We returned to the lounge to an alternative people watching spot, noting Fulham's owner, David Patterson, and his wife, Harriet. As we were sizing them up, Jack was first to notice that near them was a person we knew quite well — our very own Will, talking to another young guy. He must have somehow felt us both staring in his direction as he turned his face towards us and gave us a nod, finished his conversation and came over.

"Hello you two," Will said.

"So are you working in here today?" Jack asked. I could tell she was doubtful as all the waiters had a uniform on and Will was in a black T-shirt and chinos.

"Not in here, no. These are all Wembley's staff, not the Club's. Anyway, ladies, lovely to see you as always but I need to head down pitch side." He turned to leave.

Jack and I looked at each other, impressed.

As Will went to walk away, Jack said, "If you can, text us with any team news … " and with the most charming smile she could muster, added, "Please."

Wembley Astra Grand

At 2.30 p.m., Zac arrived in the gym for his appointment with Dario. He was still feeling excited rather than nervous about the match and was looking forward to getting this session out of the way so he could put on his fancy Final suit and join the rest of the team at the stadium.

Dario was there before him, prowling around, picking up weights and putting them down again, swinging kettle bells and smacking his fist into the punchbag every time he walked past it. He said even less than usual as he put Zac through his paces on the bike and the treadmill before taking a yoga mat out of a big storage cupboard and unrolling it on the floor.

Zac went through a long and complicated flow of movements, ending up on his back with his eyes closed, trying to concentrate only on breathing but unable to prevent himself from comparing Dario's relaxation techniques, unfavourably, to Jade's. He couldn't wait to tell Tammy that he'd enjoyed a visit to a spa. In fact, he couldn't wait to see her after the match or even to send her his customary text before it.

Which reminded him — "Can I have my phone back now?" he asked, opening his eyes.

"In a minute," said Dario, peering down at him from over six feet up, his rather oily dark fringe hanging forwards. "Are you feeling anxious now?"

It was unmistakably cruel but Zac simply frowned and said, "No, I'm feeling good right now. It was a great idea of the gaffer's for me come here. And thanks to you as well for the training."

He sat up and looked at his watch. It was 3.10 p.m. — time to shower and get ready to leave.

Before he could move, Dario said, "I knew a guy like you once, back in Croatia. He played in midfield for Hajduk Split."

"Oh yes?" Zac said. Somehow, he knew that "like you" didn't mean "blond" or "American" or "happily married"

"Yes. Really talented guy but after a while he just couldn't hack it anymore, couldn't take the pressure of having to perform in front of the big crowds, kept having panic attacks. Ended up in some dead-end job in Zadar."

"Well, thanks for telling me that."

Zac jumped angrily to his feet and was about to walk off when Dario said, "Don't forget to put the mat away."

It wasn't in Zac's nature to be petulant so even though he was fuming he bent down, rolled up the mat and took it to the storeroom.

He was focused on keeping his temper under control and not saying anything he might regret. He opened the cupboard door, stepped inside, added the mat to a pile of similar ones and —

— the door slammed behind him. Although he made an adrenaline-filled leap towards it, he heard the key turn in the lock before he could grab the handle.

"Dario!" He banged on the door. "Dario, you son-of-a-bitch! What are you playing at? Let me out of here!"

There was no reply and Zac punched the door again and then kicked it. But the cupboard was effectively a small room and the door was solid enough to meet fire regulations. His knuckles soon hurt and he wasn't quite furious enough to hurt his toes in the same way.

"Dario!" He yelled again.

Zac pressed the button that illuminated the dial of his watch — a watch that could tell the time in every capital city in the world and could measure altitude, speed and depth. But unlike so many watches these days, his couldn't be used for communication.

He saw it was now 3.15 p.m. He was due at Wembley in 30 minutes and the match would start in under two hours' time.

This can't be happening, he thought, panic rising. I have to get out of here.

Dressing Room

Marko entered the Fulham dressing room at 3.55 p.m. from a pre-match interview, which he felt had gone well. He had displayed just the right mix of ambition, hope and realism even though his actual ambitions and hopes had changed to fit in with his recently altered reality.

Charlie immediately drew him aside and spoke in a low, urgent tone. "Zac's not here," he said. "He should be here by now. I've tried his phone and Dario's phone but they're both switched off."

"OK," Marko said carefully.

"Have you heard from either of them?"

Marko already knew he hadn't, but pulled out his phone and made a pretence of checking it. There were innumerable good luck messages in both Croatian and English, and a text from Ivana that he didn't read.

"No," he replied honestly. "But they'll be stuck in traffic or going through security or something."

"They must know they're late," Charlie said. "Why haven't they phoned?" Then he had another thought, "Maybe we could phone the hotel? Check they've left? Do you think everything's OK?"

"Don't worry," Marko said. "Dario would let us know if there was anything wrong."

"Not if they've both got their bloody phones switched off!"

"They'll be here soon," Marko said reassuringly.

"But what if they're not?" Charlie glanced over his shoulder to check none of players were in earshot. "You know how flaky Zac is. That was the whole point of him going to the other hotel. What if he's bailed out?"

Charlie was sounding increasingly frantic. Marko was about to offer more platitudes when the dressing room door opened. Charlie spun towards it, obviously hoping to see Zac but it was Richard Green who entered.

Richard said, "They've said "no" to us delaying putting the team sheet in." Looking around him, he asked, "Is Zac still not here?"

The communications director was the last person Marko wanted involved in the drama. He said, "We'll deal with this, Richard."

Charlie fluttered the team sheet. "I think we need to assume Zac might not get here."

"What do you suggest?" Marko asked.

"If we leave Zac in the starting line-up and he doesn't turn up, then we haven't just lost him, we've lost a sub as well. If we promote Mitch to the starting eleven and name Zac as a sub, then we can bring Zac on as soon as we need him."

"But we may lose a sub that way as well."

"Better than losing Zac," Charlie pointed out.

Marko looked as if he was a weighing up a dilemma, which he was but not the one Charlie had just presented him with.

Charlie said, "It's due in right now."

"OK. Do it," said Marko. "You sort out the sheet, I'll speak to Mitch."

The team sheet was a typed page with the Club crest at the top. Charlie grabbed a pen, leaned against the wall and crossed out "9 Zac Miller" in the left-hand column and replaced it with "12 Mitch Masters". He then did the reverse in the right-hand column.

He handed the sheet to Richard, who took in the scribbled amendments.

"What the hell's going on?" he asked. "Surely you drilled into them that they couldn't be late?"

"Yes, of course," said Charlie. "But ... "

He let the sentence trail off, not wanting to speak his fears aloud. Their brilliant but troubled striker being late might not be the worst-case scenario.

Fulham FC VIP Lounge

Ivana endured a lot of football events with a fake smile painted on her face. Functions like this one at Wembley, however, were a different matter and her smile was almost warm as she strutted around the VIP lounge enjoying the attention due to the queen of WAGs.

At around 4 p.m., she had a useful conversation with Harriet Patterson, the owner's wife, who was stylishly dressed as always. Harriet confirmed that Marko and Ivana could borrow the Pattersons' Caribbean-based yacht for any week over the summer when David and Harriet weren't using it.

Ivana then took up a vantage point near the windows from where she could watch a group of younger WAGs chatting. Aidan Rafferty's girlfriend Niamh was among them, in a spectacular white jumpsuit with a plunging neckline, as was Pia Alvarez in a short, tight, low-cut white dress that left little to the imagination. Next to them, Tammy Miller in a simple white sundress looked initially unremarkable, until she smiled.

Ivana's gaze wandered away, over the Flower Woman — what on earth was she doing here? — and some of the Club employees too lowly to be worthy of recognition. She checked her phone but there had been no reply to her text from Marko. She didn't really expect one but the incident with the Turkish man had unsettled her. Hamarat had made her skin crawl and she didn't like the fact that there seemed to be something going on between him and Marko.

She thought back to the strange conversation they'd had on Thursday night. Was it Hamarat who had offered Marko something he thought he wanted? This was the kind of issue she had to weigh up as she edged ever closer to her decision of whether to stay or go. A week floating on the sparkly blue waters of the Caribbean was a big positive but Hamarat pawing her at future meetings was unappealing.

But here was a diversion to distract her from these difficult thoughts. A waiter was approaching the group of young WAGs with a glass of red wine.

It all happened very quickly, just like a real accident — one second, the wine was in the glass, the glass was in the waiter's hand and the waiter was steady on his feet and the next, the waiter tripped and the wine gushed all over Pia's white dress.

There was a shriek from Pia and a lot of flapping and exclaiming from the other WAGs, who went scrabbling for tissues and napkins. The waiter managed to slink off in the mayhem while Ivana turned away. Revenge wasn't sweet; it was full-bodied with herbal notes.

Loz

It was good that we'd had plenty of canapes — they were needed to soak up all the champagne we were drinking. We were, pretty much shamelessly, making the most of just having to stick our glasses out and having them regularly replenished by a friendly passing waiter. Our giddiness levels were rising as kick-off approached. We planned to leave the lounge at 4.30 p.m. so we still had fifteen minutes or so before we'd be heading for our seats. We could sense the growing buzz of the fans in the stadium behind us. The lure of the less well-dressed singing masses was starting to outweigh the free champagne and food, and WAG watching.

We were draining our glasses, having decided to leave, when we heard some sort of squeal emanating from a group of WAGs. Jack and I turned to see what the commotion was about and saw the woman of Jack's hotel flowers infamy frantically wiping down the front of her body-hugging dress, helped by a couple of the women around her. The poor woman had managed to tip a glass of red wine down herself — not what you needed when wearing a white dress! It was unsisterly of us, but Jack and I couldn't help smirking as the scrubbing seemed to make it worse.

We were still glancing over in their direction when, out of the corner of my eye, I could see the sleek Ivana Maric walking our way, as elegant as a catwalk model, her long blonde hair moving gently around her face. Her fitted white trouser suit and super-high heels contrasted with our tad more casual attire.

"Don't look now, Jack, but Ivana's heading in our direction."

Jack immediately peered over my shoulder.

There was no smile or outstretched hand. "Jack, the Flower Woman, I thought it was you. I am happy you were able to join us here today and share this occasion."

I was in awe of being up close and personal with this woman. I was conscious that I was probably staring a bit too intently at her expertly made-up face, the lipgloss looking straight out of a Vogue cover.

To her credit, Jack had composed herself and managed to have a conversation along the lines of being delighted to have Fulham as a client of hers and being even more delighted to be invited to the lounge on Cup Final day. I made no attempt to join the conversation, happy to be a bystander.

"I appreciate the task you undertook for me," Ivana said, her voice emotionless. "That was a good thing."

Jack almost blushed as she said it was nothing and was happy to help.

At that moment, another woman came towards us, clearly seeking Ivana. She looked different from many of the other women in the room, still beautiful but in a much more natural and less overtly groomed way. She apologised for interrupting and with a hand on Ivana's arm moved her to the side of us. She was trying to talk quietly but as they hadn't moved far away, we could still hear what she was saying.

"Ivana, I'm worried. I haven't heard from Zac."

Jack and I subtly shifted our position. Neither of us spoke as we strained to listen in. The American accent and mention of Zac's name meant we didn't need to be Wagatha Christie to work out who this woman was.

Ivana responded, "Well that is normal, Tammy. He will be preparing for the match. It will start in less than an hour."

"No, you don't understand." The woman, Tammy as we now knew, looked genuinely worried and on the verge of crying.

"I haven't heard from him since he was picked up from home yesterday, to go to the hotel."

Her voice started to quiver. "He always messages me before a match. He sends me black-and-white hearts — he's never *not* done it. But I've heard nothing from him, nothing at all. I just wanted to check, has Marko said anything to you? Is he ill or something?"

Tammy looked at Ivana intently, her brow furrowed. Ivana sighed before responding, "Do not worry. Marko will be taking good care of him. He is very important for this team. Zac will have lost his phone or just forgotten the time. That is all, Tammy."

Tammy nodded, looking down at her clasped hands and seemed comforted by Ivana's words and headed back across the room.

Ivana stayed put, motionless, clearly deep in thought. I noticed her fingers were clasped round the champagne flute like she was ready to throw it at someone.

Jack took a half-step towards Ivana and dared to ask, "Is everything OK?"

Ivana didn't move but under her breath, still just audible, spat out, "Ambition will be the death of my stupid husband."

Dressing Room

When Marko had informed Mitch of his elevation to the starting eleven, the American had predictably taken the news very well. Mitch wasn't short on confidence and had no qualms about using his compatriot's absence to his advantage.

Other players, however, overhearing the announcement, had been concerned. Leo immediately said, "Something's not right. Zac wouldn't just not turn up."

Javier replied unpleasantly, "Think back, Leo. Not turning up is what Zac does best."

"Only to training, not a match!" Leo responded hotly. "And it was because he was … " he cut himself off.

Charlie stepped in. "Time to get out on the pitch for the warm up."

He caught Jamie's eye and the captain led a general move towards the door. They were all eager to get outside for their final warm-up and to experience the atmosphere as the huge stadium filled up.

As the players were departing, Charlie said to Marko, "I'm really worried. I think you need to send someone to get Zac now."

"I'll do it straightaway," said Marko. "Now, go!"

He watched Charlie follow the players through the door then took out his phone. The text he was waiting for should arrive any moment but Charlie's focus on the situation was worrying. Marko began to pace the now-empty dressing room.

It was so typical of football, of everything in Marko's life, that this situation would go down to the wire.

***

The players came back in at 4.30 p.m. in a loud mix of excitement, nerves and anticipation. Their playing kits were arranged in numerical order around the room and as they dispersed to their places to change it was glaringly obvious that no one had turned up to claim the number 9 shirt and shorts.

Charlie came straight over to Marko and saw at once from his face that something was wrong. Before he could speak, Marko held up his phone and Charlie stared at the screen. Other than the word "Zac" the message was unintelligible. He asked, "What does it say?"

"Oh, sorry," said Marko who had apparently forgotten that Charlie couldn't read Croatian. "It's from Dario. It says Zac's ill and won't be coming."

Charlie compensated for his lack of Croatian by using a lot of English swear words. "Well, that's that then," he finished angrily. "We might as well go home."

But Marko shook his head. "Now's not the time for negativity," he said. "We can still do this."

Charlie looked over at the players, in high spirits as they slipped in their shin pads and adjusted their laces. "We're going to have to tell them."

"Sure. I'll do it when they're all ready."

***

In fact, though, Zac's absence was so blatant that no formal announcement was really necessary. When Charlie told the players to gather round, they had already guessed what Marko was going to say.

"I'll keep this brief," Marko said. "I've heard from Dario that Zac is ill and won't be joining us this afternoon."

"Ill?" Aidan repeated. "What does that mean?"

"I think we all know what 'ill' means when it comes to Zac," Javier said smugly.

Leo turned on Javier and was about to launch an attack, which may or may not have been only verbal, but Phil grabbed his arm and Charlie said, "That'll do, Javi."

Marko went on, "Obviously this isn't ideal. But everything we've done in training is still valid. Sharp attack, solid defence. Nothing has changed. And needless to say, this information goes no further than the group."

There was some muttering amongst the players. The excitement that was bubbling up earlier had drained away. Some of the team were despondent, some resentful. Zac was their talisman, particularly in the Cup, and they couldn't imagine winning the match without him. There wasn't the sympathy for him that there would have been if his absence had been caused by a broken leg or appendicitis.

Jamie cut through the mumbling. "Come on guys! We can still win this!"

Leo's unexpected ability to switch from exuberance to leadership in times of crisis surfaced. "Jamie's right," he said. "Zac's not here and it's going to be harder to win without him. So either go out there and prove you're better than him, if you think you are, or go out there and play *for* him and the team. I know what I'll be doing."

"Well said, Leo." Jamie looked round at the others as if challenging any dissenters. Phil and Lucas, whom nobody ever argued with, both nodded.

Marko said, "Time's getting on. Finish getting ready and then we'll get out there. And remember what I said earlier, don't play for me, play for each other."

As the players turned away to finish their preparations, he reflected that most of them would never play for him again.

Fulham FC VIP Lounge

Loz

A few minutes after Tammy had spoken to Ivana, we saw that paper copies of the team line-up had been brought into the lounge. It was evident, given the surprised looks and the chatter, that there was something strange about the team. Rather than wait to see a copy passed in our direction we took out our phones to check the line-up ourselves.

It hit us right away. Zac Miller was not in the starting eleven! But he was listed as a substitute. It made no sense to us at all; if Zac was injured then he couldn't come on as a sub, and if he wasn't injured, why wasn't our best player playing?

Not having our star striker against the Champions of Europe was disastrous, something that neither of us wanted to contemplate. We were stunned. Our bubble felt precariously close to bursting. If Zac was out through injury, it would be horrendous luck. But then there was the fact that Zac hadn't been in contact with his wife when she would have expected him to which was strange behaviour.

Ivana had suggested that he could have lost his phone. A plausible explanation, but somehow Jack and I were not convinced that it was as simple as that. There was something odd going on. Both of us had heard what Ivana had said after Tammy had left, about Marko and his ambition. We hadn't seen her face but her tone had made it sound like an accusation. So perhaps there was another explanation, something else entirely.

"I'm going to phone Will to see if he knows if Zac's OK . Can't hurt," Jack said. I agreed, not knowing what else to do.

Standing next to Jack, I could hear her explain to Will that Zac's wife hadn't heard from him. She asked Will if he'd seen Zac. She looked at me, her eyes wide, and with the phone still to her ear mouthed, "Not good news."

When Jack finished the call, she told me that Will had heard something about Zac having not turned up as he was ill. Once again, it made no sense. If he was ill, then why was he a sub? She said Will hadn't been able to talk properly as he was busy but he'd try to speak to us later.

Jack started scrolling on her phone.

"Loz, look at this. I saw this earlier but didn't think much about it."

It was a tweet from a young fan who'd posted a photo of Zac. It said, *AMAZING!! Just saw my idol in our hotel. Please score today! #COYW #FFC*

I'd seen it, too, and had thought how thrilled that young fan, smiling in his Zac Miller top, must have been to encounter his hero in the flesh on the day of the Cup Final.

We both studied the Zac picture carefully. The image had cut off Zac from the knees down but you could still make out he was mid-stride, in motion. Zac certainly wasn't posing for the shot, more a case of it being taken in haste. Zac was wearing a plain black T-shirt with the drawstrings of something resembling a small gym bag across his shoulder. His face was its usual handsome self and though it was expressionless, there was an assuredness about him — like some immortalised ancient Greek athlete.

Jack enlarged the picture. The young fan had said in his post that he'd snapped it in his hotel and from Zac's background and the lighting it must have been taken inside, probably in some fairly open communal area, like the reception or foyer. Jack enlarged it again and we continued our forensics, looking for something that might be useful.

"I think I know where this was taken," Jack said, lifting her head. "I recognise the colour scheme, the mauve and navy."

I was on tenterhooks as I took the phone off Jack and peered again at the picture.

"That's the edge of the reception desk and I can see a chair in the background. That's the hotel I delivered the flowers to. The one in Wembley that Marko uses for … who knows."

She looked towards the red-wine stained woman across the room.

She took back her phone and started searching for something.

"This makes more sense to me now," Jack said, handing the phone back to me.

It was the message from Melissa, the receptionist from the hotel, that Jack had showed me on the Tube, about the Club's room being occupied by a *'fit looking bloke'* — like, say, a tall, tanned Zac Miller!

"OK. So we know Zac was at this hotel," Jack said. "But the rest of the team were at the Grove —Will told us last night — a different hotel entirely. I've seen pictures of them there all over social media. I guess everyone assumed that Zac was at the same place, but he obviously wasn't."

Jack and I stood there, in the corner of a plush Wembley VIP lounge, everyone else around us enjoying the pre-match hospitality in blissful ignorance.

"That picture of Zac was taken this morning and he doesn't look ill to me," I paused as I tried to get my thoughts in order. "I think this has something to do with Marko, you know. Last night Will talked about Zac getting special treatment. But why would that be the case? He's part of a team and you'd think they'd all be together. Just doesn't make sense."

Jack, her linked hands resting on her chin as if praying for a miracle, said hesitantly, almost in a whisper, "I'm just putting it out there … but you don't think it's something to do with the Diamonds job? That would be *ambitious* for someone who's managing a Championship side — even if he's just won the League. He's one of their ex-players after all?"

It was starting to dawn on me what she was getting at but I had to check. "What are you saying, Jack, exactly? I know Will said something about *Marko being Marko*, whatever that means but he's hardly going to stop our best player from playing, is he? Why on earth would he do that?"

Jack shrugged her shoulders — who knew anything anymore?

We knew that we were probably mad, but the heady mixture of champagne and adrenaline made us decide that we had to be women of action.

With no one else to turn to, we were going to see if we — the florist and the town planner — could find out where our striker was. What would happen after that we didn't yet know but as we made our hasty exit from the lounge, Jack texted Will.

We told him we had a good idea where Zac might still be and were heading off to try to find him.

Wembley Stadium to Wembley Astra Grand

Loz

We ran out of the VIP lounge full of intent, straight into a concourse full of people. Jack and I threaded our way through the crowd to hop on the escalator down to the next level. We could hear that most fans were in the stands by now but on the lower floors there were still plenty of people downing drinks, making last-minute dashes for loos, filling water bottles and frantically checking seat numbers as the countdown to kick-off approached.

The excited faces around us made me feel a pang of envy, acutely aware we'd be missing the start of one of our Club's most historic matches. But Jack and I didn't have to ask each other whether we were doing the right thing.

At ground level, we headed towards the exit. A security guard looked perplexed, calling out, "Aren't you going the wrong way, ladies?"

Arnie-style, Jack responded, "Don't worry, we'll be back."

Outside, a roar erupted in the stadium behind us — the opening ceremony had just begun.

Our decision to act had been done with such haste that it was only at this point that we realised we had no real plan of action. Jack had been to the hotel before but had driven there and so we needed to get directions. We could see on their website it wasn't that far away but was still at least a twenty-minute walk.

We hadn't even had a chance to get into stride when Jack stopped and pointed towards a new form of urban littering — some abandoned lime green electric bikes. Some fans must have used them to get to the match. We both had the app so hopped on knowing the faster we pedalled, the more we'd charge up the bikes and the quicker we'd get to the hotel.

"Hope we don't get stopped by the police," Jack said, "as we definitely wouldn't pass a breathalyser test!"

I laughed, probably slightly on the hysterical side. The sun was shining, the wind was flowing through our hair, we were cycling through the homelands of Wembley on empty streets and we were on some madcap mission. Whatever happened, it was going to be a day to remember.

***

It was almost 5 p.m. by the time we got to the hotel. Our window to find Zac Miller was closing fast.

As good citizens, despite our quest, we attempted to tidily place the bikes outside the hotel entrance so they didn't get in everyone's way.

We rushed into the hotel's plush reception area. From her text, we already knew Jack's friend, Melissa, wasn't working. The on-duty receptionist was busy dealing with a family. We stood impatiently behind them, Jack with arms folded and me unconsciously clenching my fists. The parents stared intently at a map spread out across the counter while their three kids fought with each other over a mobile phone nearby.

We had decided that we'd go up to room 606 — Melissa had shared that it was Marko's usual one — to see if Zac was there but we needed a lift card to get up to the floor. Whatever the family in front us was doing seemed to involve visiting every place in central London and, despite our audible groans, they were not in a rush.

Jack looked over to the far corner towards the lifts, saw a couple approaching them and pulled me in their direction.

We smiled at the couple as they called for the lift and when the door opened, got in after them. They already had their room card in hand and hovered it over the keypad before pressing the button for floor 5. We nodded our thanks, as if that was our destination also.

We quickly arrived at floor 5 and waited for the couple to get out before us. Seeing the sign for the stairs, we ran towards them, just one flight between us and Zac.

On the sixth floor by the lifts, the signs displayed the direction of room 606 and we ran down the softly lit corridor. I knocked loudly on the door. We stepped back, the realisation that one of our favourite players could in any second be in front of us was beyond weird. We waited nervously but there was no answer. Jack put her ear to the door and I visualised it opening just at that moment. A few doors down, we noticed a maid come out of a room, her cleaning cart parked further down the corridor.

"Excuse me." The maid turned round. "Did you see the man in this room at all?" Jack asked.

"Room 606? No, sorry. I did his room not long ago and there was no one there. His stuff was still there but I have it that he should check out today."

We thanked the maid and headed back to the lift lobby, relieved we didn't need the pass to go down.

I asked, "In that photo taken by the fan, Jack, did Zac have anything with him?" We looked at it again.

Enlarging the photo, our eyes were drawn to the drawstring bag over Zac's shoulder.

"The gym seems as likely a place as any for a footballer to be," Jack said.

We had the lift to ourselves and looked for the gym floor. A temporary sign was displayed by the floor buttons.

"No lift access to the Fitness Centre," I read out. "OK. Let's head to reception and hope that annoying family have gone by now."

We headed across to the desk where the receptionist was talking to a man so we stood behind him. He was soon despatched and we stepped forward. I let Jack do the talking.

"Hi there. Melissa's off today, isn't she?"

"Yes. But I am here. Can I help you?" The receptionist, 'Anna' according to her name badge, asked, without adding a smile.

"OK. Can you please tell us where the gym is?"

"Are you hotel guests?"

"No." Jack hesitated. "But we're thinking of staying here and we'd like to take a look at it in advance."

"Not possible. It's booked for private use today."

I was standing behind Jack and while looking around me had spotted the sign for a Fitness Centre on the wall to the left of reception with an arrow pointing downwards. I put my hand on Jack's shoulder as a signal to leave it. A couple of other people were now queuing behind Jack, and I felt a tactical withdrawal would be best.

Standing back, we could see a red rope blocking the stairs down to the Fitness Centre. A small square sign hanging off it said *Closed for Private Use*. The proximity of the entrance to the receptionist meant that there was no way we could pass without being seen by her. Neither us felt brave enough to run the gauntlet near the stern-faced Anna.

"What a bloody jobsworth," Jack complained. "What do we do now?"

"I've got an idea. Let's go outside and check something out."

We sat down on a bench outside the hotel normally reserved for smokers and people waiting to leave or pick up a taxi.

"C'mon then, Loz. What's your bright idea?" Jack sounded dejected. "Have we missed the Final for nothing?"

She looked at her phone. "One nil to the Diamonds," she said, sighing loudly. "Robert-bloody-Ludwig scored on 20 minutes. Just a couple of minutes left to half-time."

I didn't look up. "If we can finish the half like that, I'd take it," I said.

“What are you doing anyway?” She could see me doing searches on my phone and flicking through web pages.

“It will just take me a minute or two, but I need to check out the planning permission details for this hotel on the Council’s website.”

I didn’t dare look at Jack’s face.

“I know you love your job, Loz, but really? Now’s not the time for that!”

Jack slumped forward, her head in her hands.

“I’ve got it!”

Jack slowly sat up. I pointed to my phone. “The hotel’s not very old and I’ve managed to download the floor plans. I know where there’s a second entrance to the gym. Come with me.”

We went back into the hotel lobby where a few people were milling about. We sloped past the reception desk where the guard dog Anna was peering at a computer screen and we headed back towards the lifts. Opposite them on the wall, there was a large gold-framed mirror and to its left, in the far corner, was a door marked *Staff Only.*

We turned the handle and walked through, gently closing the door behind us.

I could see on the ground-floor plan, now enlarged on my phone, that this was a secondary stairwell down to the basement so I led the way. After two shallow dogleg flights of steps we came to another door. I opened it nervously, not quite sure what I’d find. Behind the door was a short length of corridor that looked to be full of store cupboards. We could see that at its end it continued off to the right and so we ventured down and peered around the corner. It was empty and quiet and the carpet was soft beneath our feet, but I felt I was walking on tiptoe.

We continued, neither of us speaking. Halfway along the corridor, we saw a closed set of double doors with a sign saying *Fitness Centre.* On reflex, I grabbed Jack’s hand.

This time it was Jack who tried the door handle. She pulled it downwards and went to push the door, expecting resistance but, to our surprise, it opened. We ventured in and looked around the gym — it was empty. The door behind us clicked shut.

“I don’t know what we were expecting but there’s no one here,” I said, close to crying.

“What a complete waste of time!” Jack said, her hand to her forehead. “We were nuts to come here, Loz. We must have been drunk on adventure or something. Let’s just head back to catch what’s left of the match.”

We were about to open the door to leave when we heard a noise coming from the corner of the room. We both stopped and held our breath. There was an unmistakable banging from inside a cupboard.

We rushed over to the door marked *Yoga Store Cupboard,* its key still in the lock.

"Is someone in there?" Jack enquired, ever so politely.

Wembley Astra Grand — Gym

The first five minutes in the closet had been horrendous. Zac's heart pounded, his legs shook and he struggled to breathe. He thought he was going to faint, or be sick or have a heart attack, such was the pain gripping his chest. Then he remembered to take some deep breaths and, after a while, managed to calm himself down and almost convince himself that it was a stupid joke and Dario would let him out any second. Later, he remembered that Marko knew where he was and, when he didn't turn up at the stadium at 3.45 p.m., the manager would send someone to get him.

He periodically banged on the door and shouted but to no avail. Using the light on his watch he explored every inch of his prison but its contents weren't helpful. As well as the pile of yoga mats, there was only a bin of boxing gloves and pads, some skipping ropes and resistance bands.

At 4.15 p.m. he remembered that Tammy would miss her usual pre-match text, but would that be enough for her to raise the alarm? Might she just think he'd forgotten in the excitement of the Cup Final build-up?

The Cup Final, which he was now going to miss! Keeping calm in stressful situations was never his forte but he was more furious than scared. And, he reckoned, if he could stay angry then he could hold off the panic still nibbling at the edges of his consciousness. He gripped the water bottle he'd been holding when he'd rolled up the yoga mat. He had that, at least. He told himself that no one was around at the moment because everyone was at the match but in the evening the gym would be used again, and he'd be found.

But whilst all that meant he wasn't going to die in a cupboard, it didn't make up for the fact that he was missing the biggest match of his career.

***

By 5.40 p.m. he'd finished his water and reached the point of resignation, slumped on the yoga mats unhappily waiting for rescue. He tipped the bottle over his mouth in the hope there would be a few dregs left. At that moment, for the first time in two hours, he heard a noise that wasn't an electrical buzz or himself banging and shouting.

A woman's voice was saying, " ... let's just head back to catch what's left of the match … "

Zac leapt to his feet, propelled himself forwards and crashed into the door.

"Is someone in there?" The voice enquired.

"Yes, yes, I'm in here!" He shouted and his voice cracked with emotion.

"Oh my God," came a second female voice.

"He's behind this door," said the first one, and Zac's body flooded with relief as he heard the key turning in the lock.

The door was pulled open and he saw his rescuers: two women in white tops. He remembered to say "Thanks," as he stumbled out, blinking at the bright lights of the gym.

The dark-haired woman asked, "Are you OK?"

"Yeah," he said. "Just relieved to be out of there. And desperate to strangle someone."

The blonde one spoke up: "You OK enough to play football?"

Zac never expected to be recognised but this did away with the need for at least some explanations.

"Sure am," he said. "But isn't it too late?"

The blonde curls shook vigorously. "Nope," she said emphatically. "You were named as a sub. If we're quick, we can get you to the match for some of the second half."

Relief and resignation switched to hope, and the desire for immediate revenge lifted, temporarily.

"A sub? None of this makes sense but let's just go," he said, shaking his head.

"There are taxis out front," the dark-haired woman said.

"Great," he said. "And what's the score? Do you know?"

The brunette wrinkled her nose. "1-0 to them. Apparently, Robert Ludwig scored a worldie from outside the box."

"I'm sure it wasn't that good, Jack," said the blonde with a glance at Zac, as if she was worried he might be offended to hear of his rival's prowess.

Zac hesitated for a moment, "Sorry, but who are you? Y'all don't work here?"

Both women shook their heads. "We're Fulham fans," said the brunette, "Jack and Loz. And we need to get you on the pitch."

Wembley Astra Grand to Wembley Stadium

Loz

We took the quickest way back to the ground floor, moving the red rope at the top of the stairs, to the surprise of Anna, who watched the three of us file out. Outside, there were a couple of taxis waiting and we ran over to grab one.

We hopped in and the driver folded up the newspaper spread across his lap — he gave the air of a cabbie who hadn't had any trade that afternoon.

"Can we get to Wembley Stadium, please? As fast as you can," Jack said.

The engine started and the taxi left the hotel. I checked my watch, it was coming up to 6 p.m. already.

"I'm going to call Will," Jack said.

When Jack was on the phone trying to explain the unexplainable — that we were in a taxi with Zac Miller and Will needed to sort out getting us through security — I pulled my FFC water bottle out of my bag and handed it to Zac. He took it gratefully and downed it in one. He handed it back to me, still rubbing his wet mouth. In my head, I was thinking, I won't be washing that water bottle for a while ...

We were about half way to the stadium when the cabbie, who'd been looking in his rearview mirror for most of the journey, said, "Sorry to butt in, but shouldn't you be playing right now?"

We all nodded. "Thought so," he said smiling, "I saw you on the telly this week. I won't ask what the story is here then — I'll wait for the Sunday papers."

A traffic light turned amber and I looked at him in the mirror imploring him to go through it and he dutifully obliged.

"Me? I'm a West Ham supporter and, to be honest, I don't care much for Fulham … " Jack was sitting in the pulldown seat opposite me so Zac's long legs could be accommodated in the other half of the cab, and I made eyes at her — *can you believe this is happening?* — but she was still on the phone to Will.

The cabbie went on, "I really don't want the Blues to win the quad though, they'd go on about it for bloody ever!"

He sighed to himself and turned up the radio. The sports channel was reporting on the match — the commentator couldn't seem to believe that the Diamonds hadn't managed to advance their lead — it was still one nil!

The cab turned a sharp corner and I did my semi-best not to fall into Zac's lap. Before us, Wembley Stadium came into full view. The streets were deathly quiet apart from a few stall holders replenishing their stock.

On the phone, Jack was being directed by Will as to exactly where to go, which she relayed to the cabbie. Soon, Will came into view and he had a security man alongside him. Jack stuck her head out the window and Will could clearly see that next to me in the back of the cab was Fulham's no. 9. We saw the security man talk into his radio and the automatic bollards in the road in front of us dropped. The cab went through.

Zac didn't waste any more time — he flung open his door and ran off towards the entrance. Our West Ham-supporting cabbie put his head out his window and shouted, "Do me a favour, mate, and sort the Blues out!"

The cabbie then turned to us and said, "What a gentleman, he's left you to pay the fare!"

The security man who had been with Will said, "Come on, ladies, let me escort you to your seats."

The game wasn't over yet.

Wembley Players' Entrance

Zac sprinted through the car park, easily outstripping Will. Inside the players' entrance there was another security guard who waved him towards the lift.

Will arrived, gasping for breath, just as the lift doors opened and he jumped in after Zac.

"Which floor?" Zac demanded.

Will stabbed the button with his finger. He would have liked to ask Zac what had happened or even how he was but judging by the furious set of the striker's face Will knew he would get short shrift in reply.

Even inside the lift, they could hear the enormous crowd in the stadium. Zac raised his head at the sound, like a wild animal sensing its prey. "Is it still 1-0?"

"Yes. You ready for this?" Will dared to ask.

"Born ready," Zac replied tersely.

The lift jolted to a halt and as soon as the gap between the opening doors was wide enough, Zac leapt through it and raced down the corridor while Will shouted directions to the dressing room from behind him.

The dressing room was huge, empty and messy with drinks bottles, training kit and footwear scattered on the floor and benches. Zac spotted his own shirt immediately and had pulled off his gym kit before he reached it. Will arrived, panting as Zac was lacing his boots.

"Do you need anything?" Will asked.

"Water."

That was easy to find and Will tossed a full bottle to Zac and opened one for himself. Zac shoved his shin pads into his socks and dashed back to the door. "The bench don't know you're here," said Will.

"They will in a minute," Zac replied as he stepped through the door and turned in the direction of the pitch.

The noise of his studs clattering on the floor as he ran down the corridor to the tunnel was quickly drowned out by the thunder of the crowd. He ran faster through the tunnel, bursting out pitch side into sunlight so bright and shouting so loud that he was momentarily disorientated.

He realised the Fulham bench was to his left and turned towards it, seeing both Marko and Charlie in the technical area, the former hunched and still, the latter animated and frantic with his hands cupped around his mouth yelling something at the team.

The crowd behind the dugout spotted Zac before the coaches. A chant began, spreading like wildfire around the curve of the stadium until all 38,000 white-clad Fulham fans were singing his name in a deafening crescendo: "*One Zac Miller, One Zac Miller, ONE ZAC MILL-ER*!"

Marko and Charlie turned at the same time and it would be hard to say which one looked more astonished to see the new arrival.

It was Charlie who reacted first, grabbing Zac's arm and asking questions to which Zac rapidly replied, "No, not ill," and, "You wouldn't believe me if I told you."

The answers didn't make sense, but Charlie realised that he had never seen Zac so angry or keyed up before. It was as if the waves of sound from behind and around them were pressing Zac onto the pitch while only Charlie's hand was holding him back.

Charlie looked round at Marko who was gaping in stunned silence so the first team coach decided to take matters into his own hands. He waved to the fourth official and asked Zac, "Are you ready to go on?"

Zac shook his arm free and snarled at him. "Just get me on that fucking pitch!"

Wembley Stadium

Loz

We were out of breath as we came to the top of the steps that led down to our seats. The nice security man had jogged along with us until he could point the way to our block.

We momentarily paused to take in the incredible panoramic scene before we skipped down the steps. On reaching our row, we had to ask surprised fans — *who-comes-this-late-to-a-final* looks on their faces — to stand to allow us to scoot along to our seats. Before we had sat down, we heard a familiar voice behind us:

"Good of you both to show up and lend your support! Bar shut now, has it?"

It was Moany Man. Wembley stadium has 92,000 seats and we had to be within insulting distance of Moany Man! Not even this, though, would dent our unadulterated joy of seeing at least some of the Final. Although we had missed most of the match, from the second we became part of the White Wall, we were a committed part of its communion, enveloped in the tension and energy of the crowd.

"Still at least fifteen minutes left to go, Loz."

As Jack said that, some of the crowd started to get their feet — they were pointing to the side of the pitch and animatedly talking to the people around them. They'd seen Zac Miller run out of the tunnel and head towards the team's bench. Zac Miller, the prodigal footballer, the man missing in action, had returned.

Jack and I looked at each other, we hadn't just dreamt it. It seemed too ridiculous to contemplate. Had we really been responsible for getting Zac to the FA Cup Final?

Zac Miller was now standing on the side-line alongside the fourth official who was holding up the board indicating that we were making a substitution. Zac was jumping up and down on the spot, his eyes focused on the game. He looked like a man possessed.

The Pitch

The Diamonds players and fans had come into the Cup Final wanting, expecting, a spectacular end to their hugely successful season. They didn't just want to win the match, they wanted a big, stylish, decisive victory, worthy of the incredible team they were. All season they had played and beaten better sides than their little neighbour. Sure, Fulham had won the Championship, but that was an easy league. And OK, yes, they had beaten Arsenal and Liverpool on the way to the Final but the Liverpool result looked like luck while the Diamond Blues had beaten Arsenal both home and away in the Premier League, not just once in some neutral stadium with less atmosphere than the moon.

Lorenzo Verdi, the popular and experienced Diamonds manager, had done his best to prepare his players for the Final. But it hadn't been easy. There was little time to train effectively after the victorious return from Porto and little commitment to serious training. The players were tired after a marathon of a season, travelling the length and breadth of the continent and, despite Verdi's warnings against complacency, they felt that the hardest miles of the race were behind them. They had beaten European giants and their own domestic rivals. Fulham would surely be easy pickings.

The Final didn't go as the Diamonds planned. Far from being spectacular or even entertaining, until the 75th minute, it was a dull game in which two surprisingly well-matched teams largely cancelled each other out. The Fulham players weren't in awe of their majestic opponents and they refused to be intimidated. The only goal had come from a moment of individual inspiration and there had been no other shots on target at either end. By mid-way through the second half, the Diamonds had given up on the desire for a big score line and were willing to sit on their 1-0 lead and make it through to the final whistle unscathed.

For Robert Ludwig it was a frustrating afternoon. He disliked going into a match unprepared but while the Diamond Blues had been briefed on Fulham's strengths and weaknesses, most of their players were unfamiliar, too lowly for Ludwig to have encountered in a career spent in the highest echelons of the sport. He had come across the Swede, Karlsson, in international competition and indeed the left winger had paid him the courtesy of greeting him in perfect German before the game. He had encountered Antonio Perez Alvarez before and had crossed swords with the experienced defender Sunday Oyetoro.

But before the match, the Diamonds' sessions had been all about Zac Miller. As a fellow attacker, Miller had intrigued Ludwig and he had watched the recordings of Miller's goals again and again. The man was certainly prolific but a lot of his goals had little to do with his skill as a striker — they were created by the team working hard and combining together; Miller was simply in the right place to finish off the move. Still, Ludwig was reluctantly impressed — no one was in the right place that often by chance and Miller's neat finishing ability would be envied by players the world over.

But Zac Miller wasn't playing. Instead, another American had bludgeoned the Diamonds defence like a battering ram from kick-off. He had energy and brute strength but no flair. Meanwhile the little number 14 darted around the box, in and out, side to side, dodging, jumping, sliding but unable to make a breakthrough. Ludwig could see the defence had their hands full, but he had problems of his own. The two enormous centre-backs thwarted his every move. The captain, Crawford, managed to clear almost everything that came his way while still finding time to direct the defence and encourage the team. His defending was a bit basic, Ludwig thought, with a lot of hoofing and scuffing but it was effective.

He was pleased with his goal, but he was self-critical enough to admit the dose of luck that accompanied his strike — on another day, the ball would have flown over the bar. He would have loved to get another, but he just couldn't get the ball in the right area. Crawford had passed him on to his partner who was even bigger, stronger and more rustic. The two read the game as well as any centre-back duo Ludwig had come across, though, and seemed to have an uncanny ability to know exactly where the other was at any given moment.

As the game ground on, Ludwig, Lorenzo Verdi and the Diamonds fans felt more and more that they just wanted it to end. A score of 1-0 was enough, the quadruple was theirs, the fact that this was far from a classic final didn't matter.

But then something changed. It was a substitution, which wasn't surprising at this stage of the game, but the swap brought with it a shift in the atmosphere of the stadium. Suddenly, the entire Fulham end of the crowd was chanting one man's name in unison so precise that Ludwig, who was not normally imaginative, found chilling.

He looked at the man running onto the pitch. So, this was Zac Miller — all golden hair and 35 league goals — given 15 minutes by his manager to turn this match around for Fulham. It was a challenge Ludwig would have relished. Not that he ever played as a substitute, of course.

***

Both Eric Jovic, whom Charlie brought off in the absence of any direction from Marko, and Antonio, whom Zac sprinted past on the pitch, tried to ask Zac what was going on. To Leo, questioning him while he was passing on Charlie's directions, he said only, "Play in the hole," and then added his own instructions, "And be ready for the rebound. And don't ask."

The attacking substitution was the right move and it paid off immediately. From sitting back and seeing the game out, the Diamonds players had to ratchet up through the gears and force their tired legs and brains to defend. Zac Miller was playing like a demon and his energy galvanised his teammates. The Diamonds were under constant bombardment from Zac, Mitch and Leo, with Javier putting in his trademark crosses, Antonio arcing the ball forward at any opportunity and Lucas Karlsson confusing the opposition with his clever, defence-splitting passes and his tricky forward runs.

Be ready for the rebound, Zac had said, because he knew the only way to score today was to shoot on sight, accurately and often. They were too good for the Diamonds defence to handle — Mitch's strength, Leo's agility and Zac's finesse. But while the shots-on-target stats were climbing, so were the saves — none of them could get the ball past the Diamonds' World Cup-winning goalie. Be ready for the rebound, but there were no rebounds — every shot was either gathered by the gloves or pushed aside.

Fulham were attacking the east end of the ground. The sun was behind them and the strong, noisy, impregnable White Wall of Fulham fans was in front of them roaring them forwards again and again, desperate for a goal. But the clock was running down; 80 minutes, 83, 85 … the Diamonds' goalkeeper was keeping his team in the lead.

In the 86th minute, Zac won a corner. Antonio ran to take it, pummelled by the noise of the crowd. He swung the ball in. Zac connected with it but not quite perfectly. The shot was too high and hit the bar. But that meant there was a rebound. And Leo, who had wriggled free from his marker, leapt for it. The goalie was caught in no-man's-land and could only turn to watch hopelessly as Leo's header curled past him into the back of the net.

You would have thought it was impossible for the noise in the stadium to get any louder, especially as one half of the crowd had fallen completely silent. But Leo was deafened as he ran to the corner flag before being crushed by his teammates piling on top of him. It was minutes before he emerged grinning from the scrum.

Fulham were back in the game, the momentum of the match was with them and the Diamond Blues players, waiting to kick off, looked very worried indeed.

***

With the score level at 90 minutes, the game went to extra time. In the short interval before the restart, the two teams gathered in groups in either half of the pitch. The Fulham players looked fresh and eager, gulping water because the heat hadn't yet gone out of the day, but ready for another 30 minutes of battling. Charlie looked across at the blue huddle — most players were sitting or lying down in contrast to the Fulham team.

Marko stood with them but silent, his arms folded, looking morose. Glancing at him but seeing no sign that he was about to speak, Charlie said, "We've got them on the run here, lads. One more goal will win it. Keep it tight at the back, keep the pressure on up front and that goal will be ours. And that was brilliant, Leo, just brilliant!"

As the group broke up, Jamie turned to Zac. "We were so worried about you … "

"Not half as worried as I was."

Jamie was about to say more but the referee's whistle blew, and Zac ran to the centre circle to kick off extra time.

***

The fans in the stadium got their money's worth that afternoon. It wasn't just that they got 30 extra minutes to watch, it was that those minutes, the last half hour of the English football season, were enthralling.

After the Diamonds' long dominant but unproductive period and then Fulham's resurgence when Zac Miller entered the fray, the match turned into a real Cup tie. The Diamonds hadn't won three titles by accident and their class began to show. They were committed and organised. Robert Ludwig started to look menacing. He had two shots in quick succession — one clipped the bar and sailed into the crowd, the other was narrowly saved by Alex McKenna and Fulham only survived the chaos in the box from the resulting corner by Phil Philopoussis putting his body in the way of yet another Ludwig strike.

But Fulham gave as good as they got. Antonio had a shot cleared off the line and there was a genuine penalty shout when one of the

Diamonds defenders, tired of Mitch's brutal tactics, pulled him down in the box. The play was end to end and relentless. When the first period of extra time finished, both sets of fans were grateful for a few minutes' respite having watched the action with shredded nerves and gnawed fingernails.

As the players changed ends, Charlie and the other coaches gave the Fulham players what encouragement they could but the adrenaline was ebbing away and now they were the ones sinking to the ground. Only Zac was still on his feet and he looked across the ragged circle at Marko. The manager had said nothing so far.

In truth, Marko simply didn't know what to say. All his plans had gone awry, all his hopes hung in the balance. His future was completely out of his control. He was in a stadium with 92,000 other people but he felt totally alone.

He looked over at the Diamonds players. In 15 minutes' time, he could be their manager in all but name. The gamble wasn't over. And yet ...

"Score me a goal," he said to Zac.

And then the whistle blew and the tired circle dispersed. Marko strode back to his technical area not knowing, for the first time in his life, what he wanted to happen next.

***

Robert Ludwig kicked off the final period of the game. Immediately Zac was onto him, intercepting the ball and meeting him shoulder to shoulder as Ludwig tried to win it back. For a moment, the two number 9s grappled like wrestlers. The move set the tone for the next ten minutes — play became stretched and scrappy, passes were misplaced, tackles mis-timed and shots misjudged. Fans at both ends of the stadium gripped each other in terror, barely able to watch. One wrong move, one slip, one mistake and it would be ecstasy for one side and despair for the other. It was no longer about winning the match; it was about trying, desperately, not to lose.

Charlie began to think anxiously about penalties. Zac would take one, of course, and Mitch and Leo. Javier was a good penalty taker but would Marko trust Antonio with one? And if not him, then who?

But then he saw that he might not need to think about penalties at all. The ball was in the Diamonds half being passed around by the Fulham attackers at a pace so fast and furious that the Diamonds players could barely see it, never mind intercept. This was the moment;

this was the time to risk it all. Charlie seized it and with minutes to go he waved the Fulham defenders forwards to pile on the pressure and the passion. The addition of Aidan and Sunday to the attack made for some dizzying forward play full of intent and determination. This was exactly what Charlie had known this team could do, what Marko had coached them to create — not just a moment of magic but a whole stream of it — move after move, pass after pass, some short, some long, some disguised, some direct. The ball was getting closer and closer to the box and then deeper and deeper into it.

With two minutes left, close to the goal line, Mitch flicked the ball up, Leo darted forward and the confused defenders, thinking he was the danger man, went with him; Sunday kept his opponent at bay while Lucas created a diversion at the near post. A tiny gap in time and space opened up, the ball fell into it and Zac Miller's right foot smashed it through a churning melee of limbs and bodies and into the back of the net.

Score me a goal, Marko had said, and Zac had done it. It was a goal, in its own way, every bit as good as Robert Ludwig's wonder-strike. It was the goal that won Fulham the FA Cup.

***

To the fans in the stands, the last two minutes of the match felt like an eon. And to the exhausted players on the pitch, they felt even longer. But the seconds raced past for Marko, standing on the touch-line alongside an agitated Charlie with the unused subs already off the bench, hopping from foot to foot behind them. Marko seemed to have no time to form any coherent thoughts, to work out what he would say to the players, to the press, to — God forbid — Omar Hamarat. It was still very warm in the stadium, but Marko felt cold to the point of shivering.

When the final whistle blew and Charlie leapt on him like a bear, embraced him then let him go, he staggered. He had just come to the conclusion that the only way to deal with the situation was to escape from it when he became aware of Lorenzo Verdi in front of him.

The Diamond Blues manager was an old-school Italian gentleman and his first thought after his gut-wrenching loss was to congratulate his opponent.

Marko felt his hand wrung in both of Verdi's and tried to focus on what the older man was saying in his lyrically accented English, "… must congratulate you … such clever tactics … keeping your best player in reserve like that was a stroke of genius. I would never have the nerve for such a daring strategy. The Premier League are fortunate to be getting a young and audacious manager next season. I look forward to seeing what you do there. You will excel, I'm sure … ”

Marko managed to thank him in reasonably gracious terms but as he was turning to find his way to the tunnel, he was arrested by Richard Green and Charlie.

Richard said, "You need to come and speak to the press. Just a quick word before the presentation. They're with Jamie now."

"I ... " Marko found he couldn't complete the sentence.

Charlie said quickly, "I think Marko's a bit overwhelmed. I'll do the interview."

He clapped Marko on the shoulder with jocular sympathy and hurried away with Richard.

Marko jogged out of the sunlight into the disconcerting dimness of the tunnel. It was empty but echoed eerily with the raucous noise of the stadium. His vision clearing, Marko stumbled down it, unsure of his destination. After passing the dressing rooms, he found an empty physio room, went in and shut the door behind him.

He leaned against the wall and tried again to clear his thoughts. He still felt shaky and rather sick, which he guessed was probably normal when your plans, your ambitions and your future had all been shattered by your own miscalculation.

Physio Room

Richard Green, the communications director, was having a busy day. As busy, he thought self-importantly, as the players. Fulham winning the unusual double of the Championship and the FA Cup meant there was a lot of national and international interest in the Club and he had to make sure the right lines got out immediately. He didn't want any speculation or mixed messages.

It didn't help that Marko Maric had gone AWOL at the final whistle. Luckily, both Charlie Paxton and Jamie Crawford were articulate and compliant and were completely on message to the press. Even Leo Blake, who was interviewed as Man of the Match, remembered his media training despite being so excited he was almost incoherent. He managed to thank all the right people, even though he added an unauthorised but forgivable one to the list — his mum.

But now those initial interviews were over, and Richard needed to find Marko for the presentation and the formal press conference which would follow. He scoured the areas near the pitch, hampered by the players whose celebrations were already underway. He checked the VIP suite, which was loud and busy but devoid of Marko. He went back towards the dressing room but found Marko by chance in a small room he'd previously overlooked.

Marko looked less composed than usual. His tie was crooked, and he had clearly been running his hands through his hair.

Richard said, "It's time for the presentation now, Marko, then the presser afterwards. Lorenzo," — he wasn't really on first-name terms with Lorenzo Verdi but he never missed an opportunity to name-drop — "will be first and then you afterwards, OK?"

There was a mirror in the room and Marko used it to check his hair and straighten his tie then he nodded and followed Richard into the corridor.

There were a lot of storylines that Richard needed to get out to the press today. One of the best (although one he dare not use) would be how the usually cold and calculating Marko Maric was completely overcome by winning the FA Cup.

The Stands

Loz

Our tear-stained faces were focused on the Royal Box as we watched our players walk up the famous Wembley steps to the presentation level. Jamie Crawford led the way, his troop behind him. At the very back was Marko Maric.

Jamie shuffled along the row until he reached a smiling Duke of Cambridge and the FA Chairman. Sitting on the ledge before them was the instantly recognisable FA Cup, adorned with its hastily attached black and white ribbons. Their congratulations seemed genuine and heartfelt as they handed Jamie a winner's medal. In turn, the other players and assistants were presented with theirs and only once they had all received them was Jamie beckoned towards the trophy. The players were all bunched together looking a mixture of dazed and ecstatic. Our eager anticipation for Jamie to lift the trophy was drawn out as he signalled for Zac Miller to join him.

The striker had to be man-handled back towards the centre. The fans were holding their breath, Jamie and Zac, each holding a handle, lifted the cup skywards — to the most euphoric roar. Black-and-white confetti exploded as the players bounced up and down and passed the trophy along the line.

Marko Maric was last to receive the Cup and the team cheekily jostled alongside him, waiting for him to lift it up. He wasn't smiling, as if embarrassed by the attention. He paused before hesitantly kissing the Cup and then lifting it up. There was another deafening roar.

Jack and I were both now only capable of speaking gibberish. The joy was incomparable. We hadn't just won the FA Cup — we'd beaten the European Champions, who happened to be our local rivals *and* stopped them getting the quad. Never in our lives would anything get better than this!

Not wanting to miss out on the jubilation, we stayed until all of the pitch antics had finished — the champagne soakings, the players hanging off goal posts, the bad dances, the using the lid of the trophy as a hat, the kiddies being carried on shoulders. All of it, we lapped up. We might have had VIP passes for the day but, first and foremost, we were proper fans. With the last of the players off the pitch, we headed towards the VIP lounge.

We definitely deserved a drink!

Dressing Room and Media Suite

By the time the presentation was over, Marko was feeling much safer. The players were partying already — none of them were going to ask him difficult questions; his phone was receiving so many messages that the battery was running low. He turned it off, meaning Hamarat couldn't get to him. That still left the press, but they were going to be far more interested in the Diamond Blues losing the FA Cup Final than Fulham winning it. Luckily, he could always plead the language barrier in any tricky cross-examination.

Richard led him away from the pitch towards the media suite, which meant going back past the dressing rooms.

The Fulham team, which had been playing such refined football less than an hour earlier, was now engaged in something between a rave and a riot on the concourse. They were singing, dancing and drinking champagne out of bottles; Leo, who was still clutching his Man of the Match trophy, looked like he'd had a shower in the stuff.

They all saw Marko and swarmed over, offering bottles, clapping him on the back, trying to shake his hand and persuade him to join the party. He shook his head while Richard carved a pathway through the carnage.

On the edge of the group was a player in a blue Diamonds shirt: Ludwig, number 9. Marko was surprised to see him there but that was nothing to the astonishment he felt when the man turned around. It wasn't Robert Ludwig, it was Zac Miller. The two strikers must have swapped shirts after the presentation, but the logical explanation did nothing to cure Marko's disorientation — Zac had no idea how close he had come to wearing a Diamond Blues shirt full time.

Unlike the other players, who were having the time of their lives, Zac looked forbidding. He was drinking water, not champagne, and when he spoke his tone was hostile. "I need to talk to you."

"Not now," said Marko, trying to hurry past after Richard.

"Then soon," said Zac and it sounded like a threat.

Richard had overheard the exchange and wondered what it was about. He had been told yet again to keep Zac Miller away from the media, which was a mystifying instruction when the American was intelligent and eloquent, not to mention the star of the team. Now he wondered if he had stumbled across another story that wasn't for public consumption.

***

The press conference was a lot easier than Marko feared. It began, unusually, with the journalists applauding him as he entered the room. Once he sat down and poured himself some water, he found most of their questions were predictable and unimaginative.

"We've just been talking to Lorenzo Verdi," came the first question. "He called you a tactical genius for bringing Zac Miller on when you did. What do you say to that?"

"Lorenzo's very kind," Marko answered without in fact answering. "We've been fortunate to have a manager of his ability in English football for so long."

"When did you come up with the strategy?"

"Earlier this week," Marko replied.

"What made you think of it?"

Marko shrugged. "Sometimes an element of surprise is useful in football."

"What other surprises have you got up your sleeve?"

"I can't tell you that or they wouldn't be surprises!"

Such was the warm and friendly atmosphere that everyone in the room laughed far more than the weak joke deserved.

The questions went on: did he think Leo Blake would get a senior

England call-up? How many players did he want to bring in over the summer? What positions was he looking at? Was he excited about managing a team in the Europa League?

Eventually, Richard intervened and said, "Just one more question please," and Marko began, for the first time that day, to relax. But the last question, when it came from an experienced print journalist, wasn't one he could avoid or answer with a joke.

"You've been linked with some other clubs recently including the Diamond Blues. Any truth in those rumours?"

Marko looked from the man who had asked the question to the row of cameras along the back of the room. He sensed Richard gathering his papers and waiting for him to answer so they could leave.

"No," he answered. "I'm Fulham's manager and I'm looking forward to managing Fulham in Europe and the Premier League next season."

It sounded believable, he thought, and if he said it enough between now and August, he might start to believe it himself.

Fulham FC VIP Lounge

Loz

When we arrived at the lounge it was already packed. It felt a different place from earlier in the day, the decorum and nerves had gone, and the atmosphere had changed to a full-blown hair-down celebration.

We made our way into some space in a corner of the room and the waiter recognised us, probably from our less than exceptional attire and welcomed us back, quickly providing us with two glasses of the tastiest chilled champagne. We clinked glasses to the most remarkable day of our lives.

We were both a little shell-shocked from the afternoon's events and still somewhat starstruck from finding ourselves back again within the heart of the Fulham family elite. The players hadn't yet come up from the changing rooms and we guessed they would be a good while longer, spraying more champagne over each other and eating pizzas, or whatever else teams do after winning the FA Cup.

Jack nudged me in the ribs, "Over there. At three o'clock. It's the Diamonds owner, Hamarat, with David Patterson and his wife."

I looked over and saw the chalk pin-stripe suited Hamarat. He was shaking hands and smiling as graciously as he could, before stepping back and making a small bow as an indication of publicly conceding defeat.

Hamarat didn't overstay his welcome and made towards the door before stopping to speak to Ivana and shake her hand. Ivana had been engaged in conversation with a radiant Tammy Miller and we could see her introduce her to Hamarat. Ivana was not smiling.

"Look who's here now," I said to Jack, "just come through the door."

It was Lydia Edwards, the new mayor, looking cool. She glanced around the room and I thought she was about to head in David Patterson's direction when Hamarat sidled up to her. For a brief moment, she frowned before her smile became as fixed as Hamarat's. The music had got louder and so Hamarat was forced to move his head closer to hers, his mouth to her ear, to make himself heard. They parted without shaking hands.

We were loving the hob-nobbing, even if we were being completely ignored. The people-watching was top-drawer and our friendly waiter was keeping our glasses topped up.

Since getting Zac Miller to the stadium, Jack and I hadn't spoken about our incredible afternoon. As soon as we'd got back, we'd been caught up in the match but now it was hitting home. Our lives that afternoon had become some surreal dream and neither of us knew how to process it. But we had to start somewhere.

"Jack?"

"Yes, Loz?"

"What do you think Zac Miller was doing locked in a cupboard on Cup Final day?"

Saying it out loud made it even more bizarre. We were just at the point of trying to think of an explanation when we got diverted by seeing our Club mascot, Billy the Badger, make a dramatic entrance into the lounge waving his hands in the air. David Patterson ran over to him and gave him a badger-bear hug. Jack and I looked on and laughed.

A few others got their cameras out to take selfies with him but after a few snaps Billy pulled himself away.

Jack laughed, "He's coming over our way, Loz. He's obviously been told he has to mingle, even with the ones in jeans."

Billy came towards us and nestled in between us, wrapping a furry arm around each of our shoulders. The nearby waiter gestured Jack to hand over her phone so he could take a photo and Jack and I both laughed looking towards the camera. And then, in one swift movement, Billy lifted his black and white arms and yanked off his furry head gear.

The waiter, still with camera in hand, managed to catch our astonished faces as we looked into the laughing eyes of a hot and sweaty … Will.

Fulham FC VIP Lounge to Concourse

He was on the home straight now, Marko thought as he strode to the VIP lounge. He could be in and out of here in half an hour, then off home where he could clear his head and work out his next move. He might even have a glass of champagne.

The glass was duly offered to him at the door to the suite and he took it. The fizz was ice cold and deliciously refreshing after the last few hours in the heat of the stadium. He was immediately surrounded by people offering their congratulations and he managed not to show his impatience as he slowly made his way through the crowd to where David Patterson was standing. Someone gave him another glass of champagne, which helped.

At last, he was able to shake hands with David and kiss Harriet on both cheeks. David was ecstatic with the result and already enthusiastic about next season. "We'll sit down on Monday," he said, "And start talking about budgets."

There was no rest, Marko reflected, for the wicked, but he was able to extricate himself from the couple and cross the room to where Ivana was standing, nursing a glass of champagne and looking faintly bored.

Her expression changed when she saw him. She immediately started congratulating him but he interrupted her saying, "Shall we go?"

She looked surprised but not disappointed and said, "Sure. I'll ring the driver."

He looked around as she took out her phone and made the call. The players were going to be unleashed in here at any moment and he wanted to be long gone before they tried to sweep him up in the bedlam they were bound to create. Long gone too, before he could be cornered by Zac Miller asking difficult questions.

Ivana ended her call and said, "He'll be downstairs in two minutes."

"Let's go," Marko said. The timing was perfect, he thought — he'd shown his face, he'd spoken to the Pattersons and he'd avoided the players. He was home free.

Except that, in fact, the timing couldn't have been worse. As he and Ivana exited the lounge onto the concourse the first person they saw, leaving his own party, was Omar Hamarat.

Marko stopped dead. Sensing something, Ivana looked round in alarm. But Hamarat was as confident and urbane as ever, surrounded by an entourage, including Kerim Bayram.

"Ah, Fulham's hero of the hour," Hamarat said loudly. "Allow me to offer my most sincere congratulations on your really quite unbelievable victory."

Marko felt his hand crushed in the vice-like grip he remembered from Porto.

Hamarat dropped his tone so that only Marko and Ivana could hear his next words: "I will make sure you regret this for the rest of your life."

Fulham FC VIP Lounge

Jack and Loz

After yet more badger hugs and Will downing a large glass of water, he abruptly pulled himself away and said, "I'll be back in a minute. I just need to sort out the music."

Within seconds the music, which had steadily been getting louder since the end of the match, went up a few notches.

The song intro was unmistakable — that guitar rift was the one and only The Clash's 'London Calling'. As if hypnotised, everyone in the lounge, including the Pattersons, stopped their conversations and started to move in time with the music.

What a way to finish this meteorically unforgettable day — a Fulham family singalong at the top of our voices, confirming that we do indeed "live by the river … "

And hopefully we always will.

EPILOGUE

TWO MONTHS LATER

The Bahamas

Dario slid into the water and swam lazily over to the pool bar. He was enjoying cocktails in the Caribbean very much. He limited himself to one or two per day — any more would interfere with his training schedule which was almost as intense as usual.

When he had landed in Nassau very late on 30th May he'd immediately checked the Cup Final score. Initially, he thought he'd read it wrong and the Diamonds had won 2-1 with Fulham scoring a lucky goal. When he found a more detailed match report to read in the back of his taxi he was astonished — not only had Fulham won but Zac Miller, whom he had left locked in a cupboard, had scored the winning goal! What the hell had happened? For a moment he considered breaching his agreement with Marko and phoning him but changed his mind when he thought things through. Marko had paid him — paid him very well — to do a job and then disappear. It looked like he had failed to perform and he was panicking when he checked his bank balance.

But the money was there — Marko had transferred it before the match thinking he could rely on Dario to get the job done. But the job had been done! How had Zac Miller — too charming and courteous to be a decent footballer in Dario's opinion, never mind his other issues — got out of the cupboard and onto the pitch?

This question had been gnawing at Dario for two months. He'd read all the coverage of the Final in the press but the spin was about Marko being a tactical genius for keeping Zac in reserve for so long. Dario snorted the first time he read this but the angle didn't go away.

For a while Dario feared that Marko's wrath would reach across the Atlantic but he'd heard nothing and now with Marko busy with transfers and preparations Dario knew the threat of reprisals had faded.

For a second, slithering onto a bar stool he felt jealous at the thought of the football world turning without him but then the barmaid smiled and reached for a frosted glass and he remembered how much he was enjoying his life of luxury at Marko's expense.

And if the money ran out before he felt like finding a new job? Well, the higher Marko's reputation climbed the further it had to fall, and the greater the sum Marko would pay to protect it.

Sardinia

Sardinia was beautiful. He loved the dry heat, more comfortable than the Caribbean, and the richness of the landscape — it was almost as good as parts of Turkey. Omar Hamarat sat underneath a large parasol by his villa's pool, looking relaxed in his shades and panama hat, his pink shirt open, fresh watermelon juice in hand. Tabitha was by his side in a tiny scarlet bikini and black baseball cap, flicking through glossy magazines.

Everyone kept telling him that the Diamond Blues had had THE most remarkably successful season and this team was one that would go down in footballing history. The FA Cup defeat was brushed under the carpet, an irrelevance. It was a domestic trophy that had lost its lure and its relevance — so said fans and commentators to mollify wounds. Even if that might be so, the quadruple, that elusive, slippery, unattainable quad, had been there for the taking.

He'd accepted Lorenzo Verdi's resignation, it had been pre-ordained. There was much press speculation as to his replacement but Hamarat liked keeping them — and the contenders — guessing.

Hamarat hadn't spoken to Marko Maric since that post-match Wembley encounter. When he'd seen Zac Miller run on the pitch he had been incensed but he'd convinced himself that the match was nearly won. He still hadn't got over how the Final had been so rapidly turned on its head by the one man who wasn't supposed to be there!

No matter how good Hamarat was at putting on fronts, having to shake the Fulham players' hands and, even worse, his own team's, was the hardest performance of all. It took all his efforts to smile magnanimously, conscious of the focussed cameras, when his jaw was clenched and his blood boiling.

He was content to let Marko Maric stew in his Croatian juices for a while. Hamarat could come back to him at a time of his choosing. He had other matters to deal with first.

Things had not gone Hamarat's way at all that summer. Joe Martinez being a case in point. Hamarat was disdainful of his pathetic behaviour — dropping-out after a little heat from his wife. In retrospect it was fortuitous for Hamarat to have found out exactly how weak Martinez was before he got the job.

Hamarat put his hands behind his head and closed his eyes. He was looking forward to heading back to London the following week. It was only for a few days and Tabitha was staying on at the villa. It was always quieter at his St James's club over the summer, a perfect time for a business lunch. He smiled to himself, satisfied he had all the leverage he needed as far as the new mayor was concerned.

Austin, Texas

Zac had wanted to question Marko about Dario's actions at Wembley but he lost track of the manager during the post-match celebrations. Soon after that, reaction to everything that happened that day set in and Zac didn't stray far from his bed for the rest of the weekend.

On the Monday he and Tammy had flown to the Florida Keys where they had spent two blissful weeks undisturbed in each other's company and Zac felt himself recovering from the long and stressful season. For once, he was the one insisting they visit the hotel spa.

Now they were in Austin where he was enjoying catching up with his brothers, hanging out in their old haunts, barbecuing steaks under the burning sun and drinking beer in the back yard. The day before, Brian Stanley had phoned to say negotiations for Zac's new contract at Fulham were complete and he would be emailing the document over for signing.

So he was sitting on the porch with a pen in his hand but he was hesitating. This was the deal he wanted — he had reiterated to Brian that he wouldn't consider other options. Brian had muttered something about "comfort zones" but Zac ignored him. He knew from experience that the Premier League was most definitely not his comfort zone. As for Europe, that was an unknown quantity.

There was nothing comfortable about working with Marko Maric either and Zac thought back to Cup Final day. He had pieced together the story from what he had gleaned from Jamie and Leo — Dario had sent Marko a text saying Zac was ill and Marko hadn't questioned it. He couldn't really blame Marko — after all it was he who had gone to the manager doubting his own fitness to play in the Final — but he was disappointed. He had thought Marko knew him better than to believe he would miss a match, whatever his state of mind.

That was only part of the picture though. No way had Dario been acting alone. And who would have benefited from Zac missing the Final? Fulham's opponents obviously. The corruption was breathtaking. Of course he had no proof, but Zac wasn't going to let it lie — no one could treat him like that and get away with it.

He avoided thinking about those hours in the closet. The panic he had felt didn't bode well for the season ahead. But he had dealt with it, he reminded himself, and gone on to score at Wembley. He quickly signed the contract and went inside to scan it before he could overthink the situation any longer.

Soon, it would be time to fly back to London and start pre-season training at Motspur Park. Time to convince himself he was strong enough for the Premier League.

Cannes

Kerim Bayram had enjoyed Cannes so much at Easter that he and his wife came back for the summer. He liked to have lunch along la Croisette, on the Grand Hotel's terrace, looking out onto the azure Mediterranean and watch the beautiful people go by.

It hadn't been a good year financially so far and his lost bet on the Diamond Blues to beat Fulham in the FA Cup had topped it off. After his lunch with Hamarat in mid-May, he'd staked a six figure sum on the Diamonds winning the quadruple, such was his close friend's confidence of beating Monaco and his strategy for dealing with Fulham via their manager, Marko Maric. So much for that insight. Hamarat had been so furious after the Final that Bayram thought it would be sensible to ask what went wrong another time. He still hadn't got to the bottom of it.

As for the Fulham ground purchase, Patterson still wasn't for selling — but it might not be down to him, Bayram thought. Bayram was an old-timer when it came to picking up distressed assets at discounted prices and was content to wait it out. He'd been told by Hamarat that City Hall wasn't a problem either as losing Martinez was just a temporary setback. In the meantime, he'd enjoy his vacation.

Hammersmith

<u>Loz</u>

I still couldn't quite believe that we'd won the FA Cup — just thinking about it made me well up. I was on a permanent high even if work carried on much the same. My boss remained missing in action — she somehow managed to take most of the summer off — and every time I saw my Diamonds supporting colleague Andy, I reminded him that Fulham had stopped them getting the quad. It must have been so annoying — but I just couldn't help it.

Footie fans hate it when the season ends — we all feel bereft for a while before our Monday morning football chats are replaced with Wimbledon and athletics or whatever — and cricket if you're Dom. Having to adjust was hard at the best of times but that year it was especially tough as there had been no summer football with the World Cup rescheduled to the winter. When July was almost at an end I was happy that at least we had friendlies and possible new signings to talk about.

As for Jack and me, we couldn't wait to have Fulham back in the Premier League and go on a Europa Cup journey. Before the new season kicked off Dom and I planned a week in the Basque country — I'd always wanted to see the Gehry designed Guggenheim museum and his Rioja winery.

I hadn't told anyone at work, only Dom, about what happened on Cup Final day. The Club's comms guy, Richard, had suggested that it would be better not to. Will told us he didn't know who or what it involved or whether there was criminal activity. Who knows? Weird stuff. And talking of Will, should we now refer to him as Billy?!

A few days after the match, Jack called me to say that two bottles of champagne had been sent to her shop, one for each of us, from the Club. Another excellent result!

Motspur Park

Marko was glad to be back at the training ground, immersed in the transfer market and preparing for pre-season training. He had endured his Caribbean holiday in a state of impatience. He didn't enjoy doing nothing at the best of times and being forced into a week of inertia when he had so much on his mind felt like torture.

He had tried — really tried, he told himself — to make sure Ivana enjoyed the break and he certainly felt that they flew back to London in more companionable silence than they had left it. But yesterday she had left for Croatia and he couldn't help turning the statement, "see you when you get back," into a question.

She had paused on her way to her taxi. Her heels were so high that their eyes were level as he contemplated kissing her goodbye. "I'll call you when I land," she said.

He was relived to throw himself into his work but he couldn't get the memory of what had happened at Wembley out of his head. In Hamarat and Bayram, he had made some dangerous enemies. Hamarat's hissed parting shot worried him. The man had a long reach and powerful friends. Hamarat thought Marko had crossed him and at some point he would exact his revenge. Marko was conscious too that his arrangement with Dario wasn't watertight. He hadn't heard from his erstwhile friend since the Final and he hadn't expected to, but he was aware that back in May his ambition had clouded his judgment — he had given Dario power over him and now that felt like a mistake.

Marko still felt unsure about being at Fulham when he had been offered so much more but he knew he had to keep his counsel and get on with the job. He had already achieved a lot with this team and, despite himself, he was excited to see how much further they could go.

He had been ambivalent about the news that Zac Miller had signed a new contract — he knew he would never find a striker who suited his system better than the Texan but he remembered Zac in the Diamond Blues shirt trying to confront him at Wembley. More unfinished business.

There was so much promise in the sunlight of pre-season. And so much danger lurking in the shadows.

City Hall

She couldn't yet say she had a total grip on the role but she felt like she was getting there. Her full team was in place and, despite a few teething problems, it had the makings of a good one.

The role was beyond intense, as Lydia knew it would be. Skye was old enough to get on with her life without her mum and it had helped her become more independent. Skye's relationship with Tom seemed to be going well too, despite Lydia's reservations as to his underlying motives. As for her own, she'd hardly seen Jonathan. There'd been an article about her rich ex-banker boyfriend in one newspaper, implying Lydia was part of the same old metropolitan elite, but it didn't gain any traction. She comforted herself that Jonathan knew the score and they'd pick things up again when life calmed down.

Lydia had just arrived back in her office at City Hall after having been out to open a new social housing construction project — a perfect photo opportunity for her to be seen wearing hi-viz and a hard hat, one that her comms people weren't going to miss.

As she entered the mayoral office suite, she smiled at her secretary. Sam was on the phone and Lydia was about to pass her desk and head into her office but Sam waved at her, wanting her to stop.

"I understand, Mr Hamarat. Yes, yes, I definitely will do. Not a problem."

Lydia's smile had disappeared.

"He is one persistent individual," Sam said, shaking her head. "That was the third time he called this morning!"

"What did he say?" asked Lydia.

"He says you're old friends," Sam looked at Lydia for confirmation but none was forthcoming. She went on, "He says he won't take no for answer, you have to make time for lunch with him at his club next week when you can catch up on old times." Sam looked down to consult her notes. "He mentioned some project in Colombia you worked on together, said he'd love to reminisce about it."

Lydia felt her knees buckle and placed her fingers against the desk to maintain her balance. Before needing to respond, to her relief, the phone rang again. Lydia stepped into her office and collapsed into the first chair she came to.

This was it, she thought. The moment when her past was as close as it had ever been to catching up with her. The landslide disaster from many years back caused by her company's shoddy practices was in danger of coming back to haunt her. Not that it had ever really stopped haunting her with so many lives lost.

Her joint venture partner had dealt with the PR, hushing things up and keeping them out of the media, chucking money at the right people to make sure they stayed that way. At the time, she had asked if any compensation had reached the families involved and the people on the ground but the answer had been far from conclusive. That partner had been Omar Hamarat.

Devon

David Patterson liked to spend his summers in England if he could, saving his yachting for the winter months.

He sat back in his lounger in his garden — a place that brought him peace and tranquillity. It was beautiful at this time of year, teeming with sprays of pastel coloured wild flowers. He adjusted the volume on his headphones — his hearing really was getting worse lately but listening to podcasts was now up there as one of his favourite pastimes. At the same time as tuning into what this particular set of economists and commentators thought, he was able to watch Harriet painting at her easel nearby, her brow scrunched in concentration.

His mind drifted away from the podcast as he reflected on the summer they'd had. Fulham winning the FA Cup had changed everything. He still wasn't quite sure what happened with Zac Miller that day. All he knew was that Dario Kovatic hadn't been seen since and Marko Maric had sworn blind he didn't know where he was or what was behind his actions. Patterson suspected dirty tricks somehow but his instincts were that it was probably better to leave that Pandora's Box well and truly shut for now. One thing he did know was that if it hadn't been for those two female fans somehow knowing where Zac Miller was and getting him to the match, he doubted his beloved team would have come out the victors.

The attention that poured in from around the world had been phenomenal and the profile of the Club had rocketed. That was great news in terms of pushing up the Club's value. Just a shame the economics hadn't changed for the better on his retail empire. No matter what his advisers had said, there was no way he could contemplate selling the Club after that match and that result! No way. That was the trouble with owning a football club, it wasn't just about the money, it was mostly heart and soul.

Pimlico

Jack

I was sitting on my roof terrace doing my accounts with the help of a glass of wine when my phone pinged with an incoming text from Loz. It was a balmy evening at the end of July and the air was heavy with the scent of flowering plants and noisy with the buzz of sleepy bees. Murphy had found a pool of sun to stretch out in, his black patches burned almost bronze in the glowing light.

The text was a picture of Loz and Dom and a magnum of champagne. The caption simply read, "Fulham Promotion Party!" I recognised the bottle because I had its twin in my kitchen. They were our presents from the Club after Wembley. *Thanks for being loyal fans*, the message with the bottles had read, which translated in my view to: "Thanks for keeping your mouths shut about the cupboard thing."

I replied to the text with a series of emojis and reflected that, whilst the champagne was very welcome, the hidden message had been unnecessary. Neither Loz nor I would try to sell the story of our madcap rescue of Zac Miller. No one would believe us for one thing.

After the Cup Final, I had had a week away painting in Sicily before coming back to a series of very busy weekends when the shop had been bursting with wedding flowers. I had been particularly pleased with the bouquet of white roses and lilies I had tied for Melissa's wedding in June and she had been overcome with tears when I delivered it to her.

I finished my glass, closed my laptop and said, "Come on, Murph."

The sun had dipped below my neighbour's chimney pots and a chill breeze ruffled Murphy's fur as we both stood up. The days were already getting shorter. For football fans this was a good thing, not a sad one. The new season was about to start with Fulham back where we belonged in Europe and the Premier League.

This could be the best season ever.

North London

The summer recess was the time to catch up with yourself, to make sure you were connected into your local constituency business. At his weekly surgery, after his constituents had finished explaining their issues, they'd get round to the perplexing question of why he dropped out of the mayoral race. Joe was always prepared though and he'd got his response off to a tee — to the point he almost believed it himself.

Joe and Julie were planning on going to Puglia for a couple of weeks in August — they were already salivating over the food and wine in the masseria they'd booked. They deserved a proper break, some respite from their hectic lives at home. Julie, especially. She seemed to be spending more time than ever at work and had more overnight trips than before. He didn't like to dwell on the fact that many of these seemed to be with one colleague in particular. Still, Julie was the most trustworthy person he knew.

The Labour Party had been enraged at first. Someone else could have stood if you weren't serious, they'd said. But Joe could deal with his party, his poker face perfected. They were still a disorganised shower and the leader instilled no confidence. Things could only get better for him, to coin a phrase.

The mayoral fiasco had died down in the press — their attention quickly diverted to the Lovely Lydia, London's first female mayor. Her woke agenda had resonated with Londoners but he wondered how she could actually deliver on it, enough to convince people to give her a second term. Time would tell.

Joe was acutely aware that getting on the wrong side of a man liked Hamarat was not a good place to be. Of course, he'd been in contact with Hamarat to tell him he'd pay back his money after he remortgaged the house as quickly as he could. Hamarat had sounded weirdly relaxed about it all. His holiday would be a time to gather his thoughts. Joe was down but not completely out.

Motspur Park

What a strange and eventful season at Fulham Football Club!

I had no idea that my friendship with Jack and Loz, initially cultivated over their love of wine (and football), would lead to the most eventful year of my life. The shock on their faces when they saw me in the VIP lounge after the Final was priceless.

Because of Jack and Loz I'm now with Fleur and we're off to Greece on holiday next week and I can't wait. I'll be packing t-shirts and shorts rather than furry animal outfits.

I'd never been much bothered about football before, it had just seemed too primitively tribal to me but now I think I've had a Damascene conversion — I've become a Fulham fan! How could I not when I experienced the elation of that incredible win at Wembley, against all expectations? And how could I not when I played my part in getting the star player on the pitch?

I've managed to pass the Billy the Badger baton on to a new guy who seems a natural cheer-leader — for his sake, I hope they dry clean the costume first …

I did like being the Club's dogsbody with my access all areas pass. Now though, the Club have asked me to take on the role of Assistant Player Liaison Officer and I've accepted; it comes with a decent pay rise too.

I just hope David Patterson can keep control of the Club because hopes for this season are high now we're back in the Premier League and off on a European tour. To my surprise, it looks like Marko Maric isn't leaving, but for how long can he stay faithful to the Club — and to his wife? And how will Zac Miller cope under the spotlight in the most-watched league in the world? But who knows if our manager will be led astray by his ambitions once again?

Acknowledgements

We started our Fulham blog, *Jack and Loz at the Cottage*, in 2014 providing light-hearted reviews of matches and the match day experience at Craven Cottage and further afield. In the autumn of 2019 we had the idea of jointly writing a novel set at the Club we love from a totally fictional perspective. By January 2020, aided by cappuccinos and plenty of wine, we had agreed the plot of *Crossing the Line* and went our separate ways to start scribbling, assuming that we'd be able to meet up frequently during the writing process. But, of course, with the onslaught of the global pandemic, it wasn't to be. The time we would usually spend going to matches, we used for book development instead – virtual meetings at 3 p.m. on Saturday became our regular slot. *Crossing the Line* is therefore a product of lockdown and while this brought more than the usual challenges of novel writing, the book kept us chatting, laughing and positive through a difficult season for Fulham FC and a tough, sometimes tragic, time for everyone.

For her invaluable help with book planning and essential editing, our heartfelt thanks go to Harriet McGann. Her razor sharp skills and dedication to the cause were appreciated more than we can say.

We are tremendously grateful to our early readers, in particular Michael Waters, and Cat Skinner and Zubia Abbasi at yourbetareader, who provided useful feedback. We are also immensely thankful to our later readers: Miriam Best, Tom Lawson-Butler and Liz Mason. Their comments and insights helped us see the wood for the trees. Thanks also to Erika Bergoc for her early project management insights.

We want to thank Sammy James at *Fulhamish* for his enthusiastic encouragement and support. Our gratitude also goes to Jordan and Zoe at Jozo Collection for their creative flair in bringing the book to life so magically with their wonderful cover design.

A very special thank you to our families and friends who cheered us on in our joint venture.

And lastly, to Fulham Football Club and everyone associated with it. Thank you for all you do for your fans and your community. A share of any profits from the sale of this book will be donated to the Fulham Foundation.

Printed in Great Britain
by Amazon

63475453R00161